P9-CCX-878

Praise for *New York Times* bestselling author B.J. Daniels

"*Lucky Shot* is third in a solid mystery series with rugged cowboys and strong women who are smart characters. Fans of the show *Longmire* will find a new book to absoutely adore."

—*RT Book Reviews* on *Lucky Shot*

"Forget slow-simmering romance: the multiple story lines weaving in and out of Big Timber, Montana, mean the second Montana Hamiltons contemporary…is always at a rolling boil."

—*Publishers Weekly* on *Lone Rider*

"The first book of Daniels' new Montana Hamiltons series will draw readers in with its genuine characters, multiple storylines and intense conflict set against the beautiful Montana landscape."

—*RT Book Reviews* on *Wild Horses*

"Truly amazing crime story for every amateur sleuth."

—*Fresh Fiction* on *Mercy*

"Daniels is truly an expert at Western romantic suspense."

—*RT Book Reviews* on *Atonement*

"Will keep readers on the edge of their chairs from beginning to end."

—*Booklist* on *Forsaken*

"Action-packed and chock-full of suspense."

—*Under the Covers* on *Redemption*

"Fans of Western romantic suspense will relish Daniels' tale of clandestine love played out in a small town on the Great Plains."

—*Booklist* on *Unforgiven*

B.J. DANIELS

Hard Rain

HQN™

HQN™

ISBN-13: 978-0-373-78913-9

Recycling programs for this product may not exist in your area.

Hard Rain

Copyright © 2016 by Barbara Heinlein

All rights reserved. Except for use in any review, the reproduction or utilization of this work in whole or in part in any form by any electronic, mechanical or other means, now known or hereinafter invented, including xerography, photocopying and recording, or in any information storage or retrieval system, is forbidden without the written permission of the publisher, HQN Books, 225 Duncan Mill Road, Don Mills, Ontario M3B 3K9, Canada.

This edition published by arrangement with Harlequin Books S.A.

For questions and comments about the quality of this book, please contact us at CustomerService@Harlequin.com.

® and TM are trademarks of Harlequin Enterprises Limited or its corporate affiliates. Trademarks indicated with ® are registered in the United States Patent and Trademark Office, the Canadian Intellectual Property Office and in other countries.

www.HQNBooks.com

Printed in U.S.A.

This book is for my daughter, Danielle.
Not only has she read everything I've ever written
and always has the best advice, she is my designer.
She is always there when I need her—which is a lot.
Because of her willingness to tackle any task,
she is an inspiration to me. I wish I was half as
strong and capable and talented as she is.

CHAPTER ONE

Thunder cracked overhead in a piercing boom that rattled the windows. As she huddled in the darkness, rain pelted down in angry drenching waves. Lightning again lit the sky in a blinding flash that burned in her mind the image before her.

In that instant, she saw him crossing the ridge carrying the shovel, his head down, rain pouring off his black Stetson. It was done.

Dark clouds blanketed the hillside. Through the driving rain, she watched him come toward her, telling herself she could live with what she'd done. But she feared he could not. And that could be a problem.

Brody McTavish heard the screams only seconds before he heard the roar of hooves headed in his direction. Shoving back his cowboy hat, he looked up from the fence he'd been mending to see a woman on a horse riding at breakneck speed toward him.

Harper Hamilton. He'd heard that she'd recently returned after being away at college. Which meant it could have been years since she'd been on a horse. He was already grabbing for his horse's reins and swinging up in the saddle.

Runaway horse.

He'd been on a runaway horse when he was a kid.

He remembered how terrifying it had been. With that many pounds of horseflesh running at such a deadly speed, he prayed hard she could hang on.

He had to hand it to Harper. She hadn't been unseated. At least not yet.

Harper, yards away on a large bay, screamed. He spurred his horse to catch her and as he raced up beside her, her blue eyes were wide with alarm.

Acting quickly, he looped an arm around her, dragged her off the horse and reined in. His horse came to a stop in a cloud of dust. Her horse kept going, disappearing into the foothill pines ahead.

Brody let Harper slip to the ground next to his horse. The minute her feet touched earth, she started screaming again as if all the wind had been knocked out of her when he'd grabbed her but was back now.

"You're all right," he said, swinging out of the saddle and stepping to her to try to calm her.

She spun on him, leading with her fist, and caught him in the jaw. He staggered back more from surprise than the actual blow, but the woman had a pretty darned good right hook.

He stared at her in confusion. "What the devil was that about?"

Picking up a baseball-sized rock, she brandished it as she took a few steps back from him, all the time glancing around seeming either to expect more men to come out of the foothills or looking for a larger weapon.

Had the woman hit her head? He spoke calmly as he would to a skittish horse—or a crazy woman. "Calm down. I know you're scared. But you're all right now." It had only been a few months since the two of them were attendants at her sister Bo's wedding, not that they hadn't known each other for years.

She peered under the brim of his hat as if only then taking a good look at him. "Brody McTavish?" She stared at him as if in shock. "Have you lost your mind?"

Brody frowned, since this hadn't been the reaction he'd expected. "Ah, correct me if I'm wrong," he said, rubbing his jaw. "But I don't think this is the way most women react after a man saves her life."

"You think you just saved my life?" Her voice rose in amazement.

"You were *screaming* like either a woman in trouble or one who has lost her senses. I assumed, as any sane person would, that your horse had run away with you. No need to thank me," he said sarcastically.

"*Thank you?* For scaring me half to death?" She dropped the rock and dusted the dirt off her hand onto her jeans. "And for the record, I wasn't *screaming*. I was…expressing myself."

"Expressing yourself at the top of your lungs?"

Harper jammed her hands on her hips and thrust out her adorable chin. He recalled her sister's wedding back at Christmastime. While both attendants, they hadn't shared more than a few words. Nor had he gotten a chance to dance with her. His own fault. He hadn't wanted to get in line with all her young suitors.

"It was a beautiful morning," she said haughtily. "I hadn't been on a horse in a long time and it felt so good that I couldn't resist expressing it." She looked embarrassed but clearly wasn't about to admit it. "Do you have a problem with that?"

"Nope. But when I see a woman riding like a wild person, screaming her head off, I'm going to assume

she's in trouble and needs some help. My mistake."
Didn't she know how dangerous it was riding like that
out here? If her horse had stepped into a gopher hole…
A lecture came to his lips, but he clamped his mouth
shut. "You have a nice day, Miss Hamilton." He tipped
his hat, grabbed up his reins and started toward his
property.

"You're just going to walk away?" she demanded
to his back.

"Since you aren't in need of *my* help…" he said over
his shoulder.

"I thought you would at least help me retrieve my
horse."

He stopped and mumbled under this breath, "If your
horse has any sense he'll keep going."

"I beg your pardon?"

Brody took a breath and turned to face her again.

Her blond hair shone in the morning sunlight, her
blue eyes wide and filled with devilment. He recalled
the girl she'd been. Feisty was an understatement.
While nothing had changed as far as that went, she
was definitely no longer a girl. He would have had to
be blind not to notice the way she filled out her jeans
and Western shirt.

She shifted her boots in the dust. "I'd appreciate it
if you would help me find my horse."

"By all means let me help you find your horse, then.
As you said, it's the least I can do. Would you care to
ride…*Miss Hamilton*?" He motioned to his horse, glad
he hadn't called her princess, even though it had been
on the tip of his tongue.

Looking chastised, she shook her head. "And, please,
my name is—"

"Harper. I know."

"Thank you for not mistaking me for my twin." She sounded more than a little surprised. "Not even my own father can tell us apart at times."

He could feel her looking at him, studying him like a bug under a microscope. He wondered what she'd majored in at college. Nothing useful, he would bet.

"Thank you also for helping me find my horse," she said into the silence that fell between them. "I really don't want to be left out here on foot if my horse has returned to the barn."

He thought the walk might do her some good but was smart enough not to voice it. "The last I saw of your mare she was headed up into the foothills. I would imagine that's where we'll find her, next to the creek."

She glanced up at him. "I should probably apologize for hitting you." When he said nothing, she continued. "With everything that's been going on in my family, I thought you were... Anyway, I'm sorry that I hit you and that I misunderstood your concern." He could hear in her voice how hard that apology was for her.

And, he had to admit, her family had recently definitely been through a lot. The family had seemed to be under attack since her father, Senator Buckmaster Hamilton, had announced he would be running for president. Three of her sisters had been threatened. Not to mention the mother she'd believed dead had returned out of the blue after twenty-two years—and her stepmother had been killed in a car accident. It was as if tragedy was tracking that family.

"Apology accepted," he said as he picked up her cowboy hat from the dust and handed it to her.

As they walked toward sun-bleached cliffs and

shimmering green pines, he mentally kicked himself. He'd had a crush on Harper—from a distance, of course—for years, waiting for her to grow up, and now that she finally had and he'd managed to get her attention, he couldn't imagine a worse encounter.

Not that he wasn't knocked to his knees by her crooked smile or the way she had of cocking her head when she was considering something. Or the endless blue of her wide-eyed innocence—all things he'd noticed from the first time he'd laid eyes on her. He smiled to himself, remembering the first time he'd seen her. She'd just been a freckle-faced kid.

Somehow, he'd thought… She'd be grown-up and one day… He told himself someday he and Harper would have a good laugh over today's little incident, before he mentally kicked himself.

He'd actually thought he'd rescued the woman of his dreams—until she'd hit him.

BRODY MCTAVISH. HARPER grimaced in embarrassment. She'd been half in love with him as far back as she could remember. Not that he had looked twice at her. He'd been the handsome rowdy teen she used to spy on from a distance. She'd been just a girl, much too young for him. But Brody had come to parties her older sisters had put on at the ranch. She and Cassidy were too young to attend and were always sent up to bed, but Harper often sneaked down when everyone else, including her twin, thought she was asleep.

Several times Brody had caught her watching and she'd thought for sure he would snitch on her, but he hadn't. Instead, he'd given her a grin and covered for her. Her nine-year-old heart had beat like a jackhammer in her chest at just the thought of that grin.

She'd seen Brody a few times after that, but only in passing. He'd graduated from high school and gone off to college before coming back to the family ranch. She'd been busy herself, getting an education, traveling, experiencing life away from Montana. When she'd heard that her sister Bo was dating Jace Calder, she'd wondered if he and Brody were still best friends.

It wasn't until the wedding that she got to see him again. She hadn't been surprised to find that he was still handsome, still had that same self-deprecating grin, still made her now grown-up heart beat a little faster. She'd waited at the wedding reception for him to ask her to dance since they were both attendants, but he hadn't. She'd told herself that he probably still saw her as a child, given the difference in their ages.

Glancing over at him now, she didn't even want to consider what he must think of her after this. Not that she cared, she told herself, lifting her head and pretending it didn't matter. He probably didn't even remember the secret they had shared when she was a girl.

As they walked, though, she couldn't help studying him out of the corner of her eye. Earlier, she hadn't appreciated how strong he was. Now that she knew he wasn't some predator who had been trying to abduct her—something she'd been warned about as a girl since she was the daughter of a wealthy rancher, not to mention US senator—she took in his muscled body along with the chiseled features of his handsome face in the shade of his straw cowboy hat.

No matter what he said, he hadn't accepted her apology. He was still angry with her. She'd given him her best smile when he'd returned her hat from the ground and all she'd gotten was a grunt. Her smile was all it usually took with most men. But Brody wasn't most men. Isn't that why she'd never been able to forget him?

"I feel as if we've gotten off on the wrong foot," she said, trying to make amends.

Another grunt without even looking at her.

"My fault entirely," she said, although she didn't really believe that was true and hoped he would agree.

But he said nothing, nor would he even look at her. He was starting to irritate her. She was doing her best to make up for the misunderstanding, but the stubborn man wasn't giving her an inch.

"You can't just keep ignoring me," she snapped, digging in her boot heels as she stopped shy of the pine-covered hillside. "Have you even heard a word I've said? If you don't look at me right this minute, Brody McTavish, I'm going to—"

He swung on her. Had she not been standing flat-footed she would have stumbled back. Instead, she was rooted to the ground as suddenly he was in her face. "I've *been* listening to you and I've *been* looking at you for years," he said, his voice deep and thick with emotion. "I've *been* waiting for you to grow up." His voice faltered as he dropped his horse's reins. "Because I've been wanting to do this since you were sixteen."

Grabbing her, he pulled her against his rock-hard body. His mouth dropped to hers. Her lips parted of their own accord, just as her arms wrapped around his neck. Her heart hammered against her ribs as he deepened the kiss and she heard herself moan.

The sudden high-pitched whinny of a horse only yards away brought them both out of the kiss in one startled movement. Turning, she could see her horse in the trees. Her first thought was that the mare had gotten into a hunter's snare, because the whinny was one of pain—or alarm.

Brody grabbed her arm as she started past him to see what was wrong with her horse. "I think you should wait here," he said, letting go of her arm as he took off toward the pines.

"My horse—"

"Stay here," he said more sternly over his shoulder.

Still stunned by the kiss and anxious about her horse, she set off after him. The ground was soft under her feet. She saw where fresh soil had washed down through the pines, forming a dark, muddy gully.

Her horse was partway up the hillside near where the rain a few nights ago had loosened the soil and washed it down the hillside. As Brody approached, the mare snorted and crow-hopped away a few feet.

"She's afraid of you," she called to his retreating backside. She could hear him speaking softly to the horse as he approached. She followed, although she was no match for his long legs.

An eerie quiet fell over the hillside as she stepped into the shadowed pines. She slowed, frowning as she finally got a good look at her horse. The mare didn't seem to be hurt and yet Harper had never seen her act like this before.

"I thought I told you to stay back," Brody said as she came up behind him. "You've never been good at following orders, have you?"

So he did remember her sneaking downstairs at her sisters' parties. She felt a bump of excitement at that news, but it was quickly doused. Past him, she saw that her horse's eyes were wild. The mare snorted again, stomped the ground and shied away, to move a few yards back from them and the gully.

"What is wrong with her?" Harper demanded, afraid it was something she had done.

"She's reacting to what the hard rain dislodged and sent down the hillside in an avalanche of mud," Brody snapped. What was he talking about? As she started to step past him to get a look, he put a hand out to stop her. "Harper, you don't want to see this."

She *did* want to see whatever it was and resented him telling her she didn't. Protective was one thing, but the man was being ridiculous. She'd been raised on a ranch. She'd seen her share of dead animals, if that's what it was. She stepped around him, determined to see what the storm had exposed.

At first all she saw were old grimy, weathered boards that looked like part of a large wooden box. Then she saw what must have been inside the container before it had washed down the slope and broken open.

Her pulse jumped at the sight, her mind telling her she wasn't seeing what her eyes told her she was. *"What is that?"* she whispered into the already unnerving quiet as she took a step back.

"From the clothing and long hair, I'd say it was the mummified body of a woman who, until recently, had been buried up on that hillside."

CHAPTER TWO

SENATOR BUCKMASTER HAMILTON rubbed his temples, his headache worsening. He caught his reflection in a wall of glass on the other side of the room. He was a big man who looked like the Montana rancher he was. His blond hair had grayed at the temples. He wondered if he'd be totally gray by the election.

Often, he feared he wasn't cut out for this. He hated these staff meetings and all the minutiae that went with them. Angelina had always handled the things that didn't require his personal attention, which apparently had been most everything. His appreciation of her had gone up tenfold since his wife's death. No wonder the Silver Bow County sheriff still suspected him of her death. It was the guilt he felt that the sheriff was picking up on. The night of her death, he'd planned to tell her he was leaving her for his former wife, Sarah.

"It comes down to who can win," his campaign manager, Jerrod Williston, was saying. "Everyone thinks you have the Republican primary in the bag. Not until you're the nominee are we going to let up, though."

Buckmaster half listened to Jerrod as he looked around the conference table. Angelina had hand-picked everyone here from the finance director and press secretary to the field director, treasurer and volunteer coordinator. Under them were political organiz-

ers, schedulers, technology managers, office managers
and legal advisers. Fortunately, Jerrod had stepped up
since Angelina's death, making it possible for him to
stay on the election trail without facing a lot of the or-
ganization that came with such a huge campaign.

Angelina had hired Jerrod, saying he was the best.
He'd only run a few other campaigns for presidential
candidates, but he came highly recommended, according to her.

"He's tough, but he has charm," Angelina had said.
"He'll be dead honest with you about how the campaign is going, but lie like a pro on camera. And he
looks damn good on TV. One look at him and you see
a Republican."

Jerrod looked like a movie star and dressed like a
CEO. He was in his midthirties, had numerous degrees
and spoke as if born with a silver spoon in his mouth.
It was easy to see why Angelina had chosen him.

"He'll get you elected," she'd said as if there had
never been any doubt.

"We're out of the honeymoon period with the
media," Jerrod was saying. "They loved you, hung
on your every word, treated you like the father they
wished they'd had. But now that we're coming down
to the wire, every reporter assigned to you is waiting
for you to screw up so they can get that sound bite. Be
careful. Warn your family, too. This is the point where
we have to be scandal-free. And that applies to everyone in this room."

As the rest left, Jerrod brought him over two as-
pirin tablets and a glass of water. Buckmaster smiled
and downed them.

"Not what you expected, huh?" his campaign manager said, pulling out a chair next to him.

He had to admit it wasn't. He'd spent months traveling across the country, visiting foreign governments, eating on the run, sleeping in so many hotels that he often woke up and didn't know where he was. He'd talked until he was sick of his own voice. "I thought that if I was elected, I could help my country. Make it a better place for my children and grandchildren. Do my part in making it a better world."

Jerrod laughed. "A noble enterprise."

"Is it?" he asked. "I read somewhere that this race between all the candidates is going to cost six billion dollars. Aren't there places all that money could be better spent?"

"Look how many jobs a lot of us have because a bunch of men and women have decided to run for president," Jerrod said with a laugh. "It's democracy at work." He got to his feet. "You'll feel better after the primaries."

"Only if I win," Buckmaster said, and forced a smile.

"You will. I'll see to that. In the meantime…"

"Right. Don't *say* anything stupid. Don't *do* anything stupid."

"And keep those daughters of yours out of trouble."

The senator got to his feet with a chuckle. "No problem. My six daughters have always been perfect in every way."

Jerrod chuckled. "Right. Perfect angels. We're so close now, we can't let anything stop us." He hesitated only a moment, his blue-eyed gaze sharpening. "I wanted to talk about your former wife."

Sarah. The woman who, twenty-three years ago, had tried to kill herself, and failing that, had disappeared only to return with seemingly no memory of where she'd been or why she'd done what she had. Buck had hated her bitterly for leaving him to raise their six daughters alone. But when she'd returned from the dead after twenty-two years, he'd also realized that she was the only woman he'd ever truly loved.

"About Sarah…" Buckmaster said, but was interrupted by the ringing of his cell phone.

SARAH JOHNSON HAMILTON tried the number again. The wind had come up outside. She watched a dust devil whip across the yard of the old farmhouse. Closer, she studied her reflection in the glass. On the surface, she looked like a shy, fiftysomething, blonde, blue-eyed, ingenuous woman. Not like a woman who had dark secrets.

The phone at the other end rang a fourth time and then went to voice mail.

As grit pelted the front window, she stepped back and disconnected. She didn't leave a message this time. Russell hadn't called her back after her other messages. She doubted he would now.

Sarah knew she shouldn't be calling Russell, especially after she'd broken their engagement. If Buck knew, he would have a fit and make more of it than it was.

She just needed to hear Russell's voice and know that he was all right. But, if she was honest with herself, that wasn't the only reason. After fainting at her daughter Bo's wedding, she'd been running scared. Maybe there was more wrong with her than the neurologist said. Or maybe he was right, and it was all in her head.

She couldn't remember why she'd fainted but when she'd opened her eyes, her daughter Kat had been leaning over her. "What?" Sarah had said at her daughter's angry expression.

"She's all right," Kat said as she'd helped her mother to her chair. "Everyone just move back and give her some air. You, too, Dad."

It wasn't until they'd all stepped back that Kat had said, "Who was he? The man you saw standing outside the reception who made you turn ghost white and faint?"

"I don't know what you're talking about," Sarah had said. "I don't remember seeing—"

"That's right. You don't remember *anything*," Kat had said sarcastically.

She had gritted her teeth, reminding herself that Kat had always been the impossible child, but also one of the smartest. Kat had seen something. "What did this man look like?" she'd asked.

"Handsome even after all these years. He looked like your former lover from The Prophecy, Joe Landon. Ring any bells? No, that's right, you didn't recognize anyone in the photo I showed you. Not even the image of the alleged former Sarah Johnson. Or should I call her Red?"

She hadn't recognized any of the people in the photograph—even the redheaded woman who held a slight resemblance to herself—let alone the handsome man standing next to the woman.

"Kat," she'd said impatiently. "I wasn't a member of some anarchist group."

"Keep telling yourself that, Sarah. But you just saw one of the men and fainted. Try to explain that away."

She'd been shaken throughout the rest of the wedding festivities and had had to hide it from her husband and her other five daughters. As far as she could tell, Kat hadn't told her sisters about her suspicions. No one believed her that she couldn't remember the twenty-two years she'd been gone—let alone something Kat believed she'd done in college.

Wasn't that why she desperately needed to talk to Russell? He had always been able to calm her down. Mostly, she needed someone that she could trust to talk to. But could she still trust Russell after breaking his heart?

"I'm worried about Russell." In retrospect she shouldn't have voiced that worry to Buck the last time he was home from his presidential campaign. He was still jealous of the man who'd found her the day she returned to Beartooth. Not only had Russell rescued her, but he'd taken her in, made sure she had everything she'd needed, and offered her kindness and, months later, love and marriage.

Buck, who'd remarried in her twenty-two-year absence, was jealous even though she'd recently broken off her engagement to Russell.

"I heard he's on a cruise, probably visiting some tropical island and you are the last person on his mind," her former husband had snapped. Because she was believed dead those years, their marriage had been declared null and void. Otherwise, Buck would have been a bigamist when he'd remarried.

She'd had six daughters with Buck so she should have expected this reaction. Still, she had a bad feeling that Russell might be in trouble. She needed someone to talk to and Buck was gone so much of the time…

"It's just that Russell took it really hard when I gave him back his ring," she'd said, hoping to make him understand. "He was…angry. Which isn't like him." Nor was it like him to go on a cruise. He was Montana born and bred. If he'd left the state, then he was even more upset with her than she'd originally thought. So why did she suspect he hadn't left?

"I'm afraid of what he might do," she'd said, trying to get her husband to see that she was truly worried and possibly for a good reason. "Maybe you could say something to the sheriff. Russell has a daughter here. I can't imagine him leaving her and his grandchildren, even for a short time. You don't know how kind Russell is, how caring and forgiving."

"He's a saint," Buck had said impatiently. "Can we please not talk about him? He's gone. You're with me now."

Not exactly, she thought as she pocketed her phone now and glanced out the window again. She *was* on Hamilton Ranch again but not living at the main house as Buck's wife. Instead, she lived in a ranch house that had come with one of his land purchases. She couldn't even see the main house from where she lived, and she certainly couldn't move back in. Not with Buck's wife's only months in her grave. The media would have had a field day if they knew about her and Buck.

Not to mention how much more suspicious it would make the sheriff up in Silver Bow County. He already suspected Buck had something to do with Angelina's car accident.

Distractedly, she watched the gale sway the tall

pines next to the house. Beyond them, a wide swatch of expansive land ran for miles before colliding with the unforgiving Crazy Mountains. All of it Hamilton Ranch.

It had been hers and her husband Buck's twenty-three years ago. The ranch was larger now. Buck didn't understand the word *enough*. He had to conquer, to control, to lead, she thought, thinking of his success at ranching and politics. Now he was hurtling toward the White House like a minuteman missile—that was, if nothing detonated his campaign before he reached his goal.

She'd nearly done that when she'd returned after letting everyone believe she was dead for all those years. It only made more copy for the gossip columns that she couldn't recall any of it, including why she had evidently driven her car into the Yellowstone River in the middle of winter in an attempted suicide several months after the twins were born.

When her body wasn't found, she was ruled legally dead. Somehow, she had survived, though she'd had no idea how or where she had gone after that. The last thing she remembered was giving birth to Harper and Cassidy, who were now out of grad school. She'd missed all six of her girls' lives. She'd missed years with Buck. Worse, in her absence, he'd replaced her.

Some days, it all seemed too much. Her daughters didn't know her and didn't seem to want to get to know her. She'd come back to find her husband remarried. He'd been the only man she'd ever loved—at least as far as she could recall—and to return to find Angelina Broadwater Hamilton living in her house... The media had tried to paint a love triangle between the three of them.

But neither her astonishing return from the dead nor Angelina's death in a car accident four months ago had derailed Buck's propulsion toward the presidency. Instead, the polls had him rising even higher seemingly because of it.

Where Sarah fit into it, though, was still to be decided.

"It's too early for us to announce that we're getting back together," Buck had said. "But I have my staff ready to put a spin on our reunion as soon as it is time." Jerrod Williston was his campaign manager. She'd never met him, but she knew from what Buck had said that he didn't approve.

"I'll keep after Jerrod," Buck had told her. "He always comes down on the cautious side in these things. But it won't be long, I promise," he'd said as he'd taken her in his arms. "We will be together as husband and wife in the White House."

Sarah had tried to see herself there with him and couldn't, and that frightened her. Sometimes, like now, alone in the middle of the huge ranch Buck had built, she thought she should have married Russell. He had promised her a "normal" life. Isn't that what she'd always wanted?

Outside, she saw with growing concern that a storm was rolling in. Dark clouds shrouded the Crazies, as the locals called the massive mountain range. The wind wailed, making the tree limbs lash the house. She shuddered at the thought of another thunderstorm like the one from a few nights before.

She'd always hated storms—just like her daughter

Bo had when she was young. Russell knew how she
hated the thunder and lightning, the unrelenting rain.
He would never have left her alone with a storm coming in. Not that Buck could have come to her even if
he'd been in town. He was at some caucus or other and
not expected back for days.

Her phone rang. She hurriedly pulled it out, hoping
it was Russell. She needed to hear his voice, to know
he was all right, to be assured that he had forgiven her
for hurting him. Forgiven Buck for drawing her back.

Russell was determined that the reason she'd tried
to kill herself all those years ago was because of something unforgivable that Buck had done, something she'd
pushed into the dark recesses of her memory, unable
to face it. Or worse, Russell had a crazy theory that
Buck had somehow had her brain purposely "wiped"
so she couldn't remember.

Russell's hatred of Buck scared her. Her fear was
that she'd changed the loving, caring man and that now
he might do something crazy in an ill-conceived attempt to save her from Buck.

She glanced at the phone, saw who was calling and
felt a rush of guilty disappointment that she quickly
smothered. It was her daughter Harper calling. The
only one of her six daughters who had reached out
to her.

SHERIFF FRANK CURRY shoved back his Stetson and
gazed up the hillside. He was a big strong man, even
now that he was in his midsixties, with a gunfighter
mustache that was more gray than blond anymore.

Earlier, he'd been having lunch with his wife, Lynette, on a picnic table outside the Beartooth General Store when he'd gotten the call.

"One of these days we're going to get through a meal without being interrupted," he'd said as he'd tossed his half-eaten sandwich into the small brown bag.

"And you would be bored to tears and driving me crazy," Lynette had said. She'd said it jokingly, but there was underlying worry in her expression.

He'd been threatening retirement but hadn't been able to quit just yet. There was one case—not even an official one—that he couldn't leave until he saw it through to the end. But after that...

The return of Sarah Johnson Hamilton from the grave had been like a pebble thrown into a quiet pond. The ripples just kept getting bigger. He knew he was waiting, all his instincts telling him there was more to her return. The fact that her former husband was running for president only made him more concerned.

But when he'd had the FBI look into it, they had found nothing that threw up any red flags for them. Some people saw Sarah as a nutcase. Others were convinced she'd been suffering from postpartum depression after giving birth to the twins. Still, it left a lot of unanswered questions.

Unfortunately, Frank was left to worry alone. Now standing at the bottom of a hillside on Hamilton Ranch, Frank had a bad feeling that this was another ripple that eventually would be like a tsunami, threatening to drown the entire community, if not the country.

"I figure that gully washer of a storm we had the other night loosened the soil up on the hilltop," Undersheriff Dillon Lawson was saying. "The old wooden casket swept right down the hill to end up broken open in the pines."

Frank nodded in agreement at Dillon's assessment as he shifted his gaze to the corpse. He'd seen photographs of mummified bodies, but this was his first in the flesh. The skin was dark and hard, stretched over the bones in a gruesome grimace. The victim had shrunk to skin and bones, her clothing pooling around the shriveled torso and limbs.

What made the sight even more ghastly was the long hair still attached to the skull. Now, covered with mud, the woman's hair lay in muddy waves above her.

"This is remarkable," Coroner Charlie Brooks said as he knelt next to the corpse. "I've never seen one preserved quite this well. The body had apparently been buried in this wooden box, which kept it from animals, but the fact that it didn't decompose..." He scratched his head. "Remarkable."

Frank thought about what a shock it must have been for Harper Hamilton and Brody McTavish when they'd found it. He'd taken both of their statements after getting the call and rushing to the scene. While the two had come by horseback, he and Dillon had taken an old logging road that ended at the top of the hillside— and the original burial site, given the hole left there.

Brody had assured him that they hadn't touched anything. "We called as soon as we saw what it was."

Harper had been visibly upset. "Who is it?" she'd asked in a whisper.

"We don't know yet, but it appears to be an old grave," he'd told her.

"So, not anyone we might know," she'd said, sounding relieved.

"More than likely not," Frank had said, though he couldn't be sure of that until after Charlie did his job. Unfortunately, he had his own suspicions. He just hoped he was wrong.

"You're both free to go, but we're going to treat this area as a crime scene until we know more," he'd told them.

"What would make it mummify like that?" Dillon asked Charlie now.

"Probably a variety of things. There are two kinds of mummies, anthropogenic, those created by the living, and spontaneous, which are created unintentionally due to natural conditions. I'd say this one is spontaneous."

"Spontaneous?" Dillon asked.

Charlie looked up from his inspection of the corpse. "The internal organs are removed from the anthropogenic mummies and chemicals are used to preserve the bodies. Spontaneous ones have occurred in extreme heat or cold or conditions such as those found in bogs."

"This certainly isn't a bog," Dillon pointed out.

"True," the coroner agreed. "In order for the body to mummify under these conditions, I'd say she was buried at the top of the hill where there is little vegetation and the soil is much drier than the soil down here in the trees. The body would have had to go into the ground in late fall before the soil was completely frozen and then the weather would have had to have gotten very cold after that. The winter temperatures would explain the absence of flesh-eating organisms, like maggots. Cold also slows or completely stops the body's bacteria from decomposition, resulting in a mummified body that could last thousands of years."

"So it could be an old settler's grave, right?" Dillon

asked. "Wouldn't be the first time we've uncovered one in Montana."

The coroner shook his head. "The nails in the coffin aren't that old. Also, the clothing's all wrong. She's wearing *jeans*."

"Don't blue jeans date back to the late eighteen hundreds?" Dillon pointed out.

Charlie considered the corpse. "If I had to guess, I'd say she hasn't been here that long. I could be wrong. She *is* well preserved."

Frank said nothing. He had a bad feeling he knew exactly how long this woman had been here. "Any way to estimate how old she was when she was buried?"

The coroner considered the mummified corpse for a moment. "Young. Maybe teens, early twenties. I'll know more when I get her on the autopsy table."

"What are the chances of getting any DNA that we could use to try to identify her?" Frank asked.

"I'm hopeful," Charlie said. "Scientists have been able to extract DNA from mummies a whole lot older than this one. Maybe we'll get lucky."

"Will be interesting to find out who she was," the undersheriff said as he motioned to the shattered remains of the wooden box the body had been buried in. "Wasn't much of a burial."

"Looks like an old feed box found on places all around this county," Frank said. "Let's make sure we take the box in as evidence."

"Wait," Dillon said. "You're thinking foul play?"

"Just covering all bets." Nothing like a hard rain to loosen the soil and unearth all kinds of things, he thought.

Charlie reached out to take some strands of the victim's hair between his fingers. Rubbing off the mud, he said, "I can tell you one thing. She was a redhead."

Frank stepped away, needing to take a breath. Dread had settled like a bad meal low in his belly.

Behind him, he heard the coroner ask Dillon, "Have you taken all the photos you need? Then I'm ready to move her." An assistant who'd been waiting patiently in the pines at some distance now moved in with a body bag. "Let's roll her over. Easy… Hold up."

Frank had been lost in thought when he heard Charlie say, "Sheriff, I think you might want to see this."

With growing dread, he stepped back to the scene.

"She was wearing a leather Western belt," the coroner said, looking up at him. "Assuming it's her belt, her name is tooled into the leather. It says Maggie."

CHAPTER THREE

THE SHERIFF SWORE, pulled off his hat and raked a hand through his graying blond hair. "Maggie?" he repeated. It appeared that he hadn't jumped that far after all to the conclusion that had his stomach roiling.

"Do you know who she is?" Charlie asked. He was new to the area. The undersheriff was also looking at him quizzically. Dillon, too, wasn't from around here so neither of them would know.

"A teenager went missing, hell, it must have been almost thirty-five years ago now," Frank said. "She just up and disappeared. A lot of people thought that she'd run away. It wouldn't have been unheard-of, especially this girl. Her name was Margaret Ann McTavish or Maggie as everyone called her."

"*McTavish?*" Dillon said. "A relative of Brody's?"

"His cousin. I was in my midtwenties when she vanished. Maggie was eighteen." He shook his head at the memory of her and avoided looking at the remains lying in the mud. It broke his heart to see her like this.

"She was a beauty. Green eyes, long red hair, with a wild streak. So it was no wonder that everyone figured that she'd taken off. Rumor was that she'd headed out to Hollywood to become a movie star or to New York to become a model."

Frank called up an image of her from one hot summer day. He'd been driving along the dirt road near her ranch when he'd spotted her. She'd been on a horse, tearing across the pasture like the devil himself was after her. Her long red hair was blowing out behind her. She'd been wearing a white T-shirt, cutoff jeans and cowboy boots. He remembered the sheen of the sun on her bare browned limbs. She'd had a body that should have been illegal, at least that's what all the young men around here said. But it had been the look on her face that he thought of now.

"I've never seen anyone who lived life to the fullest as much as she did," he said, overwhelmed for a moment by the deep sorrow he felt as he finally looked down again at her mummified corpse. "We all thought we'd see her on television or maybe in some late-night movie." He shook his head. "But we never heard anything about her again."

"No one suspected she'd met with foul play?" the coroner asked.

Frank had had a couple of theories of his own. "I thought there might have been more to the story of her disappearing like the way she did. I hadn't been a deputy with the sheriff's department long at that point. Maggie's father, Flannigan McTavish, filed a missing persons report. The sheriff at the time looked into it."

Now he could admit to himself that he'd thought the sheriff hadn't really investigated the case and Frank knew why. "I was worried something had happened to her, but there apparently wasn't any evidence of foul play."

"Didn't her father suspect she hadn't run off?" Dillon asked.

Frank put his Stetson back on his head and sighed.

"Maggie McTavish was like a wild horse that had to run free. There was no corralling her. That's why I think everyone thought she'd taken off for greener pastures or had gotten herself into trouble and had to leave. She'd apparently packed a few clothes, because they were missing along with a duffel bag," he recalled the sheriff telling him. "That was the end of it. I think even Flannigan finally believed she'd run off."

"Why do I get the feeling there's more to the story?" Dillon said, studying him.

"There were more rumors." He thought about those now and swore under his breath. "There was talk that Maggie had been seen with Senator John David 'JD' Hamilton."

"Senator Buckmaster Hamilton's father?" Dillon asked in surprise.

"The one who is now running for president," Charlie said, nodding as if seeing where this was going.

"The Hamilton and McTavish ranches had access to each other," Dillon was saying. "But wasn't JD a whole lot older—and *married*?"

Frank nodded. "He would have been about forty-two. She was eighteen. His son, Buckmaster, was older than Maggie. His wife, Grace, was confined to a wheelchair by then."

The undersheriff let out a low whistle. "Sounds like a scandal waiting to happen, especially with JD running for president just like his son is now. So if the rumors were true about him and this teenaged girl…"

"He might have had to do something about it," Charlie said, and looked down at the corpse. "While JD Hamilton's presidential race is obviously history, Maggie turning up now seems like the worst possible time for his son, Senator Buckmaster Hamilton."

Frank nodded. "On top of that, I'm worried about what Flannigan McTavish will do when he finds out. There was no love lost between him and the Hamiltons even before the rumors started about Maggie and JD."

"HARPER, YOU SHOULD go home," Brody said, needing her to leave so he could get back to the ranch. It wouldn't take long before everyone in the county had heard about the woman's body being found. He needed to reach his family before that happened and yet he was hesitant to leave Harper.

The two had led their horses back to the spot where he'd been mending the fence. Neither had said much on the walk.

Brody felt sick to his stomach. Had he not known whose body it was the moment he saw it… He struggled now with the implications and what this was going to do to his own family.

Harper pocketed her cell phone after making a call. Standing next to her horse, reins in hand, she still didn't move.

He could see how hard this had been on her and she didn't have a clue how much worse it was going to get. He swore under his breath thinking of the kiss earlier, back when he thought the two of them had a chance.

Harper's wide blue eyes shimmered. "I've never seen anything like that before." Her voice broke. This had been a shock for her. But it was going to be more of a shock when she found out who's remains they'd found.

"Did you reach your father?" he asked, wondering how the senator was going to take the news.

"It went to voice mail. He's really busy right now. He's in DC so there isn't anything he could do anyway." Her eyes welled with tears. "My morning started off so good, and then you scared the life out of me jerking me off my horse like that, and then my horse ran away and then—"

"You do realize that if I hadn't mistakenly *rescued* you, you would have ridden right past me—until your horse caught a whiff of that back there and bucked you off onto your perfect little…backside. Now, please let's just go home."

"I wasn't blaming you." He saw her swallow and fight tears as she swung up into her saddle. She looked so beautiful sitting up there, chin up, head thrown back so her mane of windblown blond hair tumbled down her slim back. The sun kissed her face, making him ache inside at the memory of his mouth on hers.

As desperate as he was to get to the ranch, Brody couldn't help but see the vulnerable young woman under the Hamilton girl facade. He thought it must be hell being one of the Hamilton Girls, as they were called. And now, with her father running for president, it had to be even worse. The pressure was really on the Hamilton sisters to be perfect.

When he thought of the girl she'd been, it always made him smile. He'd fallen in love with that girl. He had surprised himself when he'd told the adult Harper Hamilton that he had been waiting for her to grow up. That was exactly what he'd been doing, he realized. It had always been Harper he'd wanted. And now this.

"I called the ranch. There's no one there," she said,

her voice breaking again. "The staff must be off or running errands."

He understood now her hesitation. She didn't want to go home, because there was no one there for her. He felt a piece of his heart break. He'd always thought she had everything and right now she didn't have the one thing she needed most. He had both his father and uncle. He'd known all his life he could depend on them when he needed them. Now they would need *him*.

"There must be someone you can call. One of your sisters? Or your mother." He hated that he couldn't stay with her, but right now, he had to get to his father and uncle.

Harper pulled out her phone again. Brody tried not to listen to the phone call to her mother as he gathered up his tools and loaded them into his saddlebags. He felt badly since her mother hadn't been her first choice. But then, the woman was almost a stranger to Harper.

As Harper finished her call and pocketed her phone again, he saw her expression. Like him, she was having second thoughts about her going to her mother. As much as he needed to get home… "Look, if you don't want to—"

"No, it's fine. She's staying at one of the houses on the ranch. I can go by horseback."

"You're sure you don't want to call one of your sisters?" he asked. "Not that I'm butting in or bossing you."

She smiled at that. "I think it just comes naturally to you. Just as it comes naturally to me to rebel when someone treats me like a child."

"We've both agreed you're a grown woman," he said. Their gazes met, the attraction flashing like ground lightning between them. "You should get to your mother's, then." His head and heart ached with even the thought of what this was going to do to his family. He couldn't think about what it would do to Harper and her family. Not right now.

As if she hadn't heard him, she looked back at the hillside where they'd found the body. "I know it's silly since I've lived on this ranch from the time I was born and I've never been afraid of anything, but I feel..."

"Spooked," he said, and nodded as he glanced back toward the hillside in the distance before turning to her. That was only one of the emotions ripping through him right now.

"I've always thought I was pretty strong and could handle most anything."

"You are." He'd never seen her this vulnerable. A part of him wanted to protect her, but there was no protecting her from this.

"I'm sorry how this day turned out for you," he added, remembering that she'd said the reason she was screaming was because she had been in such a great mood. It was that free spirit in her that he'd seen when she was a kid that had endeared her to him.

Now he wanted to wrap her in his arms and tell her that everything was going to be all right. That he would help her get through this. But it would have been a lie. This was going to tear them apart before they even got the chance to be together.

"If you want, I could ride—"

"No," she said with a shake of her head. "I'm fine. My mother's isn't far from here." She started to rein her horse around to leave but stopped. "You know you *did* rescue me, Brody. Thank you. I don't know what I would have done if you hadn't been here."

He said nothing around the lump in his throat as he tipped his hat and watched her ride west. *Just let her go.* But it was the last thing he wanted to do. Unfortunately, he had no choice now. He looked back at the pine-covered hillside where the authorities were now loading the remains, and quickly turned away.

"Who was that you were with?" Sarah Johnson Hamilton asked her daughter as she glanced out the window. On the phone, Harper hadn't told her mother about what had happened earlier. She'd just asked if Sarah was going to be home and could she stop by.

Harper frowned. "I rode here alone." Stepping to the window, she looked out to see Brody riding away. He'd *followed* her? With a pang, she realized that he'd been more worried about her than he'd wanted her to know.

"Then who was that?"

"Brody McTavish. We…ran into each other earlier." Harper was surprised to see her mother's disapproval and challenged her. "Why, what's wrong with him?"

"Nothing," Sarah said, and turned away from the window. Her smile never met her eyes. "What was he doing on the ranch?"

"He was mending fence on that lease property next to ours. If there is some reason you disapprove of him… But then, why would you? You don't even know him. He was just a boy when you left." She hadn't said it to hurt her mother. She'd just been thinking out loud.

Her mother looked as if she'd been slapped. "I didn't mean to find fault with him. I'm sure he's nice."

"He is." Well, most of the time, she thought. She

still couldn't understand why he'd wanted to get rid of her so quickly after they'd found the body.

Her mother moved to her to brush dust off the shoulder of her shirt. "I'm so glad you didn't get caught in that thunderstorm. You're not even wet."

"It went to the north," Harper said distractedly.

"Let's go into town and get lunch. A girl day, what do you say?"

Harper stepped back. She couldn't help being annoyed. "Why don't you want me seeing Brody?"

Sarah looked frustrated. Harper could tell that she wished she hadn't brought it up. "I would hate to see you get interested in a boy so soon since returning home. I want to spend more time with you."

She really doubted that was the reason. "Brody isn't a boy."

"No, he's a grown man and quite a bit older than you," Sarah said.

"Eight years. He used to come to parties that my sisters threw at the house. He seemed…nice."

"These parties happened when your father was gone," her mother guessed. "I don't think he would have approved."

"Approved of Brody or the parties?"

"I'm sorry if I've upset you. I didn't mean—"

Harper waved away their disagreement. This wasn't why she'd come here. "Don't you want to know why I asked if I could come see you? When Brody and I were riding earlier, we discovered a body."

"What?"

"That's why I'm here. I didn't want to go to the house with only staff there at best. I was upset—"

"What do you mean you discovered a body?"

"It had been buried on a hillside. I guess the rain washed it down." She shuddered. "It was the creepiest thing I've ever seen." Harper looked to her mother for comfort, but there was none coming.

"What hillside?" Sarah demanded.

Harper waved a hand in the direction of the other end of the ranch. "Next to the McTavish land. That's where I ran into Brody."

"Whose body?" Her mother had gone pale.

"The sheriff doesn't know yet. I don't want to talk about it. It was…gruesome." She shuddered again. "I'm going to have nightmares."

"That's horrible," her mother said as she moved to the window again.

Harper looked past her mother. Brody was a dot on the horizon, his horse kicking up a small cloud of dust that settled behind him. She couldn't help but think of the kiss and the thrill of finally being in his arms. It had turned out to be the only good thing that had happened today.

"I suppose I should call Dad before he hears about it from the sheriff," Harper said.

"Let me tell him," her mother said, turning from the window.

She still couldn't get over her mother's reaction not only to Brody, but also to the news about the body. "Why is there bad blood between the Hamiltons and the McTavishes?"

"I didn't say—"

"It's clear from your reaction to Brody and the news about the body being found on our land." Harper was just beginning to realize what a sheltered life she'd led so far. She would have laughed if anyone had told her that her family had secrets—until today. "Why do I get the feeling that you know who the woman was?"

CHAPTER FOUR

JD HAMILTON SQUINTED in the sun as he cast his fishing line into the crystal clear lake. This high-mountain lake was his favorite one in the Crazies. It was where he came when life below these mountains started getting the best of him. He thought of himself as a reasonable man, but lately his life seemed to be spinning out of control.

He and Grace had argued again this morning. As he reeled in his line, he couldn't help but remember some of the things she'd said about Buck's bride.

"For hell's sake, Grace, they're married. Can't you just accept Sarah?"

"Never. If you weren't so blind, you'd see that she took advantage of him. You can bet it was her idea to elope. She trapped our son, the gold-digging—"

"Grace! When did you become so hateful?" he'd demanded as he'd stared at a woman he no longer recognized. Sarah, their son's bride he'd surprised them with only days before, reminded him of Grace as she'd been when they'd first met. Both were petite blue-eyed blondes.

"Hateful?" Grace had laughed. "When do you think I changed?" He'd seen the tears in her eyes only moments before she'd left the room. Her son's elopement had hit Grace hard. He'd been her baby, the true love *of her life. And now he could see that she felt he'd betrayed her.*

A fish struck his line as he heard the sound of a horse whinny nearby.

Reeling in the cutthroat, he turned to see a bay horse come out of the trees being ridden by a young woman. He recognized Maggie McTavish and thought of the gangly girl who used to ride across the pasture next to his ranch. She'd always ridden hard and fast as if running from something.

Over the years, he'd watched her go from pigtails to ponytails and finally the thick single braid that swung against her slim back as she thundered past. She'd changed from gangly to sleek and beautiful, and still she seemed to be running either from something or toward it. He never knew which.

He just knew that one day she wouldn't ride past and that he was going to miss seeing her.

She reined in now, slipping off the horse with graceful ease. That she was beautiful was only part of the young woman's appeal. There was something strong and determined in the way she held herself. Almost defiant.

"Nice trout," she said as he brought the cutthroat the rest of the way in. "Dinner?"

Grace didn't like him to bring fish home. She said they stank up the house when he fried them.

"Not tonight," he said, and held up the beautiful fish. The colors caught in the sunlight as bright and multihued as a rainbow. "You interested?"

She shook her head and looked toward the lake. "I didn't mean to disturb your fishing." She turned as if to leave.

"Don't leave on my account," he said as he carefully lowered the fish into the water at the edge of the lake and watched it swim away in a ripple of clear water. "I have to get back. You can have the place to yourself."

She turned to look at him then, her green eyes luminous. Her long plaited red hair hung down almost to her waist. She reached back to unbraid it. Waves of crimson fell around her slim shoulders. She was even more beautiful up close.

"If you're sure," she said.

He nodded and began to break down his rod so he could pack it and his gear into his saddlebag.

"This is where I come when I need to think," Maggie said, gazing out at the lake. "There is something so peaceful about this place."

He looked past her to the small mountain lake ringed in huge boulders left by the last ice age. Mirror Lake was so clear he could see submerged rocks down a good ten feet, then nothing but bottomless dark water.

"I've been dreaming of a swim all morning," she said turning back to him.

"Swim?" He laughed. "Do you know how cold that water is?"

She smiled and for the first time looked like the teenager she still was. There was something timeless about her. But when he gazed into those green eyes, he saw an old soul, a young woman wise beyond her years. What had made her that way? he wondered. Or had she been born knowing truths that should have been saved for much later in life?

He watched her sit down on a nearby rock and pull off her boots and socks. As she reached to unbutton her jeans, he turned away to finish loading his horse for the ride back to the ranch. In truth, he wasn't ready to leave the lake. The thought of going back to that house, back to Grace and her anger and hatred, back to the decision he'd been putting off for weeks...made him want to stay here forever.

But he felt uncomfortable being here with Maggie. She made him feel old and full of regrets, as if he'd wasted his life.

Out of the corner of his eye, he saw her slip out of her jeans and drop them beside her boots. She was unbuttoning her shirt when she said, "Dare you to go in with me."

That made him laugh and turn toward her. She stopped unbuttoning her shirt for a moment to give him a challenging grin. "Chicken?"

"I don't think—"

"So don't think. Just do. We all think way too much." She peeled off her shirt. Barefoot and down to her underwear, she ran up the smooth surface of a large boulder at the edge of the water. There she stopped to look back at him. "You really don't know what you're missing."

He might have argued that, but she didn't give him a chance. She dived off the rock. He would always remember her long sun-browned body clad only in white bra and panties caught in an arc over the glistening water. She looked like a sea nymph, her long red hair floating out behind her as she sliced through the clear water.

JD felt such a moment of supreme loss that his heart ached with it. He wanted desperately to jump in with her. He wanted to feel young and free like her. He *wanted to feel that jolt of ice-cold to awaken the man he'd been.*

Instead, he stood on the bank and watched her glide through the water. At that moment, he knew that life was captured in fleeting moments, choices taken and not taken, opportunities lost. As he watched her swim, he knew he'd just made a choice he would regret.

"You shouldn't swim alone up here," he called to her.

"I know. There are a lot of things I shouldn't do," she called back.

RUSSELL MURDOCK CHECKED his phone, turned it off and replaced it in his pocket. "I'm sorry, you were saying?"

The elderly woman sitting in the chair next to him raised her head and looked around as if not recognizing her surroundings. Millie blinked in the bright sunshine before giving him a radiant smile.

"You know, I can't remember what we were talking about," she said with a laugh. "It happens more and more all the time."

"Don't feel bad, it happens to us all," he said. She was a slim, pretty woman with white wispy hair that covered her head like a protective cloud. Her hair was in stark contrast to the vivid blue of her eyes. Her face was soft, her skin only lightly creased. She looked like a kindly grandmother.

"We were talking about Dr. Venable. He rented from you when he worked at the clinic outside of town."

She frowned and looked around the courtyard as if again wondering how she'd gotten there.

"Ralph," he suggested.

She turned toward him then, her face brightening.

"He was such a polite man. Nicest tenant I ever had. He would bring me little treats," she said confidentially as she leaned toward him. "Don't tell my children. They worry about my health. He knew I loved chocolate."

Russell saw that he'd lost her again. She seemed to have been transported as if by time machine to twenty-five years ago. He tried to imagine what Dr. Venable had looked like back then. According to Russell's calculations, he would be close to Millie's age now, seventy-two. But unlike Millie, maybe he wasn't now suffering from dementia.

"Did he ever talk about his work?" Russell asked. He desperately wanted to ask about Sarah Hamilton and if Ralph had ever mentioned her. "When Ralph brought you treats, chocolate, did he mention his patients?"

He wasn't sure which word did the trick, but Millie was back. The nurse had told him she was having a good day and might be able to help him.

"He liked helping people," Millie said. "He hated to see them suffering. When I told him about my nightmares after my husband died, he got tears in his eyes. He told me he could help me forget." She shook her head.

"You weren't interested in having your memories erased?" Russell said, trying hard not to sound too eager.

"No, our memories are all we have at the end. We don't get to pick or choose. The bad ones make us stronger—at least that's what I tell my children." She smiled sadly. "You know he lost his wife. So tragic. Suicide is a terrible thing for those left behind. He said he tried to take away the bad in her life, but had failed.

He swore on her grave that he wouldn't let it happen to anyone else."

"So he succeeded?"

She seemed to wander away from him again and he'd thought he'd lost her, when she said, "I don't think he could get rid of anyone's bad memories any more than he could get rid of his own."

Russell disagreed. He would bet his life that Dr. Venable had stolen Sarah's memories and he was going to prove it or die trying.

WHEN HARPER RETURNED to the main ranch house after seeing her mother, the guard at the gate buzzed to tell her she had a visitor. The name didn't sound familiar.

"Did she say what it was about?" Harper asked suspiciously. Often the media would try anything to get inside the house for a story.

"She says she has information about your mother."

Still annoyed with her mother's attitude toward Brody, she told the guard to let the woman in. If it turned out the visitor was lying, she could call the guard and have him escort her away.

Harper felt anxious. She'd gone to her mother's hoping for some reassurance after the grisly scene she'd witnessed earlier; instead, she had left even more upset.

Now she opened the door to find a young, pretty woman standing there. "I'm Ariel Crenshaw." When Harper didn't react, she added, "I'm Ace's sister."

"I'm sorry, I don't know who Ace is," Harper said, wondering now if she had been too quick to let in a complete stranger. Since her father had joined the race for president and her mother had returned, they'd been inundated with reporters. Harper hated that they had to have guards at the front gate. She yearned for the days when they came and went without being under such scrutiny.

"Addison 'Ace' Crenshaw, the private investigator your mother hired," the woman clarified.

Her mother had hired a PI? "I'm sorry. This is news to me." Harper was just beginning to realize how much her family kept from her. "Won't you come in," she said, moving aside. "You say my *mother* hired your sister?"

"Before she was killed," Ariel said. "My condolences, by the way."

"Wait, no. You're referring to my *stepmother*, Angelina."

"My mistake. I'm so sorry." Ariel had stopped in the middle of the large living room as if not sure what to do next.

Harper wasn't sure there was anything she wanted to know about the Ice Queen, as she and her sisters called Angelina. They had never been close to the woman their father had married. She had always treated them as if Buck's six daughters were a burden she had to bear.

"Let me start at beginning," Ariel said. "My sister was murdered. I'm trying to find out why. It seems to have had something to do with an anarchist group called The Prophecy?"

Harper shook her head. "I've never heard of it."

This surprised Ariel. "Your father didn't tell you that two members of the group have been implicated in the death of my sister, as well as the death of your stepmother?"

She couldn't believe what she was hearing. "I was

out of the country, but the last I heard, it was an accident." She motioned the young woman into a chair. "Would you like something to drink?"

Ariel declined but took a seat. She sat on the edge and leaned eagerly toward Harper. "My sister was investigating a woman by the name of Sarah Johnson. Is that anyone you know?"

Harper hesitated. "That *is* my mother."

"Oh." Ariel sat back, wariness replacing the earlier eagerness. "I'm sorry. I didn't know. This is all quite confusing."

Their family had been in the news for months, especially because of her mother. "You must not read newspapers or watch the news."

"I had been working with my church group in a remote part of Africa until my sister's death. We had neither newspapers nor television and little news filtered in from outside."

Harper didn't like talking about her family's situation since her mother's return, but this young woman had lost her sister possibly because Angelina had hired her to dig up dirt on Sarah.

"I grew up believing my mother was dead," Harper explained. "She drove into the river when I was only a few months old and drowned. At least that's what we all thought. Apparently, she was trying to kill herself for some unknown reason and failing that, she disappeared for twenty-two years. She suddenly reappeared a year ago. What makes it even more bizarre is that she swears she doesn't remember anything from the birth of my twin and me until she 'woke up' in the middle of a dirt road outside of Beartooth. According to her, she has no idea where she'd been those twenty-two years."

"She still hasn't remembered?"

Harper shook her head. "Not that I know of."

"That's interesting, but it doesn't explain why my sister was looking into not those missing years your mother lost but your mother's college years."

"Really?"

The young woman nodded. "All her inquiries were from the mid– to late–nineteen seventies."

Harper had no idea and said as much. "So where does this anarchist group come in?"

"The Prophecy? Apparently, my sister thought that your mother had been part of the group and that's what got her killed. Back in the seventies they blew up some government buildings, killed some people. A couple of the group went to prison. The others were never caught, until recently. The leader was believed to be the only woman in The Prophecy, a woman who resembled your mother, Sarah Johnson."

She stared at Ariel in shock. "I had no idea." She'd been kept in the dark. Who else knew about this? Her father obviously. But did her sisters? "If my mother really was part of the group…"

"That's just it. Turns out apparently that some members of The Prophecy were trying to only make your mother look like she was the one called Red. Another woman confessed to being Red when some of the male members were caught. Another one was killed."

"Wow, I'm beginning to realize how much I've missed being away at college and then abroad all these years," Harper said. She wondered what else her family hadn't told her and instantly thought of Brody and his family—and the body buried on the ranch.

"I know I should let it go, but it just feels…unfinished," Ariel said as she got to her feet. "I was hoping someone in your family might have heard more about this anarchist group and how investigating your mother might be tied to my sister's death."

"Your sister didn't leave any information?"

"No. The file on your mother was incomplete. That was another reason I was suspicious. My sister took copious notes on her cases."

"That *is* odd."

"Well, I'm sorry to have bothered you with this." She reached into the side pocket of her purse. "If you don't mind, can I leave my card with you? Should you hear anything…"

"I'll let you know. I'm so sorry about your sister."

"Thank you."

Harper glanced at the card. It only had Ariel's name and number on it. She walked her to the door. "So, are you a private investigator, as well?"

Ariel laughed and shook her head. "Good heavens, no. I'm a community planner. It was bad enough having a father and sister as gumshoes."

Ariel stopped and pointed to a photograph of Buckmaster and Angelina. "I recognize your father. He's running for president."

Harper nodded. "That's my stepmother with him. We don't have any photos of my mother." She knew that was odd and saw that Ariel did, too. "We think my stepmother got rid of all of them when she married my father."

Ariel raised a brow.

"There was no love lost between them, even before my mother came back from the dead." She saw the change in the young woman's expression. "But I'm sure my mother had nothing to do with Angelina's death or your sister's. Like you said, it turned out she wasn't a member of The Prophecy."

"Right." Ariel looked skeptical. "But if your mother had been, given the apparent animosity between her and your stepmother, she might have wanted to get rid of her competition."

BRODY FOUND HIS father in his blacksmithing shop. A blast of heat hit him the moment he opened the door. Silhouetted against the fire that burned hot in the furnace was Finn McTavish. Finn was smaller than his older brother, Flannigan, with a shock of dark hair and lightning-blue eyes. He was also a gentle man with a hearty laugh and an affable personality.

The three of them lived on the McTavish Ranch, which would someday be Brody's. It was large enough that they each had their own homes some distance apart. While Brody worked the cattle part of the ranch, his father and uncle worked as blacksmiths, their family trade.

Hearing him enter, his father shoved back the helmet he wore and laid down the piece he'd been working on. Motioning for him to follow, he stepped out the back door. Brody walked through the blast furnace of the shop into the cool of bright spring sunlight outside. His father had pulled up an old crate and sat down. He motioned for Brody to take one.

As he pulled up a crate and lowered himself onto it, he could feel the older man's gaze on him. He'd never been able to hide anything from his father. Finn McTavish had second sight. At least that's what the family said about him. Brody believed that his father "saw" things that other people didn't because he paid attention.

"What's wrong?" Finn asked.

Brody met his father's gaze. "We uncovered something on that stretch of land we lease between the ranch and the Hamiltons."

"We?"

"Harper Hamilton."

Finn nodded. "One of the twins."

Brody said nothing. He'd done his best to hide how he felt about her. She'd been too young for him for years. Now that she was home and age didn't matter so much… He was sure his father knew what he'd hoped but appreciated him not saying anything.

"We…ran into each other." He saw no reason to get into the whole story. He was embarrassed enough by it. "Her horse had gotten away. When we found the mare…we also found a grave that had been uncovered. Rain had washed it down, the wooden casket breaking open in the pines."

His father said nothing as he turned to look out at the Crazies in the distance as if imagining the scene. This early in the spring, the mountains were still deep in snow. The rain that had unearthed the corpse had turned to snow in the high peaks of the Crazy Mountains. They stood brilliant white against the blue of the Montana sky, as inaccessible as Harper Hamilton now was to him.

The melt hadn't started yet this year. Soon the rivers and streams would be swollen and brown with silt and the valleys would green up as if overnight. Spring brought a newness to the land. The green was almost blinding under the warm sun and the clear blue sky.

Brody loved this time of year. It had always felt as if anything was possible in the spring. At least until this spring.

"The body?" Finn asked without looking at him, as if he already knew.

"A woman."

His father's gaze shifted back to him. Tears welled in that sea of blue, eyes so much like his own. "The sheriff identified her yet?"

He shook his head. "But it's her. It's Maggie, isn't it?"

Finn got to his feet and headed back inside his shop. As he passed his son, he put a big hand on Brody's shoulder and gently squeezed. There was sorrow in his eyes, and pity. His father knew somehow that his son had been in love with Harper Hamilton for years. He also knew how impossible it would be for the two of them to be together now.

But Brody wasn't thinking about that right now. His thoughts were with his uncle and the unbearable news he was about to receive. Maggie had been his only daughter, the sunshine of his life.

Shaken, Brody stood as the door closed behind Finn. He heard him inside shutting down the furnace. How long had his father known it would end like this? Brody hadn't wanted to believe it and yet the moment he'd seen the broken casket, the body of the woman, he'd known. Just as he'd known who had killed and buried her there.

Brody was born after Maggie disappeared. But he'd learned about Maggie when he got older, even though his uncle and father didn't like talking about her. He shook his head, anger making him fist his hands at his sides as his heart ached. For thirty-five years the dirty secret had lain as silent as Maggie's grave. But the Mc-Tavishes had known the truth. Now, what JD Hamilton had done would come out. Both families would suffer. He didn't want to think about how his uncle would react. Maggie's name would be dragged through the mud. But so would the Hamiltons.

Brody thought of Harper. All these years of waiting for her to grow up and now this. He was a damned fool for thinking the two of them stood a chance. Not a Hamilton and a McTavish.

AFTER DIGGING OUT the old missing persons report, the sheriff no longer deceived himself that the body that had been found could be anyone but Margaret "Maggie" McTavish. The clothing she'd been wearing the last time she was seen matched exactly the clothing found on the remains.

Frank knew he couldn't wait until the autopsy report came back to notify next of kin. Because the remains had been mummified, Charlie had called in several doctors to assist. That meant that the autopsy would take longer than normal.

"Not that many doctors get to do an autopsy on a mummy," Charlie had said. "Because of the ancient ones that have been found and autopsied, we have some techniques available that we didn't have that many years ago. But it will take time."

Time was the one thing Frank didn't have. Word had gotten out, just as he'd feared it would. He'd already received several calls. He'd put them off with the usual "we won't know anything until the autopsy results are in."

Not wanting to give this kind of news over the phone, Frank drove out to Flannigan McTavish's home to tell him before he heard it from someone else. Charlie Brooks had offered to make the trip, since the coroner was often the person who delivered news of a death. But the sheriff couldn't put this on anyone else.

Flannigan was a big Irishman who'd come to this country as a teenager with his parents and much younger brother, Finn. His family had settled in the valley, farming and ranching and blacksmithing. When Flannigan's wife left him, he'd raised their only child, Maggie, alone.

By the time his brother, Finn, had married and was expecting their first and—as it turned out, only child, Brody—Maggie had already disappeared.

Frank had been a deputy when the call had come in that Maggie McTavish was missing. He hadn't been assigned to the case. The sheriff at the time had handled it himself. But he remembered seeing the eldest McTavish after Maggie's disappearance. Flannigan had looked like a broken man.

The man who walked from his shop out to the patrol car as Frank parked and exited looked strong as a bull moose. He'd aged well, as if determined not to let what had happened defeat him. Or maybe he wanted to live because in his heart he had to believe that Maggie would come home one day.

If so, Frank hated to think what this news would do to him.

"Sheriff," Flannigan said, extending his hand. As they greeted each other, Flannigan glanced in the backseat of the patrol SUV as if expecting to see someone there. Pushing eighty, his face was weatherworn and wrinkled, but like his work-strong body, the keenness in his piercing green eyes belied his age.

"Flannigan, I'm afraid I have some bad news."

The older man nodded. "It's Maggie, isn't it?" he asked as if he'd been expecting this news for the past thirty-five years.

"We don't have a definitive identification yet, but based on what she was wearing the day she disappeared and other evidence found at the scene, it's her. We're investigating her death as a homicide."

Flannigan took a step back before slumping against the vehicle. Frank started to reach for him, but the older man waved him off. After a few moments, Flannigan pulled himself together.

"I'd like to ask you some questions, but those can wait," the sheriff said. "I understand, though, that her room was left as it was thirty-five years ago. I'd like to take a look in it, if you don't mind."

To his surprise, Flannigan shook his head. "No reason to talk about it that I can see. No reason to go snooping in her room, either. What's done is done." He started to turn away.

"I'm going to need your help to find her killer. If there is anything you know about what happened to her, now is the time to tell me," the sheriff said.

"Just let me know when I can bury my daughter," Flannigan said.

"I'm not sure how long it will take after the autopsy."

He spun back around, his once-handsome face a mask of fury. "She hasn't been through enough? You're going to let them cut her up?"

"We're looking for evidence that will—"

"Bring her killer to justice?" Flannigan spit out the words. "Her killer is dead and buried. There is no bringing him to justice."

"We don't know who killed her without—"

"Everyone knows who killed her and why," the big man erupted. "You're looking for a way to save him— *and his senator son.*"

"You're wrong. If her killer is dead, it may seem like hollow justice to you. But I'm determined to find your daughter's murderer. That's why I need your help. You were one of the last people to see her alive. If you—"

"I already said no." The elder McTavish shook his head and walked away. Over his shoulder, he said, "You're on private property, Sheriff, and it's time for you to leave. My daughter's been through enough. Please leave before I do something I might regret."

In the distance, Frank could see a pickup headed this way, moving fast. He recognized it as one driven by Finn McTavish, Flannigan's younger brother. The sheriff waited a little longer, watching the staggering steps of Maggie's father, not wanting to leave the man alone. Then he got into his patrol SUV and drove away as Finn pulled up in the yard.

Frank only got a glimpse of the man's face. Finn already knew. Which could only mean Brody knew the victim's identity the moment he'd seen the body.

CHAPTER FIVE

Grace Hamilton watched the young lovers cross the pasture arm in arm.

"That conniving bitch."

"Grace," JD said in that reprimanding, disappointed and impatient way of his. He put all his disgust into her name so he didn't even have to bother to say more.

Her husband was always taking up for that woman her foolhardy son had brought into their home as his wife. Not for long, though, if Grace had anything to do with it.

"Give Sarah a chance," JD said. "Buck loves her. Isn't that good enough?"

"His name is Buckmaster. If I had wanted him called Buck, I would have named him Buck."

Her husband gave her a weary look.

"You may be fooled by her because she's pretty and nauseatingly coy, but believe me, there is nothing sweet or helpless about that woman. She knew exactly what she was doing when she married our son."

"I don't have the energy to argue with you about this," JD said. "I'm going to ride up into the Crazies and fish for a while." He stepped to her and planted a kiss on the top of her head.

She clutched his arm, desperately wanting back the

man she'd married. She felt JD slipping out of her grasp as he pulled away to leave. He'd been pulling away now for what? Months? Or was it years?

"I didn't mean to—"

"Grace, please try to make our son and his bride feel welcome here in our home. I'm begging you." He turned and left before she could respond—no doubt why he'd left so quickly.

She turned back to the window. Buckmaster and his bride had stopped in the pasture to embrace. She watched them kiss and then draw apart. Sarah Johnson Hamilton looked back toward the house as if sensing she was being watched. Could she see Grace standing before the window?

Grace didn't think so until she saw Sarah give her a self-satisfied smile before turning back to Buckmaster.

Her heart began to pound harder. The woman was evil. Grace had felt it the moment she'd met her. There was something dark and...broken in Sarah. Why didn't JD believe her?

Because JD prided himself on seeing the best in everyone. Because her husband was a fool—just like her son, she thought uncharitably.

She watched her son and his wife head back toward the house. She had tried to talk to Buckmaster, but, like his father, he'd cut her off, saying she just needed time to get to know Sarah. Not wanting to alienate her son, she'd backed off.

But now as she hurried down to her room, closing the door behind her, Grace knew she had to find a way to save her son from this woman. And she would have to do it alone since she couldn't depend on JD to help her.

In fact, she wasn't sure she could depend on JD anymore at all. He'd promised that he would never leave her, but a part of him had already left to be a senator, she thought as she moved to the window in time to see him ride away toward the mountains.

First her son, and now she was losing her husband.

SENATOR BUCKMASTER HAMILTON got the call in the middle of a staff meeting. He'd put his phone on vibrate, pulling it out almost unconsciously since he had no plan to answer it. The primaries were coming up in June. That didn't give him much time to secure his place in the race for president.

Listening to his advisers on what else needed to be done, he glanced at his phone to make sure it wasn't one of his daughters calling. When he saw that it was the sheriff calling from Montana, he excused himself and took the call out in the hallway.

"Frank?" he said into the phone. "What's wrong?"

"Nothing to do with your daughters," he told the senator quickly. They'd had a lot of calls like this lately. Buckmaster's only concern had always been the same. Were his girls all right? "I'm sure you've heard about the recent…incident on your ranch from Harper."

"Incident?" He had talked to Sarah earlier but only briefly. When he'd told her he was in a staff meeting, she'd said it was nothing and he'd promised to call her later.

"Harper didn't tell you about the remains she and Brody McTavish found on the ranch?"

"I haven't spoken with Harper. What's this about remains? On my ranch?" His first thought was a homeless person traveling through on the rails.

"I wanted to give you a heads-up," Frank was saying. "Based on what she was wearing when she disappeared and other evidence, the remains appear to be Margaret McTavish's. We'll know more after the autopsy."

Buckmaster blinked a couple of times. At first the name rang no bells. Then it hit him. *Maggie. Maggie McTavish.* He swore silently. "I don't understand." But he feared he did.

"She'd been buried in a wooden box on that hillside next to the McTavish place. Buck…" Just the use of his first name by the sheriff told him the news was about to get worse. "We're investigating this as a homicide. As a professional courtesy, I wanted to call you myself. We should have a positive ID soon. But you know me well enough that I don't believe I have to tell you I intend to find her murderer, no matter where that trail leads."

He didn't hear anything Frank said for a few seconds. Maggie McTavish. Murdered… Buried on Hamilton Ranch…? Dear God, no.

"…so I'm going to need to talk to you, and Sarah, as well."

Buckmaster shook his head as what the sheriff was saying finally registered. Frank was warning him. He swore again. What was the point of an investigation? There wasn't a person in the county who wouldn't have already dug his father up and hanged him for the murder. "Sarah and I don't know anything. That was years ago."

"Thirty-five this fall," Frank agreed. "But with most everyone else who was connected with Maggie gone…"

"You mean with my father dead." He leaned against the hallway wall and closed his eyes. "You can't believe that he had anything to do with this." Even as he said it, though, he realized how little he had known about his father. Maybe JD Hamilton had a side that he'd kept hidden from all of them.

"Quite frankly, I don't know what to believe."

"How was it that her body turned up now?" he demanded. With him so close to winning the primary election, it felt as if his opponents had to have literally dug this up.

"We had a bad storm the other night. The body had been buried in a wooden box up on a hill near the fence between the properties. The rain must have loosened the earth… Harper happened to be riding her horse in the area when—"

"Wait." Buckmaster opened his eyes and pushed off the wall. "You say my *daughter* found the body?"

"She and Brody McTavish."

"What the hell were those two doing together?" The words were out before he could call them back. He heard a door open.

"You'll have to ask your daughter," the sheriff said.

One of his advisers motioned that they were waiting on him.

"I'll do that. In the meantime, you'll keep me informed on your investigation."

"Of course. Are you planning to be home soon?" Frank said quickly, as if hearing in Buckmaster's voice that he was anxious to get off the line. "I really do need to talk to you. I'll call Sarah—"

He didn't want the sheriff talking to Sarah alone. "I'll fly home. Don't bother Sarah with this until I get there." Silence. "She doesn't know anything anyway." When the sheriff still didn't say anything, he swore.

"No matter what you suspect about my..." He almost said *wife*, but he caught himself before he did. Even though he thought of her as his wife, he and Sarah weren't married. Not yet anyway. "Sarah, she isn't strong."

"Like your mother," Frank said.

Buckmaster could hear in the silence that followed that the sheriff hadn't meant to say that. "My mother is a suspect, as well as my father?" He swore.

"Everyone is a suspect until I find out who killed her. Call me when you get in," Frank said.

Buckmaster disconnected and started back toward his meeting. His stomach roiled. He straightened his tie and reached for the doorknob. For years he'd been following in his father's footsteps. First senator, now a candidate for president...

His father's damned legacy, he thought with a bitter laugh. He'd thought any secrets had been buried with JD. *What did you do, Dad? What the hell did you do?*

STILL REELING FROM the morning she'd had, Harper called the one person she'd always been able to count on—her older sister Ainsley. She quickly told her about their gruesome discovery.

"Oh, Harper, I am so sorry. Are you all right?" Her sister had quit law school to find locations for movie sites in Montana. Their father hadn't been happy about it, Harper had heard that much at least on the family grapevine. But Ainsley seemed happy and swore it was only temporary.

"It was awful, but I'm okay. I'm just glad Brody was there."

She heard a smile in her sister's voice. "I am, too."

They fell silent for a moment. "Do they know whose body it is?"

"The sheriff said they won't know anything definite until the autopsy," Harper told her.

"So it could have been there for years?"

"Apparently it was. You should have seen it," she said. "It was the creepiest thing I have ever seen. I haven't told Dad. Mother wanted to do it. I don't know if she was going to wait until we knew something definite or not."

"Probably a good idea. No reason to upset him until she has all of the facts," Ainsley agreed. "He has enough going on. I'm sure if there is something to worry about, the sheriff will let him know."

Harper thought about that. "I had a visitor when I returned today. Ariel Crenshaw, the sister of the private investigator Angelina hired to dig up something on Mother."

Ainsley groaned. "Angelina. That woman, rest her soul. Why would the PI's sister come by to talk to you?"

"She's looking into her sister's death. She said some members of an anarchist group called The Prophecy were connected to both Angelina's death and that of her sister, the private investigator Angelina hired to look into Mother's past. Did you know about this?"

"No. Angelina thought Mother was involved with this group?"

"Apparently. She hired the PI to find out something about Mother's *college* years, in particular, the late seventies."

Ainsley was quiet for a long moment. "That *is* odd."

"I can't believe we didn't hear something about this."

"There must not have been anything to it," Ainsley said. "So, was it nice seeing Brody again?"

SARAH HEARD SOMETHING in Buck's voice when he called to tell her he'd already heard the news about Maggie McTavish. She braced herself. With the primaries coming up, she knew the kind of stress he was under. He didn't need this. Worse, he didn't have anyone he could lean on in DC.

She couldn't be with him and that worried her. The problem was that she knew Buck only too well. He was already having second thoughts about his run for president. With this latest news, he would start having even more doubts. He could still pull out before the primaries. She couldn't let that happen. Somehow, she had to give him the strength to continue, because she knew how much the country needed him. And how much he needed this, even if he was starting to question it.

"I'm flying in tomorrow morning. Meet me at the airport," he said to her surprise. "It will give us extra time to talk. I can't stay away long."

"I thought you were in meetings with your advisers for the next few days?" That he wanted her to meet him at the airport was odd. He always left his SUV at the airport. Unlike a lot of politicians, he didn't have a staff car or hire limos to take him places. He drove himself because, at heart, he was a Montana rancher. No private jet. No driver. No expenses that would raise eyebrows from his constituents.

"What's this about a body Harper found on the ranch? I assume that's why you called me earlier."

"I didn't want to upset you and since there is nothing you can do here—"

Buck swore. "Frank says the remains are Maggie McTavish's. He wants to question the two of us in connection with *murder*."

Something hard and cold settled in her stomach. "Question us? About *what*?"

"What the hell do you think?" he snapped. "I knew all this was going to come back someday and bite me in the ass, but I never expected this. Pick me up at the airport. We need to get our stories straight before we meet with the sheriff."

BRODY HAD HEARD his father's pickup engine rev and knew he was on his way over to his brother's place to give him the news. He'd hurried around the shop building, but he was too late. He realized as he saw his father racing toward his brother's house that if he needed him to come along, he would have asked him.

Of course, Finn would want to tell his brother the news alone. Brody couldn't bear the thought of how his uncle was going to take it. From what his father had told him, Maggie had been Flannigan's pride and joy. This news would break the old man's heart—as if Maggie hadn't done that when she was alive.

He hurried to his pickup. What would happen now? He hated to think. But he needed to talk to his dad and uncle. It wouldn't be long before the news was all over the county. He needed to know what they were going to do about getting Maggie justice.

His uncle and dad had started the ranch, but their hearts had always been in the blacksmithing part of the operation. When he turned twenty-one he'd taken over the ranching and farming. They'd both been at the age where they were happy to hand over the reins.

He had tried to make their lives easier, since both of them had worked hard their whole lives.

Now as he drove down the road toward his uncle's place, he wished there was a way to spare them what was coming. Turning into his uncle's place, he passed the sheriff and drove a little faster, worried.

As he pulled up in front of his uncle's house, he spotted his father sitting on the porch alone. "What's going on?" Brody asked as he joined him. His uncle was nowhere in sight. Brody felt his heart lodge in his throat as he saw his father's expression. "Is he all right?"

"The sheriff was here," Finn McTavish said. While only in his midsixties, he looked older suddenly, his face drawn and haggard. "He told your uncle that the body was Maggie's and that it was now a murder investigation."

"Where is he now?" Brody asked, thinking he shouldn't be alone.

"Inside the house."

He started in that direction but his father stopped him.

"Leave him be. He'll come out when he's ready," Finn said.

"The sheriff… So it's Maggie, just as I'd feared." He'd grown up wanting to believe that the beautiful cousin he'd never known had run away to make a better life for herself. He'd actually looked for her in late-night movies since from the photographs he'd seen of her, she was so striking that she could have been an actress or a model. She could have been a lot of things.

A wave of nausea washed over him. He'd heard stories about his cousin since he was a boy. In fact, his

first fistfight in grade school had been over what Billy
Loring said his father had said about her. At that time,
he'd never seen more than photos of her that his uncle
kept on the mantel, but she was family and family was
worth defending even if Billy Loring was older, bigger and stronger.

"When Harper and I found her horse... The rain had
washed the wooden box down the hillside. She was
buried on Hamilton Ranch, just yards from our land,"
Brody said, and turned as the screen door was flung
open and his uncle stepped out. Flannigan McTavish
looked as if all the air had been knocked out of him.

"Uncle Flan—"

"I don't want to hear another word about my Maggie." His uncle's green eyes flashed with anger. "Nor
do I ever want to hear you've been with that Hamilton girl."

With that, he descended the porch steps and walked
across the yard toward the shop.

"Let him go," his father said. "You heard him. He
needs to grieve in his own way."

Growing up, neither his father nor his uncle had
liked to talk about Maggie, but when pushed, his father had told him that Flannigan had doted on his only
daughter and "that was part of the problem."

"Nor does he want to hear about Harper, it seems,"
Brody said, realizing that he'd known this would be the
case. "Don't you think I heard the rumors growing up
about Maggie and JD Hamilton? But even if it's true
and JD killed her, it's no reason to hold it against the
rest of the Hamiltons."

His father looked toward the shop. Flannigan had

stopped and turned to look back at them. Brody saw
the two men exchange a glance.

"Or is there another reason the two of you don't
want me with Harper?" he asked.

CHAPTER SIX

JD KNEW SOMETHING was wrong the moment he opened the door to the ranch house. "Grace?" Maybe it was the quiet, the sense that no one was home, and yet Grace's car was in the drive. "Grace?"

He had already started toward the kitchen when he heard the moan and retraced his steps to the living room, hurrying now, suddenly afraid.

She lay at the bottom of the stairs, her body twisted, her face pressed into the hardwood.

"Grace!" he cried, running to her. His first thought at seeing her lying there was that he would never forgive himself. She must have fallen down the stairs while he'd been gone. If he had been here...

Her eyes flickered open and he saw the pain and the fear. How long had she been lying here? Where were Buck and Sarah? He silently cursed himself for leaving her. He knew how upset she'd been at the news that Sarah was pregnant. "It's all right. I'm here now."

"I can't feel my legs," she cried, and gripped his arm. "JD, I can't feel my legs."

"Lie still. Don't move. I'm getting help." He quickly stepped to the kitchen wall phone and called 9-1-1 for an ambulance.

Grace had begun to cry, muttering something through her tears that he couldn't make out.

"Please hurry," he pleaded into the phone before going back to her and kneeling with her on the floor. *"Don't talk,"* he insisted when she tried to tell him what had happened. *"They said you should lie very still. An ambulance is on the way."*

She closed her eyes and he prayed she didn't die. At the hospital he paced the floor, too upset and too guilt-ridden to sit. She had begged him to resign as senator his second term. She'd never minded his involvement in politics as long as their son was home. But now...

"Your wife has sustained an injury to her spine," the doctor said when he finally came out.

"She said she couldn't feel her legs," JD said. *"Is she—"*

"I think the paralysis is temporary. There is some swelling. Once that goes down..."

"But you don't know if she will be able to walk again?"

"Let's wait and see after the swelling goes down. If you like, you can see her now."

He walked down the long hallway to her room, mentally kicking himself for not being there, though he doubted he could have prevented her fall even if he had been home. That logic didn't make him feel much better. He'd been distancing himself from Grace and her angry bitterness for weeks now.

"How are you feeling?" he asked as he stepped through her door and moved quickly to her side. He'd promised to love and honor this woman until death did they part. He desperately didn't want to break that oath. He'd always been a man of his word.

Grace gave him a wan smile. *"I might never walk again."*

"The doctor is hopeful that when the swelling goes down, you'll be fine. You were lucky. It could have been much worse."

"Lucky?" she demanded. "JD, I was almost killed."

"What happened to make you fall like that?" he asked.

"Is that what you think happened?" she cried. "She tried to kill me."

"What?"

"Sarah. I was upstairs. I heard Buckmaster leave. I thought she'd left with him, but instead, she came upstairs looking for me. She was acting strange, talking crazy. I told her I didn't want to argue. I started down the stairs and I felt her hand in my back. JD, she pushed me!"

He stared at his wife. "Grace—"

"You don't believe me?" Her voice had risen. It broke on every word. "I just told you that my daughter-in-law tried to kill me and you're calling me a liar?"

"There must be some other explanation. Maybe you just thought—"

She turned her face to the wall. "Get out of my room."

"Grace—"

"Get out!"

He took a step back, telling himself she'd had a scare. Once she was feeling better... "I'll check on you later."

"Don't bother."

BRODY KNEW HOW stubborn his father could be. He waited, determined to get answers that he felt he'd been denied all his life.

He'd wanted to know about Maggie from as far back as he could remember. Once when he was very young he'd asked about the beautiful woman's photo on his uncle's mantel. Flannigan had been drinking and was surprisingly talkative. He'd said that Maggie was "the sweetest girl God ever put on this earth."

"Where is she?" he'd asked. His uncle's green eyes had filled with tears.

"She's in my heart."

When he'd asked his father how Maggie could be in his uncle's heart, he'd been told, "She's gone and it breaks your uncle's heart and mine to talk about her."

Now, as he waited for his father to speak, he felt that old frustration. Everything he'd learned about Maggie had been either on the playground at school or whispered gossip. All of those stories had been about a wild, reckless young woman with the morals of an alley cat.

"Leave it alone, son," Finn said as he got to his feet and started to walk past him.

Brody grabbed his father's arm, making Finn look at him with alarm. He'd never talked back, let alone laid a hand on the man who'd raised him.

"I'm sorry," he said, letting go. "But I've heard that my whole life. Don't you think it's time I knew the truth?"

"The truth?" his father repeated, suddenly looking tired. "I'm not sure you want to hear that this woman you've taken a fancy for…"

"Harper?" He couldn't imagine what she could have to do with any of this. It had all happened so long ago.

"Her grandfather, Senator JD Hamilton, killed your cousin as sure as I'm standing here. And now Maggie's name will be dragged through the muck all over again. If this doesn't kill my brother… I'm sorry, son, but the best thing you can do is stay away from Harper Hamilton."

"If it's true and JD Hamilton killed Maggie, then why didn't he go to prison for it?"

His father sighed. "Even if we'd known then what he'd done with her, he would never have seen a prison cell. He was a senator who was in line for the presidency of the United States."

"You don't know that. Still, if there had been any proof that something had even happened to her—"

"You think he would have let any proof surface? Maggie's killer went free. Just as his son will make sure that JD Hamilton's reputation stays intact while Maggie's is…" His voice broke. "Please, Brody, leave this alone. Leave Harper alone." With that his father headed toward the shop his uncle had disappeared into earlier.

Brody stood on the porch, shell-shocked by everything that had happened. He'd never heard his father talk like this. Finn loved America, the only home he'd known. Did he really believe there would be no justice for Maggie? Worse, did he paint Harper and her grandfather with the same brush?

He balked at the idea, not wanting to believe it. Not wanting to let go of the hope that, as bad as it was, he and Harper might defy the odds and have a chance of a future. But hadn't he known when he'd seen Maggie's body buried on Hamilton land that their chances had gone from bad to worse? All he could think about was what this would do to Harper when the truth came out.

Brody heard his father call out, "Flannigan?" and watched as his uncle came out of the shop and met his brother. He couldn't hear what his father was saying.

Flannigan had always seemed like a giant. His eyes welled with tears as he saw the big man stagger. Finn laid a hand on his brother's shoulder as Flannigan bent his head and wept.

RUSSELL LEFT MILLIE Hansen staring unseeing out the window in the lounge and walked down the rest-home hallway. If Millie was in her right mind—even momentarily—then she believed that Dr. Ralph Venable had returned to the States.

Since the doctor had sent Millie a postcard from Brazil after he'd left Montana, Russell was betting that he would do the same on his return. Apparently the doctor had been as fond of Millie as she had been of him. Dr. Venable wouldn't know that anyone was onto him.

The doctor had been working in a hospital in South America, assisted by a woman named Sarah Johnson. Russell's Sarah. He thought of all the times he'd been afraid of what her past would reveal. And then it had turned out that there was no big secret. Except for the fact that Dr. Venable dealt in wiping away memories. He seemed to have done a great job on Sarah since, as far as Russell knew, she still hadn't remembered those years.

What Russell wanted to prove was that the real villain behind the brain wiping had been Sarah's own husband, presidential candidate Senator Buckmaster Hamilton.

Sarah was blind when it came to her former husband. She still loved him—a sentiment that could have been sublimated into her mind by Dr. Venable.

Not that it mattered. Once Russell exposed Buckmaster, Sarah would finally have to face the truth. Russell told himself that he wasn't doing this to hurt her. He was doing it to save her. It didn't matter that she'd broken his heart. Russell would be there to pick up the pieces because if he was right, Sarah was going to need him.

But first he had to find the proof that would free Sarah of Buckmaster once and for all.

He stepped quickly into Millie's room, headed for the bulletin board beside her bed. There were so many cards and papers tacked to the bulletin board that it was covered a good quarter-inch thick.

He scanned the board quickly, hoping that Dr. Venable had sent another postcard recently and it would be on top. Seeing everything Millie had tacked up, he was certain that if the doctor had sent her another postcard, it would be here.

He doubted there would be a return address, but there would be a postmark. Was Millie right? Was the doctor back in the States? Or was she confused? He'd lucked out catching her on a good day, but still...

There was no postcard visible. He would have to take everything down. Looking toward the open door, he heard several patients walk past, the legs of their walkers making scraping sounds as they passed.

He told himself he would look more guilty if he closed the door, but he had no choice. Quickly moving, he took a peek out into the hallway before closing the door. There was no lock.

Back at the bulletin board, he began taking down the myriad cards and letters and printed affirmations. He found the postcard under a half dozen birthday wishes.

The words were printed in neat script: "Hope to

see you soon now that I am stateside." It was simply signed "Ralph."

The postmark was smudged but he could make out part of the date. The card had been sent over three weeks ago.

Russell flipped the card over to see a photo of Miami's art deco area of the city.

Dr. Venable could already be back in Montana. Russell knew what had brought him back. Sarah. The question was how long before he contacted her? Or had he already? Was he going to restore Sarah's memories? Or steal more of them?

FRANK HAD SPENT the day fending off curious residents who'd heard about a body being found on Hamilton Ranch. He'd put them all off. Now, as he entered the house, he saw his wife, Lynette, standing in the kitchen. One look at her expression and he knew she wouldn't be as easy to dissuade. Once considered the worst gossip in three counties, Lynette had a way of attracting news like metal to a magnet. He could tell that she'd been waiting all day to grill him.

"Who is she?" his wife wanted to know the moment he walked into the kitchen.

He pretended not to know what she was talking about, curious how much of the story was already on the wind. Fortunately, the assumed identity of the corpse hadn't gotten out, but he was sure there had been speculation and that Maggie McTavish's name would come up—if it hadn't already.

"Won't know anything until the autopsy," he said, hanging up his Stetson on the hook by the back door. "What's for dinner?"

"Roast beef. I heard it was a woman's body buried on Hamilton Ranch and that her body had been mummified."

"*Roast beef* and *mummified* should never be used in the same sentence," he joked as he headed toward the refrigerator for a beer.

"How long has the body been there?" Lynette asked, standing on the other side of the open refrigerator door. He could see the top of her head. Her last trip to the beauty shop had left her hair the color of eggplant. Since he doubted anyone her age would dye her hair that color on purpose, he'd kept his mouth shut, hoping she'd go back to the brunette she'd been when he'd met her.

"Again, won't know anything until—"

"You can't put me off with that procedural jargon," she snapped as he closed the refrigerator to find her standing there with her hands on her ample hips.

Frank leaned in for a kiss. He couldn't help but smile. Lynette was the love of his life. She drove him crazy, but it was a nice kind of crazy.

"You know the rumor that's already spreading around?" she asked as he twisted off the cap on his bottle and took a long drink. "Maggie McTavish."

He'd known it wouldn't take long. It was a logical jump from the mummified body of a woman to Maggie, the young woman who'd disappeared thirty-five years ago.

"The roast smells wonderful," Frank said as he turned away to open the oven. "You cooked potatoes, carrots and onions with it. My favorite."

"So it *is* her," Lynette said, seeming to need to sit as she dropped into one of the padded kitchen chairs.

He didn't waste his breath telling her again that they wouldn't know anything definite until the autopsy.

"I heard she was in a wooden box, so someone murdered her and buried her on Hamilton Ranch," his wife was saying. "I heard the spot was close to McTavish land. Do you think that's where they used to meet?"

He didn't have to ask whom she was referring to. Senator John David "JD" Hamilton, Senator Buckmaster Hamilton's father.

When he realized she was waiting for an answer, he said, "I'm trying hard not to jump to any conclusions though I see you don't suffer that same fate."

"If the rumors were true from back then—"

"And we all know that if you can't trust a good rumor, then what can you trust," he said.

"Seriously, he was twice her age—not to mention *married* and about to run for president." Lynette shook her head. "You know he killed her. But what I'm wondering is how you're going to prove it. JD's long dead. So is his wife, Grace, not that she could have done it from her wheelchair—unless, of course, she was faking her inability to walk. There is always that since she definitely had motive."

Frank groaned. He loved—and hated—the way Lynette's mind worked. It took so little to get her imagination going. "It appears you've already got it solved."

"With Maggie dead," his wife continued as if he hadn't spoken, "who does that leave that might know the truth?"

He took another drink of his beer. His thoughts had already ridden along this same path. "I love watching the wheels turning in your head. It is an amazing thing to see."

"I suppose Buckmaster could have learned about his father's affair and killed Maggie? Or..." Lynette's eyes went wide and luminous. "*Sarah*. Sarah and Buck were living in the same house during at least part of that time. Maybe she killed her to protect JD and his candidacy for president."

"Wow," Frank said. "Let me write this all down."

"Make fun if you will, but you have to admit, there are more suspects than ever when you think about it. Especially given what we know about Sarah."

That was just it. They knew just enough about Sarah and her return to give him heartburn. "I had better eat well to keep my strength up, then. Is the roast about ready?"

She mugged a face at him as she got to her feet and went to the oven.

He put down his beer to help her with dinner as he thought about what she'd said. She'd made some good points. But until the autopsy was complete and the DNA results were in...

"Assuming that the body is Maggie McTavish's," he said as they sat down to eat. Frank dished them both up roast beef and vegetables. "What do you remember about her?"

Lynette shot him an I-knew-it look. "Too beautiful, too wild, too...easy. Not to mention the difference in age between her and JD." She made a disapproving face. "He was old enough to know better. If it had come out... But that's why he had to kill her, wasn't it? He would have lost the election. A wife in a wheelchair, a teenage lover on the side at his age. He would have been lucky to get a single vote."

"He was forty-two," Frank had to point out. "That's not exactly elderly."

"And Maggie was eighteen."

"Legal age of consent."

"Not even the age of JD's own son."

"She knew her own mind by that age." He couldn't help defending her, even though he knew it would get a rise out of Lynette.

"How do *you* remember her?" she asked suspiciously.

"Uninhibited, free-spirited, brazen and definitely too tragically beautiful. I remember thinking that she'd get her heart broken and come to a bad end." He could feel Lynette staring at him.

"You were in love with her."

Frank shook his head. "I was in love with you. Actually, I felt sorry for any man who fell for Maggie. I think they would have definitely gotten to know heartbreak as well, but—" he shrugged "—what do I know?"

"I suppose someone could have resented her free spirit, or maybe it was her beauty, and killed her."

"That's one theory," he agreed.

She stopped eating to look at him. "You know something I don't."

He grinned across the table at her. "I hope I know a lot of things you don't," he said with a laugh. "If the corpse is Maggie McTavish's, I have no idea who killed her. Does that make you feel better?" He reached for the knife to cut more roast. "Let's not talk about murder. It gives me indigestion. Let's talk about the store and what else is new."

Lynette had once owned the Beartooth General

Store. But after she was almost killed in a fire at the store, she'd sold it, the land and her house she'd once shared with her first husband, Bob Benton. When the new owner had the store rebuilt as it had been, Lynette had gone back to work there part-time. Frank had seen that she missed working and was glad. It gave her an opportunity to get out of the house—as well as hear what was going on in the county.

"Mabel Murphy stopped by. You know she used to clean for Grace and JD Hamilton," Lynette said now, getting her cat-that-ate-the-canary look. "She told me something interesting."

Frank put more roast and vegetables onto her plate and, smiling, helped himself. He could tell that his wife had been sitting on this little tidbit all evening. "I suppose there's no stopping you. Mabel already has the murder solved?"

"Mock, but Mabel swears that she overheard Grace arguing with JD about Maggie not long before the girl disappeared." Lynette licked her lips and met his gaze. "So Grace *knew*. And what's more, Grace couldn't stand her daughter-in-law, Sarah. She blamed her for eloping and stealing her son, Buck, and for encouraging JD to run for president. Mabel overheard her say something about wanting to kill both of the women she claimed had destroyed her life—if one of them didn't kill her first."

He did find that interesting but did his best to hide it. "I'm amazed Mabel got any cleaning done with her ear to the door all the time," Frank said. He made a mental note to himself to find out how Grace had died.

"Say what you will about Mabel, but she is one of the only people still alive who might have information about what was going on in that house. Buckmaster and Sarah lived with his parents for a while—until Grace and Sarah had a huge row and the newly married couple moved out—so how can you trust anything they tell you?"

SARAH WAS WAITING for him at the airport when Buckmaster flew into Bozeman the next morning. He hadn't been able to take a decent breath since the sheriff's call. But when the plane touched down, he felt some relief. He was home. Back in Montana.

Out the plane window, he caught sight of the Bridger Mountains, the tops frosted with fresh snow. He took a breath, then another. He'd come too far to let the past destroy him and his family. Unfortunately, he had no idea how to keep that from happening.

Maggie McTavish.

Hadn't he known that she would take the whole family down?

"You can't leave now," his campaign manager had said, pulling him aside and lowering his voice when Buck told him he had to go home. "We have to prep you for this debate. Whatever is going on at home, this isn't the time."

"I have no choice." He hadn't wanted to get into it with Jerrod. "I'll be back in time for the debate." He'd started to step away when his campaign manager had grabbed his arm.

"I can tell something has happened. How bad is it?" Jerrod had demanded.

"Just let me take care of it."

The younger man had sworn under his breath. "One of the girls?"

"I really don't have time to get into this right now, but I'm afraid there will have to be some damage control. How much, I don't know yet. I'll call you." He'd pulled free and left, afraid there wasn't enough damage control in the world to stop the storm that was about to hail down on them.

Now he looked up and saw Sarah waiting for him parked at the curb. Just the sight of her hit him like a two-ton truck. She made him feel weak in his knees. All he could think about was taking her in his arms. But, he reminded himself as he looked past her, this wasn't the place.

You're just like your father. Your life is nothing but lies and secrets.

The thought made him grit his teeth. With his carry-on in one hand, he reached for the door handle and quickly jumped in the vehicle.

He'd been a fool to ask her to pick him up. He was too well-known. So was Sarah by extension. Had they embraced, it would have been in the news within the hour—complete with quickly snapped cell phone photos, if not a photographer who might have heard he was flying in.

"Drive!" he ordered.

"Buck, you're scaring me," Sarah said.

"I don't know what I was thinking asking you to come here," he said as she pulled away from the curb. "I just wanted to see you as quickly as possible."

Sometimes he wished he'd never gotten into politics. He'd taken away any privacy he had—not to mention the privacy of his family. But politics were in his blood, he thought bitterly as they left the airport.

"I'm sorry," he said as he looked over at her. "I

wanted to take you in my arms. I wanted to kiss you and…" He shook his head. "One day soon we won't have to hide anymore."

Sarah didn't look convinced.

"I swear to you," he said, reaching over to take her free hand. He caressed her palm with his fingers, tracing her lifeline. "I love you, Sarah. Somehow, we're going to get through all of this. Right now, though," he said, letting go so she could tend to driving, "we have to wade through the quagmire of my father's legacy."

AFTER WHAT SEEMED an interminable amount of time, the sheriff finally got the call from the coroner's office.

"We have some preliminary results down here," Charlie Brooks said. "I thought you might want to stop by my office."

"I'll be right there." Minutes later, he pushed open the door to find Charlie behind his desk. Frank pulled out a chair and sat, surprised how weak his legs felt. He could tell by the look on the coroner's face that they'd found out something that had upset him.

Charlie, a former veterinarian turned coroner, was new at this murder business. He'd thought because he loved mysteries, he would enjoy the work. Often he looked disappointed in mankind—and a little sick to his stomach.

"Were you able to find a cause of death?" Frank asked. He could see the report on Charlie's desk, his hands resting over it. He worried that because of the mummification of the body they wouldn't be able to get any definitive answers.

"She suffered a severe brain injury…"

The sheriff sat back. "So she could have fallen off her horse, hit a rock—"

Charlie shook his head. "From the angle of the wound, she was hit with a heavy object in the back of the head, but apparently it wasn't sufficient to kill her."

"You can tell that from the mummified body?"

"Her internal organs were intact, including her brain, lungs and womb."

He stared at the coroner. "What are you trying to tell me?"

Charlie sighed and looked away for a moment. He'd been almost excited to be able to do an autopsy on a mummified body since they were so rare. Now, though, he looked more than sick to his stomach.

"She was five months pregnant," the coroner said after a moment.

Frank swore under his breath as his mind raced with possible suspects given this information. Who would have known about the pregnancy? Had Maggie told the father of her baby? Rubbing a hand over his face, he sighed. "I was worried it would be something like that. Will it be possible to get a DNA sample from the fetus?"

"We're hopeful."

"In that case, we'll need to get DNA samples from anyone who might have fathered her baby." Frank was already thinking of how difficult that was going to be given that their chief suspect—JD Hamilton—had been buried not long after Maggie.

"But wait a minute. You said the blow to her head wasn't enough to kill her."

Charlie nodded. "We found something under her fingernails."

Frank frowned. "I can't believe there would still be skin or fibers."

The coroner shook his head. "There were splinters."

It took him a moment to understand what that meant. He felt his pulse leap with horror as his breath caught in his throat. "No," he said, shaking his head, but the look on Charlie's face told him it was true. His stomach did a slow, sickening roll.

"I checked the wooden box she was buried in," the coroner said. "There are gouge marks on the inside of the top of the coffin. Whether by accident or on purpose, Maggie McTavish died from a lack of oxygen. She was buried alive."

CHAPTER SEVEN

JD DIDN'T GO back to the lake. Grace noticed, narrowing her eyes at him, making him feel as if he had something to hide.

The animosity between his son and daughter-in-law and his wife had seemed to escalate as Sarah's pregnancy became more advanced.

"Now she has him where she wants him," Grace said bitterly. "And she has you, too, doesn't she? She's talked you into running for president."

"You know it's been something I've considered," he said in his defense. A part of him wondered if he'd latched on to the idea because it would get him away from the ranch, from the feuding and fighting, from Grace.

He felt guilty and yet he wanted to see if he had a chance of winning the Republican primary. His supporters seemed to think he did. He had his doubts, but the more he thought about it, the more he wanted to run.

"If I could get out of this wheelchair, I would kill her," Grace said.

He didn't even bother to reply, simply walked out of the room. He'd talked himself hoarse trying to get her to make peace with her daughter-in-law. What had happened to the woman he'd married?

"I'd kill that other one, too," he heard her say as he started to close the door. That other one? His heart lodged in his throat. Maggie? Is that who she was talking about? He turned to look back at her.

Grace smiled and nodded. "Why don't you go fishing, JD. At least we know what makes you happy, don't we?"

WHEN SHE'D HEARD that her father was flying in today, Harper swung by the Beartooth General Store to pick up the homemade cinnamon rolls he loved. She was anxious to see him after everything that had happened and was disappointed when he said Sarah would be picking him up at the airport.

She needed to talk to him about not only the body that had been found on the ranch, but also the events four months ago involving Angelina and her mother. Even if her mother wasn't a member of this anarchist group, she had to admit it all sounded suspicious to her. She was realizing how little she knew about her mother. Was her father realizing the same thing? Or was he blinded by love?

As she pushed open the door to the grocery, the bell jangled and Lynette Curry or, as everyone called her but her sheriff husband, Nettie looked up. Surprise registered on her face, but nothing like the surprise on the face of the woman Nettie had been visiting with.

As the door closed behind her, Harper said hello to Nettie and Mabel Murphy. The two older women returned the greeting, but it was clear as Harper walked toward them that she'd interrupted something. She guessed it was about the body that had been found on the ranch. It was no surprise that the news had already gotten out.

"What can I get you, Miss Hamilton?" Nettie asked.

Harper could tell that she didn't know which twin she was. "I'm going to need a half dozen of your wonderful cinnamon rolls," she said, and Nettie quickly turned and began cutting into the huge pan of rolls. She seemed nervous. So did Mabel. The tension in the air could have been cut along with the cinnamon rolls.

"Is everything all right?" Harper asked, hoping to clear the air.

"I was about to ask *you* that," Mabel said.

Nettie tried to hush her as she wrapped the cinnamon rolls up and put them on the counter, but Mabel didn't seem to hear. "How did your family take the news?"

"The news?" Harper asked, pretending she didn't know.

Mabel leaned forward to whisper even though they were the only people in the store. "About Maggie's body being found on your ranch."

"Maggie?" So the sheriff had already ID'd the body? The name didn't register.

"Maggie *McTavish*. I heard her body was…mummified." Mabel shuddered. "It must have been ghastly to find—"

"What?" Harper said as she grabbed the counter for support. "The body we found was Brody's *cousin*?" She'd heard stories about Maggie. In fact, she'd thought that Maggie's alleged reputation was probably why her mother didn't like her being around Brody and the McTavish family.

"You hadn't heard?" Nettie asked, even though it was clear she hadn't.

"Does Brody know?" Harper asked, sick at heart for him.

"I would imagine he knows by now," Nettie said.

"If he didn't know when he saw the body to begin with," Mabel added, one brow shooting up.

Harper stared at her. "How would he have known?"

"It isn't like some of us didn't suspect, under the circumstances, that she'd gotten herself murdered and buried on the ranch," Mabel said.

"Circumstances?" Harper was in such shock that none of this was computing.

"Surely you know about your grandfather and Maggie," Mabel said, even though Nettie was trying to shush her. "True he was married and twice her age, but everyone in these parts—"

"That was only a rumor," Nettie broke in. "There's no reason to jump to conclusions. I'm sure my husband will sort it out all in good time."

Harper felt numb. *Her grandfather JD and Maggie McTavish?* She thought again of Brody. Had he known about this? She recalled how distant he'd gotten after they'd discovered the body and mentally kicked herself. *He'd known.* Or at least he'd suspected it was Maggie. No wonder he'd been so upset. No wonder he'd been so anxious to get away from her.

"I have to go," she said, and turned toward the door.

"What about your cinnamon rolls?" Nettie called to her, but Harper was on a completely different errand now.

BRODY LOOKED UP to see a vehicle roaring up the road. He'd just finished chores and was headed for the house he'd built on the McTavish Ranch some miles from his father's and uncle's.

He watched from under the brim of his straw cowboy hat. Whoever was driving that SUV was going way too fast. He braced himself for more bad news as the SUV came to a dust-boiling stop just feet from him.

"What the hell?" he said as he moved to confront the driver. When he saw who it was through the open window, he swore again. "What are *you* doing here?"

"That body we found…is it…"

"My cousin Maggie's." He nodded slowly.

"I'm so sorry. I just heard at the Beartooth General Store."

"So it's all over the valley by now," he said with a curse. He really didn't want to talk to her about this. Seeing her made it all that much more painful.

"I understand now why you just wanted to be alone yesterday. If I had known—"

"I'm fine. Thanks for stopping by. You should get on home now." He turned away. Behind him he heard her car door open and let out an oath under his breath as he heard her come after him.

"If you think being rude will make me go away, you're wrong."

He shook his head and turned back around to face her. "How does a man deal with a woman like you?"

"I know why you're acting like this. But you don't have to protect me. I can handle the truth."

Brody sighed. "What is it that really has a bee in your bonnet?"

"Other than one minute yesterday you were rescuing me—" She held up a hand to stop him before he could correct him. "And kissing me and telling me it was something you'd wanted to do since I was sixteen and the next you were telling me to get lost. A little explanation would have been nice. Then I hear at the store that my grandfather and your cousin Maggie were..."

"Lovers?"

"Is it true?"

He shrugged. "You should ask someone who knows. I wasn't even born yet."

"Neither was I. But that doesn't keep it from affecting us, does it."

He wanted to tell her there was no "us" and he couldn't see how there ever could be. His uncle and father had made it clear how they felt already. Wait until all this hit the fan.

She squinted in the sun for a moment. "Your uncle never mentioned—"

"He didn't like talking about Maggie," Brody said.

"If you think my grandfather killed her, well, you're..."

He raised a brow, waiting.

"That is what you think!" she cried.

"Look," he said, holding up his hands. "This is why I didn't want to get into it with you. I don't know who killed Maggie. We may never know. But I don't think it's a good idea for you to be here. My uncle could stop by. He's upset enough without seeing you here."

She stared at him, looking as if she might cry. "So you and I can't even talk or be seen together? And you're good with that even though all this happened before we were born?"

He raked a hand through his hair. "It's complicated. Anyway, you and I are like oil and water. It's just as well we don't take things between us any further."

"I see." She took a step back. Anger had dried her

tears. He was thankful for that. If she had cried, well, he would have been tempted to take her in his arms and he was afraid where that would lead. "Just for the record, I'd been waiting years for you to kiss me."

"Glad I got that taken care of, then."

Harper narrowed her gaze at him. "You can just accept all this if you want, but I'm going to find out who killed Maggie and clear my grandfather's name," she said defiantly.

"That's your worst idea yet. What if you find out that he killed her?"

"The one thing I won't do is let other people tell me who I can see and not see depending on their last name."

"It's not that cut-and-dried. Harper, you have no idea what you're getting into."

"Well, it won't have anything to do with you so I wouldn't worry about it."

He groaned inwardly as he watched her stomp to her SUV. Damn that woman. As she left in a cloud of dust, he told himself that it had been an idle threat. Once she drove away, she'd realize she didn't have the first clue as to how to go about finding a killer from thirty-five years ago and give it up. At least, he hoped that would be the case.

What if they were all wrong and JD Hamilton hadn't killed Maggie? What if her killer was still alive? Brody swore again. If Harper went through with her threat, she could be putting herself in danger.

But more than likely all that would happen was she'd get her heart broken when she learned the truth.

THE MOMENT HARPER reached home, she called her mother, but had to leave a message. She'd just hung up when she heard someone behind her. She turned to find her sister Kat, hands on hips, giving her one of her narrow-eyed looks.

"What do you think you're doing?" Kat demanded.

"I beg your pardon?" Harper said. Kat had always been bossy growing up, but if she thought she could still tell her what to do...

"I heard you on the phone telling Sarah that you want to talk to her about Maggie McTavish."

"Sarah? You mean our *mother*? You're the only one of us who calls her Sarah."

Kat ignored that. "Whatever you're doing, stop it. You have no idea what you're doing or how dangerous it could be."

Harper stared at her sister. "You sound like Brody."

Kat groaned. "He's involved, too?" She shook her head.

"Everyone, including Brody, believes that our grandfather killed Maggie McTavish. So I really can't see how it could be dangerous, since JD Hamilton has been dead for years. Unless you're suggesting Dad would harm me to keep the awful truth a secret?"

"Not *Dad*."

Harper was taken aback. She'd expected Kat to tell her how ridiculous Brody's claims were, that their grandfather, as well as their father, was innocent. But the way she'd said "not Dad."

"*Mother?* Are you saying Mother might harm me to keep me from finding out the truth?" Even as she asked the question, she recalled her mother's reaction to seeing her with Brody McTavish. Also Ariel Crenshaw's questions about Sarah Johnson Hamilton. "You think Mother knows something about Maggie's death?"

Kat shrugged. "Sarah lived in the first ranch house with our grandparents at about the same time as this thing with Maggie would have been going on. That was before Dad and Sarah moved out and he built this house."

"What is it with you and Mother?" She knew her sister too well. "*You know something?* What? You think Mother killed Maggie McTavish?"

"I didn't say that. But I think she's capable of it."

Harper couldn't have been more astonished. "*What? I* knew you had a problem with Mother but—"

"I found out some things about Sarah around Christmastime." It annoyed her that Kat called their mother Sarah, but she listened as her sister related the investigation that Kat's boyfriend, Max, had initiated. It had been Max, the journalist, who'd discovered that, during her college years, Sarah Johnson had allegedly been involved with a radical group called The Prophecy.

"I thought some other woman confessed?"

Kat looked surprised that Harper knew that.

"I had a visit from Ariel Crenshaw, the sister of the PI Angelina hired to find out about Mother's past. But she said Mother was cleared."

Her sister looked away for a moment. "Dad didn't want you knowing this, but… When Max and I started looking into Sarah's past, several of the members of The Prophecy tried to kill us."

She couldn't believe what she was hearing. "Where was I when all this was going on?"

"Europe. Finishing your education."

"It was a rhetorical question. I know where I was geographically. How it is no one thought to tell me?"

"Dad didn't want to worry you and Cassidy."

"But the rest of you knew?" she demanded.

"Not everyone."

"You still believe that Mother was a member of this anarchist group back in the seventies?"

"Not a *member*, a coleader—or possibly the real leader—and the only woman in The Prophecy."

"Red," Harper said, wondering if anyone would have told her if Ariel Crenshaw hadn't. "So what did they do that was so terrible?"

"They blew up buildings, killed innocent people."

She was having a hard time believing her mother had been involved. "If that is true, then why isn't Mother in jail? Why would this other woman confess?"

"Her name is Virginia Handley and it turns out she was involved in social unrest in the seventies. I've recently found out that she is dying of cancer."

"You think she took a bullet, so to speak, to save Mother."

"Crudely put, but yes."

"How could they get some random woman to confess to such a thing if it wasn't true?" Harper asked.

"She wasn't random. According to Dad, Sarah knew her. They…resembled each other and had lived in the same dorm at college. The woman was an activist and tried to get Sarah involved, but according to Sarah, she had refused. At least, that is her story."

"This is why you don't call her Mother?"

"I feel more comfortable calling her Sarah."

"You think she's lying. What does Dad think? Never mind—he believes her, doesn't he? But you can't think she would have been involved in killing innocent people."

"Max and I visited the prisons where two of The

Prophecy are locked up. If you had seen their expressions when they saw me—because of my resemblance to Sarah at that age… I hadn't wanted to tell you this. But you need to know. Digging in the past is…dangerous. Take it from me."

"Wait a minute. You talked to two members of the group who are in prison? They told you Mother was one of them?"

"Not in so many words, but they did tell us that they aren't finished. They have something planned and they led us to believe that…Sarah is in on it."

Harper shook her head. She thought of the woman who'd returned to them. Their *mother*. She couldn't be involved. This was all crazy. "Why would these people…" She didn't finish her question as it came to her. "*Dad*. This is about him running for president? Wait, they wouldn't have known that when Mother was in college. And what could it have to do with Maggie McTavish's death?"

"You might recall that our grandfather was also planning to make a run for president—shortly after Sarah came into the family. Dad admits that Sarah encouraged him to run. We think JD was actually her first target."

Harper stared at her sister. "You and Max are still trying to prove Mother is Red." The thought shocked her. "And, what, now *Dad* is her target?" She felt sick to her stomach.

"You see why I want you to stay out of Maggie's murder? And don't bother Cassidy with any of this," Kat warned. "Not about Maggie McTavish's body being found buried on the ranch or rumors about our grandfather and her, let alone what we suspect about Sarah."

"We used to be a family without any secrets," Harper bemoaned.

Her sister laughed. "You are so naive. We have always been a family of secrets. If you don't have one, you're the only member of this family who doesn't."

It wasn't until after Kat had left that Harper stood at the window looking in the direction of the burial site she and Brody had uncovered, thinking about her own hard-kept secret.

SARAH WAS RELIEVED when Buck suggested they stop by her house on the ranch before calling the sheriff. She made them each a cocktail and carried the sweating glasses to the porch, where she found Buck staring out at the ranch.

"I keep thinking about back then," he said as he accepted the glass she offered him. She watched him take a long drink before he looked at her. "Do you remember how it was between my parents?"

She gave a little laugh and took the seat next to him. "I was so head over heels in love with you that I wasn't paying any attention to anyone but you."

As she looked past him in the direction of the main house, she wished she *couldn't* remember. Buck had seemed in denial back then, as if he didn't want to admit what was going on.

"I'm sure you were too busy running the ranch and building our house to remember much, either," she said, offering him a way out.

He looked over at her as if surprised. "So that is the tack we take? We lie?"

The sun beamed in a cloudless sky to the south of the Crazy Mountains, but it held little warmth even though it was afternoon. A cold spring breeze swept down from the snowcapped peaks, bringing the chill with it.

"Let's go inside," she said, knowing that it wasn't just the breeze that chilled her. The last thing she wanted to do was relive the past. Was that why she couldn't remember much of it?

She pushed open the door, moving to the gas fireplace. Turning it on, she waited for warmth to come out of it as Buck finally made his way into the house. He moved slowly, as if old and tired. Or perhaps just not wanting to face what was coming.

"I'd brought you back to the ranch with me after we eloped," he said, as if the past were puzzle pieces that didn't quite fit together. "I should have known my mother would never forgive me for not giving her the big wedding she'd apparently always wanted for me."

Did he really believe that was the only problem Grace had with the two of them getting married? Was he that naive? Or was he trying to rewrite history just as she suggested?

"I'm sorry things were so rocky once we returned to the ranch," he said.

"We did have that short honeymoon *before* we went to Vegas," she said, not wanting to dredge up Grace and that part of the past. There were some things best left buried. Like Maggie McTavish.

Buck smiled at her as he came to stand in front of the fire. "Those were some of the happiest days of my life."

His words surprised her. She remembered feeling anxious. A part of her had thought those few days might be all they would have together. She'd been half-afraid that she'd given him too much of herself too fast.

Give away the milk and a man has no reason to buy the cow. Her mother's words. Shacking up in a motel for a few days of wild, passionate lovemaking was fun, but she'd expected Buck to come to his senses. They were both young, him twenty-five, her twenty-four. And yet, he'd fallen for her. It still amazed her on some level even after all of these years. She'd never felt that lovable.

"I couldn't let you go," Buck said simply. It was why they'd eloped. She'd put the idea into his head. Had she been afraid even then that JD and Grace Hamilton wouldn't accept her? Or had she wanted it finalized before Buck changed his mind? She'd always thought he'd look at her one day and realize he'd made a mistake. She still felt that way, though here he was, still in love with her.

The gas fireplace was finally putting out some heat. Sarah finished her cocktail and put down the cold, wet glass to hug herself. So much of the past worried her—and not just the twenty-two missing years. She couldn't trust her memories. People told her things, but she didn't feel them skin-deep, let alone bone-deep.

"I still can't believe we eloped," she said into the silence.

He laughed softly. "We were crazy for each other."

"Or just plain crazy, according to your father."

Buck's expression darkened. "He was worried because his own marriage hadn't turned out like he'd hoped." Buck's father, the senator, had been upset, saying he hoped his son hadn't jumped into something without thinking first. But it was his mother's reaction that Sarah would never forget.

"I'm sorry about the way my mother treated you," Buck said as if he could no longer deny how bad it had been. "I'll never forgive her for that."

Sarah stepped away from the fire, her back to Buck. "She and I finally understood each other before she died."

"I'm glad."

A silence fell between them. They'd avoided the one subject she knew the sheriff would be questioning them about. JD and Maggie McTavish.

"Do you think he did it?" Buck asked after a moment.

"We ARE TRYING to retrieve DNA from the preserved fetus," the coroner told the sheriff when Frank stopped by his office. "As I told you, the victim was about five months pregnant."

"I still can't believe she was that far along," Frank said, wondering how she'd been able to keep it a secret—and who might have known. "You think it's still possible, then, to find out who fathered her child." Isn't this what he'd been hoping to hear? It wouldn't prove who the killer had been on its own, but it would definitely add to the suspects, he thought, if the baby wasn't JD Hamilton's.

"I'm still hopeful, since everything was well preserved. Chances are that you might be able to make a DNA match. Because it's been so many years, you may be dealing with the progeny of the baby's father, though."

Buckmaster Hamilton, Frank thought.

"I don't envy you that job."

He smiled at that. Buckmaster had called earlier to say that he and his former wife, Sarah, would be coming by the office this afternoon. "How long will it take to compare the DNA once I get samples for you?"

"We can put a rush on it. It will depend on the quality of the sample we get from the fetus if we can get a close match. Also, it depends on how many samples you bring us. How many are we talking about?"

Frank stood, settled his Stetson on his head of thick graying blond hair and turned toward the door. "I have no idea at this point. That was thirty-five years ago. Obviously, I have at least one suspect in mind. Unfortunately, if I can't get DNA from progeny, then I am going to have to get a court order to have JD's body exhumed. But if there were others, which, according to the rumors, there were…"

"Good luck."

"Yeah," he said, thinking of how this was going to go down when he asked the presidential candidate Senator Buckmaster Hamilton for a DNA sample—let alone threatened him with the exhumation of his father. By law, Frank wouldn't be able to force Buckmaster, so that might take a court order, as well.

As he left the coroner's office, he figured the senator had to have known about the alleged affair between his father and Maggie McTavish. But maybe he didn't know about the baby. Frank thought it would be telling to see the possible future president's reaction to providing a DNA sample.

CHAPTER EIGHT

JD HAD GONE to his son's house after he left Grace at the hospital following her second accident. Sarah opened the door. She was wearing an apron that did little to cover her protruding belly. There was flour on her hands and a dusting of it smeared across one cheek. She was laughing as if Buck had said something funny just before she opened the door.

"JD," she said. "I'd give you a hug but I'm making biscuits and Buck is giving me instructions."

"I'm just trying to help," he called from the kitchen. "Can you believe the woman has never made biscuits from scratch before? Don't tell Mother."

JD followed Sarah into the warm sunny kitchen. When the two had moved out of the homestead house and into this small cabin on the ranch, Sarah had gone to work and quickly spruced it up. With the construction of their new house coming along quickly they wouldn't be here long. The new house was a good distance from the old homestead—and Grace.

He looked around, admiring what Sarah had done. It felt like a home. He experienced a pang, thinking of his own home. Grace had lost interest in it after Buck was born, just as she'd lost interest in a lot of other things. Her whole life had revolved around her son and now she felt she'd lost him.

*But how far would she go to get him away from his
wife? He hated to think.*

"Don't let me keep you from your biscuits," he said
as he took a stool at the kitchen table where the biscuit-
making was going on. He could smell beef stew bub-
bling in a pot on the stove. His stomach growled, but he
didn't want to impose so he decided to make this quick.

"Sarah, did you happen to stop by the house
today?" he asked.

She looked up from the dough she was wrestling into
a large round ball. "No, was I supposed to?"

"I just thought you might have seen Grace earlier,"
he said.

"No, is something wrong?"

"She took another fall."

"Is she all right?" Buck asked, quickly concerned.

"She's going to be fine. The doctor wanted to keep
her overnight—"

"We should go to the hospital," Sarah said, putting
down the biscuit dough and starting to wipe the flour
from her hands.

"I think it would be better if she got some rest tonight. Maybe the two of you could stop by tomorrow
after she's home." He prayed that Grace would have
come to her senses by then. This time she'd sworn
that Sarah had come by and, insisting that she needed
fresh air, had pushed her wheelchair out on the deck.
Screaming for help, but with no one around to hear,
Grace said her daughter-in-law had shoved her off the
deck, wheelchair and all. Fortunately, it was only a
three-foot fall. But she'd gotten skinned up and she'd
hurt her back again.

"Are you sure there is nothing we can do?" Sarah asked.

He met her blue eyes and saw nothing but concern. But for a moment... Grace was going to poison him against Sarah if he let her. "Just learn to make biscuits," he said, getting to his feet. "That will make your husband happy."

Sarah exchanged a private, intimate look with Buck. "Making him happy is all I ever want," she said, and placed a hand over her swollen belly.

JD thought of Maggie. He had a sudden image of her pregnant, her face radiant, her smile dazzling as she met his gaze.

AFTER HER ENCOUNTER with Brody, Harper had tried to think of a logical way to learn as much as she could about Maggie McTavish. When her mother returned her earlier call, she said she couldn't talk then because she and Buck were going to meet with the sheriff. But she could tell from her mother's voice that she wasn't happy about the prospect of talking to her daughter about JD and Maggie and the past.

Harper knew this wasn't going to be easy. Both Brody and Kat had tried to talk her out of looking into the murder. But Kat didn't know what was at stake. And as for Brody...

She tried not to think about him as she drove into town to the library, parked and entered the old brick building.

A woman in her midfifties was at the desk. She looked up as Harper approached. "Can I help you?" Her name tag read Karen Parker, Librarian.

"I'm looking for a Sweet Grass County High School yearbook."

Without a word, the woman led her back into the stacks. Harper loved the smell of books and the feel of libraries and always had. That was probably why she'd stayed in school for so long instead of returning to the ranch after her first degree.

"What year?" Karen Parker asked.

"Nineteen seventy-nine."

The librarian turned to look at her in surprise. "That's the year I graduated."

"Really? Then you must have known Maggie McTavish."

The woman looked as if she'd just tasted a lemon. "No."

"No? The classes were so small I thought for sure—"

"I knew who she was, but that was all. She didn't... associate with girls much."

Harper opened the yearbook to the senior class of 1979.

Her gaze fell on a young man named Kyle Parker. She looked up at Karen. "Any relation to Kyle Parker?"

"My husband." With that, the woman turned and went back to her desk.

Harper found the other three high school yearbooks, took a chair and looked through the annuals, still a little perplexed by Karen Parker's unfriendly attitude once she'd mentioned Maggie. It had been years. Wouldn't she have gotten over high school by now?

It wasn't until she found a photo of Maggie with Kyle Parker from her freshman year that Harper thought she might have discovered the reason for Karen's reaction.

The shot had been taken at a dance. Both were crowned with a caption that read: Couple of the Year.

Sophomore year there was another photo of Maggie, this time with Will Sanders. Junior year Maggie was with Bobby Barnes. Senior year there was no photo of Maggie with anyone that Harper could find—not even in the array of senior prom photos. Had Maggie not gone to her prom? Was she already involved with JD?

She found one photo that caught her eye, though, and had to flip back to it. A school dance? Maggie was in the distance. Closer were two boys glaring in her direction. Harper recognized them both from their senior photos—Kyle Parker and Will Sanders.

Wanting Brody to see these, she took the yearbooks and approached the desk. But one look at Karen and she had a bad feeling that she wasn't going to be able to check them out.

Karen barely looked up. "You can't check those out."

"But I can make copies, right?"

"The self-serve machine is broken." When Harper said nothing, the woman sighed and said, as if put out, "Mark the pages and I will copy them for you."

Harper would rather have copied them herself, given which pages she wanted. But she took the scraps of paper Karen gave her, marked the page numbers and stuck them in the yearbooks before handing them to her.

Looking even more put-upon, Karen disappeared into the back. At one point Harper thought she heard her on the phone talking to someone. She'd sounded upset, angry. After what seemed like more time than necessary to make a few copies, Karen returned. She definitely looked upset.

If Karen had appeared unfriendly before, she appeared so livid that she was actually shaking as Harper paid for the copies. "Can I ask what you want with these?"

Harper tried to think of a reasonable lie and, short of that, went with the truth. "I'm trying to find out who killed Maggie McTavish."

The woman let out a surprised snort. "Isn't that the sheriff's job? And why would you want a photo of my husband?"

"I was curious about who she dated in high school."

Karen huffed. "You're trying to lay the blame somewhere besides at your own family's door, that's what you're trying to do. Well, it won't work. Everyone already knows who killed her." With that, she turned and disappeared into the back again.

This time there was no doubt. She was on the phone and talking quickly, although Harper couldn't make out her words.

Once outside, she got into her SUV and looked again at the photos from the yearbook. Wasn't it possible one of these boys had never gotten over Maggie? What would he have done if the woman he loved began seeing someone twice her age? She looked again at the photo of Kyle and Will glaring at Maggie. Photos didn't lie. There was animosity in their stares.

Putting the copies aside, Harper started her engine and pulled out. She hadn't gone far when an older model Chevy pulled in behind her. She'd seen the car before, though she didn't know whom it belonged to. Nor did she think much about it until the vehicle stayed with her as she left town.

She was on the narrow road that led to Beartooth

when the driver looked as if he was going to pass. Instead, he pulled up beside her for a moment, laid on his horn, startling her, and then gunned the car, swerving in front of her as if to force her off the road. She hit her brakes as the car's tires boiled up gravel and dirt that pelted her windshield.

Wondering what the driver's problem was, Harper called him a name under her breath as he disappeared up the road in a cloud of dust. Then she put it out of her mind. She had more important things to think about. She couldn't wait to show Brody the photos.

"I KNOW WHAT you want to talk to us about and it's bullshit," Buckmaster said the moment he and Sarah walked into the sheriff's office.

Sarah looked shocked that he would start the conversation like that. "Buck—"

He waved off her interruption. "There is no reason to beat around the bush here. Frank wouldn't have called us both in unless he wanted to talk about Maggie and my father."

"So, they did have a relationship?" Frank said, also surprised that they were getting straight to the point. He'd been dreading this meeting.

"*No.* It was all one-sided," the senator said with authority. "Maggie tormented him. She threw herself at him shamelessly. I have no idea why she wanted him when there wasn't a man in the county who wouldn't have taken her up on her offer."

Frank raised a brow. "Yourself included?"

"Don't try to twist my words on me. Maggie was trouble. I knew to stay away from her." He seemed to realize that Frank was having a hard time believing that. "I know what you're thinking. She wasn't interested in me because she was after my father. Okay, that's probably true. Maybe I would have taken advantage of the situation if it had been offered to me. But I can tell you my father didn't. He was devoted to my mother. He would never have even been tempted."

The sheriff sighed and Buckmaster seemed to realize he'd gone too far again.

"Fine, he was probably tempted, but I *know* he didn't act on it."

"How do you know that?" Frank asked.

The senator seemed at a loss for words for a moment. "I saw the battle that was raging inside him," he said with a curse. "My mother had been ill for so long. She was confined to a wheelchair and, let's face it, she wasn't an easy woman. She refused to have a nurse living in the house with us to take care of her, so he resigned from his post as senator near the end of his term to stay home with her."

"I thought he resigned because he was planning to run for president?"

"That was later. It was clear that he missed politics, so my mother encouraged him to run. She knew how much being a senator had meant to him. She wanted him to have the presidency. She didn't want to stand in his way. She knew he would make a good president."

"You say she knew him," the sheriff said. "Then she knew about Maggie McTavish? Was that why she wanted him to run?

Buckmaster swore and started to deny there was anything to know, but Frank stopped him.

"Did she know what he was going through with Maggie?" the sheriff asked. "Isn't it possible that Maggie was why your mother wanted to get him away from the ranch, away from Montana?" Frank noticed that Sarah hadn't said a word. "Is this how you remember it?" he asked her.

Sarah looked startled that he'd dragged her into the conversation.

"Leave Sarah out of this," Buckmaster said irritably. "I hope my mother didn't know what Maggie was doing, but I guess it's possible. Look, what you're really asking is if my father killed her." Sarah laid a hand on his arm, but Buckmaster shrugged it off. "You didn't know my father like I did. He…was the most honorable man I've ever known." His voice broke. He looked away as if embarrassed. "That's how I know he didn't act on any…feelings he might have had for Maggie."

Feelings? Buckmaster knew that there was more going on between his father and Maggie McTavish than her simply tormenting the man.

Frank looked to Sarah. "You were there. Do you think JD had feelings for Maggie?"

She shook her head. "Buck's right. Maggie just wouldn't leave JD alone. It was…shameful the way she behaved. But JD wasn't the only man she threw herself at. If you look at her track record… As I recall she and Bobby Barnes were an item. I can't remember the names of the other boys I heard she was with in high school. Bobby might be able to give you some names."

Frank studied the two of them for a long moment before he got to his feet. "I think that will be all for now. If I have any more questions—"

"Since your investigation has nothing to do with my father, I'm sorry but I can't be coming home every time you have a question," the senator said.

He'd expected this reaction. "In that case, you might want to give the lab a sample of your DNA now, then."

"What?" Buckmaster demanded.

Frank met his gaze and saw confusion and then panic in the senator's eyes. "I need your DNA, but I also need your permission to have your father's body exhumed."

"Like hell."

"I can get a court order, if I have to."

The senator looked beside himself. "Why would you need—"

"Maggie was almost five months pregnant when she was murdered."

SARAH HAD NEVER seen Buck this upset. "I knew I should have had the bastard cremated," he swore as they left the sheriff's office.

A baby. She silently cursed Maggie for what she'd done to the Hamilton family. "Buck, you don't mean that. Maggie is the one to blame for all of this."

He stopped at the SUV and leaned against it for a moment as if to catch his breath. "What if it was *his* baby?"

Sarah didn't answer. They both knew the answer to that. "The state would have to prove that he killed her."

Buck looked up at her. She could tell that he was scared. His father had dropped out of the presidential race at the last moment without any explanation and only days later had died in a car accident. His car had gone into the Yellowstone River and, trapped inside, he'd drowned. At least they'd been led to believe it was an accident.

She knew Buck hadn't missed the similarities between his father's "accident" and her own. Except she'd gotten out of the car and survived. JD hadn't. But had he purposely driven into the river because he couldn't live with what he'd done?

"I think you were smart to give the sheriff your DNA," she said as they approached her SUV. Buck reached for the keys to drive. She could see that he was still shaken as she climbed in.

He opened his door and slid behind the wheel like a man headed for the gallows. He'd aged since getting the call about Maggie McTavish's remains being found on Hamilton Ranch. He looked defeated. She knew she had to do something. She couldn't let this beat him. Worse, she couldn't let him quit the presidential race.

"You aren't your father," she said as he started the engine. "No matter how all of this turns out—"

"Are you serious?" He let out a bark of a laugh. "You think I can continue the presidential race if it turns out that my father not only had an affair with a woman half his age but also killed her to hide the fact that he'd knocked her up?"

"They won't be able to prove that he killed her."

"It won't matter. They will crucify him in the press." He shook his head as he pulled out of the parking lot. "Can you imagine the damage this will do? And what about the girls? They will have to live with this."

"You're assuming he was guilty."

Buck shot her a look. "Don't be naive. Not even the sheriff believed that my father wasn't guilty of at least having an affair with that woman."

Sarah looked at the passing scenery as he drove them out of town and toward the Crazy Mountains. A spring squall bloomed over the peaks, promising a rain shower before the day was over. The landscape had begun to turn green. New leaves popped from buds on the trees, and early wildflowers broke through the dried fall grass.

She hated to be the one to tell him that there was another problem. "I think you should talk to Harper."

Buck looked over in surprise. "About what?"

"Brody McTavish."

"Brody McTavish?"

"He was with her when they found the body."

"So what?"

"I think she likes him and has for some time now."

He shook his head. "That is the least of my concerns. Harper's too young to be serious about anyone."

Sarah sighed. "She's twenty-three. Have you looked at your daughter lately? She's definitely not too young to be serious. She's a *woman*, Buck. And Brody... Brody is a McTavish. He's quite a bit older and probably more experienced. I suspect there is more going on between them than you might think. Worse, what happens when Flannigan finds out his nephew is interested in a Hamilton?"

CHAPTER NINE

"GRACE, WHAT IS it going to take to make you happy?" JD paced the bedroom, his hands thrust deep into his pockets, his body rigid with anger.

She thought about when JD had been so in love with her, he would have moved mountains to make her happy.

"I want you back." The words were out before she realized she'd said them.

He stopped pacing to stare at her. "What in heaven's name are you talking about? Grace, I'm here."

"I feel like I'm losing you," she said, her words choked with tears.

He spread his arms wide. "Losing me? Grace, I'm here. I've told you I will never leave you. What more do you want from me?"

Clearly more than he could give, she thought as she looked at him through her tears. "I want you to believe me." She saw his expression harden. "Why would I lie?"

"We both know why. You want your son all to yourself. You'd do anything to get rid of Sarah. Grace, you're going to be a grandmother soon. I thought you would love that."

She made a sour sound and looked away.

"If only you could find something that would make you happy," he said.

"What would make you happy?" she countered.

He looked at her for a long moment as if considering that. "You being well and content again. You were once, weren't you?"

"You make it sound as if I put myself into this wheelchair. I told you what happened."

He looked away then as if he couldn't bear to hear this again. He didn't believe her and no matter how many times she'd tried to warn him, he refused to listen. "You have to stop telling these lies about Sarah."

"She's tried to kill me twice. Next time—"

JD shook his head. "Well, our son and his wife have moved out of the house so you should be safe and happy now." His words were laced with sarcasm.

Buckmaster hadn't believed her, either. She'd wanted to call the sheriff after the first time, but JD wouldn't let her.

"Grace, this obsession you have with breaking up Buck's marriage, it has to stop. That girl did not push you down the stairs or off the porch. You did this to yourself and look where that has gotten you." He motioned to the wheelchair.

"She hates me and wants me dead," Grace cried. "I'm trapped in this wheelchair. What if next time she succeeds?"

He only shook his head in disgust. "Stop. Just stop. I can't take much more of this."

"Don't you think I know she's been talking to you about running for president? She wants to get you off the ranch, out of this house, away from me, so she can finish the job."

He'd walked away from her and, later, she'd seen him ride off toward the Crazies. When she'd asked him what he did up there, he said he fished.

"But you never bring fish home."

"Because you don't like me frying it and stinking up the house. Isn't that what you always say?"

Was it? She couldn't remember saying that, but maybe she had only because she resented the time he spent in the mountains away from her fishing or whatever else he did.

HARPER SHOULDN'T HAVE been surprised when, after she returned home, Brody showed up at the ranch house demanding to see her father. News of his return traveled fast. Often there would be more reporters outside the ranch gate. Everyone was looking for a story. How soon before they picked up on what could soon make horrible headlines?

"I just got home myself. He isn't here," she told him.

"Or did he tell you to say that?" He tried to look past her into the living room.

"You think I'm lying? Or that he told me to lie? You don't know me or my father."

"When will he be back?"

"He and my mother have gone in to talk to the sheriff. I don't know when he has to fly back to DC or what his plans are while he's home."

"I should have known," Brody said angrily. "Your father is going to try to quash this investigation. He can't let the truth come out."

Her own anger spurred her words. "You're assuming that my grandfather had an affair with your cousin and then murdered her."

"It's a damned good assumption. He was the one who had the most to lose if the truth came out. She was half his age."

"And if you're wrong and he didn't have an affair with her? Didn't kill her?"

He met her gaze. His angry look softened. "I know this is hard for you and I'm sorry. But I need some answers."

She raised a brow. "I thought you already *had* all the answers."

Brody swore and, taking off his Stetson, raked a hand through his dark hair.

"If Maggie was as beautiful and desirable and as wild as I've heard, then I'm betting she broke some man's heart other than my grandfather's."

"You don't know that she broke his heart."

"That's my point," she said haughtily. "We know nothing of her life. But I am going to make it my personal mission to find out *everything*."

He shook his head. "And if I'm right and all your investigating leads you to your grandfather?"

"Then so be it."

"Even if it hurts your father's chances of being president?"

"I would hope voters wouldn't condemn him for something my grandfather might have done."

"You really aren't that naive, are you?"

She glared into his handsome face. "At least I don't jump to conclusions based on circumstantial evidence."

He laughed. "Circumstantial? She was buried on *Hamilton* land."

"If my grandfather was guilty, I would assume that he was smart enough to bury her far from the ranch."

"Unless he was so arrogant that he thought he would never get caught, which is what happened."

She shook her head. "You really are impossible. While you're busy pointing fingers, I've been working to find the truth just like I told you I would." She stepped back and started to close the door.

Brody caught the door in his large hand. "Your father already *knows* the truth. Ask him why JD pulled out of the presidential race when he did. There's your answer right there. My cousin Maggie disappears, your grandmother dies and your grandfather drives into the river. You don't have to be a rocket scientist to figure this out."

"Just a mule-headed cowboy, apparently."

"You think your father didn't know what was going on?" he scoffed. "I wouldn't be surprised if he pulls out of the race now because he knows he was part of it."

She was so furious she could hardly speak. "You'd like to see that, wouldn't you?" she demanded angrily. "Is that the justice you're talking about? The son paying for his father's mistakes? Would that make you happy?"

"No." He suddenly looked bereft. He put his hat back on and glanced away for a moment. She felt her own temper cool, as well.

"If you had seen my uncle when he heard about us finding his daughter's body… Maggie was his life. To find out that she'd been murdered and lay in an unmarked grave all these years…" He looked away again and she felt a piece of her heart go with him.

"I want the truth, too."

"Are you sure about that?" he said, meeting her gaze with a pained one of his own. "All I see is this ending in more heartbreak."

She nodded. "This situation hurts us already. I can't see how the truth is going to be any worse."

He seemed to finally notice what she was holding in her hands. "What is that?"

"It's copies of photos from the high school year-books the years Maggie attended." She'd had her finger holding her spot in the pages when he'd knocked at her door. Now she flipped them to the sheet with the photo of Kyle Parker and Will Sanders and handed it to him. "Check out the way they're looking at your cousin. I'd say there was no love lost between them."

"This doesn't mean—"

"There are also photos of her with other boyfriends. On top of that, the librarian is married to one of those boys in the first photo. Boy, did she get upset when I told her what I was looking for."

He glanced up from the sheets of paper she handed him and shook his head. "You are going to piss off the entire town."

She let out a laugh. "I already have. Some guy in an old car chased me out of town and pelted my SUV with rocks as he flew past me. At the time, I didn't think much of it. I just assumed he was some jerk in a hurry. But, since then, I think he might have been Karen Parker's husband, Kyle." She pointed at him in the two photos she'd had copied.

Brody swore. "Are you crazy? You could have been killed. Isn't it obvious the trouble you're stirring up and how dangerous it is?"

"Exactly. You're assuming the only people who have something to hide are in my family. This proves that isn't true. More people than you think might have wanted to kill your cousin."

"Oh, that's great to hear," he said sarcastically. "Tell me about the car the man who harassed you was driving."

"It was old. Vintage. Blue and white with…" She made a sign with her hands.

He pulled out his phone. "Like this 1957 Chevy Bel Air?"

She nodded. "Only this one was blue and white."

"Got it," he said as he put away his phone.

"I'm going to talk to the boys she dated in high school and then—"

"What?" he demanded. "Are you just going to drop by and ask them if they killed her?"

"It's better than what you're doing. Maybe they know something. Or at least they can tell me who her friends were. Do you have a better plan? Oh, that's right, you came by here to what? Demand answers from my father? If he knew anything, he would have already told the sheriff."

He groaned under his breath. "I'm sure."

"That's just it, you're not even considering that there might have been someone else in her life. What are you afraid of? That you might be wrong?"

"I wish I was wrong for a lot of reasons." His gaze bored into hers. She felt heat rise up her chest to her throat. All he had to do was look at her like that and—

"Look, I'm sure the sheriff is already checking into everyone associated with Maggie. So knock this off, okay? I don't want to have to worry about you."

"You worry about me?"

He shook his head. "What am I going to do with you?"

She leaned against the doorjamb. "I have some ideas."

"HARPER." SHE LOOKED SO damned sexy leaning against that doorjamb. Brody fought the attraction, telling himself that she just didn't understand how bad it was going to get. He shook his head at her. "This can't happen."

"So you keep saying. But I know you want to kiss me again."

He had to laugh. "Oh, yeah?"

She raised her chin. "I told myself when I was nine that I was going to marry you."

He raised an eyebrow. "At the ripe old age of nine, huh? How many others have you planned to marry since then?"

"You're the only one, but don't let it go to your head."

"What if I have other plans?" he asked, playing along because it felt good to pretend—even for a little while.

He saw her expression look doubtful. Until that moment apparently she hadn't even considered that he might have a girlfriend, even a fiancée she didn't know about.

"Do you?" she asked, straightening and looking worried.

He shook his head. "But let me give you a little piece of advice. Most men like to do the chasing."

"Well, most men would have caught me by now."

He looked into those big blue eyes. This woman really was impossible. "You are aware that our families hate each other, right?"

She nodded. "I'm getting that impression. Like Romeo and Juliet, except I'm not planning to kill myself."

"Well, that's good to hear."

"Brody." She caught his sleeve as he started to step away. He couldn't keep doing this. It was killing him.

He turned to her. The look on her face turned his resolve to jelly. He stepped closer, wanting to take her in his arms and hold her tight. "Let's get something straight. If I decide to kiss you again, you'll know it."

She smiled at that. "*When* you kiss me again," she said. "I'm going to win your heart, Brody McTavish, against all odds."

Harper already had his heart. "What can I say to make you stop playing detective?"

She tilted her head and gave him that crooked smile. "You could come with me to talk to Maggie's old boy-friends."

RUSSELL CALLED THE sheriff after he left the nursing home. He'd taken the postcard he'd found in Millie's room down to the office and asked for a color copy of both sides. The secretary who worked there was kind enough to comply and didn't question why he would want a copy of Millie Hansen's postcard.

"I talked to Millie," Russell said when the sheriff answered.

"I warned you that she has dementia."

"I guess I caught her on a good day. We had a nice chat about brain wiping. She said that Ralph just liked helping people. He even offered to help her forget about her husband's death. She passed on his offer, then again, she didn't really believe he could wipe brains. But she did tell me something interesting. Dr. Venable is back in the States." He sensed the sheriff's skepticism even though Frank hadn't uttered a word. "As it turns out, she was right. He sent her a postcard. I had a copy made of it. I thought you might want to see it. I can be at your office within the hour."

When he arrived, Frank was waiting for him. "Where was it sent from?" the sheriff asked anxiously.

"Miami." He handed over the copy.

Frank inspected it for a long moment. When he looked up, he said, "You think he's headed for Montana."

"Don't you? I suspect his work isn't finished."

"But what work is that?" Frank said, clearly not expecting an answer.

"Whatever Senator Buckmaster Hamilton has hired him to do." He could hear what the sheriff wasn't saying, that he'd heard this theory before and was still doubtful. But Russell believed Buckmaster was capable of unspeakable things to get what he wanted.

"Just for the sake of argument, why would Buckmaster want the doctor back now?"

"Maybe to give Sarah back her memory so they can be the happy couple they used to be," he said sarcastically. "To make sure she never remembers what happened before she went into the river that night. If it came out now, it could end his career. He wouldn't want to take that chance."

Frank sighed. "I guess only time will tell."

"Apparently, all we can agree on is that whatever the doctor is doing back in the States, it involves Sarah," Russell said.

"Just keep in mind, for all we know, Sarah is the one who called him back to the States."

Russell shook his head. "I heard about Maggie Mc-Tavish's remains being found on the Hamilton Ranch.

That should tell you everything you need to know about the Hamilton men."

"Let's not forget that Sarah was in that house when Maggie disappeared."

Russell couldn't believe his ears. "You can't think Sarah would kill her. What possible motive could she have had?"

"She was the one who encouraged JD to run for president. And now she's encouraging Buck to do the same thing. If it meant that much to her thirty-five years ago, she might have realized that Maggie was a roadblock and decided to take care of it herself." The sheriff shrugged. "Truthfully, I don't know what to think. But at this point, everyone involved is a suspect in Maggie's murder, including Sarah."

LYNETTE "NETTIE" CURRY glanced down the road for a sign of her husband's pickup's headlights. He must be working late, she told herself. In the yard light, Frank's crows were lined up on the telephone line that hung between the house and barn.

Her husband had studied crows since he was a boy. The ones who'd settled on his ranch were like his children. He'd given them names, actually seemed to understand the sounds they made. Nettie couldn't deny that the crows reacted to him as if happy to see him whenever he came home.

Like now, when they, too, were looking down the road, expecting to see a cloud of dust. Frank was usually home by now and the crows knew it.

As she moved away from the window, she wondered if it was the Maggie McTavish case that had delayed him. Something had been nagging at her all day.

Now, as she walked into the kitchen, she knew what she had to do.

The small box was hidden in the back of one of the kitchen drawers because she didn't want her husband to know about it. Frank would make fun of her. For now, what was inside was her secret.

Taking out the box, she held it carefully, as if its contents were precious or breakable. Moving to the kitchen table, she opened the box and gently took out the pendulum that hung from a thin cord. It felt warm cradled in her palm.

"This is silly," she'd told herself numerous times. She'd ordered the stupid thing after it had been discovered that Sarah Johnson Hamilton had returned to Montana after twenty-two years with a pendulum tattoo on her tush. Nettie had been intrigued as to why the woman would have something like that permanently needled into her flesh. So she'd ordered a pendulum just for the fun of it.

Logically, did she really believe that this thing could tell the future? Unfortunately, the other times she'd tried it, the pendulum had told her things that had proved true.

Since then, she'd experimented with it. Holding the end of the cord now, she positioned the pendulum a few inches over the tabletop and took a deep breath before letting it out.

The pendulum stilled as if waiting.

First, she asked it a question that she already knew the answer to. "Is the body that was found Maggie Mc-Tavish?" she asked in a whisper.

For a moment, the pendulum didn't move, then slowly it began to circle. Yes.

She let out a breath she hadn't realized she'd been holding. She wanted to ask who had killed her, but the pendulum, while nothing short of amazing, could only answer yes or no.

"Will her killer be caught?"

The pendulum wobbled for a moment, then began to circle. She felt a huge sense of relief. Of course, Frank would catch the killer.

"Is the killer someone I know?" she asked.

The pendulum had come to a stop again between questions. As it started to move, she heard the sound of a car door slamming. She dropped the pendulum on the table, her heart pounding. Shooting to her feet, she quickly scooped it up and shoved it into the small box. As the front door opened, she hurriedly hid the box in the back of the kitchen drawer.

She'd just slammed the drawer closed, when she heard her husband come into the kitchen. Spinning around, she cried, "You worked late." Her voice came out too high, too cheery.

He stared at her, then toward the back door. "Why do I feel as if you just sent your lover scurrying out the back door." He glanced past her to the window over the backyard.

"You just startled me," she said, wiping her perspiring hands down the clean apron she'd put on earlier. "My mind was a million miles away."

"Uh-huh," he said, clearly not believing it for a moment.

"I made tuna salad earlier," Nettie said as she moved to the refrigerator. "I can toast the bread, if you like."

"No need. Just plain bread will be fine." He sat down on the chair at the table that she'd only abandoned moments before. She could tell he was still watching her. It was the sheriff in him. He saw through people, maybe especially her.

"If there is something I should know, Lynette…" he said as she put a sandwich in front of him. He took a bite, his eyes focused on her.

She was about to confess about the pendulum. So what if he made fun of it and her for being so silly about the stupid thing. This was the second time he'd almost caught her playing with the darned thing.

Fortunately, she was saved by the bell. His cell phone rang. He glanced at it and said, "It's work. I have to take this."

Nettie listened as the dispatcher relayed the message. All the time Frank was on the phone, he was watching her suspiciously.

She chuckled to herself. He didn't really think there was someone else, did he?

SARAH AND BUCK drove to the main ranch house.

"I'd like to spend the night with you, but I need to be sure that Harper is all right and the others if they've heard about this latest situation," Buck had said.

She understood. He had a flight out soon. But he'd said he'd get a ride to the airport.

As she drove away, she felt like crying. It surprised her that she could feel this lost. The truth was that she was tired of waiting in the wings. It made her think of Russell and the life she could have had if she had married him. She felt instantly guilty. Before she'd dropped him off, Buck had talked about how he wanted his campaign manager to step up the process of getting her back into his life.

"Jerrod is determined that it can't come out about the two of us until after the primaries," Buck had said.

"Maybe he's right."

"I want you standing next to me the day I'm elected. *If* I'm elected. That was what I had planned, but now this thing with Maggie McTavish…" He'd sworn. "It's always something. Sometimes I think I should just withdraw from the race so we can be together and to hell with everything else." When she hadn't said anything, he'd looked over at her. "What?" he'd demanded.

She'd said what she knew he'd wanted to hear. "You're going to be the next president of the United States. You aren't going to let anything keep you from it. And when it happens, I will be standing next to you."

Relief had washed over his expression, softening it. He needed her with him. She had to be there with him. He'd reached for her hand and squeezed it. But sometimes she didn't understand why it meant so much to her.

Now alone again, she drove home only to pace the floor. How long could she keep Buck in the race with the way things were going? It wasn't just this latest news that worried her. Going into her bedroom, she took out the copy of the photo from the back of the drawer. She'd requested it from the sheriff after he'd found what he believed to be proof of where she'd been during the missing twenty-two years.

She stared at the woman in the photo as if looking at a stranger. It was a much younger version of her and not just someone who resembled her. But she had no memory connected to that younger self—or to the location or the story that went with it.

Apparently she'd gone to Brazil with the man in the

photo, Dr. Ralph Venable, a psychiatrist. He looked to be much older than her. According to what the sheriff had found out, she'd worked with him in a hospital for twenty years as his assistant. It seemed inconceivable since she had no training. She wondered how exactly she had "assisted" all those years.

It scared her that she didn't recognize the man.

More frightening was the realization that this wasn't the man from her nightmares.

So who was Dr. Ralph Venable? According to the sheriff, a suspected member of The Prophecy, the anarchy group that she'd sworn she knew nothing about. And yet, she'd spent more than twenty years with this man?

Sarah rubbed at her temples, remembering what Buck had said.

"These people set you up because you looked like that woman Red—Virginia Handley. She and the rest of them are responsible for what has happened to you, including wiping your brain and giving you false memories. No wonder you're so scared. You don't know what is real and what isn't."

That they'd tried to frame her, she could believe. But that they'd somehow stolen all memory of the past from her and given her false memories… "But how is that possible?"

"The sheriff found out that Dr. Venable was experimenting with brain wiping," Buck had told her. "He thinks that's what happened to you."

Russell thought the same thing. He'd been the one to suggest the idea to her in the first place. It still didn't explain why she'd tried to kill herself in the Yellowstone River that winter night only months after her twins were born.

"The night you drove into the river, you survived and called someone to come pick you up," Buck had told her, based on what the sheriff had been able to piece together.

She'd heard the veiled anger in Buck's tone and wondered if he would ever be able to get over what he saw as her betrayal. Not just that she'd tried to kill herself. That could have been because of postpartum depression, so he couldn't blame her if that had been the case.

No, what he blamed her for was that she hadn't called her own husband after failing at suicide. Instead, she'd called someone she trusted. Or only thought she could trust. But who had that been? This Dr. Venable?

She had no memory of any of it. When Buck had talked to her regarding what the sheriff had found out about those years, it was as if he was talking about a stranger.

"Whoever this man was who you called, he took you to a clinic up by White Sulphur Springs where Dr. Venable was doing his experiments. The clinic closed a few days later and both you and the doctor disappeared."

Not disappeared. Took off to Brazil where Dr. Venable continued his experiments. That's what the sheriff thought. That's what Buck thought. And one of the people Dr. Venable had experimented on apparently was her.

So had she gone to Brazil willingly with this crazy doctor? Was there some reason she'd wanted—or needed—her memories wiped away?

Sarah put the photo back in the drawer where she kept it hidden. Her head ached as it often did when she tried to remember the past. She didn't know what to believe. She thought of the happy memory of her and Buck riding horses across the pasture, the sun on her face, the breeze blowing back her blond hair.

A false memory. Buck had said it had never happened. Apparently, she'd been thrown from a horse soon after she and Buck were married and refused to get on one again. She had no memory of it.

What made it worse was that Buck said the incident had taken place near Horsethief Creek—in the same area where Maggie's body had been found.

She rubbed her temples, her head aching. The harder she tried to remember, the more the past hid in the darkness and the more she realized she had no idea who she really was or what had really happened to her.

What glimpses she had of her memory terrified her, because if those memories were true, then there was a good chance she was not only a member of the anarchy group The Prophecy, but that she was a killer.

CHAPTER TEN

IT HAD BEEN several weeks since JD had gone back to the lake. He knew it was foolish. But the temptation was too great. He was too old for her, more than twice her age. That he'd thought of the difference in their ages was telling enough. That he saw himself diving into the lake, cutting through the icy water and coming up to find her next to him haunted his dreams nightly. He wanted to see her again, so he stayed away.

When he was around Maggie, he felt alive, as if anything were possible. He forgot for a while about the problems at home. He recalled other summer days when he was a boy, lying in the sun next to the lake, watching clouds float past and daydreaming about the future.

A woman by the name of Mabel Murphy cleaned once a week for them. She often chattered on without him paying any attention, but at the mention of Maggie McTavish, he tuned in to what she was saying.

"Huge argument right there at the Creamery. You know Bobby Barnes, good-looking kid, star athlete, works at his dad's car dealership? Maggie McTavish could certainly do a lot worse. The two were an item last year. Bobby was trying to get her back, though I can't imagine why. Put his hand through the wall. I *heard he broke some bones. That girl. She is nothing but trouble."*

JD felt Grace's gaze on him.

"I've seen her on our property riding that big bay of hers headed up into the mountains," his wife was saying. "I wonder what she does up there in the mountains? Maybe she's like my husband and enjoys fishing."

"Fishing." Mabel made a rude sound. "What that girl is hooking into ain't no fish." She laughed heartily at her own joke.

JD excused himself to see to one of the horses.

A week later, he rode up to the lake with his fishing rod. He'd desperately needed time away from the ranch. Grace had become even more disagreeable since Sarah had given birth, and Buck was busy working on their new house.

"You should see the way Sarah looks at me," Grace had complained. "I swear she hates me."

"Maybe if you were just a little more welcoming to her..."

"You always take her side," his wife had said in disgust. "Why don't you go fishing," she'd added, and wheeled away.

Why not, he'd thought.

Now, though, as he neared the lake, he hoped Maggie wouldn't be there. He felt...vulnerable. Grace's relentless complaining and constant bickering with her daughter-in-law had him wanting to escape the house more and more.

But as he rode up to his spot where he liked to fish, he saw her horse and heard the beckoning splash of water on the other side of the huge boulder.

He reined in and, for a moment, almost turned his horse around and left. Then he heard her voice and felt a pull like gravity.

"Came back for a swim, did you?" Maggie asked as she glided into view.

"OH, GOOD, YOU'RE HOME," the senator said as he walked in the front door of the ranch house. "I have to catch a flight back to Washington, but I was hoping to see you before I left. Are you all right? You look flushed."

She felt like she had at sixteen when she'd come home from a date to find her father waiting up for her. "I— It's hot out," she said, the best she could come up with.

Just seeing Brody had put a flush in her cheeks, let alone arguing with him. Even the thought of him sent a wave of heat through her. Did he actually think he'd talked her out of continuing her search for Maggie's killer?

"I was hoping you were staying the night," she said to her father.

"Have to get back, big debate coming up." He looked distracted for a moment before he focused on her and smiled. "You appear to have adjusted to being home again," he said as he took in her Western attire. She did a twirl for him just as she'd done as a little girl, only today there was no frilly dress. Today she wore jeans, boots and a Western shirt.

"So you're enjoying being on a horse again?" he said as they both sat down.

"I am."

He seemed to remember that it was out riding when she and Brody had found Maggie McTavish's remains.

"I'm sorry you had to see that yesterday. Damned shame."

She was thankful he'd brought it up. "I wanted to ask you about Maggie and…" Harper knew that her father was pressed for time. Also, there was no easy way to ask the question. "Did my grandfather have an affair with her?"

He held up both hands. "Please, I don't want to talk to you about this. I just had to go through this with the sheriff."

"I'm sick of not knowing what is going on with my family. Did my grandfather have an affair with Maggie McTavish?" Harper demanded. "The truth is going to come out. Stop trying to protect me."

Her father sighed. "Harper, I don't have time for this." He started to get up.

"Dad, I need to know. I've been looking into her murder."

He sat back down. "What?"

"Someone has to."

"The sheriff is looking into this as we speak. You have no business—"

"*No business?* JD Hamilton was my grandfather. This is my family. You have all kept me in the dark about the goings-on here for too long. I know what everyone is saying, but is there any truth to it?"

"I'll tell you what I just told the sheriff. I have no idea."

She knew he was hoping she would let it go at that. But she couldn't. "How is that possible? If anyone should know, it would be you. You lived with your parents for a while, right? After you and Mother got married."

Her father turned to her, his face a mask of pain. "I honestly… Something was going on, that's all I can tell you."

"*Something?* Why do you say that?"

He raked a hand through his graying blond hair. She saw his gaze turn inward. "I overheard them arguing. My father wasn't the kind of man who even raised his voice, so I was shocked."

"Did you hear what they were fighting about?"

Her father groaned. "Harper, I don't want to drag all that up again."

"You aren't going to have a choice. Maggie was murdered and buried on our ranch. The sheriff has been asking questions and pretty soon the media is going to get wind of it. We need to know the truth so we can—"

"You mean *you* need to know the truth. Is this about Brody McTavish?"

She bit down on her lower lip for a moment, surprised when her eyes blurred with tears. "What if it is?"

"Baby girl," her father said, getting up to come over and sit next to her. "You can't be in love with this man." He took her hand.

"Why can't I?" she demanded, pulling her hand free of his. "Tell me. If you know something…"

"You can have any man you want."

"What if I want *him*?"

THE SHERIFF WASN'T surprised that the news about Maggie having been buried alive was already in the wind. He'd hoped to contain the gruesome details, but from the look on his wife's face, Lynette had already heard.

"Is it true?" she demanded when they met for

lunch. They were sitting on the picnic table outside the Beartooth General Store as they often did on the days that she worked.

He nodded and finished his sandwich, scrunching up the plain brown bag she'd brought it in. He was still wondering why she'd been acting so strangely when he'd come home last night. She'd acted if as she were hiding something from him. He'd never understand her completely, he told himself, and tried to let it go.

"Mabel?" he asked.

"She called me first thing this morning with the news. You know I hate being the last one to learn about these things."

That he *did* know about her.

"Did Mabel tell you where she was?"

"At home."

"Wearing her phone out calling people with the news," he said, resigned that there was no containing news like this. He glanced at his watch.

"It's just so…awful," Lynette said.

It was. He tried not to think about the vivacious young woman and how her life had ended. "I have to go," he said, getting to his feet to take his paper bag and Lynette's over to the trash can.

"You have to catch her killer."

"I will."

"I know," she said, smiling at him.

"Are you sure you're all right, Lynette?" he asked frowning. "You've been acting strangely even for you."

"I'm fine." She got to her feet. "I should get back to work."

This was the woman he knew. She had to get back

in the store so she could keep her end of the grapevine oiled and running smoothly.

"I love you, Lynette," he said impulsively. "If there is anything you need to tell me…"

She met his gaze and laughed. "I don't have a lover if that's what's worrying you."

He couldn't help but smile. He truly did adore this woman. "I'm glad to hear that. I already have one murder on my hands as it is." But it hadn't skipped his attention that she hadn't told him what it was she was hiding from him.

Frank decided to pay Mabel Murphy a visit. He found her getting ready to go into town. She wore a large-print bright flowered dress and too much perfume. Her lips had been painted bright red and there were two matching patches of red rouge on her cheeks.

"Special occasion?" he asked when he saw how she was made up.

"I'm sorry?" She frowned as if she didn't know what he was talking about.

"You're all dressed up. I must have caught you at a bad time."

"Just on my way into town to do some shopping."

More than likely to gather and dispense gossip. "If you could spare a few minutes, I wanted to ask you some questions."

Her expression brightened. "I have all the time in the world." She motioned him in excitedly. "This is about Maggie McTavish, isn't it? I knew it when I heard about that body being found on the Hamilton Ranch."

She led him into a living room furnished with antiques handed down by family members. Mabel didn't spend much time at home so there was a fine layer of dust on everything.

Frank took the chair she offered and got right to it. "I understand you used to clean for Grace and JD Hamilton."

Mabel looked pleased as a peacock. She sat, folded her dimpled hands in her lap and said, "I certainly did and I got an earful."

"About Maggie McTavish?"

"About her and the daughter-in-law. Grace hated Sarah." Mabel leaned forward conspiratorially. "Grace lived in fear that Sarah was going to kill her." Looking pleased with herself, she said, "The fall down the stairs that killed her wasn't her first. Of course, JD and her son thought Grace was getting senile. I wasn't so sure. But then again, she would have done anything to free her son of his wife."

While interesting, the sheriff needed to know about Maggie. "Did Grace mention Maggie?"

Mabel nodded quickly. "She saw her riding her horse by the house on her way to the mountains. That's where they met, at some lake up there. JD pretended he went up there to fish. Posh! He never came home with fish, but he looked pretty pleased with himself after an afternoon up there in the mountains."

He could see that Mabel didn't know any more than the other gossips in town, but he had to try. "So you never actually saw Maggie and JD together?"

"No, but I wasn't born yesterday. One of them would ride by and then the other would take off. Same coming back down from the mountains. Grace knew. She'd sit at that window, so mad she could have eaten nails."

"They might not have gone to the same place."

Mabel shook her head smugly. "I saw the drawing Maggie did of JD."

"Drawing?"

"It was of him fishing at some lake in the mountains. She couldn't have drawn that if she wasn't up there with him."

"What happened to the drawing?"

She shrugged. "I saw it while cleaning his room, you know they had separate rooms after Grace's fall down the stairs and her needing a wheelchair. The drawing was lying on his bedside table. Maggie had even signed it. He caught me looking at it. After that I never saw it again. I think he hid it."

Frank hated to even ask, but did anyway. "So who do you think killed Maggie?"

"It's obvious, isn't it? JD. He had the most to lose if the truth came out."

"What about Grace?"

"Oh, she wanted to, I know that. But how could she, being confined to that wheelchair?"

Yes, how could she? Frank realized he needed to talk to Grace's doctor.

BRODY WORRIED ABOUT HER.

Harper found herself smiling as she drove into town to pick up a few things. His worrying about her, though, hadn't changed anything. He wasn't interested in helping her find out the truth, apparently. Nor did he think they had any hope of ever being a couple.

She intended to prove him wrong. The way she saw it, they had only one chance. All she had to do was find out the truth. It was the rumors, the accusations, the speculation, that would keep them apart forever if she didn't. The truth—no matter how bad it was—would put an end to the rumors. They would face whatever it was and everyone would move on. At least that was her hope, naive or not.

It was late afternoon, the sun disappearing behind the Crazies, when she saw the car Brody had said was a 1957 Chevy Bel Air. It sped past, the driver seeming not to notice her sitting at the stop sign. She didn't get a look at the driver because of the sun glinting off the windshield, but she was bound and determined to find out who was driving.

She hesitated only a moment before she flipped a U-turn in the middle of the street and followed the car. To her surprise, the driver didn't go far. She saw him turn into Bill's Auto Repair and park. As she drove slowly past, she realized she'd been holding her breath.

It came out on a gasp of surprise as she recognized the man who stepped out.

If she was right about Karen Parker calling someone, then she had expected it would be Kyle, her husband. But the man who climbed out of the Chevy and entered the shop was the owner, Collin Wilson, the son of the auto repair shop's namesake, Bill Wilson, and a classmate of Karen's—and Maggie's.

She frowned as she drove on past. Could she be mistaken about why Collin had chased her out of town? But if not, why would Karen call Collin instead of her husband?

Turning around again, she drove back and parked where she had a view of the auto shop. She could see Collin start toward his office when a customer pulled up. Harper waited. Collin talked for a few minutes and then handed off the customer to one of his employees before going inside.

She could see him in the small office and watched as he began to rummage through his files as if searching for something. Whatever it was, he didn't seem to find it. She saw him slam the file cabinet, then look around his office. His gaze lifted to the window—and to where she was parked. Hurriedly, she started her SUV and pulled away without looking back.

But she had a bad feeling that Collin had seen her.

She couldn't help thinking about Brody's concerns— as well as her father's. The senator had told her enough to make her worry that there might be some truth in the rumors about his father and Maggie.

"My parents' marriage wasn't going so well," her father had said before he'd left for his flight back to DC. She'd known how hard it was for him to talk about this, but she couldn't let him keep trying to protect her. She had enough of that with Brody.

"My mother was in a wheelchair by then. They argued a lot." He'd looked up. "That was about the time that your mother and I moved out. Mother had become…more than difficult. Looking back, there's a chance she might have been suffering from early Alzheimer's or dementia. So, even though she accused my father of having an affair with Maggie, maybe it wasn't true."

"Why would you say that?"

"She also accused your mother of things that she didn't do." He'd shrugged and looked at his watch. "I really do have to go." He'd pushed to his feet. "My father was good man. But he wasn't the kind of man I could ask outright about what was going on."

Harper had seen defeat in her father's shoulders. "Whatever comes out, it isn't about you."

He'd smiled at that. Everyone thought she was so naive.

"People are more understanding than you think. We're not the only family with possible skeletons in our closets," she'd told him.

"The truth is, Harper, I didn't want to know what was going on with my parents. I've regretted that decision for years. Now I have no way of knowing what happened in those months before, first, my mother died and then my father pulled out of the presidential race. Shortly after that, he had the car accident and died. I should have asked. Maybe I could have done something. But I didn't. Your mother and I were newlyweds and I was running the ranch while Dad was first away in the senate or later taking care of my mother."

"You can't blame yourself." But she could see that he did.

"I'm glad you're spending some time with your mother. She needs you more than ever right now."

Of course, she'd read between the lines to what he had really been saying: *Stay away from Brody McTavish and the past.*

But she could do neither, she thought as she glanced at her watch and wondered what time Collin Wilson would be closing the auto shop.

WHEN SARAH ANNOUNCED that she was pregnant so soon after the birth of Ainsley, Grace was beside herself. "One child wasn't enough for her?"

She and JD had wanted more than one child. But after Buckmaster was born, things had changed be-

tween them. Then she'd found out she wouldn't be able to conceive again. It shouldn't have mattered, but she didn't feel the same about JD after that. She devoted herself to her precious son. When JD had gone into politics, she'd been glad for the time he was gone and she and Buckmaster were alone together.

That someone like Sarah could conceive so easily...it felt like a slap in the face. She hated the young woman even more. Now her son was even more trapped by the evil woman.

"Mother?"

Grace started at the sound of Buckmaster's voice. "In here," she called, praying he'd come alone.

She smiled as he entered the room. He was so handsome, so much like his father, at least in looks.

"Are you alone?" *she asked, looking past her son to the doorway.*

"Mother." *His voice was full of reprimand.* "Please don't start."

She bit her lower lip, nodding and forcing a smile. She had so little time alone with her son, she wasn't going to spoil it by spending it arguing.

"You look so tanned and handsome," *she said, patting a spot on the couch next to her wheelchair for him to sit.* "Ranch work suits you."

He smiled and sat down. "I'm enjoying it," *he said, as if it surprised him.* "How are you doing?"

"Fine," *she said quickly. The last thing she wanted was Buckmaster to think she needed him to move back in with his pregnant wife and a baby.* "I have a private nurse who comes each day."

"I suppose Dad told you that Sarah is pregnant again."

"He mentioned it." Her smile actually hurt. "Another girl?"

Buckmaster laughed. "I'll take as many as I can get. Sarah feels the same way."

Grace just bet she did but held her tongue.

"That's one reason I stopped by. You haven't seen the house Sarah and I are building. We're going to need the added room."

"Your father has promised to take me to see it one of these days," she said, not in the least interested.

"It's up the road from here by the creek. It's more open there, more room to expand."

"You're anticipating having that large a family?"

He grinned and shrugged. "We'll see. Mom, I've never been happier." His grin faded as he looked at her. "I just wish you and Sarah—"

"No woman would ever be good enough for my son," she said quickly.

"I suppose not. Sarah is going to bring Ainsley by later. You haven't seen her for a while. I thought you might enjoy that."

Grace hadn't taken to being a grandmother even though she had always thought she would. She told herself it was because she could see Sarah in Ainsley.

"That will be lovely," she said to her son, and didn't even try to smile as he got up to leave.

"So you don't have a problem with me building a house?" he asked.

"I just want you to be happy."

"Then you've gotten your wish." He looked around the room before his gaze fell on her again. "Where did you say Dad was?"

She hadn't. "He's gone fishing." At least that's what

he called it. She'd noticed lately how different he was when he returned. She would be a fool not to know that his trips involved more than fishing.

CHAPTER ELEVEN

HARPER SAT OUTSIDE the auto shop sipping an espresso and hoping she wouldn't have to pee before Collin Wilson finally closed up for the night. Earlier she'd seen him searching for something. It might have nothing to do with Maggie's death, but Harper wanted a look in that office. If there was evidence that might incriminate him...

She knew she was grasping at straws, but after talking to her father she was even more determined to learn everything she could. She wasn't sure how the pieces fit together, but Maggie and Collin had dated in high school, and Karen had called someone from the library after making the copies of the photos. Harper was betting that Collin Wilson had been at the other end of that phone call. Why else had he chased her out of town like that?

So what was the connection between Karen and Collin? Why wouldn't Karen have called her husband? She told herself that it was a small town. Maybe Karen and Collin were friends from high school or had been neighbors growing up. Maybe there was nothing suspicious about it.

But she did wonder if Karen's husband would have thought so.

She glanced at her watch. When she looked up

again, a car drove up and two men got out. They'd changed since high school, but she was still able to recognize them from their yearbook photos. As Will Sanders and Kyle Parker got out and went into the auto shop, they both looked over their shoulders as if afraid someone was watching them.

Harper sat up a little straighter. Collin didn't seem that happy to see them. Even from a distance she could see that the conversation between them was confrontational. They kept glancing out the window. Who were they worried was watching them? Not her, Harper thought. The sheriff?

Collin moved to the window and lowered the blind. Fortunately, half of the blinds were old and bent, so she could still see the muted animated conversation. If she was closer, she might have been able to read lips. It was a talent she'd picked up living with five sisters who thought they could keep secrets from her.

The conversation ended. None of the three appeared happy about its conclusion. A moment later the two emerged and drove away and the light inside the shop office went out. She slid down in her seat. Peering over the edge of the side window, she watched Collin come out of the business, lock the door behind him and walk toward his Chevy parked out front.

Harper slid farther down in the seat as his headlights filled her car. She held her breath as he drove past. She waited until the sound of his engine died off in the distance before she sat up, opened her car door and got out.

She didn't bother with the front door since she'd just seen Collin lock it. Instead, she went around back. The alley was dark, no streetlights, just some abandoned buildings behind the shop. The other businesses along the street were also closed in this part of town.

Nothing moved in the alley. The abandoned buildings cast black shadows over the narrow dirt alley, making the night even darker. She could hear the occasional vehicle engine a street over, but nothing else. Walking down the alley, she thought about turning on the flashlight she'd brought from her car. The alley was full of potholes, some deep enough that she almost fell. The body shop had three bays with two rear doors that opened to the alley.

Harper remembered seeing one of them ajar earlier when she'd driven around the block after Collin had seen her. One of the mechanics had the door propped open and was outside smoking. Just as she'd feared, the door was no longer propped open. She wasn't sure she was up to breaking in even if she knew how to. She tried the first door. Locked. She stepped to the second one and tried the knob. It turned in her hand. A draft of cold, oily-smelling air rushed out.

Reaching into her bag, she pulled out the flashlight and flicked it on. That's when she saw the small rock that had kept the door from closing all the way. She made sure it stayed where it was as she stepped in and let the door close partway behind her.

Avoiding the pits where Collin and his employees worked on the cars, she headed for the office.

If only she knew what she was looking for, she thought as she opened the door to find a desk and a half dozen filing cabinets against one wall. Shelving covered another wall. The shades were already drawn, but she knew they provided little cover.

She turned on her flashlight and had only just begun

searching when she heard a sound. Snapping off the light, she dropped behind the desk as the door opened and someone stepped inside.

"You can come out now," a familiar male voice said.

"Brody?" she asked as she popped up.

Brody flicked a flashlight beam over her. "What are you doing here?" he demanded.

"I could ask you the same thing—you almost gave me a heart attack."

"Better than what could have happened if it hadn't been me."

Her heart was still thudding wildly against her chest. But was it from being startled or from seeing Brody again? "What are you doing here?"

"I've been watching the place after you described the car that you say chased you out of town. I'd left to get something to eat and came back in time to see you sneaking around back."

She waved that off, wanting to get to something more important. "Remember when I told you that Karen Parker called someone as I was leaving the library and moments later the driver of an old Chevy harassed me? Well, guess who drives that car?"

"Collin Wilson," they said in unison.

"The point is, why would Karen call him and not her husband? And that's not all." She told him about Collin searching for something in the office earlier and then Will and Kyle arriving.

"They're probably friends," he said, sounding not in the least impressed. "They went to school together. I'm not sure anything about that is necessarily suspicious."

"If you had seen them, you wouldn't say that. They were huddled together, looking upset and talking fast.

They kept glancing around as if afraid someone was watching them until Collin pulled down the shades."

"Someone *was* watching them. *You.*"

She mugged a face at him. "I'm telling you they're hiding something and if I had to bet, I'd wager they were talking about Maggie."

"I'm sure they probably were, but that's only normal. They all dated her and the discovery of her remains has to come as a shock."

"I'm sure it does, especially if they are responsible for putting her in the ground."

"All *three* of them?"

"Why not? If you had seen how guilty they looked, you'd be as suspicious as I am." When he said nothing, she took that as positive and added, "Even I know it would have been very difficult for only one person to have handled the burial alone."

"I know you want to believe that, but if he had already dug the grave before he killed her…"

She shuddered, aghast. "Who would be that cold-blooded?"

"A desperate married man who would have lost everything if it came out that he'd impregnated an eighteen-year-old."

"Maggie was *pregnant*?"

"Five months. Which gave your grandfather even more motive."

"I knew it," she said angrily.

"What?"

"You already have your mind made up. You aren't even willing to consider that the killer could be anyone but my grandfather."

"That's not true. I'm not even saying you're wrong

about those three men and what they might have been up to. I'm just trying to keep you from jumping to conclusions without any proof."

"I know what I saw," she said stubbornly. "How about trusting my instincts? Can you do that?"

He studied her for a moment as if making up his mind. "That would depend. How good are your instincts?"

She looked at him, hearing a lightness to his tone. He was trying to defuse the tension between them, along with her anger. And it was working. She eyed him as he had done her. "Want to know what my instincts tell me about you?"

He raised an eyebrow. "I'm not sure I want to hear this."

"Yes, you do," she said smiling. "You're…kind, trustworthy, loyal—"

"I sound like an old dog."

"—and smart, but—"

He laughed. "Oh, I was afraid there would be a but."

"But…you also have a self-deprecating sense of humor that keeps you from being too perfect. I like that you don't take yourself too seriously." She liked so much about him and knew it must show in her gaze, because he looked almost embarrassed. The magic that she felt sparked between them as she spoke from her heart. "You're a man who can be trusted. I trust you with my life."

THE WEIGHT OF her words fell heavily on his shoulders. "Now I know your instincts shouldn't be trusted," he said, and looked around. "So you're here doing what exactly?"

She wasn't sure exactly. "Looking for Maggie's killer."

"I thought that was an idle threat."

"If you knew me at all, you'd know I don't make idle threats."

"Still, what do you hope to find in an auto repair shop?"

"I won't know until I find it," she said haughtily. "But earlier I saw Collin in here searching for something. He didn't find it."

"Great." Brody shook his head. "He could have been looking for a misplaced bill or an invoice or his grocery list. Harper, I have to tell you, this wasn't your best idea. Did you ever consider that you'll be arrested for breaking and entering if the sheriff catches you? Worse, if you're right about what you think the three men were up to, then you could have three killers after you. Did you ever consider that?"

She shivered. "Collin could have run me off the road the other day, but he only tried to scare me."

"There is always next time."

Harper ignored that. "You have to admit it makes a person wonder why he would feel threatened by me looking into Maggie's murder."

"You're assuming Karen called Collin and that the incident on the road was a scare tactic. Karen could have called anyone. Even someone from your own family."

While touched by his concern, she felt a shot of anger. "So now you're saying that not only was my grandfather a murderer, but also there are others in my family who won't hesitate to take me out, too?"

He sighed. "I don't know why I bother trying to protect you from yourself."

"Why do you? I was here first. So leave."

"Shh." He waved her to silence. "Did you hear that?" he whispered.

Obviously she hadn't. If this was a trick— She heard a clank, like a door closing. Brody grabbed her and jerked her back against him as he turned off his flashlight and pressed them to the wall behind the file cabinet.

"Don't make a sound," he whispered, his warm breath tickling her ear.

BRODY HELD HARPER close as footfalls echoed in one of the auto bays in the room next to them. He waited, expecting the office door to bang all the way open, the light to come on and the two of them to be discovered hiding behind the file cabinets.

How had he let himself get into this position? Worse, he was unbearably aware of Harper's lush body pressed against his own. He began to silently recite words to the first song that came to mind so he didn't think about her nipples, which unless he was wrong, were now hard as pebbles against his chest. This woman was going to be the death of him.

He tried to concentrate on what was going on in the garage next door. What sounded like a wrench being dropped echoed through the wall, then the rustle of tools in a toolbox and finally retreating footfalls on the concrete before a door slammed closed.

"Do you think he's gone?" Harper whispered. She sounded breathless and he realized he was probably crushing her.

He stepped out from behind the file cabinets but didn't turn on his flashlight until he heard the sound of a car engine. The roar of the motor died off, leaving them in silence again.

He snapped on his flashlight and looked at her. She looked a little flushed. Or maybe he was thinking of his own heat. "I think that was enough excitement for me for one night."

She let out a breath and stepped from the hiding place. He could see that she wasn't ready to give up. Did the woman have no sense at all?

"Since I'm already here…" She turned on her flashlight.

"Seriously?"

"You don't have to stay."

"What do you hope to find? You said yourself Collin searched earlier and didn't find whatever it was he was looking for. Which might have been a customer's bill, for all you know."

She nodded, but he could tell his words didn't make a dent.

"I had no idea you were so stubborn."

Harper laughed at that as she opened the top file cabinet and shone her light inside. "Yes, you did."

He stood there, fuming for a moment. "Fine, I'll look in the desk. I can't very well leave you here to get caught. With two of us, it will go faster."

She smiled but quickly hid it when he shot her a look.

He found nothing of interest in the desk drawers. By that time, she'd finished going through two of the file drawers.

"This one drawer is stuck," she said from behind him. "Can you help me?"

Brody felt anxious. They'd been here too long. Someone was bound to notice the lights behind the drawn blinds. But he knew Harper wasn't about to leave until she'd looked into the bottom file cabinet.

He motioned her out of the way and grabbed the drawer handle. She was right. It was stuck. He gave it a jerk. The drawer came open but something fell behind the filing cabinet.

Harper quickly stepped back into the space they'd occupied earlier to see what had fallen. Hurriedly, he made short work of the bottom file cabinet, seeing at once that it held nothing but a bunch of old bills. He was about to close the drawer, when she came out from behind the cabinet holding what looked like a yearbook and smiling broadly.

"I think we found what Collin was looking for," Harper said grinning.

"A YEARBOOK?"

Harper ignored Brody's tone and opened the book almost reverently. Her hope was that this was what Collin had been looking for, which would mean there was something in here that he was afraid might incriminate him.

It had been her idea to go to the truck stop. This time of night, it wasn't busy. Brody had followed her there in his pickup. Once inside, they took a booth in the far corner, ordered coffee and, sitting side by side, she opened Collin's senior yearbook and began to read what his friends had written in it.

Most of what was scrawled on the pages was what could be found in any old yearbook. "Have a great summer... So glad we got to know each other this year… Stay cool… Keep in touch… You rule!… We're free!"

Those were mostly notes from girls Collin had known. Karen Jones now Parker had signed "Friends Forever." So maybe that was all there was between the two of them.

The male classmates had written less poignant mementos. "You suck!… Keep it in your pants… You owe me $10… Dork!… Up yours."

Disappointed, Harper started to close the book. On the back page, someone had written, "Take it to your grave. Or wish you had, Buddy."

"Do you recognize the handwriting?" she asked Brody. The script was distinct. So was the pen he'd used, a wide black one.

Brody took the book from her and flipped through until he found several other spots where the student had signed with the same pen. Most of what he'd written was silly stuff.

But under his own photo he'd written with the same pen "I know, I'm awesome. :)"

"Will Sanders?" Harper said. "Do you know him?"

Brody shook his head. "You do realize that something as cryptic as 'Take it to your grave. Or wish you had, Buddy' could mean just about anything."

She nodded.

"Nor do we know that this yearbook is what Collin was looking for earlier."

"I know what you're saying." Harper agreed. "But it does make you wonder, doesn't it? I wonder if Maggie had a yearbook?"

CHAPTER TWELVE

JD HELD HIS *breath as he neared Mirror Lake. It had been a long winter. Now he hoped that Maggie would be waiting for him. All through last fall, their visits had become something he looked forward to. She made him laugh. He felt alive up here with her.*

The days he couldn't ride up to the lake seemed interminable. Grace had been getting steadily worse as Sarah's second pregnancy had progressed. He'd done his best to keep peace in the family, but Grace's insistence that Sarah wanted her dead had finally made him explode and storm out.

He let out the breath he'd been holding as he spotted Maggie's horse in the clearing by the lake.

Dismounting, he found her sitting on a rock looking troubled.

"Anything I can do?" he asked as he joined her.

She smiled, her face lighting up as if she was just as glad to see him. "I just needed a friendly face."

They sat and talked. She'd be graduating soon, but she didn't know what she wanted to do with her life. She said she'd just hang around for now, riding her horse, swimming in the lake.

"Everyone I know is getting married." She shook her head.

"Isn't there a boy you're interested in?"

She laughed. "Boy, exactly. They are so immature. So boring. So single-minded."

He could well imagine and said as much. "I used to be one." They laughed, then fell silent, the only sound the gentle lap of the water against the rocky shore.

"You can talk to me," Maggie said as she distract-edly brushed dried pine needles from the soles of her bare feet. He could see that she'd already been in the icy water. Her hair was wet and there were spots on her Western shirt where her wet bra had bled through.

"I thought I was talking to you."

She looked over at him. "You can tell me what's wrong."

He smiled at that. "And bore us both to death? No, thanks."

"I'm a good listener." She had begun to replait her hair.

"Where does your family think you go on the days you ride up here?" he asked. He knew that Maggie was Flannigan McTavish's only child. She lived with her father on the ranch that he and his younger brother, Finn, owned. Both men were blacksmiths and kept to themselves.

"You're asking if they know about you?" Maggie finished braiding her hair, tying off the end with a rubber band she'd pulled from her cutoff's pocket. "They don't know where I go or what I do. Does that make you feel better?"

"I wasn't trying to hide the fact that we see each other." It was a lie and her look called him on it. No one would understand their connection.

"What if they did know about you?" she challenged.

"They wouldn't approve. I'm a married man old enough to be your father."

She smiled. "If you say that to yourself enough times maybe you will quit riding up here to meet me." Before he could object, she said, "I look forward to our visits as much as you do, so please don't deny that you come up here to see me."

He didn't. He couldn't. He looked out at the lake. A weak spring sun cast a patina over the surface as a hawk circled above them.

"I like this," he admitted, feeling the pinch of guilt and telling himself he could live with it. "I like being here with you."

She rested her shoulder against his. "So tell me what's wrong."

He closed his eyes, hesitating only a moment before he opened his heart to her.

THE NEXT MORNING, no one was more surprised to see Brody than Harper was. "You're *still* determined to play detective, right?" He didn't give her a chance to answer. "Fine. Come on. At least when you're with me, I know you aren't getting yourself into trouble. There also might be a way to find out what was going on with Maggie before she died without you stirring up the whole town." He turned and headed for his pickup.

She wanted to dig in her heels and demand to know where they were going. But as she watched him stride to his truck, she found herself hurrying to catch up. Wherever he was going, she was going with him.

"I don't like doing this," he said as they both climbed into his pickup. "I feel disloyal to my cousin. Worse, to my uncle."

"Now you know how I feel, especially knowing how much my father has to lose if I'm wrong."

He glanced over at her and had the good grace to look chastised as they drove out of the ranch and down the road toward Beartooth. "No matter how this ends, it's going to be bad."

She looked up and saw where he was headed. "What are we doing?"

"My dad and uncle were meeting with the sheriff to see when Maggie's remains will be released for burial. So there won't be anyone on the ranch—at least for a while." He glanced at her. "My uncle left Maggie's room exactly as it was the day she disappeared."

"Seriously?" Harper felt a shiver.

"So if there are any clues as to where she went that night…"

"Or if there was someone else…"

He nodded. "But I wouldn't get your hopes up. I'm sure the sheriff searched the room thirty-five years ago. By now, Sheriff Curry has probably already been there, as well."

"It won't hurt to look, though, right?"

His expression was doubtful. "We just can't let my uncle catch us."

Brody pulled up in front of a small older house. As Harper got out, it felt as if an eerie silence had fallen over the place. She knew that both Brody's uncle and father had houses on the ranch. After college, Brody had built his own house miles down the road from the two brothers. But she'd never been on the ranch before.

She had to run to keep up with Brody as he hurried to his uncle's front door. Like most houses in rural Montana, the door wasn't locked.

"Are you sure we should be in here?" Harper asked, hanging back in the doorway, suddenly worried they would get caught.

Brody didn't answer as he moved deeper into the dim light of the old farmhouse. Harper glanced over her shoulder and then stepped in. The house felt cool and smelled of what could have been last night's roast beef dinner. Brody had gone down a short hallway and stopped to wait for her.

She followed, feeling that she was trespassing. Brody had made it clear that there would be hell to pay if they got caught. Worse, because he was in Maggie's room with her, it would be much worse if he was caught with a Hamilton.

Harper joined Brody as he opened the door to his cousin's room. The scent that escaped was one of age and dust and a faint smell of a sweet perfume. Her stomach roiled. "We shouldn't be here."

"No, but now that we are, let's do this."

She stared at the horse posters on the walls, the straw cowboy hat hanging on the bedpost, a worn guitar leaning against the wall.

"Harper," Brody said, getting her attention.

She nodded and moved cautiously to the desk, not wanting to disturb the dust any more than necessary. There was a thick layer of it on everything. It seemed that Flannigan McTavish had closed the door and not opened it again in all this time.

"So the room is exactly like it was the night she disappeared?" Harper asked. She could see that Brody wasn't anxious to disturb the dust or anything else in the room. "It doesn't look as if Frank Curry or anyone else has been here," she said, pointing to the undisturbed dust on the floor.

"I guess not," Brody said. "But I would assume that the former sheriff searched the room thirty-five years ago. Apparently he didn't find anything."

"So what makes you think *we* will?" she had to ask.

"Because he wasn't looking for a murderer. We are."

"Your uncle will know someone's been here."

"I'll deal with that when I have to."

Harper didn't like the sound of that as she took in the room.

"Start with the desk drawers, I'll look under the bed and the top shelf of the closet. We're looking for her yearbook—or anything else that might give us a clue to what was going on with her before she was killed."

Harper moved cautiously to the desk. Grasping the knob of the bottom drawer, she pulled it open.

Notebooks and three-ring binders. She opened one after another only to find schoolwork, nothing else.

She tried the next drawer. This one had what appeared to be mementos. Report cards, numerous dried flower corsages, a plastic tiara, Halloween masks, and under it all was a small wooden box.

Carefully, she pulled out the box and opened it. Inside was a bundle of what appeared to be wildflowers. Most of the petals had fallen off the stems. The flowers had been tied together with a thin piece of hair ribbon. Clearly they had meant something to be placed alone in this box. But unfortunately there was no card or note. Who had given them to Maggie? she wondered.

"Any luck?" Brody asked.

"Not much." She closed the box, put it back and opened the last drawer.

There were a few cards and papers in this drawer. Several drawings that, even to Harper's amateur eye, looked as if they'd been done by someone with talent.

"Was Maggie artistic?" she asked.

"Not that I know of, why?"

"Oh, I found some drawings. They're quite good."

She pulled out all the papers and went through them but found nothing that could be considered helpful. No love letters. No notes that girls often did as they tried out a boyfriend's name to see how it looked with her own. No appointment book with plans for the week or even the next day.

As she started to close the drawer, it caught on something. Pulling it all the way open again, she saw what had kept it from closing—a framed photo of two girls of about twelve. One was a beautiful redhead, the other a dark-haired brunette. Both appeared to be early teens. They stood squinting into the sunlight, their arms locked around each other, both smiling broadly. Best friends, Harper thought, recognizing times in her life when she'd taken a photo like this.

She held the photo up for Brody.

"Maggie and…" He took the framed photograph from her and looked at the girlish writing at the bottom. "Amber? The only Amber I know of is Amber Jenkins."

"Ty Jenkins's sister?" Another boy she'd seen in the yearbook. "Wouldn't her friend know what was going on back then?"

"I guess it would depend on how close they were at the time Maggie disappeared."

"Or how close Maggie was with her brother. Didn't Ty Jenkins kill himself?" Harper took the photo back.

She'd found no other photographs of the two young women. Had they still been friends when Maggie was murdered? And where did Collin Wilson fit into the picture? Or did he?

"I'm beginning to realize how different things were thirty-five years ago," Harper said. "We would know if they were friends if Maggie had had a cell phone back then. There would be text data, phone numbers and appointments, and possibly even GPS to track the last few places she went."

As Harper started to put everything back in the drawer, the light caught on something small and metal in the very back.

"With us knowing nothing about her, it's impossible to know what we're even looking for," Brody said as he continued to search. "You're right. If this had been recent, everything, including photos, about her would have been posted on Facebook. Thirty-five years ago—"

"She would have kept a diary." Harper held up the tiny gold key she'd found in the back of the drawer.

Brody turned from where he'd been going through the closet. "How do you know that's what it is for?" he asked, stepping to her to take the key.

"Are you kidding? I had five sisters. The only way I could keep anything to myself and secret was a locked diary. I would hide the key—and then hide the diary somewhere else."

He looked around the room. "We've looked most every place. Without tearing the room apart…"

"Wouldn't a diary have been the first thing that was found after she disappeared? Either the sheriff found it after the missing persons report was filed or…"

"Or my uncle did." Brody pulled an item out from under the bed. "I found her yearbook from senior year."

Harper hurried over to him as he flipped it open. There were a few places where it had been signed, but very few. What was written under photos of girls Maggie had gone to school with was innocuous enough. "Best of luck in the future… Stay cool always… Keep the faith… Have a great summer."

Under Maggie's photo, though, someone had printed the words: "Bitch. You deserved it and worse."

Brody shook his head and started to close the book. Harper took it from him and opened it again to the photo of Bobby Barnes and Maggie in some class where they sat next to each other. Under it, he had written, "Not over by a long shot." The other boys Maggie had dated hadn't commented in her book.

BRODY DROVE OUT of his uncle's place through the back way. The last thing he wanted was for Flannigan to find them in Maggie's room—let alone be caught with Harper. It would be bad enough when he saw the footprints. His uncle would know Brody had been there—and not alone.

He looked over at Harper, mentally kicking himself for getting caught up in her quest to find out the truth. The sun shone in through the side window of his pickup, lighting up her beautiful face and making her long blond hair shine like summer wheat.

After waiting years for Harper to return to Montana and the ranch… He'd never wanted any other woman the way he did this one. If anything, her stubborn determination to face all of this head-on had made him fall even more in love with her.

She was strong and he liked the way she stood up to him. The woman knew her own mind, no doubt about that. But for the life of him, he couldn't see how they could ever be together—not if they had any hope of their families being a part of their lives. It had been bad enough before, but once they'd found Maggie's remains on Hamilton Ranch…

He felt her gaze and glanced over at her as the pickup bumped along the narrow dirt road behind the ranch. "What?" he asked, forced to quickly return his attention to his driving. Ahead was a stand of cottonwood trees and a small creek they would have to ford.

"I know what you said about the man doing the chasing and all that. I had hoped that we would have all summer to get to know each other, to…" She waved a hand through the air. "But now I feel we might not have much time. I don't want to waste any of it by being coy or waiting around for you to make the next move. So let me say it. I've had a crush on you for years. When Bo told me that you weren't dating anyone…"

He slowed the pickup as they entered the stand of trees. It was cooler in here, the sun peeking through the branches. Ahead, he saw that the creek was higher than he'd hoped it would be. This felt like a bad idea—all of it, he thought as he brought the truck to a stop under the canopy of trees and looked over at Harper.

"Before you go any further, I think it's probably better if we don't see each other again until this all blows over," Brody said.

Harper looked as if she couldn't believe what she was hearing. "This is what you have to say after I told you how I feel?"

He sighed and looked out at the creek. "You know

it's for the best. Sit here. I need to take a look at the creek before we try to cross it." He got out. Two seconds later he heard the passenger side of the pickup open.

"Because of the bad blood between our families you're going to waste this time we have together?" Harper demanded behind him.

He picked up a branch that had fallen from one of the trees and tested the water level at the center of the road. When he turned, her blue eyes were narrowed.

"I can't believe that the cool teenage boy I knew grew up to be a coward."

"A coward?" he repeated, tossing the stick away.

"I call them the way I see them," she said, hands on her hips.

Did she not realize that he'd just gone out on a limb back there at his uncle's house and all because of her? He took a step toward her. "A coward? Those are fighting words."

She laughed mockingly. "So far I haven't seen much fight in you."

He met her challenging gaze. "You really have no idea what is good for you," he said as he caged her against the side of the pickup with a hand on each side of her.

"I used to think *you* would be good for me," she said quietly, her voice rough with emotion.

"But now?" he asked.

She gave an almost imperceptible shrug before her gaze locked with his. "When are you going to quit pretending that you don't want me?"

"Remember when I told you that the next time I was going to kiss you, you'd know it?"

Harper nodded.

His mouth dropped to hers, her lips parting in welcome. He stepped closer, pressing himself against her, against the truck. He'd never wanted anyone like he wanted Harper right now. He'd been waiting for years for this, he thought as he forced her mouth open with his tongue. All his senses told him to stop. Only heartbreak would come of this if he was right about her grandfather and his cousin.

But then Harper flicked the tip of her tongue across the inside of his lower lip. He let out a moan, one hand going to her full, rounded breast. His thumb found the nipple's hard tip and flicked it. She let out a groan in answer as he deepened the kiss.

The sound of an approaching vehicle brought him out of the kiss. He cocked his head, listening as he tried to catch his breath. His hand was still on her breast. Her arms were still locked around his neck. He could hear the roar of a motor.

"Someone's coming." He swore as he drew back, his gaze going to hers. He could see the heat in all that blue, hear her ragged breaths, feel her trembling as he removed his hand from her breast. A few minutes longer and he would have had her clothes off and—

He turned and opened the pickup door. She slid in, him following. The vehicle was coming from the direction they had. That meant it was probably either his uncle or his father. The creek was high, but now he had no choice. They had to cross. He was in no mood for a confrontation with his uncle—not with Harper here.

Throwing the truck in Reverse, he backed up, shifted into First and tromped on the gas. The truck shot out of the trees. The front tires dropped into the creek bed, water swept down each side of the truck as they roared across and up the other side. At the top of the hill, he looked back. His uncle's truck had stopped some distance away.

Brody knew there was no doubt that Flannigan had seen them.

CHAPTER THIRTEEN

WHEN JD RODE up to the lake, he could tell that Maggie had been waiting for him. He hoped she was all right. He worried about her.

As he dismounted, she looked excited as she rose to go to her horse. Watching her, he saw her pull something from her saddlebag. "This is for you."

She held out the piece of heavy paper almost shyly. He frowned questioningly as he took it. His surprise was obvious as he saw that the drawing was of him.

"Did you do this?" he asked.

"It's just something I play at."

"You're good, really good. You have talent. Have you thought about doing something with this talent?"

"Like becoming an artist?" She smiled at that. "They're just doodles. They aren't worth anything."

"Who told you that?" he asked, angry with whoever it had been.

She shook her head. "Don't make more of it than it is."

He looked again at the drawing. She had captured him casting his lure toward the shimmering surface of the lake. The lines of the sketch were powerful in that she had captured the essence of not only the scene but also of him and the mood he'd been in that day. She was more than talented, he thought as he looked up to

see her walk to the edge of the lake. She was percep-
tive. She seemed to see him more clearly than anyone
ever had.

That thought shook him. She had her whole life
ahead of her. He wanted to see her get out of here
and make something of herself. At the same time, he
hated to see her go.

"Have you thought more about college?" he asked.

She turned to look at him. "Is that what you want?"

"It isn't about me."

Maggie said nothing as she turned her back to him
again.

"You're young. You can make something of yourself."

She let out a sigh. "What about you?"

"What about me?"

Maggie turned to look at him again. "You make it
sound as if your life is over."

Is that how he felt? Some days, most days lately,
after resigning his senate seat to stay home with Grace.
"I've already made choices that affect my future. You
haven't yet."

She raised an eyebrow. "Haven't I?"

He swallowed back the lump that rose in his throat at
the look she gave him and shook his head. "Maggie—"

"What do you want, JD?" she asked as she stepped
toward him. "If today was the first day of the rest of
your life and you could have anything you wanted,
what would you want?"

WHEN BRODY DROPPED Harper off at home, she opened
the door to find Kat waiting for her. "You and Brody
McTavish?"

Harper sighed. "I'm in love with him."

Kat shook her head. "Is that all?"

"Isn't that enough? Look what love has done for you." Kat had changed over this past year. There was a softness to her that hadn't been there. Max's doing, Harper thought. Also Kat dressed and acted differently. She wasn't so…closed up. *This is what love does to you*, she thought, and wanted the kind of contentment she'd seen in her sister's face.

But right now there was worry in Kat's expression. "Harper, I thought we discussed this before. I told you why you can't get involved in Maggie's death, and now I suspect you've dragged Brody into it, as well."

She crossed her arms. Kat had always been bossy. Harper wasn't going to let her boss her now that they were both adults. "I'm already involved because I'm a Hamilton and JD was my grandfather."

Kat sighed. "Then there's something you need to know about our grandparents." She sat down on the couch and patted the cushion next to her.

Harper quickly joined her. Kat would have been old enough that she might remember what had been going on back then.

"I was only a child, but I remember Dad and Sarah talking about our grandfather and grandmother when they thought I wasn't listening," Kat said. "I got the feeling there was a secret, but what was clear was that JD and Grace weren't happy, but then again I can't imagine anyone being happy with our grandmother. Even photographs of Grace scared me. She looked mean. I remember Sarah saying that grandmother wanted nothing to do with Ainsley when she was a baby. In the photos Grace was in a wheelchair wearing black and this look on her face…" Kat shivered.

"So you think our grandfather did have an affair with Maggie?"

Kat made an impatient face. "Let me finish. I wouldn't have blamed JD if he had found some happiness away from that house. But I also think Sarah played a role in all this."

Harper made a disgusted sound. "And I think you want to blame her for everything. But Maggie McTavish's murder? Really?"

"I think she was more of a…catalyst. I know she pushed our grandfather to run for president. I heard Dad talking about it once with Angelina. He'd been drinking and he was saying how it is often the woman behind the man who makes the man. I think he meant it as a compliment. But he said his grandmother hated politics and if she'd had her way, JD would never have even run for the senate—let alone considered running for president. It was after Dad married Sarah that she talked JD into running. Apparently, like Dad, he had a good chance of winning.

"Don't you think it's odd that Sarah did that?" Kat asked.

Harper shrugged. "Maybe she could see that he needed to get away from his wife—if she was that awful to him."

"Maybe. Or maybe Sarah had her reasons for wanting him to be president."

She groaned.

"She is determined to put at least one Hamilton in the White House. She is certainly encouraging Dad and has been ever since she came back. Why would she care?"

"Because she loves him and knows it's something he wants."

"Does he? Or is this all tangled up with his own father and his near run for president?" Kat said with a sigh.

"And Mother is determined that Dad be president so she can…what?"

Kat shook her head. "All I know is that she encouraged our grandfather and now she is encouraging our father. I really doubt the reason is because she wants to live in the White House."

Harper couldn't believe what she was hearing.

Her sister had given her a look that chilled her. "I'm telling you to leave it alone. I'm serious. I think our mother is capable of just about anything. If she's involved in this…" Kat shook her head. "Not to mention what you might find out. You won't be able to un-ring that bell."

Brody was certainly convinced that if she found out the truth, she would regret it. Maybe he was right. But a part of her was tired of being kept in the dark, of being protected and pampered as if she would break in a strong wind. She told herself that she would face whatever that truth was, but she wasn't going to stop digging.

Too antsy to stay inside, Harper saddled up and rode over to her mother's. All the way, she kept thinking about what Kat had told her. She didn't know what to believe. The one thing that she knew, though, was that her mother had been living in the same house, the old homestead, with JD and Grace Hamilton before Maggie disappeared. They'd moved out when Buck was building the house he lived in now.

If anyone knew what had been going on back then, Harper was betting it was her mother.

"Are you all right?" Harper asked when her mother opened the door. She looked pale, almost scared. "I should have called to remind you I was coming by." Her mother looked past her to where Harper had tied her horse.

"No, it is always wonderful to see you. You just startled me. I didn't hear a vehicle and then when you knocked…" She hugged herself.

Now as she looked at her mother, she couldn't help thinking what Kat had told her couldn't possibly be true. Sarah Hamilton was a small woman with a timid bearing. Right now she looked as far from dangerous as anyone could. She looked scared of her own shadow.

"Are you afraid, living out here by yourself?" Harper asked, concerned for her mother.

"No, of course not. I was merely startled. I was reading. I must have dozed off. Come in."

"Could we sit out on the porch? It is such a beautiful day."

"Of course. I can get us something to drink. A cola? Or I could make some lemonade."

Harper started to decline, but she sensed her mother needed the time to regain some control. No matter what Sarah said, she *had* been scared—not just startled. "I'd take some lemonade."

"Go on out on the porch, I'll be right there." Her mother disappeared into the kitchen.

Harper walked to the front porch and took one of the chairs, her thoughts on her mother. She had no memory of what her mother used to be like since Sarah had allegedly died when Harper and her twin were only a few months old. But this small, nervous woman who scared so easily definitely seemed at odds with what Kat had told her. Unless Kat was right and her mother had something to fear from her past.

Minutes later, her mother returned with two tall glasses of lemonade.

Harper took a sip of her lemonade as her mother pulled up a chair and sat. "I was hoping you would tell me about my grandparents."

Her mother sounded relieved when she spoke, as if she was glad they wouldn't be talking about Maggie. "I'm sorry you never got to know my parents. They both died in a house fire the year I graduated from college. They would have adored you and your sisters."

"And Dad's parents?"

It was evident from Sarah's expression that she realized these were the grandparents Harper was really interested in learning about. "I didn't know them well since they both died shortly after your father and I married."

"You and Dad eloped."

"We did. He knew his parents would insist on a big wedding and with his mother ill and his father busy as a senator…we decided not to wait."

Harper studied her for a moment, detecting something in her voice. "Were they upset with Dad for eloping?"

Sarah looked away for a moment. "Buck was their only son so, yes, they were disappointed," she said as if carefully choosing her words.

"My grandmother was already in a wheelchair by then?"

"Not yet." Her mother looked uncomfortable.

"How did she end up in a wheelchair anyway?"

SARAH REALIZED SHE must have given away more than she had intended with her answers. She let out a short laugh, hoping to cover up whatever it was that Harper had sensed. Her daughter surprised her at how... insightful she was. She warned herself to be more careful around her.

"Why are you asking me all these questions?" she said, trying not to sound defensive and failing.

"Isn't it obvious? The sheriff isn't the only one trying to prove that my grandfather killed Maggie McTavish. Brody is determined to find proof, too."

Brody. She let out an oath under her breath. "I didn't think you were seeing him anymore."

"I was never *seeing* him, as you put it." Her daughter looked away, a slight blush creeping up her neck that made Sarah realize she had reason for concern when it came to Brody McTavish. "We're trying to find out the truth."

Sarah attempted to hide not only her shock, but her displeasure, and failed. *"You and Brody? Why would you do that?"*

"Because someone has to."

Sarah shot to her feet. "Harper, you have to stop this," she said as she moved to the porch railing and looked out on the ranch. Why did history have to repeat itself? "We should go inside. A storm is coming." She could smell rain on the warm wind.

"You didn't answer my question about my grandmother Hamilton," Harper said doggedly when they were inside sitting in the living room.

"Harper, I'm begging you to leave the past alone."

"That's what Kat said I should do."

Sarah froze. She could feel her daughter's intent gaze on her. "It's good advice."

"Don't you want to know why Kat gave me that advice?"

Sarah could feel the noose tightening around her neck. "She told you about The Prophecy and that she thinks I was the leader, a woman called Red. I wondered how long it would be before she shared that with you. Did she also tell you that the real Red confessed?"

Harper nodded. "Kat's afraid that more about The Prophecy is going to come out. She thinks it might have had something to do with my grandfather pulling out of the presidential race—and maybe even his death."

"Did she say that?"

"Not in so many words. But if you weren't involved, then you can't help me, right? But you know more than you're telling me. Please, Mother, help me."

She looked at her daughter and gave up trying to shelter her. "Kat's right. We don't know what those people did or what they still might do. Did Kat mention that not all of the group have been found and arrested?"

"Then she's right about them being dangerous, since apparently they tried to frame you," Harper said. "Why would they do that unless they were trying to make Dad look bad before the election? But if they were somehow involved as far back as when my grandfather was a senator planning to run for president, isn't it possible that one of them—not my grandfather—killed Maggie McTavish?"

Sarah saw that this had been where Harper had been headed all along. "That's quite the stretch. It sounds more like you just don't want it to have been your grandfather who was responsible for Maggie's death."

"*Don't you?* I'm worried what it will do to Dad's campaign if it ends up that JD Hamilton was not only an adulterer but also a murderer."

"We might never know what really happened," her mother said.

"Maybe. Did you know that Maggie kept a diary?"

THE RAIN CAME on a spring squall that swept down out of the Crazies. The sky darkened an instant before droplets began to pelt the windshield.

Brody turned on his pickup's wipers, his mind on Harper and the kiss and the feel of her in his arms. He couldn't deny his feelings. And yet… Mentally he kicked himself for agreeing to help her look for the truth about his cousin and her grandfather.

Earlier Harper had promised to talk to her parents. He'd told her he would talk to his father, and was headed to the ranch now.

He couldn't help feeling anxious, though. His father and uncle had made it clear they didn't want to talk about Maggie or her death. It was as if everyone was hiding something. He had tried to question them but had only managed to make them angry and even more closemouthed. This time he wouldn't settle for being put off again. Harper was determined to find a killer. On the off chance that Maggie's killer was still alive…

What worried him was the way his father and uncle had been acting since Maggie's body was found. What could they possibly know that made them seem almost…afraid?

Admittedly, he knew Harper was right. Her family, he was sure, had their own secrets. The two of them couldn't get the whole picture without putting both sides of the stories together. He'd been a fool to go charging over to the Hamilton Ranch thinking he would accomplish something by demanding to see the senator. The presidential candidate certainly wasn't going to admit anything to him. But he might tell his daughter the truth.

Brody was still convinced that the only way they would ever know the truth was if he and Harper did the digging themselves. Buckmaster had too much power and influence to suit Brody. Maybe Sheriff Frank Curry couldn't be bought. But Brody had no doubt Buckmaster could put all kinds of pressure on him during this investigation.

Brody also knew that he and Harper had more access to their families than even the sheriff. While his father and uncle might not tell Frank everything, Brody might be able to get them to talk. He was damned sure going to try.

Because if Brody and Harper had a hope of ever being together, given the way their families felt, they had to find out the truth—and pray that it wouldn't destroy what they felt for each other.

The rain turned to sleet and then hard kernels of snow. Icy pebbles pounded the pickup and whitened the road ahead. Dark clouds obscured the Crazies. Wind whirled tumbleweeds across the road into his path. He slowed as he neared his uncle's place.

As quickly as the squall had blown in, it moved on

past. The barrage stopped, leaving the sky a white-washed blue overhead. There was nothing like spring in Montana, he thought as the sun came out again.

Seeing his father's truck parked outside, he turned down the drive to his uncle's house.

Good, he would be able to talk to them both, he thought as he parked and climbed out.

He heard raised voices as he neared the front door. He'd never known the brothers to quarrel—let alone fight. Without knocking, he stepped in. The moment his father and uncle saw him, they stepped apart and fell silent.

"Don't let me disturb you," he said, closing the door behind him.

"You should learn to knock," his father said, clearly agitated.

Brody ignored that as he moved into the room. "I can only imagine what the two of you were arguing about. What's going on?"

"It doesn't concern you," his uncle said, and started to leave the room.

"Like hell," Brody snapped, motioning for his uncle to stay put. "It's time the two of you told me what you've been hiding all these years. I know it has something to do with Maggie. So what is it and why do you both look scared? Does it have anything to do with Maggie's diary?"

HARPER COULD SEE that she'd upset her mother, but she couldn't stop now. Brody had gone to talk to his father and uncle. The only way they were ever going to know what happened thirty-five years ago was if they could get the people who were there to tell them.

"Talk to me. I'm not going to give up. I *will* find out the truth."

Her mother groaned. "What is it with this family and the truth?" She met Harper's gaze. "There are many truths."

"You had to know if JD and Maggie were having an affair. When you and Dad first got married, weren't you living in the same house with him and Grace for a while?" Sarah nodded. "You probably even knew Maggie."

"I'd seen her go riding by on her way up to Mirror Lake," she admitted as if seeing that Harper wasn't going to take no for an answer. "JD fished up there occasionally. But if they had a…sexual relationship, I really can't say." She sighed.

Picking up her lemonade, the ice nearly melted, she took a drink. "JD was angry at your father for running off and getting married to a complete stranger. Apparently, there was some girl in the valley whose family had a large ranch that he had wanted Buck to marry."

Harper thought she finally might be getting somewhere. "What about my grandmother?" she asked, positive now there was something her mother didn't want to tell her. "Was she angry, too?"

"Grace was more angry than JD, but she hid it behind a sweetness that would have given a person a cavity. At least that was the way she was around JD and Buck."

Harper thought she was finally getting somewhere. "So the two of you *didn't* like each other."

"Not to speak ill of the dead or—worse—your grandmother, but Grace was the most manipulative, controlling, stubborn, domineering woman I've ever met. If she was protective of her husband, she was worse when it came to her son. No one would have been good enough for Buck."

Harper saw her mother's eyes seem to glaze over, as if she was back there, the new bride coming home to the ranch to meet her in-laws for the first time and not under the best circumstances.

"Grace had insisted Buck be called Buckmaster— just as she had named him. She'd insisted on a lot of things and JD did his best to make sure she got what she wanted. I saw at once that Grace Hamilton wasn't as helpless as she wanted her husband to think."

"I get the feeling you've never talked about this with anyone," Harper said.

Her mother smiled, tears in her eyes. "There were a lot of things I've never told anyone, not even your father." She let out a bitter laugh. "You asked for the truth? There was one time when I accidentally walked in and found Grace standing a few feet from her wheelchair. She'd gotten up to get something, thinking no one was home."

"So she *could* walk."

"At least a few steps. She looked startled when she saw me. Then we both heard JD coming down the hall calling Grace's name. I saw a change in her expression. She grabbed for her wheelchair, but it rolled away. I reached for her, but she fell, knocking the chair over as she hit the floor. JD had rushed in, demanding to know what had happened. 'That girl,' Grace had cried, pointing a finger at me. 'She tried to kill me.' JD didn't believe her, but Grace never changed her story of how her chair had gotten stuck on the rug and she'd asked for my help. That I'd purposely dumped her out of the chair."

"That's horrible," Harper said, almost too shocked to speak. She'd heard of awful mother-in-laws but nothing like this.

Her mother laughed. "You think that's horrible? Grace told everyone I was the one who pushed her down the stairs to begin with. I was the one who put her in that wheelchair. She would have done anything to get rid of me. Even lie."

"But surely Dad and JD saw through it."

"JD wouldn't let her call the sheriff. Your father didn't believe it and I don't think JD did, either. Still, when I became pregnant with Ainsley, that's when we had to move out of the old homestead. I didn't feel safe around her. We moved into a cabin on the ranch until the main house was finished. Buck told his mother we just needed more space, but she knew why we moved out."

"What a nasty woman."

"That's what I thought then, but now? Now I think she was just afraid of losing her son—*and* her husband," Sarah said.

"If that was the case, then she must have known someone was after her husband," Harper said. "She must have suspected there was someone else and if she was desperate enough to try to keep her husband and son by lying about you trying to kill her… What if she knew about Maggie? Unless there were other women. Was my grandfather a womanizer?"

"He was handsome enough, that's for sure. I wish I knew more but Buck and I didn't see that much of them after we moved out. Grace took my pregnancies very badly."

Harper frowned. "So what happened to the old homestead where my grandparents lived?"

"It's still there. Like a lot of early settlers, the original house was built down by the creek in the trees to shelter it from the storms. It's only today that people build so they have a view."

"Wait, where is this house?"

Her mother described how to get there.

"My grandparents lived in what we call the old Maynard House?" she asked in surprise.

"Is that what your father calls it? Probably because his grandfather, Maynard Hamilton, built it."

Harper sat back, considering everything her mother had told her. "So if my grandmother could walk, and she stayed in the wheelchair as a way of trying to hang on to her husband, she must have known about Maggie and the affair—if there was one. Was there, though?"

Her mother shrugged. "Maggie was young and beautiful and carefree and probably fun, everything that Grace wasn't. I'm sure JD was tempted. But if he acted on it, I don't know."

"Dad said the same thing. That he didn't know."

Sarah looked uncomfortable. "I do know that if the two of them were lovers, your grandfather didn't kill her."

"How do you know that?"

"He was a good, kind, peaceful man as honest as the day was long and he would never have left Grace. He was committed to her."

Harper felt confused. "But if he was running for

president in four years and he'd fallen in love with
Maggie McTavish, then wouldn't he be—"

"Living in his own private hell."

"So what would he have done?"

Her mother shook her head. "That's just it, I have
no idea. Love can be blind, especially when you fall
in love with the wrong person. Or, maybe to him, she
was the right person but the wrong circumstances."

Like Brody McTavish, Harper thought. "What if
Maggie wasn't the wrong person for him? What if she
was…the love of his life?"

Her mother gave her an impatient look. "There could
never have been a happy ending for them. The differ-
ences in their ages apart, Grace would never have let
that happen."

BRODY WAITED. HE saw his father and uncle exchange a
look. "I'm not going to leave until I get some answers."

"He's correct," Finn said, over the protests of his
brother. "Brody has a right to know."

Flannigan started past them. "I won't be part of
this."

"You *are* part of it," Finn said grabbing his brother's
arm. "We *all* are. Brody has to know the truth. Don't
you see that? We can't hide it anymore—especially
from my son."

Brody looked from his uncle to his father and felt
his heart drop to his boots. "What is it you've been
hiding from me?" he said, his voice sounding strange
even to him.

Flannigan swayed on his feet like a large pine in

a fierce wind. "We swore on the Bible that we would never—"

"We did what we thought was right then because Maggie insisted," Finn said. "I have to do what is right *now*. I told you no good would come of it. But you were so hell-bent on saving Maggie and look how much good that did."

Flannigan pulled free of his brother's grasp. "She was my *daughter*. She was—" his voice broke "—my life."

"Yes, we all know that," Finn said. Brody heard the pain in his father's voice. "And I am your brother."

"You want to drag her name through the dirt like everyone else?" Flannigan demanded.

"No, I want to tell the truth, something I should have done a long time ago."

"I was trying to protect her. It's what she wanted."

"Maybe protection wasn't what she needed."

"You don't have to remind me of the mistakes I made with Maggie. I've had to live with them for all these years." There were tears in his uncle's eyes.

Brody had been trying to follow the conversation. As his father turned to him, he was suddenly afraid that the last thing he wanted to know was the truth.

His father cleared his throat. "Maggie was raped. Not that she told us. We wouldn't have known at all, except that she'd written something in her diary and your uncle found it."

"So she *did* keep a diary," Brody said. Harper had been right about that.

"You were only guessing when you asked about a diary?" his father asked, frowning.

"She said in the diary that she was raped?" he asked. "She used that word?"

"No," Finn admitted. "She'd been to a doctor. Apparently, there was some…damage."

"She was *raped*," Flannigan said.

Brody rubbed a hand over his face. "Who?"

"We don't know. She refused to tell us, but there was also a mark on her face where she'd been hit," Finn said. "And bruises on her wrists…"

"We damn sure knew who," Flannigan snapped.

"We didn't know," Finn argued. "We *still* don't. But we suspected."

"Senator JD Hamilton," Brody said.

His father nodded. "Then we realized that Maggie was pregnant. Your uncle tried to talk her into going away and having an abortion, but by the time we found out, she was too far along to have a legal abortion." He stopped to clear his voice again.

Brody didn't like what he was hearing. "Tell me you didn't—"

"The day she disappeared…" He looked to his brother before continuing, as if he hadn't heard his son speak. "We found a doctor who would perform the abortion."

No longer able to stand, Brody dropped into a chair. He felt sick. He could tell by the looks on their faces what had happened. "She didn't want an abortion. You were going to what? Force her?"

"If that's what it took. I wasn't going to let her ruin her life over…" Flannigan waved a hand through the air. "We were just going to do what was best for her," his uncle said, silent tears rolling down his cheeks. "In time, she would have—" He looked away. "Instead, she went to *him*, told *him* she was keeping his baby…" His voice broke again. "And he killed *her*— and the baby—so don't be looking at us like that. We were trying to *save* her."

Brody shook his head as he took in the two men he'd grown up wanting to emulate. He couldn't have been any more surprised if they'd told him he'd been left on their doorstep by aliens. "What could you have been thinking?"

"You don't know what it was like," Flannigan cried. "I did everything to make her see that this man was going to destroy her. She wouldn't listen. Even after what he'd done to her… If I had only killed JD Hamilton before it went this far." His uncle broke down for a moment before he angrily stormed out.

His head spinning, Brody turned to his father. "So you don't know for sure that JD Hamilton took her by force or that the baby was even his. Maggie never told?"

"No, but we know that they use to meet at a high mountain lake in the Crazies. Flannigan saw a drawing she did of JD fishing up there."

"What about her diary?" Brody asked. "Is it possible she wrote in it during those last days that—"

"After Flannigan read it and confronted her, Maggie must have done something with it. We've never been able to find the diary. That isn't all. She took some belongings with her the day she left. As far as I know, those haven't turned up, either."

"Belongings? You mean as if she was running away and wouldn't be back?"

Finn looked away. "She took her best dress and

some things that her mother had worn on her wedding day."

Brody swore. *"She thought she was getting married?"*

CHAPTER FOURTEEN

THE WATER SHOCKED his system the moment JD dived into the lake. For a moment, he thought it might stop his heart and he would die up here in this crystal clear lake with her. The thought had been almost comforting.

The freezing water cleared his head as quickly as it chilled him. What the hell had possessed him? He knew the answer as he climbed out shivering. Behind him, she splashed him and laughed. "I knew you'd find it refreshing."

"That water is nothing but melted snow." He laughed as he grabbed his shirt to wipe the icy water from his face.

"When was the last time you laughed like that?" she asked joining him.

He shook his head. He honestly couldn't remember.

"Well, I'm glad I got to hear it," she said. They stood like that, both smiling at each other, the sun warming their bare flesh.

She cocked her head. "You're quite handsome when you smile. You should smile more."

JD felt uncomfortable. He'd never been good at compliments. But from this young woman especially. He didn't want her to get the wrong idea.

"Stop looking so worried," she said with a laugh.

"Now you may never laugh or smile around me again. I shouldn't have said anything." She climbed up the rock and jumped in again, letting out a cry of exaltation before hitting the water.

"You're a glutton for punishment," he said as he watched her swim toward him. Water beaded on her lashes like jewels and ran down her flushed skin. Goose bumps dimpled her arms and legs and flat stomach as she climbed out. He turned away, but not before he'd seen hard brown nipples pressing erect against the fabric of her bra, the hint of a red V through her wet panties. Worse, she'd seen him looking and he'd seen the challenge in Maggie's green-eyed gaze.

He felt her warm hand on his back. He turned and she stood on tiptoe as if to kiss him. He grabbed her wet, bare shoulders and held her at arm's length. *"This can't happen,"* he said with a groan.

"What is it you think is going to happen?"

He gave her a sideways glance as he let go of her. *"You're trying to seduce me."*

She laughed, letting her head fall back before she looked at him again. Those green eyes narrowed. *"How am I doing?"*

He shook his head and released her. As he started to put on his shirt, she stopped him with her hand on his arm.

"What are you so afraid of?" she asked, as if truly concerned.

It was his turn to laugh. *"You."*

She smiled at that. *"I'm not that scary."*

"Like hell."

Her hand moved to his face. She cupped his jaw. *"I've watched you for years,"* she said, her eyes dark-

ening. "I know you, just as I know why you come up here, and it isn't to fish. You're like me. You've been headed here for years."

Her hand was warm, the skin soft and silky against his stubbled jaw. He took hold of it and pulled it away from his face an instant after her thumb brushed the corner of his mouth.

"Tell me what you're running from," he said.

She shook her head. "Not from. To. I think I've been running to you for years."

"No." He let go of her hand. "I'm too old for you."

She smiled at that. "Actually, I'm probably too old for you." Maggie turned her back to him as she walked over to the rock where she had undressed to go swimming the first time they'd met up here.

He pulled on his shirt, knowing that if he hesitated it would be his downfall.

"You can leave, but one of these times," she said, over her shoulder, "you're going to realize that you and I are lost souls destined to be together."

He shook his head as he finished dressing, swung up into the saddle and spurred his horse forward a couple of steps. She'd climbed back up on the rock, standing there half-naked in the warm sunlight. He didn't want to leave her and yet he couldn't stay. He should never have let her talk him into going in the lake with her.

"Maggie, I really wish you wouldn't swim alone," he said as she peeled off her wet underwear and dropped it on the warm rock.

"So do I," she said, and dived stark naked into the water.

THE SHERIFF GOT the call he'd been hoping for late in the afternoon.

"We were able to get DNA from the fetus," Charlie said, sounding tired. The job was obviously wearing on him, especially with a case like this one. "Did you get DNA from any suspects yet?"

They both knew who the leading suspect was, which was one reason Senator Buckmaster Hamilton's DNA couldn't be the only one sent to the lab.

"I am going to pay several other suspects a visit today. I'll get back to you when I have more DNA for the lab. You think we can have the preliminary results quickly?"

"In this case, I do."

He hung up, looked at his watch and headed for his patrol SUV. With luck he could catch Bobby Barnes before he headed home.

Bobby Barnes was just getting off work at the sawmill. He came out of a large metal building carrying an old-fashioned metal lunch box. His head was down, his worn boots shuffling along like a man who couldn't wait to sit down after a long, hard day's work.

The sheriff was within feet of Bobby before he looked up. He smelled of fresh-cut pine and sweat. Fine sawdust clung to several days' growth of beard. There were lines around his eyes, a paunch making his dirty flannel shirt protrude at the belly and a stoop to his shoulders that erased all memory of the high school quarterback who everyone said had potential. Bobby looked all of his fifty-three years.

"Sheriff?" Bobby said, grinding to a stop. His eyes narrowed like a man debating what he might have done to warrant a visit from the law.

"Bobby, I was hoping to have a few words with you before you left for home."

"This isn't about Claudia, is it?"

Frank could only guess what Bobby was referring to. Claudia had called deputies on her husband a few months back over a domestic dispute, but then had refused to file charges. "It's about Margaret McTavish."

All the tired seemed to go out of the man. For just a moment, he glimpsed the young man Bobby Barnes had been.

"Maggie?" Bobby said, as if even her name filled him with vitality. "She turned up?"

"She did," Frank said, wondering if he really hadn't heard. "Mind if we chat in my patrol car?"

Bobby headed for the SUV with purpose in his step. It wasn't until the two of them were seated inside, Bobby holding the old metal lunch box between his knees, that he said, "Maggie. After all these years." He frowned then, seeming to realize the sheriff wouldn't be bringing good news. "Is she all right?"

Frank shook his head. "Her body's been found where it was buried thirty-five years ago."

All the spirit went out of Bobby in a breath. He sank into the seat, his blue eyes cloudy with pain. "Oh, hell. You mean she never left?"

Frank shook his head. His reaction seemed real, but Bobby had dated Maggie. Everyone in town had known about their argument at the Creamery.

"Bobby, I need to ask you a few questions about that time before she disappeared."

He nodded, but he looked far away, as if already back there, his face full of regret.

"You and Maggie dated."

"Dated?" Bobby shook his head as he looked over at him. "I asked her to marry me." He seemed to be fighting the painful memories. "I saved for months for a ring. The day I put it on her finger was the happiest of my life, but she wanted to keep it quiet. I don't think her old man approved of me."

Frank was glad he'd decided to talk to Bobby alone. It wouldn't have been good for Bobby's wife, Claudia, to hear any of this. He guessed Claudia had been living in Maggie's shadow for years as it was.

"So she agreed to marry you?" He thought of the duffel bag and missing clothing that he'd seen in the missing persons report.

Bobby nodded. "We were going to elope. But the night we were supposed to meet, she didn't show. I figured she'd changed her mind." The regret in his voice was palpable. His voice broke as he asked, "But she died? That's why she didn't show?"

He nodded. "Someone murdered her and buried her not far from her family ranch."

Bobby seemed to pull himself out of the past with great reluctance. "He killed her."

"Who?" Frank asked, although he knew what was coming.

"That senator, JD Hamilton." Bobby sat up a little straighter. "I knew she was seeing him. I wouldn't have been surprised if she wasn't in love with him and was going to marry me only because of the baby."

"You knew about the baby?"

He nodded. "It wasn't mine. But I didn't care. I would have loved the kid because it was hers." He shrugged.

"Did Maggie tell you who had fathered the baby?"

"Naw," he said with a shake of his head. "But I knew what I was getting myself into. It wasn't like I didn't know she was only marrying me because he wasn't going to."

"You loved her."

Bobby let out a bitter laugh. "I never stopped." He looked out the side window for a moment as if pulling himself together. Even after thirty-five years, Frank could see the pain. Men had killed over less pain than that.

"Then how can you be sure it was JD Hamilton's baby?"

"I wasn't. Until I happened to see them together once on the main street in town," Bobby said with a curse. "The bastard was old enough to be her father." He shook his head.

"You confronted her?"

"She didn't even deny what was going on." Bobby seemed to realize where the conversation had gone. "You think I killed her?" He sounded shocked.

"She hurt you."

Bobby laughed. "She fricking killed me. If it hadn't been for Claudia… I won't lie and say that I didn't think about murder. But had I acted on that feeling, it wouldn't have been Maggie I killed. As it was, the bastard killed himself." Bobby seemed to start. "Oh, hell. He did kill her, didn't he." He looked up at Frank. "He killed her because he couldn't be president—not with some pregnant teenager he'd been having an affair with. Then he couldn't live with what he'd done."

"We don't know that," Frank said. "That's why I'm asking everyone who dated her to give me a DNA sample."

Bobby reached for the door handle, suddenly angry. "You want *my* DNA." He let out another bitter laugh. "You're just hoping it will turn out to be someone else's kid, not Hamilton's." Bobby opened the patrol SUV's door and shot an angry look at the sheriff. "You and Buckmaster have always been thick as thieves."

Bobby was so far off base that it was laughable. "That's not true. All I'm trying to do is find her murderer."

"Well, you're barking up the wrong tree. I *loved* Maggie. I still love her." His voice broke. "If it wasn't for that damned Hamilton…"

"Then let me clear you by giving me your DNA."

"She was pregnant with his baby and you want my DNA? Kiss my—"

"I can get a judge to force you, but I don't want to do that."

"We weren't even together in the months before she disappeared," Bobby said.

"There is one way to prove it." Frank handed him the kit.

Angrily Bobby ripped it open, swabbed the inside of his mouth and stuffed the stick back into the container. "There. The sooner the truth comes out, the better."

Frank thought the same thing as Bobby climbed out of the SUV, dragging his lunch box with him, and slammed the door. He watched him walk toward an old pickup parked nearby. Bobby got in and sat for a long while, his head on his arms on the steering wheel, before he started the engine and left.

When Frank reached Big Timber, he wasn't surprised to see Bobby's pickup parked at the bar.

He drove on past, hoping for a chance to talk to Claudia before Bobby came home.

WHEN HARPER CALLED Brody to tell him what she'd learned from her mother, he'd listened but said little.

"So what did you find out?" she asked. She could hear him hesitate. "Don't forget. We had a deal. I'm not happy with everything I've found out, either. We knew going into this that it could be bad."

Silence, then finally he said, "It isn't anything I want to talk about on the phone."

"Fine. Then let's meet somewhere."

"I am on my way to talk to Doc Franklin," he said. "Maybe after—"

"Dr. Ella Franklin?" She couldn't help her surprise. "She was my grandmother's doctor. If anyone would know whether or not Grace could walk… I'll meet you there," she said, and hung up before she could ask why he wanted to talk to Ella. No doubt he already knew that she was Grace's doctor.

Dr. Ella Franklin was in her late seventies. She'd retired years ago after being a country doctor and had now become what they called a local character. But back in the day, Harper had heard that she had made house calls. Often on a horse when the roads were impassible. No one had ever said she wasn't tenacious. Most people, though, said she'd lost most of her marbles.

Ella now lived alone in a small house at the edge of town. She was said to walk five miles a day—no matter the weather. Everyone considered her quite eccentric. Bold and brash, she wasn't one to mince words, which made some people cross the street to avoid her, Harper had heard.

As the woman let her and Brody into her house, Harper just hoped that the doctor would remember her grandmother. From the moment he'd driven up, Harper noticed that Brody looked as if he hadn't gotten any more sleep than she had last night.

Looking at him now, she saw that his jaw was set. Did he think she would try to cover up the truth? Was that why he'd planned to come here? Nor did he seem that happy to see her.

Ella, wearing a flannel shirt and canvas pants, led them into the living room. The furnishings, like her, looked practical. Her gray hair was short in a no-nonsense cut and there was an air about her that said she didn't like wasting time.

"So what can I do for you?" she asked, eyeing each of them.

"We're here about my grandmother," Harper said.

"Well, your grandmother's out of luck. I'm not doctoring anymore."

"My grandmother was Grace Hamilton."

"I see."

"I'm Harper Hamilton and this is Brody McTavish. We need to ask you some questions about Grace's... health."

"Seems a bit late to be worried about that now," Ella said. "She's been dead..."

"Thirty-five years," Harper supplied, and got right to the point. "My grandmother was confined to a wheelchair before her death. Was there a medical reason?"

Ella Franklin nodded. "You want to know if she

could walk. You've heard of doctor-patient confidentiality, I'm assuming."

"But she's dead," Harper said. "Not to mention there is now a murder investigation."

Ella sighed and looked from Brody to Harper. "Your grandmother, by her own choosing, was an invalid. Could she walk?" The doctor tilted her head. "Let me just say there was no medical reason she couldn't."

"So her illness was all in her head?" Harper asked in surprise.

"Don't act as though that doesn't make it real. Psychological or not, she made herself sick because she believed it was true. I can't swear that she could even stand, let alone walk." She narrowed her eyes. "What you really want to know is if she was capable of killing Maggie… That I can't say. But couldn't we all, under the right—or is it wrong—circumstances?" The doctor moved toward the door as if the interview was over.

"One more question," Brody said, speaking for the first time. "You were also Maggie's doctor. I need to know if she came to you after she was raped?"

"MAGGIE WAS RAPED?" Harper said, looking over at him in shock.

Brody didn't answer and for a moment he thought the doctor wouldn't, either. "Please, I have to know."

Ella seemed to weaken. "I wanted her to go to the hospital," she said as she came back into the room. "They have rape kits…"

"But she refused. Did she say who did it?" Brody asked.

She shook her head. "She wouldn't even have come to me if he hadn't insisted."

"He?" Harper said.

"The man who brought her to see me. I got the impression he'd insisted she get checked out. He stayed in his vehicle, but I recognized him. Senator JD Hamilton."

Brody couldn't believe this. "But if he'd been the one who—"

"He didn't rape her. From the marks on her wrists and ankles, it was more than one man," the doctor said.

"But she wouldn't tell you who?" Brody said again.

"No. I got the feeling she planned to take care of it herself," the doctor said. "I advised her to call the sheriff, but again she refused."

Brody's head was still spinning when he and Harper left the doctor's home. Once inside the truck, they sat for a long moment, neither speaking. Like him, Harper seemed too shocked to speak. It was all too much to take in.

"How did you find out?" Harper finally asked.

"My dad told me, but they didn't know who was responsible. They'd read something in her diary…"

"So she did have a diary." She still had the key in her purse, she realized, where she'd put it after Brody had given it back to her.

"They said the diary disappeared after they confronted her. They definitely didn't know what the doctor just told us."

"That there was more than one. Or that my grandfather was the one who insisted she see the doctor?"

"Neither," Brody said as he started the engine and pulled away from the Ella's house. "There's more." He told her what he'd learned from his father and uncle.

"You think she was planning to get...*married*?" Harper said. "To whom?"

He shook his head.

"JD was already married. Even if he'd promised to divorce my grandmother, it would have taken time."

Brody looked toward the Crazies. The sun glowed on the snowcapped peaks against a cobalt blue sky dotted with white puffy clouds.

"I talked to my father, and from everything he told me about JD..." she said. "He wasn't the kind of man to have hurt Maggie. Nor was he the kind who would have left an invalid wife. But it sounds as if Grace might have been losing it. Now that we know from my mother and the doctor that she probably was able to walk...and that JD wasn't happy in the marriage. If he'd fallen in love with Maggie—"

"Apparently, the sheriff is getting DNA together to find out whose baby she was carrying," Brody said. "Once we know that..."

"Promise me that we aren't going to let this keep us apart," Harper said.

He glanced over at her, his expression solemn, pain in his gaze. "I wish I could."

CHAPTER FIFTEEN

JD COULDN'T BELIEVE *how late his flight had come in. He was exhausted from the days of meetings about the possibility of him running on the Republican ticket for president. All he wanted now was to get home. He reached Big Timber and took a back road toward the ranch, hoping to make it home a little sooner.*

As he passed an old section of town, a beat-up flatbed truck came roaring out, almost hitting him and throwing gravel and dirt across his windshield. He'd seen that there were three boys in the front of the truck an instant before he threw on his brakes to avoid the crash. Now he skidded to a stop as the pickup disappeared in a cloud of dust.

"Kids," he grumbled under his breath, still shaken from the close call. He had started to drive on when he saw her in a shaft of moonlight and his heart dropped.

She came stumbling out from between two of the abandoned houses, her long red hair around her shoulders in disarray. He could see that she was hurt, her clothing torn, blood on her face. He quickly pulled over and, jumping out, ran to her.

"Maggie," he cried. "What happened?"

She shook her head, but it was clear what had happened.

He'd never felt such fury. "Those boys... Who were those boys?" he demanded.

"It doesn't matter."

"Like hell it doesn't. I'm taking you to the hospital, then I'm going to call the sheriff."

"No!" She grabbed his arm. "I'm fine."

"You're not fine. You have to go to the hospital. You have to press charges against those boys." He was breathing hard, seeing red as he helped her to the car. If he'd known what they'd done when they first came tearing out, he would have chased them down and— He hated to think what he might have done.

"I'm all right," she said more quietly as he got her into the passenger seat. She looked concerned for him. "There is no reason to call the sheriff. I won't press charges."

"They have to be punished for what they did."

"No, they won't ever be punished, and all it would do is embarrass my family."

"You can't let those boys get away with this." He stared at her in the ambient moonlight coming in the car windows. "Look at you. I could tear those boys limb from limb. Tell me who they were."

She shook her head. "You should get home. If you could just drop me at my car. It's a few blocks from here." He started to argue, but she cut him off. "Please. I hate having you see me like this."

"Maggie." It came out a cry. He touched her shoulder. She winced and he pulled away. JD knew that this would be something he would regret to his grave, but he could see that her mind was made up. "Maggie, I won't call the sheriff, but I'm taking you to the hospital."

She shook her head.

"Then your father."

"No, I can't. Please, I can't."

"You need to see a doctor."

"Ella, then... I'm sure I'm fine, but you can take me to her."

"That quack doctor?"

"Please. It's the only place I will go. Otherwise, you can just take me to my car or let me out and I'll walk."

Dr. Ella Franklin would have been burned at the stake a hundred years ago, JD thought. While she'd become a medical doctor, she dealt in strange concoctions. Grace swore by her, but JD thought of her as a witch doctor.

Maggie held her head up high, tears in her eyes. "Well?"

"I'll take you to her."

AFTER LEAVING HARPER, Brody returned home in even more turmoil than before. He wasn't that surprised when he heard a pickup tearing up the road toward his house a few hours later. He hadn't seen either his father or uncle since they'd told him about Maggie being raped.

He'd been expecting a confrontation. It had made his already sleepless nights even darker knowing that he'd gone against their wishes and that there would be hell to pay for it.

Stepping out onto the porch, he watched the truck come to a dust-boiling stop in front of his house. His uncle was out before the commotion settled.

"You've been talking to people about Maggie," Flannigan boomed as he advanced on Brody.

His father climbed out of the truck behind his uncle and tried to intervene. "Flan, wait."

Flannigan ignored him, shoving him aside when Finn got in front of him. "I told you to keep out of this, Brody, and stay away from those Hamiltons. I warned you not to tell anyone because I didn't want Maggie dragged through the dirt." His voice cracked. "You were with that woman, that Hamilton woman."

Brody knew he should tread carefully but doubted it would make any difference at this point. He couldn't let his uncle railroad this investigation—and not just for Harper's sake.

"It's better if everyone just assumes it was JD Hamilton's baby? That he killed her?" Brody demanded as he came off the steps to face his uncle. "You want to make sure he is blamed for her death. Don't want the truth coming out and possibly the real killer caught?"

His uncle made a grab for him as if to hit him.

Finn stepped between them, his back to Brody as he tried to calm his brother. "Enough! We aren't going to let this tear our family apart."

"He's already done that," Flan said. "If he wants to stay on this ranch—"

"He's my son. This ranch is his. You always said—"

"That was before he betrayed his family," Flannigan yelled. His voice broke again. "He betrayed us. Betrayed Maggie."

"I seem to be the only one who wants true justice for her," Brody said.

"Justice?" Flannigan wheeled around and took a few steps away as if trying to calm down, before he whirled around again. He pointed his finger at Brody,

his face livid. "You're chasing that Hamilton girl. You're the last one to get Maggie justice."

"You're wrong. Harper wants to find out the truth as badly as I do."

His uncle's laugh had an edge to it that cut through the air like a hatchet. "She wants to protect her family and she's using *you*."

Finn turned to look at his son. "What *are* you doing? Are you willing to give up everything for this girl?"

Brody looked toward the horizon. "I guess I am."

"I begged you to stay away from her," Finn said quietly.

He shook his head as he met his father's gaze. "I *can't*."

"Then get the hell off my property!" his uncle yelled.

"It's also my father's ranch," Brody said. "A ranch I've worked all my life that was to be mine one day."

Brody looked to his father, saw the answer in his pained face. "I guess I was wrong about that, as well." He turned and headed for his pickup. He could hear his father behind him trying to calm Flannigan down, but the message had been clear.

CLAUDIA DUNCAN BARNES answered the door to the sheriff with a baby on her hip and a toddler clinging to her leg. Both children were crying along with what sounded like several others in the background.

Frank did some quick math. Bobby and Claudia's oldest, Tamara, was in her early thirties and doing time for drugs in the state pen in Deer Lodge. Which meant at least some of these children had to be grandkids unless Claudia had opened her own day care.

She looked confused to see the sheriff standing on her doorstep, then angry. "If this is about Tamara—"

"It's not." Before Claudia could ask if it had something to do with Bobby, he said, "I need to ask you some questions about Maggie McTavish."

Claudia looked momentarily stunned. She shifted the baby on her hip. "She's dead?"

"You hadn't heard?"

She let out a bark of a laugh. "No, but you wouldn't be asking about her if she wasn't." Her expression seemed to take years off her face. "Does Bobby know?"

Frank nodded.

She looked away, her mouth tightening into a hard, thin line, before she said, "Well, then I won't expect him home for dinner, huh." She stepped back. "You'd best come in. But I have to warn you, I'm not going to mince words."

He hoped that was true as he entered the house, closed the door behind him and followed her through the obviously financially strained houseful of children.

Claudia put the baby she'd been holding into a high chair, unlatched the toddler clinging to her leg and set him in a playpen, then turned to deal with three older children seated at the kitchen table.

"Watch the baby," Claudia ordered a girl of about ten who it appeared had been arguing with the other two children at the table. "Bobby Joe, quit teasing your brother and you, quit sniveling," she said, pointing at the younger brother. "Both of you, get out front and pick up your toys before your grandpa gets home."

She headed for the back door, motioning for Frank to follow her. They stepped outside onto a creaking wood deck. Claudia went to the far end of it, reached in a cubbyhole and pulled out a package of cigarettes and a lighter.

"I'm trying to quit, but I suspect this conversation will call for making an exception." She offered him one. He shook his head and moved upwind as she lit up and took a long drag.

"So you want to know about Maggie." She coughed out a laugh and picked a piece of tobacco off the tip of her tongue before she said, "I could have killed that bitch."

Frank cocked his head at her, making her laugh at his surprise.

"You wouldn't be here unless you thought I was capable of it."

"Actually, I wondered if Bobby was capable of it."

"Bobby?" she said with a snort. "He couldn't do it, even if he wanted to, which of course he didn't, did he?" She sighed and looked at her watch. "I would imagine he's down at the bar nursing his broken heart right now."

He heard the bitterness in her voice.

She turned away to take a long drag on her cigarette. Her body was rigid with anger. "Bobby wasn't her first, although he might not know it."

"Who was?"

Claudia smiled. "Kyle Parker for one."

Frank listened to her tick off on her fingers the boys Maggie had been with in high school. What he heard was the story of a troubled, beautiful girl who gave herself away too easily. Claudia's portrayal of Maggie, though, was of a heartless tramp.

"Do you think she cared what she did to Bobby, the boy I had loved since grade school?" She cursed under her breath. "I gave her a piece of my mind, for all the good it did, if that's what you're asking."

"When was this?"

Claudia shrugged. "A few months before she disappeared. I thought maybe I was the reason she left town. I guess not, huh."

"The confrontation didn't get physical?"

She looked at him almost sadly. "I wish I'd killed her. I wanted to. Did Bobby tell you he asked her to marry him?" She nodded to herself. "Maybe I would have killed her if he'd gone through with it. But she disappeared and Bobby…" She shook her head and looked out at the mountains in the distance. "Our marriage might not be perfect, but I love him."

He watched Claudia savagely grind her cigarette into the wooden deck before hiding her cigarettes and lighter again. "He saved for months to buy her that damned diamond engagement ring." There were tears in her eyes, in her voice. He glanced at her ring finger. She wore a slim gold band. He silently cursed Bobby for being a fool.

She straightened and dried her eyes. "I love him, but I'll never understand him." Frank couldn't, either, but reminded himself how he'd hurt his first wife by marrying her when he was still in love with Lynette. He had helped bring out the psychosis in Pam and would always feel guilty for that, not to mention what it had done to her daughter Tiffany.

Just the thought of the daughter he'd once thought was his made him feel vulnerable and a little afraid. Tiffany was still locked up in the mental ward, but he knew that one day she would find a way to get out and when she did, she would come after him and Lynette.

"Who would have wanted Maggie dead?" Frank asked, pushing Tiffany as far from his thoughts as possible.

"Who wouldn't?" Claudia snapped. "How about all the people she hurt?"

"Will Sanders, Kyle Parker, Collin Wilson. Not to mention the women who loved them." She narrowed her eyes at him suddenly. "Are you purposely not asking about JD Hamilton?"

"I'm covering all the bases. I've heard the rumors, but do you or anyone else know for a fact that Maggie McTavish and Senator JD Hamilton had an affair?"

One of the kids inside the house yelled, "Grandma!" Claudia didn't seem to hear. "Maggie used sex to get what she wanted. Everyone knew she wanted JD. I'm betting she got him and, faced with her ruining his life…" She shrugged. "Or maybe she broke his heart and, finally, here was a man who had the balls to put her out of her misery for the rest of us."

"Grandma!" a child called from the back door.

"Thank you for your help," Frank said. As he walked back through the house to leave, he noticed the photo album open on the coffee table and a dozen others piled off to the side. "You have a lot of photos."

"I always wanted to be photographer," Claudia said wistfully.

"These are from high school?"

She nodded.

"Would you mind if I borrowed them? I'll get them back to you. I might have more questions down the road."

"Don't worry, I'm not going anywhere and neither

is Bobby now that Maggie is finally put to rest once and for all."

The sheriff didn't correct her as he gathered up the thick photo albums. Maggie was far from put to rest. He thought of her trying to claw her way out of her grave. At night, he would wake up thinking he had heard her screams.

BUCKMASTER KNEW HE'D done fine in the debate so he didn't wait to get the poll results. He caught the first flight home. All he'd been able to think about was the past. He knew memories were often tainted and that he shouldn't trust them. But he kept remembering little things, strange bits of conversation overheard, odd looks he might not have paid any attention to at the time and, of course, his mother's accusations against Sarah.

As much as he hated to admit it, he still often had warring emotions when it came to Sarah. He hadn't forgiven her for trying to kill herself and—worse—disappearing for twenty-two years after failing in her suicide attempt. She'd missed seeing their six daughters grow up. He'd missed her.

Even now he felt the barb of guilt that often jabbed at him when it came to his second wife, Angelina Broadwater Hamilton. He'd never loved her the way he had Sarah. But Angelina hadn't seemed to mind. She'd been determined to see him in the White House and worked continually to make that happen.

He felt another stab of guilt. Had he really planned to tell her he was leaving her the night she died? Their marriage had been on the rocks by then because of Sarah's untimely return and Angelina's inability to give it some time. She'd been determined to dig up dirt on Sarah. That's why she'd hired the PI in Butte to begin with. And look how that had turned out.

No wonder the sheriff in Silver Bow County thought he'd had something to do with Angelina's death. Her car accident had definitely worked out in his favor, he thought guiltily. If Angelina had just let it go…

"I'm sorry, but aren't you Senator Buckmaster Hamilton?"

He turned in his first-class plane seat to look at the woman next to him. They hadn't spoken since the plane took off. He'd been staring out the window, lost in his own thoughts.

"I'm surprised you fly commercial," the pretty young blonde said.

He laughed. "I'm a Republican from Montana," he said by way of explanation. "My constituents expect me to be frugal. They wouldn't even approve of me flying first-class."

She had a nice smile as she held out her hand. "Lacey Montgomery. I confess I don't pay much attention to politics. I just happened to see you on the television."

"The debate."

Lacey laughed. "I guess. I had the volume turned down."

It was refreshing to meet someone who didn't want to talk politics, Buckmaster thought as they discussed what it was like living in Montana, the size of their families, what it had taken to raise six daughters.

"Wait a minute," Lacey said suddenly. "I do remember something about a wife you thought was dead coming back?"

He nodded. "Sarah."

"Oh, I'm embarrassed. I did hear that you lost your current wife just months ago. I'm so sorry. My goodness, you really have been through a lot."

He had to laugh. "You have no idea."

"I'm a hopeless romantic so I have to ask," she said, leaning toward him conspiratorially. "Do you think you and your first wife will get back together?" When he didn't answer right away, she said, "I'm sorry. That was rude. Forget I asked. It's just that I love a happy ending."

He smiled at her. "Me, too. Sarah is the love of my life. As for the two of us being together again... Only time will tell." He gave her a wink.

"I'm so glad," she whispered. "I want true love to win out."

By the time he reached the ranch, his cell phone had begun to ring. He saw that it was Jerrod Williston, his campaign manager, no doubt calling with poll numbers. He declined the answer prompt only to have Jerrod call back and text several more times saying it was urgent.

No one was home except some of the household staff, so he wandered down to his den and poured himself a drink. He planned to ride his horse over to Sarah's. Right now he just wanted Jerrod to quit bugging him. He took a gulp of his drink as he settled into a deep leather chair and closed his eyes.

His cell phone rang again. With a sigh, he took the call. "Jerrod. Can't the poll numbers wait?" he said when he answered.

"This isn't about the debate results. It's about the interview you did with some reporter by the name of Lacey Montgomery."

"Reporter? I didn't do an interview with—" The name didn't ring a bell for a moment. Then it did. He swore under his breath. The woman on the plane. "How bad is it?"

"Bad. She said that you told her you were getting back with Sarah because she was the love of your life."

THE CLANK OF tools and the smell of oil filled the air as Frank stopped by Bill's Auto to talk to son, Collin. He found Collin under a minivan, grease up to his elbows. The radio played a country song about a man losing his woman, his house and even his dog. It made Frank think of Lynette, which made him swear under his breath.

"Collin," he called over the noise to the man in the hole.

A moment later Collin climbed out from under the van, wiping his blackened hands on a rag as he did. "Sheriff?" he said. "You got car trouble?"

"Sheriff business. Can you spare a few minutes so we can talk?" Frank asked, glancing around. The shop had three bays. A mechanic was working on a vehicle in the next bay and Collin's twentysomething daughter was manning the counter in the shop office.

"Let's step out back," he said over the racket.

Frank followed him out to the alley and around the corner of the building where there was a picnic table on a small patio. Since the shop was on the edge of town, the view down the alley away from town was of a field with Interstate 90 in the distance.

"What's up?" Collin asked as he sat down at the table. He was average build with a boy-next-door face on a man in his fifties. His hair was still blond except at the temples, his blue eyes faded, his pale skin freckled. He looked like a man who worked a lot so didn't get outside much.

Twice divorced, he had a grown daughter, and from what Frank had learned from Lynette, had been dating Amber Jenkins, who owned and worked at a local diner as a waitress. But they'd broken up recently—Amber's doing, according to Lynette.

It was the joy of living in a small town. Half the people were related; the other half had tangled relationships. Everyone knew everyone and their business. Sometimes Frank thought it would take a scorecard to keep it all straight.

"I wanted to ask you about Maggie McTavish," he said, joining the man at the table. He was pretty sure Collin already knew about Maggie's remains being found. He didn't seem surprised to be asked about her—even though he tried to pretend he was.

"Maggie? You have to be kidding."

"Why do you say that?" Frank asked.

"Because it's been…years." He frowned and picked nervously at a spot on the table where the paint was coming off. "Why would you be asking about her after all this time?"

"Because her remains have been found."

He stopped picking at the paint but didn't seem to know what to do with his hands. "I heard that, but why talk to me about it?"

"The two of you dated."

"Seriously?" Collin said. "Are you questioning everyone who 'dated' Maggie, as you call it, in high school? I hope you have a lot of time. Maggie got around."

"So I keep hearing. You and Maggie were intimate?"

Collin laughed a little too hard. "Let's just say we had a short intense relationship before she dumped me for Ty Jenkins or was it Will Sanders or Kyle Parker or Bobby Barnes? I can't remember. I suppose you've already talked to them."

Clearly, Collin had been expecting this visit even though he tried to pretend surprise. Frank didn't answer his question but asked one of his own. "Is there any chance the baby Maggie was carrying when she was killed was yours?"

Collin opened his mouth, then closed it. His face lost all color, leaving only his freckles. "Maggie was pregnant?" he finally managed to ask.

"Five months along. Is there a chance the baby was yours?"

The mechanic looked away for a moment as if needing to catch his breath. "I can't see how that's possible."

"Right, you'd already broken up with her," the sheriff said.

Collin turned back to him, appearing a little less shocked but maybe more worried.

"Then there shouldn't be a problem with you giving me a DNA sample."

"You have to be kidding?" Collin rose from the table, wiping his hands on his dirty overalls. "What is this really about? Everyone knows that Maggie was with JD Hamilton before she disappeared."

"So far that is nothing more than rumor," Frank said. "But don't worry, I'm looking into it." He pulled out the DNA sample kit.

Collin shook his head. "Is that really necessary? I

mean, what would be the point? I told you, we'd broken up long before then."

Frank could see that Collin didn't like the idea. "It's just routine in an investigation like this one. Unless there is some reason you wouldn't want to give me a DNA sample."

Collin looked around the alley as if it might provide some way to get out of this. Finding none, he said, "Sure, it isn't like I have anything to hide."

"I WANT YOU to move in with me," Buck said the moment Sarah opened the door.

"What?" She'd been waiting for this for months and, yet, now it seemed too fast. "What are you talking about?"

He stepped into the old farmhouse and looked around as if he'd never seen it before. "You shouldn't have been living here," he said with a shake of his head as he turned to her. "I'm so sorry. I should have taken a stand right at the beginning. I should have left Angelina and taken you back to our house, your house, and to hell with this election crap."

He was talking nonsense since they both knew he couldn't have done any of that. But she loved hearing it. She loved this Buckmaster Hamilton, a man determined to have what he wanted. And he wanted her.

She stepped into his arms feeling as if she was finally where she belonged.

"I'm taking you home. I'm announcing to the world that I never got over you, that you are the love of my life." He drew back to look into her face. "You've been so patient. Thank you. Tell me you'll be my bride."

That took her by surprise. *"Marriage?"*

"Not right away. Jerrod is having a fit as it is. Plus you'll need time to plan the wedding. I'm thinking right after the primary. Even Jerrod will get on board. Really play up the second chance at love and all that."

"So this is just about politics," she said, her earlier euphoria slipping away.

"No," he said, pulling her back as she tried to step away. "This is about us finally being together. You know I would quit this damned race tomorrow if push came to shove. The past year has been hell, you know that. All I've wanted is to be with you. If you had married Russell…" He hugged her tighter. "I want you where you belong. Right by my side."

She swallowed back a well of tears. Isn't this what she had wanted since the moment she returned? "What about the girls?"

"They'll be fine with it," he said, letting her go. "I could use a drink."

Sarah stepped away to get him his favorite Scotch. She poured them each a shot. Normally she didn't drink, didn't think she liked alcohol. But at the back of her mind was a memory of ice-cold vodka going down so easily that it made her wonder. Another planted false memory? Or one she should fear like those of her holding an AK-47 and feeling excited about what would happen when she touched her finger to the trigger.

"Are you all right?" Buck asked as he took the drink she handed him. Her hand was shaking and he'd seen it, she realized.

"I'm just excited." She smiled up at him as she took her own glass. "To us."

"To our future," he said, and clinked his glass with hers. "Now there is nothing standing in our way."

She took a sip, wondering if he'd forgotten about Maggie McTavish. She certainly hadn't.

CHAPTER SIXTEEN

JD DIDN'T SEE *Maggie again for three weeks. She didn't ride up to the lake and he had no way of contacting her. He couldn't very well call her house and ask for her.*

It was in town at the grocery store that he finally saw her. The bruise on her cheek was gone, but there was a darkness in her green eyes that filled him with a deep sorrow.

"How are you?" he asked, his gaze locking with hers. They'd been standing in the produce section. He could smell apples and floor cleaner.

She put on a brave smile. "Fine and you?"

"Not so fine."

Maggie shook her head and looked away for a moment. "How's the fishing been?"

"Slow and not very fun."

"I'm sorry to hear that." Her look made him ache. They might have stood there much longer except for the sound of someone clearing his throat behind them.

"Ready to go?" Flannigan McTavish asked his daughter. His green eyes, so much like his daughter's, were narrowed in a glare.

"Flannigan," JD said.

"Senator."

"WE HAVE TO tell the sheriff what we know," Harper said when Brody stopped by the next morning. She'd had a restless night, waking with the knowledge that they couldn't keep this information to themselves—no matter what Brody and his family said.

She knew he was still in shock after what they'd learned. "We have to. This isn't just about murder anymore. Whoever did that to Maggie, they have to be held accountable. The sheriff needs to know."

His jaw tightened under a day's worth of stubble. She couldn't help herself. She reached out and ran her fingers along his strong jawline. He caught her hand, then brought it to his mouth to kiss it before he released it.

"I'm not ready to do that," he said without looking at her.

"Because of your family."

He glanced over at her. "They didn't go to the sheriff when it happened because Maggie refused to tell them anything. They can't see any reason to drag her name through the mud now since it won't bring her back."

"Surely they want her killer caught, as well as her rapists. The ones who raped her might still be alive."

"I know. That's why I thought we would talk to Amber Jenkins first. She might know who the boys were. Even if she and Maggie hadn't been friends for a while... I already called her. She said she'd talk to us this morning."

Brody said nothing as he drove them toward town and Amber Jenkins's place on the river.

"I know yesterday didn't go well," Harper said. She could tell that something much deeper than the news about Maggie was bothering him.

He nodded. "I talked to both my dad and my uncle. They are furious with me for digging into her death.

They kicked me off the ranch. I spent last night in a motel."

"Oh, Brody, I'm so sorry. If you don't want to—"

"Oh, I want to find the men who hurt Maggie, trust me. And you're right. We have to go to the sheriff. I'm hoping Amber knows something since, it seems, at some point they were friends."

Like Brody, she was sick about what had happened to Maggie and wanted to track down the boys who had done it to her and fix them good. That her grandfather had been the one to take Maggie to the doctor was still confusing. How had that happened? Had Maggie called him?

Harper doubted it had slipped Brody's mind that one of the boys in high school that Maggie had dated for a short time had been Ty Jenkins, Amber's brother.

She looked over at him as he drove, her heart breaking. He'd gone against his family. She could see how this was killing him and regretted dragging him into it. When she said as much, he laughed, and said, "I got involved of my own free will, so don't be sorry. You were right. We have to find out the truth."

Amber lived on a tree-lined street in Big Timber close to the river. She opened the door wearing her uniform from the Dixie Cup Diner.

There was little resemblance to the woman in the photo they'd found in Maggie's bedroom. The girls in the photo had looked happy, young and carefree. Amber looked harried and tired. Her hair was dark and cut in a fringe that brought out her dark eyes—and the bruised-looking circles under them.

After opening the door, she glanced at them and

then at her watch. "Like I told you on the phone, I have to be at work in an hour."

"This shouldn't take long," Brody said.

With obvious reluctance, she invited them in.

"I'm Brody McTavish, I don't think we've ever met," he said. "And this is Harper Hamilton."

"I know who you both are," she said, and motioned to several threadbare chairs in what appeared to be the living room. "I heard the two of you were asking questions around town."

Harper wondered who'd told her that as they entered the house. The place was small and sparsely furnished as if decorated by someone who had just gone through a divorce and had split the furniture.

"We need to talk to you about my cousin, Maggie McTavish," Brody said.

"As I told you on the phone, I can't imagine what help I will be. I hardly knew Maggie."

Harper was surprised when Brody pulled the photo of the two girls from his pocket. She realized he'd been planning to talk to Amber all along.

"You were friends at some point," he said, showing her the photo.

Amber shook her head. "That was back in junior high. I hardly saw her after that."

"But she dated your brother, didn't she?" Harper asked. "I saw a photo of them in her yearbook."

"The year Ty died." Amber looked away, clearly angry. "She was the reason he hung himself." She turned back to them, her face stony, her dark eyes just as hard. "So, no, Maggie and I *weren't* friends."

"I'm sorry about your brother," Harper said. "How

do you know she was the reason he killed himself?" she asked before Brody could.

"He left a note to her saying how sorry he was."

"Sorry for what?" Brody asked.

"Over some stupid fight they'd had before she broke up with him," Amber said.

Harper shot Brody a look, wondering if he was thinking the same thing she was. "So you didn't keep track of what Maggie was up to after that?" Harper asked.

"I heard the rumors." Amber turned up her nose. "I wasn't surprised."

"You weren't surprised about which rumor?" Brody asked.

"I'm sorry. I know she was your cousin, but Maggie…" Amber seemed to struggle to find the appropriate words. "She used her looks to get what she wanted and once she got it, she moved on."

Harper noticed several framed sketches on the wall. "Did you do those?"

Amber looked surprised, as if she'd forgotten about them. "Maggie drew them. She liked to draw. I don't know why I hung on to them." She let out a bitter laugh. "Maybe I thought she'd be famous one day and they'd be worth something."

Harper heard hurt in the woman's words. "You kept the drawings, and even framed them and put them on your walls. You were good friends at one time."

Amber shrugged, but clearly it was true.

"She hurt you."

"Not as much as she hurt my brother."

Or as much as your brother hurt her, Harper thought. "You don't happen to have a copy of the suicide note—"

"The sheriff took it." Amber made a face as if the

note would be the last thing she would keep. She looked at her watch.

"If you could just tell us what you remember," Brody said. "I don't know anything about her. I wasn't born when she died. I was hoping you could tell us what she was like back when you *were* friends."

Amber looked surprised. "Why don't you ask your father or your uncle about her?"

Harper could see the pain in Brody's face. His talk with them hadn't gone well. She hated to think how hard that had been for him.

"They saw a different side of her, I suspect," he said simply.

Amber seemed to think for a moment. Her expression softened as if remembering the girls they'd been. "Maggie was different. She felt things more deeply than anyone I knew. She was driven no matter what she was involved in, like her art. She could draw for hours and then get on her horse and ride as if she believed her horse could fly if she went fast enough." She shook her head. "I always thought she was searching for something that would complete her."

Harper thought she saw where this was headed. "A man."

Amber looked up and nodded solemnly. "Yeah, once we hit high school, there were lots of boys who wanted to date her. She had the pick of any boy. All she had to do was snap her fingers. They all wanted Maggie McTavish."

Harper heard the envy in Amber's voice. She guessed that Brody did, too, because he said, "That's enough to make anyone jealous of her."

Amber let out a laugh. "Jealous? Is that what you

think? I loved Maggie. I wanted to *be* Maggie. Just breathing the same air around her was enough when we were young."

"Did she ever confide in you after that?" Harper asked.

Amber sighed. "Did she tell me she was seeing Senator JD Hamilton?" She shook her head. "But I saw them talking to each other in the grocery store. I'd heard the rumors, but I hadn't really believed them until I saw it for myself."

"What were they doing that made you think they were…together?" Brody asked.

"They were just looking at each other," Amber said, and unconsciously hugged herself. "I could feel the chemistry clear across the grocery store. So could her father. He got her out of there lickety-split. I could tell he was furious with her. It was kind of sad. I remember watching the senator. I think he really loved her." Her expression hardened. "But then so did my brother and look where it got him."

"Did you know Maggie was raped about five months before she was killed?" Brody asked.

Amber's eyes widened. "No."

"It seems there was more than one of them," Brody said.

"She would have been raped shortly before your brother died," Harper said.

Suddenly unable to sit still, Amber got to her feet. "I don't know anything about that." She looked at her watch. "I really need to get to work."

THE SHERIFF FOUND Kyle Parker in his real estate office downtown. He had been a football star in high school, playing on the same winning team as Bobby Barnes, Will Sanders and Collin Wilson.

He looked nothing like the photographs of himself from those days that now graced his office walls. He'd grown soft, his face ruddy, his body a little too large for the suit he was wearing.

But he shot to his feet when he saw him and extended a hand. From the look in his eyes, Frank knew that his teammates had already told him about their official sheriff's department visit.

"I wondered when I'd see you," Kyle said. "Have a seat."

"I'm sure you've heard about Maggie McTavish's remains being found," the sheriff said.

Kyle nodded. "I was sorry to hear that. I always liked Maggie."

"You dated."

"In high school." He shrugged. "She was beautiful."

"But the two of you broke up."

Kyle let out a short laugh. "Maggie had more wild oats to sow." Unlike the others, he didn't sound bitter.

"Did you see her after high school?"

"Just around town," he said with a shake of his head. "Karen and I got together and—" he sighed "—have been together now for, gad, how long has it been. Thirty…four years?"

"Anyone you knew who might have wanted to harm Maggie?" Frank asked.

Kyle shook his head. "Everyone wanted Maggie." He smiled. "But some of us were smart enough to know you can break a wild horse, but you can never trust it."

The sheriff thought that was an interesting comment and said as much. "Did you try to break her?"

"Not me," Kyle said, holding up his hands.

"Bobby?"

The Realtor sat back in his chair as if he didn't want anything to do with this question. "Bobby...he was heartbroken when they split up. It made things tough on the team back then. But obviously he got over it. The others, too, since we'd all been through it."

"I'm not sure if you've heard, but Maggie was pregnant at the time of her death. That's why I'm collecting DNA samples from those who knew her well."

Kyle blinked and shook his head. "I just told you I hadn't said two words to her since high school."

"Then you should have no problem with giving me a DNA sample."

"Actually, I do." He lumbered to his feet. "I have a showing in five minutes. I really should get moving."

"I can talk to the judge—"

"Talk to him, but I don't think you can force me to take a DNA test without some evidence. Good luck trying." With that, Kyle stormed out of his office, leaving Frank staring after him.

THE SHERIFF SAT back in his chair an hour later and took in the two across from his desk. "So," he said. "I understand you've been doing some investigating on your own."

"We thought between the two of us, we might have more access than you did," Brody said.

Frank thought there could be some truth to that. "And you're here because..."

"We've discovered some things we thought you'd want to know," Harper said. She looked over at Brody. He motioned for her to go ahead.

He listened with interest as she told him what happened after she'd gotten copies of the yearbook photos at the library. "You don't know for sure that Collin Wilson was driving the car that day?"

"No, but my digging into the past definitely got them all excited about something," Harper said.

His ears perked up when she outlined their search of Maggie's room, a search he'd been denied by the girl's father. What they found hadn't been earth-shattering, but it had led them to the boys from high school who Maggie had dated—and Amber Jenkins.

"Here is Collin Wilson's yearbook," she said, opening it to the last page.

"I won't even ask how you got it." Frank glanced at the page and the cryptic message written there.

"Will Sanders wrote that. We think it has something to do with Maggie being raped about five months before she was killed. She didn't report the rape but it was more than one individual. We wouldn't have known about it except that Brody was able to get his uncle to tell him."

He tried to hide his surprise at the rape and the five-month inference since Maggie had been five months pregnant.

"With that information, we found out from Dr. Franklin, who was Maggie's doctor, that there had been more than one rapist."

Frank mentally kicked himself. He'd been planning to talk to the doctor about Grace. He hadn't known Maggie had been a patient of hers. They were right about being able to get information he hadn't been privy to.

"Well, you two have certainly been busy," he said as he closed the yearbook.

"Also, Maggie kept a diary. It seems to be missing," Brody said.

Frank nodded. "You think she named her attackers in the diary?"

Brody shook his head. "My uncle found it and read some of it, he told us. He said it didn't name the men. But I think Maggie wrote how she felt about JD Hamilton. I think that's what my uncle doesn't want coming to light, but I can't be sure. He swears he doesn't have the diary anymore."

The sheriff sat back, considering the two of them. They'd done a hell of a job gathering information. But they'd also taken quite a chance. This new wrinkle in Maggie's story proved something he'd known was possible—that her killer might still be alive.

Which meant these two had already put themselves in danger. "I appreciate what you both have done and that you've brought this to me. However, this is an ongoing homicide investigation, and you don't want to get on the wrong side of the law."

Harper laughed, then quickly apologized. "I'm sorry, but being on the wrong side of the law right now is the least of my worries."

"I will find out who killed Maggie McTavish," Frank said, hoping to hell it was true. Otherwise innuendo and gossip would condemn JD Hamilton forever. They might anyway, even if Frank found out JD was innocent. People believed what they wanted to.

"Also, what you're doing could be very dangerous."

Harper shook her head. "You're the second person to mention that. Who is it you think I have to fear?"

"That's just it…we don't know who's responsible, and while that person may already be deceased there could be family members who don't want the truth coming out."

"If what everyone believes is true and my grandfather killed her, then it seems I have nothing to worry about," Harper said.

Frank raised an eyebrow. "Even people in your own family might be reluctant for the truth to surface."

"You mean my father? Or are you referring to my mother."

The sheriff rose. "I hope you take my advice. I don't want to see anyone else get killed."

"You have to find the boys who raped her," Harper said.

"I'm going to do my best."

"Do you know whose baby she was carrying?" Brody asked.

Frank shook his head. "Not yet."

"There's one more thing," Brody added. "The night Maggie left home we believe she thought she was getting married."

Frank remembered what Bobby Barnes had told him. Had Maggie planned to elope with Bobby? If so, what had happened?

The rape changed everything. Now, more than ever, he needed to know whose baby Maggie had been carrying.

CHAPTER SEVENTEEN

JD FOUND MAGGIE *curled into the warm spot between
the rocks. He had followed her up to the lake after seeing her ride by earlier. She'd ridden the way she had
as a girl, hell-bent for leather. A glimpse of her face
told him that there was trouble at home.*

*"Are you all right?" he asked as he knelt down be-
side her.*

*She angrily wiped away her tears. "I'm fine." Her
face was red from crying and he could see that she was
anything but all right.*

*When he touched her chin and turned her face up
to his, he saw the bruise. "Who did that to you?" he
demanded.*

"It doesn't matter."

"Like hell it doesn't. Tell me."

*She met his gaze, holding it as she said, "My father
found my diary."*

"Oh, Maggie." He groaned.

*"Don't worry. I didn't mention you by name. But
now he knows that I'm in love with a man who will
never leave his wife and that I don't care. That I will
take whatever time I can have with you." She reached
for him, but he caught her hands and held them and
her away.*

"It's wrong. We've known that from the start. Nothing good can come of this."

"That's what my father said. He said you would destroy me."

JD nodded. "That is my fear. You need to go to college. You need to—"

She jerked her hands free as she got to her feet. "I need you and if you had the guts, you'd admit that you need me," she said, bringing her fist down over her heart. "This is beyond age, beyond all the bullshit in our lives. You know how you feel about me and I know how I feel about you. That isn't going to change no matter how many times you push me away."

"We shouldn't have gotten so close," he said, pushing to his feet. They stood only inches from each other in the shelter of the rocks. The wind sighed in the tops of the pines that formed a canopy over them. Patches of summer-blue sky peeked through the boughs as puffy white clouds floated past on a warm breeze.

"But we did get close," she whispered.

He'd known that if he kept coming up here, if he kept spending time with her, if they kept opening up to each other, it would happen. He reached over, hooked his hand behind her neck and drew her to him, holding her in his arms. Her skin felt warm from the sun. She smelled of the outdoors and the Montana summer day.

"I love you, too," he said from his heart. "God help me, I love you."

A STIFF WIND blew from the north as Brody drove out of town. "Harper, you heard what the sheriff said."

"I know. But there is one place I have to go before I can quit searching for the truth."

He shot her a look.

"The homestead house where my father and mother lived with JD and Grace for a while right after they got married. I know it's a long shot, but maybe there is something there that will clear him." She shrugged. "I know I'm naive. Everyone tells me so. But after what we've found out I'm more convinced than ever that he had nothing to do with her death."

Brody nodded. "Tell me how to get there."

The Maynard House, as Harper's father called it, was at the end of a narrow dirt road lined with thick tumbleweeds that had gotten caught in the fence.

Harper had worn a jacket, the temperature below freezing this morning. Since it had snowed every month of the year at one time or another, spring in Montana was iffy at best. One day it was hot, the next it was freezing.

But the cold that Harper felt as she watched Brody maneuver the abandoned road had nothing to do with the weather. When she'd told him about the old house, he'd insisted she not go alone.

"If I find something—"

"A house that has been sitting empty that long could be dangerous," he'd said, cutting her off. "Not to mention, there could be rattlers nesting in there, rotten boards, old wells you might stumble into."

"I'll try not to stumble into anything dangerous." She couldn't help the edge to her voice. There had been moments when he seemed to see her for the woman she'd grown into. Other times, though, he treated her like a child. Worse, a harebrained one.

"I want to go with you," he'd said as if realizing he'd misspoken. "I…worry about you, okay?"

She supposed that was okay, though in truth, she wanted more. "Fine. But I want to go down there right away." She couldn't explain her hurry. Just a feeling that…that what? That they and the sheriff weren't the only ones searching for evidence into Maggie's death.

Now as Brody's pickup rattled along the rough, abandoned road, she felt her tension climbing. Growing up, no one had ever mentioned that her grandparents had ever lived in this house—the original homestead that her father had grown up in. It seemed strange to her that they wouldn't keep it up even a little.

Through a break in the pines, she saw a roofline. Brody slowed the truck as the house came into view. To her surprise it was built of stone and was much larger than she had expected it to be. Two stories, it sat in a gully surrounded by tall trees. No wonder she hadn't known it was here.

"So you've never been here before?" Brody asked, also sounding surprised by the house.

"I had no idea it was even here." Hamilton Ranch was massive in size, so that was one reason. Also, she and her sisters had never been interested in the houses that had come with the numerous smaller ranches that her father had bought up over the years. Often hired hands would live in them.

But this house was nothing like the others. First it was stone. The others were all wood frame. Also it was much older, much more…foreboding. The stone walls had grayed, and the wood shake roof was almost black. In the shade of the trees, there was something ominous about the structure.

Brody cut the engine. "So this is where they lived."

Harper nodded. "I'm sure this is a wild-goose chase.

The house is probably full of snakes and mice, like you said." Now that he was here with her, she was relieved. She would have gone in alone but was glad she didn't have to.

Brody let out a breath and opened his door. "Let's go see what's inside."

As he walked down a short overgrown path, Harper followed. The wind swayed the tree boughs over their heads, moaning and creaking loudly. The front door was a large wooden door. She just hoped the house wasn't locked now that they were here. She hadn't thought to look for a key to a house she hadn't even known existed until recently.

"The glass in the windows is still intact," he commented as they reached the front porch. The wooden planking groaned under their feet as they moved across it. Brody tried the door. It swung open. Icy cold air smelling of age seemed to rush out at them.

Harper couldn't believe her eyes. The house was full of furniture; in fact, it looked as if whoever had lived here had walked out one day and just forgotten to return or—

"You're sure no one is living here?" Brody asked, sending a chill through her.

"Just ghosts." She moved deeper into the large living area, but pulled up short when she saw the wheelchair in front of the fireplace. Her breath caught in her throat and her pulse bumped up.

Beside her, Brody let out a soft curse. "Okay, this is creepy."

"I wanted to see where they'd lived, but I never expected this."

He shook his head. "Your father and mother lived here for a while, right?"

"The first few months of their marriage, according to my mother. Then she got pregnant and they moved into one of the other houses on the ranch while Dad was having our house built."

"So your grandparents were living here alone when your grandmother died." He looked over at her. "She died in this house?"

Harper nodded and looked toward the stairs. "Then my grandfather had his car accident shortly after that…" She looked around. "I thought that if there is a clue to what was going on with them before they died, then it might still be in this house."

He nodded. "Where do you want to start?"

She looked toward the stairs again. "If my grandfather had something to hide and my grandmother was confined to that wheelchair…"

"Let's start upstairs, then."

They had started across the hardwood floor when Brody suddenly grabbed her arm and said, "Look!"

She turned to see what he was pointing at. Footprints in the thick layer of dust that covered everything. At first all she saw were the two sets—hers and Brody's. Then she saw the boot prints.

"Someone else has already been here."

WILL SANDERS WORKED as an insurance agent in a small office off the main drag. Today he was dressed in jeans, boots, a white shirt and a turquoise stone bolo tie, and had the look of a man who had only stopped into his office and was about to leave.

Frank had tried to call him several times to make an

appointment to talk to him, but Will hadn't answered his phone. Today, after talking to Harper and Brody, he'd decided to surprise him.

Surprise was the first expression that crossed Will's face. Regret was the second. "Sorry, but I'm on my way out," Will said, grabbing up some papers as he took a step toward the door.

"I get the feeling you've been avoiding me," Frank said as he sat down on the edge of Will's desk. "We can either talk here or I can take you to the station, but we *are* going to talk."

Will sighed and turned to face him. "I have an appointment—"

Frank shoved the phone on the desk toward him. "Why don't you call and tell your...appointment that you're going to be a little late. This won't take long. It will take longer if I have to ask you to accompany me down to the sheriff's office."

"Fine." He slammed the papers down on the desk. "If this is about Maggie—"

"You know it's about Maggie, which makes me wonder why you've been avoiding me. Makes me wonder if you have something to hide."

Will did his best to look innocent. He'd been a local athlete who'd made a name for himself in high school. He still looked pretty good even after all these years, his dark hair not showing any gray, his body still trim and fit.

"I don't know anything about Maggie's—"

"Murder? Or her pregnancy? Or her burial on Hamilton Ranch?"

"As I was saying, I don't know *anything*. I hadn't

dated Maggie in years by then." He shrugged. "If that's all you want…"

"Actually, I want something else." Frank pulled the DNA sample kit from his pocket.

Will licked his lips as he stared at it.

"Given what you just told me, you shouldn't have a problem giving me your DNA."

THE DAY HAD started out cold but was heating up fast. Inside the old farmhouse it was sweltering. Harper felt her clothing stick to her as she climbed the stairs to the second floor of the old homestead house. There were two bedrooms upstairs with a small bath between them. She peered in the first one. It contained two bureaus and a bed. The wallpaper, a yellow flower print, had faded almost to white.

Harper moved to the first dresser and opened one drawer after another, finding them all empty. She could feel Brody watching her from the doorway. This floor was hot and smelled musty. Like the lower floor, everything was covered with a thick coat of dust.

She thought of Maggie's room. Flannigan had left it exactly as it was out of love for his daughter. Why had her father left this house like this? It felt as if he'd simply abandoned it, wanting to forget the people who'd lived here.

The second chest of drawers was also empty. She checked the closet and when she turned, Brody was no longer in the doorway.

As she left the room, she glanced in the tiny bathroom. She could hear him in the second bedroom. Drawers opened and closed methodically. When she joined him, she found him standing by the window.

"This place has already been searched," he said before turning around. "Whoever it was might have already found whatever he was looking for."

Or *she* was looking for. Harper thought of her mother. Even though she knew Brody had probably already looked, she stepped over to the closet and peered in. It was larger than the other one so she had to step inside to see if it was really empty. There appeared to be several old shirts still on hangers. Her grandfather's? She felt in the pockets. Nothing. The floorboards creaked under her feet as she turned to step back out.

Brody looked up at her as if something had suddenly come to him. "Did you hear that?"

Obviously, she hadn't. She shook her head and listened, assuming he'd heard a vehicle coming, but she heard nothing.

He stepped to her, motioning her aside as he stepped into the closet. Again the floorboards creaked. He dropped down to run his hands over the boards before pulling out his pocketknife.

Harper watched him pry at the boards until he was able to free one. As he felt around in the hole, she held her breath. A moment later, he pulled out what looked like a rolled-up sheet of thick paper bound with a rubber band.

"What is it?" she asked as he rose and carried it over to the bed before removing the band. "A drawing," she said, answering her own question. "A drawing of my grandfather." She didn't need to ask who had drawn it even before she'd seen that it was signed, "With love, Maggie."

She felt her heart drop. JD had hidden the drawing

in the floor of the closet. There was no longer any way of denying that he and Maggie had had a relationship of some kind. That he'd hidden it—and this drawing—couldn't have made him look more guilty.

"YOU LOOK TIRED," Nettie said when her husband came home. She'd waited up for him, worried but also curious. Everyone now knew the body that had been found on Hamilton Ranch was Margaret "Maggie" McTavish's and the rumors were flying like grasshoppers in July.

"How is the investigation going?"

He groaned in answer.

"You talked to the boys she dated in high school?" Nettie knew her husband too well. He would cover all his bases before he headed for JD Hamilton and that Pandora's box.

"The main suspects. They all swear the baby couldn't be theirs." He took the cold beer she handed him. She didn't know exactly when things had changed. Frank had never talked about his cases with her—until recently. She suspected it was because he was tired of law enforcement and thinking about retiring.

She hoped it was because her insight often came in handy. Also he knew she would wear him down eventually anyway.

"I thought I had a pretty good idea of who I was dealing with going in, but it turns out I didn't have a clue. Harper Hamilton and Brody McTavish stopped by my office. They've been doing some private investigating of their own." He shook his head. "They'd learned a whole lot more than I have."

"Harper and Brody," Nettie said in surprise. "Well,

they are both closer to it than you are, though it aston-
ishes me that they're working together."

Frank chuckled. "Their families can't be happy
about it."

"So who's the baby's father?" she asked.

He shook his head. "You'll probably know before I
do. We seem to have more leaks in my office than an
old wooden rowboat."

"So you're no closer to finding out who killed her?"

"Sure doesn't seem that way."

"I'm betting that the trail keeps leading back to
Hamilton Ranch and Senator JD Hamilton," Nettie
said. "The whole county thinks he did it. He had motive. Opportunity, with their ranches so close to each
other… And considering where she was buried…"

"I think the county might be surprised. I hope so. I
hate to think what effect all this could have if JD ends
up being the killer."

"You're thinking of Harper Hamilton and Brody
McTavish."

He smiled. "I do love the way your mind works. I
suspect my warning them to quit snooping around fell
on deaf ears, but I sure hope not."

"You could arrest them," she joked.

"Don't tempt me. I may have to before it's over.
They've already talked to Ella."

"The crazy doctor?" Nettie said. "Yeah, I heard that
she thought Grace wasn't wheelchair-bound. That she
could have walked if she had wanted to. Grace, even if
she could walk, was a small woman. How could she…
bury Maggie in a wooden box? Well, she couldn't.
Not without help. So, the way I see it, it keeps coming back to JD."

Her husband seemed to be studying his beer bottle, but she knew he was listening. He just wasn't going to tell her anything.

"If Grace killed Maggie, he'd have to help her," Nettie continued. "JD would be torn up with guilt. No way would he turn her in to the sheriff since he would feel responsible. He'd help her cover up the murder. Then Grace dies, JD can't live with his guilt…"

Frank took his beer and rose.

"Where are you going?"

"To talk to my crows. They, at least, don't resort to wild speculation."

She laughed as she watched him go, then rushed to the door to holler, "If not JD, then who else would Grace turn to for help? *Buckmaster.* She would have gotten her son to help her. Or her daughter-in-law. Maybe that's Sarah's real secret."

SARAH WOKE FROM the dream with a start. Ever since Harper's visit, she hadn't been able to get the past off her mind. She sat up in bed, half expecting Buck to be lying next to her. The bed beside her was empty. Buck had gone back to DC.

She clutched the sheet and glanced wildly around the dark room before her gaze went to the window. A pine bough slapped against the glass making her jump.

A thin shriek died on her lips as she heard the wind. The pine bough hit the glass again. She sat, trying to still her thundering heart, the dream still alive in her mind and in the room.

The mystery man from her nightmares. He'd been here again. She could feel his presence, almost smell the scent of him, almost feel his touch on her bare skin.

Sarah shivered and pulled the sheet and blankets up around her neck as she leaned back. Her eyes still searched the room, the nightmare still too real. It always started the same way. She and Buck married, holding hands, laughing as they ran out of church in a hail of white rice.

The joy of the glimpse into what she had known was the future, the way a person always knew things in dreams, had filled her to overflowing. She and Buck finally, truly back together and the world celebrating with them.

Then she would see the man standing in the shadows and stumble, her laughter dying on her lips. He would be at the edge of the crowd. He never said anything. He didn't have to.

She knew the moment she saw him that he was there to destroy her happiness, her life, destroy Buck. The man had something in his hand. He was smiling as he—

That's when she woke up.

At her daughter Bo's wedding reception, that was apparently why she'd fainted. When she'd come to, Buck and her daughter Kat were leaning over her.

"Sarah, what happened?" Buck had cried, concern in his voice, in his expression.

"I...I don't know." Her gaze had gone to Kat. What she saw in her daughter's expression brought it back. She'd seen the man from her nightmare standing just outside the barn door where the reception was being held. Then darkness.

"I should have eaten something," Sarah had said to Buck. "I've just been so excited about the wedding…

Would you be a dear and get me a small plate from the buffet?"

Buck had hurried off, leaving her alone with Kat.

"Who is he?" Kat had asked, stepping closer so Sarah could hear her whispered words.

She had wanted desperately to deny that she'd even seen anyone. "I don't know."

"Someone from The Prophecy? Your coleader? Your lover?" The last word stung with its bitter bite.

"I don't know. I swear—"

Kat had given an angry shake of her head. "I don't believe you," she'd said, and had walked off. They hadn't mentioned it again.

But Sarah had been waiting, knowing in her heart he would show up again. Only next time—

She threw back the covers and got up, knowing she wouldn't get a moment's rest until she searched the house. The farmhouse had been built back in the fifties. It had come with a ranch purchase that Buck had made.

Sarah felt as if she'd been in exile since her return. She'd had to hide out from the media. Now she was hiding out because she and Buck couldn't be together. Not yet.

She understood why they couldn't let anyone know about their…arrangement. His wife—the woman he'd married fifteen years ago—had only been dead four months. Intellectually, she knew it was too soon for them to be seen together because of the presidential campaign. But she was getting tired of being stuck away, waiting.

Give it time. When he becomes president, you will be together.

Her heart beat a little faster at the thought since

she still couldn't imagine it. She moved through the house, turning on lights as she went. There was little furniture, little decor at all. Buck would have bought her anything she wanted. But she had wanted only the bare necessities, telling herself that she wouldn't be here long.

The lack of furnishings made it easy to search the house for the man. Even as she went from room to room, she knew she wouldn't find him. Common sense told her that if he showed up again, he wouldn't be hiding in a closet in some spare room.

Not if. *When* he showed up again, she thought, snapping off the lights as she went.

Arriving back at the point where she'd started, she turned out the bedroom light, then moved soundlessly through the house to the front window that looked out on Hamilton Ranch and the Crazy Mountains.

The wind groaned in the darkness. Pine boughs scraped against the old siding and clouds scudded across a midnight blue sky speckled with stars and a sliver of moon.

Her eyes had just begun to adjust to the darkness when she saw something move only yards from the house. She walked soundlessly to the spot by the door where she kept the gun. It was only a .22 caliber. Even if she emptied it into a man, it might not stop him. She would have liked something more powerful, but that thought brought with it its own anxiety.

She reminded herself that she was one hell of a shot. She would have to be.

Returning to the window, she waited. More movement. She gripped the gun, telling herself she would use it if forced to. Her daughter Kat already thought she was a killer. Sometimes Sarah felt a heat inside her that scared her into believing her daughter might be right.

She eased the front door open and raised the gun. Her breath caught in her throat before the deer stepped out from behind the pine tree and made its way across the yard.

Sarah shrank back into the house. Next time, what if it wasn't a deer?

CHAPTER EIGHTEEN

JD THOUGHT HER *a fool. That hurt more than anything,
Grace told herself. She'd seen the way he was when
he came back from one of his fishing trips. She knew
the signs. He'd fallen for that redheaded harlot from
the ranch next door. Did he think she didn't see the
half-naked young woman riding her horse toward the
mountains? The tramp had been trying to seduce him
for years.*

*And now she'd succeeded—and Grace doubted any-
one would believe her.*

*"Your father isn't here. He's busy having an affair,"
she told her son when he stopped by that afternoon
looking for JD.*

*"Mother," Buckmaster said, instantly looking
pained. He spent so little time in her company as it
was. Now she could tell he wished he hadn't stopped
by. "Where do you get these ideas?"*

*"It's that woman from next door, Maggie McTavish."
Belatedly she realized that her son hadn't come alone.
He'd brought his so-called wife. As Sarah stepped into
the room, Grace groaned under her breath. One tramp
was chasing her husband and another had snared her
son. If she wasn't trapped in this wheelchair...*

*"What's this?" Sarah asked as if it was any of her
business.*

"*Mother thinks the teenager next door is having an affair with Dad.*"

Her daughter-in-law laughed. "I really doubt that. He's too busy. If he hopes to be a contender for the presidency—"

"*He doesn't,*" Grace snapped. "*You're the only one who is encouraging him to run. Why is that? Why do you care? Isn't it enough to be the daughter-in-law of a US senator, even a retired one? Maybe it isn't good enough for you and that's why you're so determined that he has to be the next president.*"

"*Mother,*" her son reproached.

"*Someone needs to encourage him to follow his dreams,*" Sarah said.

"*His dreams?*" Grace demanded. "*He quit being a senator to be with me and now you want to take him away again? Thanks to you, he quit sooner than he planned, but now that you put this foolishness into his head, he's gone all the time.*"

"*We're here for you,*" Sarah said, and gave her a fake smile.

"*So you can try to kill me again?*"

"*When JD becomes president, he'll move you into the White House with him,*" Sarah said as if she hadn't heard. As if she didn't know it was true.

Buckmaster sighed and said, "Tell Dad we stopped by. I'll try to catch him later."

Grace wanted to grab his arm and plead with him to stay, but she knew it wouldn't do any good. He didn't believe that his wife was dangerous any more than he believed his father was having an affair. He was wrong on both counts.

"I THOUGHT I MIGHT find you here," Harper said as she climbed up onto the bar stool next to Brody.

He shook his head at her. "Sometimes you have to know when to quit." After finding the drawing and proof that Maggie and JD had a relationship, he thought she'd give up. He sure had. He went back to staring into his beer glass.

"I can't stand to see you drinking alone," she said and motioned to the bartender for a beer.

"I *like* drinking alone. Anyway, are you even old enough to drink?"

"Funny."

"What do you want, Harper?"

"Why didn't you ask me to dance at Bo and Jace's wedding?"

"Really? That was months ago." He saw that she wasn't going to let it go. "Maybe I didn't want to."

"Seriously. I was waiting for you to ask me."

He looked into her eyes and felt himself weaken. "I didn't want to wait in line." He felt his expression soften. What was it about this woman that made him want to leap tall buildings for her? "Come on, Harper, what man wouldn't want to dance with a woman like you?"

"There was only one man I wanted to dance with that night."

"Harper—"

"Well, there is no line now and the way I figure it, you owe me a dance."

He held her gaze. "Is that all you want from me?"

"For the moment." She picked up some change from the bar and walked over to the jukebox. A few moments later a slow country song began to play. The dance floor was empty. The whole place was pretty much that way this time of the day.

She looked to Brody. "Well, cowboy?"

He sighed and slid off his stool to step out onto the floor with her. "You don't know what you're getting yourself into."

"You keep telling me that," she said as he pulled her to him. "But what if I set my sights on you a long time ago and nothing can change that?"

He met her gaze and slowly shook his head. "I suggest you set your sights a lot higher."

"Come on, Brody, you said you've been waiting for me to grow up."

"That was before…"

"Before what?"

"Harper—"

"Come on, you know you're half in love with me already."

He laughed. He was a lot more than half. "Kind of full of yourself, aren't you?"

She gave him that crooked smile of hers that melted his heart like warm chocolate. "Do you remember what you told me when I left for college? You had stopped by to pick up a horse and we were alone in the stables. You told me to go after what I wanted in life and not let anyone stand in my way."

"I must have been just full of advice back then."

"I want *you*."

"You don't know what you want. I've got boots older than you and right now, I'm not worth two cents. All I have in the world is an old truck and a saddle to my name."

The song ended and he let go of her.

"I know you want me, too."

He shook his head. There'd never been anyone who captured his heart like Harper Hamilton. He couldn't speak for a moment because of how much he wanted her. How much he wanted to kiss her again, sweep her up and carry her out of this bar.

"Sometimes we don't get what we want." He tipped his hat. "Thanks for the dance."

"Did I hear right?" Undersheriff Dillon Lawson asked as he entered Frank's office and closed the door. "We're looking into Grace Hamilton's death?"

"Not just hers, but her husband's, as well," the sheriff said.

Dillon pulled out a chair and sat. "What exactly are we looking for?"

Frank hated to voice what he'd been thinking. "I suspect the former sheriff might have…"

"Covered up for the Hamiltons," Dillon said. "Those are pretty strong words."

He laughed. "And you're the one who said them."

Dillon nodded, smiling. "The way he handled the McTavish girl's case already had me wondering just how far it went. I looked through the case as you asked. Either he was told to back off or he really did believe she was a runaway and didn't bother taking it any further."

The former sheriff was long dead so they couldn't ask him. But Frank knew that Chuck Rush had stayed sheriff for years because he didn't ruffle feathers.

"Grace Hamilton's death, according to the death certificate, was ruled an accident. But what woman who has been confined to a wheelchair falls from the top of a second-story staircase? I've spoken with her doctor. Apparently she was capable of walking, no physical reason she couldn't have. So I suppose…"

"And JD Hamilton?"

"I doubt I'm the first to think he might have purposely driven into the river."

"Guilt?"

Frank shrugged.

"We might never know the truth about either death," Dillon said.

"Talk to the former coroner. Bud Turner signed off on both of them. See if after all these years he might remember something. He lives up in Boulder. Maybe we'll get lucky. And one more thing, Dr. Franklin confirmed what I heard. Maggie was raped five months before her death and, from the bruises on her wrists and ankles, there was more than one man."

Dillon lifted a brow. "The baby?"

"Your guess is as good as mine. I need to get DNA on several more suspects before we check it against the baby's DNA. Unfortunately, two of my suspects are dead."

"JD Hamilton. Who's the other one?"

"Ty Jenkins. He killed himself a few weeks after the rape. Also, I'm not sure how Collin Wilson might be involved, and Kyle Parker has refused to give me a DNA sample. The story behind Maggie's death is turning out to be a lot more involved than we first thought."

HARPER HAD WATCHED Brody leave the bar, leave her. Her heart ached. She wanted to help him, but it was clear there were things he had to work out himself with his family. Had they really disowned him? Kicked him off the ranch he'd worked all these years believing it would one day be his?

She couldn't help but feel responsible. Maybe if she hadn't pressed him to looking into his cousin's death...

Distracted, she left the bar and started home. A set of headlights flashed on behind her. Like the time before when a car chased her out of town, this one roared up behind her, startling her. Blinded by the bright headlights, she couldn't see the driver.

She sped up, but the car stayed with her. She turned off at the next road, hoping the driver wouldn't follow her. No such luck.

The headlights filled her car as the driver rode her bumper. She hit her brakes, hoping to make him back off. Instead, the driver raced up on her left side as if to pass her.

But, at the last minute, the car swerved into her. She heard the screech of metal and felt the jarring collision as the car hit her again. The wheel jerked in her hand. She fought to get control as the tires caught in the soft gravel at the edge of the road and pulled her toward the ditch.

Fortunately she wasn't going very fast when she hit the embankment. Her airbag exploded in her face as her car came to a bone-crushing stop.

"You didn't get a look at the driver?" the sheriff asked.

Harper shook her head even though it hurt to do so. She felt bruised all over from the impact. "It might have been the same one that chased me out of town before. In that older model Chevy Bel Air I recognized as the car Collin Wilson drives."

The sheriff mugged a face. "I believe I warned you about getting involved in this."

"I wasn't doing anything this time."

"Do you think it was the same car this time?"

"It could have been. It was dark and it happened so fast."

He closed his notebook. "You do realize I can have you arrested for interfering in my investigation."

"I wasn't doing anything but driving home." She gave him her most innocent look.

He shook his head. "I'll have a deputy take you home since your car has been hauled to the repair shop."

"Thank you."

"Are you sure you don't want to go to the emergency room just to get checked over?"

"I'm fine," Harper said.

"Is there anyone I can call for you? Maybe you shouldn't be alone."

She thought of Brody. "I'll be fine."

The sheriff still looked worried, but he let it go.

BRODY HAD TRIED to sleep but couldn't. He'd returned to his motel room after the bar, mentally kicking himself for not kissing Harper again. She'd been asking for it, he thought with a wry grin. But he knew that if he had he wouldn't have been able to leave it at one kiss. And right now, he couldn't commit to anything.

Tomorrow he'd go out to the house he'd built on the ranch to get his things. He couldn't believe how this was turning out. He'd had an understanding when he took over the ranch. Unfortunately, he hadn't gotten anything in writing.

That seemed foolish now, but he'd never thought his family would turn on him. That was probably how his father and uncle felt. Betrayed.

He raked a hand through his hair as he looked out at the night. The snowcapped Crazies glowed silver in the moonlight. A few clouds scudded across the midnight blue canvas studded with stars. Harper. She was probably tucked in bed right now.

That thought did nothing to help him settle down and get some sleep.

When his cell phone rang from where he'd dropped it earlier, startling him, he crossed the room in two strides to pick up the call. His heart was already beating fast. He'd been hoping it was Harper and he accepted the call without even checking to see who it was from.

If she suggested he come over, he would be in his pickup in two seconds flat.

It wasn't Harper.

THE HOUSE WAS eerily quiet when Harper returned home after the deputy dropped her off. "Hello? Anyone here?" she called only to have the words echoed back at her.

Usually there was at least one staff member around at this time of the night. Had her father given them the day off?

She told herself she was being silly. She'd grown up on this ranch in this house, and had never been afraid. But after everything that had happened recently, she felt spooked, as if everything had changed. Or maybe now she was finally aware that her life wasn't as safe and secure as she had thought.

She climbed the stairs, suddenly exhausted. The moment she hit the sheets, she was sound asleep. And then she was sitting up in bed, suddenly wide-awake.

Heart pounding, she listened for what had awakened her. A bad dream? Or a sound? She was just about to lie back down when she heard a thud from down the hall.

She froze, her thoughts scattering. No wonder she'd awakened so abruptly. She'd sensed that she wasn't alone. Or heard something...

Was it possible that it was only one of the staff?

Another thud, this one closer. She grabbed up her cell phone from the bedside table. Her first thought was to call 9-1-1, but several things stopped her. One, the sheriff couldn't get here for at least twenty minutes, and by then it could be too late. And two, whoever was up here could be staff or even one of her sisters.

The wood floor felt icy cold as she padded soundlessly toward her open bedroom door. Reaching it, she peered cautiously down the hallway.

Another thud. With a shock, she realized the sound had come from the attic. Moving down the hallway, her heart thundering in her chest, she saw that the stairs to the attic had been dropped down.

She tried not to panic. It was entirely possible that one of her sisters was digging around in the attic at three in the morning. Though highly unlikely.

If not one of them, then who?

Backtracking, she moved down the hallway to the top of the staircase to the first floor. She wanted to take the steps three at a time but was afraid she would make too much noise. Or fall and break her neck.

At the bottom of the stairs, she stopped short when she saw that the front door was standing open. She could feel the cold breeze coming in. Past the open doorway, she half expected to see a vehicle.

But not even her own was out there.

With a shock, she realized that whoever was upstairs must have thought she wasn't home. No car in the driveway. Whoever it was didn't know about her accident. Didn't know she was home.

That gave her little comfort. While someone had tried to kill her on the road, someone else was upstairs doing what? Searching for something, she thought as she heard another thud. Maggie's missing diary? But why would they think the diary would be in *this* house? Because it wasn't in the old Maynard House, she realized with a start.

Hurrying out, she stood in the faint moonlight and dialed 9-1-1. "There is someone in my house. I can hear them up in the attic."

The dispatcher said she would send a deputy out. "Is there a place you will be safe until someone gets there?"

Harper looked toward the barn and stables. "Yes."

"Don't go back into the house."

"I won't." The words were barely out of her mouth when she heard the phone begin to ring inside the house. Who would be calling at this time of the night? Brody?

The ringing suddenly stopped. Whoever was in the house had picked up the phone. She moved quickly back inside and reached for the closest landline. As she picked it up, all she heard was breathing, then the click as the person hung up.

Dropping the phone back in the cradle, she turned again for the door.

Her cell phone still clutched in her hand, she looked down at it as she stepped back out into the night. She wanted to call Brody. She knew he would come. But he was staying in a motel in Big Timber. He wouldn't be able to get here any sooner than the sheriff.

The sound behind her didn't register quickly enough. A black-clad figure came tearing out of the house, crashing into her and knocking her to the ground.

By the time Harper could look up all she saw was someone rounding the corner of the house. A few moments later, what sounded like a four-wheeler engine roared to life and took off into the night. The only thing that lingered was the faint hint of perfume on the breeze.

CHAPTER NINETEEN

JD COULDN'T STOP *worrying about Maggie. He'd been to the lake several times since the day they'd finally admitted how they felt about each other. The same day that she'd come to the lake with a bruise on her face after her father had found her diary.*

But she hadn't shown up since then and he couldn't help but be concerned. Unfortunately, he couldn't call or stop over to her house. Had she come to her senses? He hoped so. And yet he couldn't bear the thought that he might never see her again—even if it was the best thing for them both.

So he did the only thing he could do. He rode up into the Crazies to their lake. That's how he thought of it now. He missed their visits. He missed seeing her, hearing her voice, listening to her laugh. Mostly, he worried about her.

He'd just dismounted and was reaching for his fishing pole when he heard a horse whinny from the pines. Against his will, his heart did a little hop. He hoped it was her and not someone else. He wasn't up to the disappointment today.

He'd had another argument with Grace. She'd become irascible. Her hatred of Sarah had reached a rabid peak. He'd left her crying, saying she feared for her life and that Sarah would be the one to kill her.

*How did a man deal with something like that? Sarah
and Buck had suggested he take her to a psychiatrist.
He supposed he would have to.*

*JD heard the horse break out of the pines and
turned to see her. The sunlight caught her red hair
and set it on fire with light. She shot a knowing smile
and everything felt right in the world—even though it
was far from it.*

*He returned her smile, unable to hide how happy
he was to see her, as she reined in and slid down from
her horse.*

"Nice day for a swim," he said.

She laughed at that. "Won't I scare away your fish?"

"Probably." He sobered. "How are you?"

*Maggie looked away but not before he caught pain
in her expression.*

*He put down his fishing rod and stepped to her,
stopping within a few inches. "What is it?"*

*She shook her head and tried to smile as tears filled
her green eyes.*

"I can help you."

*"No one can help me," she said with a bitter laugh.
"I'm pregnant."*

*He rocked back on his boots. "Pregnant? Do you
know who—"*

*"That would be hard to say, huh." She finally met
his gaze. Her tears spilled over and he reached for her,
drawing her to him and holding her tightly.*

BRODY COULDN'T HAVE been more surprised when he
realized his late-night call was from Collin Wilson.
"You and your girlfriend have been asking a lot of
questions around town."

For a moment, he thought Collin was going to threaten him, since the man sounded drunk.

"You want to know what really happened to Maggie?" Brody realized that the man wasn't just drunk. He was scared. "Come to my shop."

"Now?" Brody glanced at the clock on the wall. It was three in the morning.

"I can't do this anymore."

"Why not go to the sheriff?" Brody asked, wondering if he might be walking into a trap. But Collin had already hung up.

Swearing, Brody considered calling Frank. But he had a feeling that Collin would clam up if the sheriff showed up. He stood for a moment debating what to do. If there was a chance that Collin really did know something...

Grabbing his keys, he headed for his truck. Still not trusting Collin's call, he drove past Bill's Auto without stopping. Only a dim light burned deep inside the shop. Collin Wilson's old Chevy was parked out front. He didn't see anyone on the street. No other cars were parked nearby.

After driving around the block, Brody stopped and got out. The street was dark at this end of town. He could hear the train on the nearby tracks, but no other closer sounds as he walked toward the shop.

Brody told himself that Collin Wilson had no reason to set him up. But then again, the man had tried to scare Harper. Or at least someone who'd been driving his classic old Chevy.

As he neared the shop, he saw in the moonlight that the right-hand side of the old Chevy had been in an accident. He slowed, looking from the damaged car to the shop entrance. The front door stood partially open.

Wary now, Brody listened for any sound coming out of the repair shop but heard nothing. Something was wrong. He sensed it as he neared the open doorway. Was he walking into a trap just as he suspected? Were Collin and his jock buddies from high school inside there waiting to jump him?

The smell hit him first. Being a rancher, he'd found his share of dead animals. Blood had a distinctive scent. He cautiously stepped inside the doorway, afraid he already knew what he would find.

"Collin?" he called as he took another step inside the door. Groping for a light switch, he heard movement off to his side. As he turned, he felt rather than saw the cold steel connect with his temple. The dark shop swam in an array of colors. Brody remembered hitting the floor as someone rushed past him and out the door. Then everything went black.

ON THE WAY back to town from the Hamilton Ranch, the dispatcher contacted Frank to let him know he had an urgent call from Brody McTavish.

"I'm at Bill's Auto. I think you better get down here."

Brody was waiting for him, sitting outside on the ground, his back against the outside wall of the shop, holding a rag to his head.

"What's going on?" Frank asked as he drove up and got out of his rig. He glanced toward the damaged Chevy. Brody was bleeding. He was thinking car accident. Hit-and-run? "What happened?"

As he listened, he tried not to ask what the hell

Brody was thinking coming down here in the middle of the night to meet Collin Wilson. "Where is Collin?"

"Inside. I never got to talk to him. I smelled blood. I started to turn on a light when someone hit me." He held his head, clearly in pain. "I woke up to find myself lying next to a dead man."

"You didn't see the person who hit you?"

"No. When I woke and saw him, I got out of there and called you," Brody said.

The sheriff moved to the open doorway and, pulling his flashlight, peered in. He let out a curse and got on his two-way to order backup and a call to the coroner and paramedics.

Thirty minutes later, Bill's Auto was wrapped in crime-scene tape. The paramedics were tending to Brody and the coroner was bent over Collin's body.

"Can you give me an idea of how long he's been dead," Frank asked.

Charlie rubbed his chin for a moment. "I'd say he was killed no more than an hour ago." Not long before Brody McTavish came on the scene, according to him.

Frank walked over to where paramedics were tending to Brody. "Did you happen to talk to Harper Hamilton in the past few hours?"

"No, why?" Brody instantly looked worried.

"She was run off the road earlier. Given the paint color on the side of Collin Wilson's damaged Chevy, I'm betting this vehicle was involved."

Brody tried to get up, but the paramedic pushed him back down saying he wasn't quite done. "Is she all right?"

"Bruised up a little, but fine when I had a deputy take her home. Since then someone broke into her house. You wouldn't know anything about that, would you?"

"No. Where is she now?"

"I took her over to her sister Bo's place for the rest of the night," the sheriff said. "Do you know of any reason Collin Wilson would want to run her off the road?"

"Other than the obvious?"

Frank sighed. He repeated what Brody had told him Collin said during the short phone call. "He didn't give you any idea what he was talking about?"

"No, but the other day, Harper said she saw Will Sanders and Kyle Parker stop by to talk to Collin. According to her, the conversation looked heated."

The sheriff nodded as the paramedic finished and Brody got up.

Brody seemed to hesitate. "Also, after Harper and I talked to you, we went by her family's old homestead house where JD and Grace lived. We found a drawing Maggie had done of JD. But there were also tracks in the dust. Someone had been there before us. If it wasn't you—"

"It wasn't. You still think someone's searching for the missing diary?"

"That's all we can figure."

"Where are you headed now?" the sheriff asked.

Brody considered the toes of his boots for a moment. "Thought I'd go by Jace and Bo Calder's and see how Harper is doing."

Frank couldn't help but smile. "Might be a good idea for you to stay there the rest of the night. At least I'll know where the two of you are. If you get any more calls like this one, you let me know before you go taking off on your own."

THE LIGHTS WERE on at the Calder house because Harper had awakened her sister and brother-in-law and then she'd had to tell them everything that had been going on. Bo had decided they should open a bottle of wine since none of them could sleep right then anyway. Harper noticed that her sister didn't have any.

They were talking when they heard a vehicle approaching. They looked at one another for a moment, before Harper rushed to the window.

"It's Brody," she said, unable to keep the pleasure from her voice. Then she realized he hadn't come out to see her. He didn't even know she was here. He'd come to see his best friend, Jace. But at four in the morning?

She hurried to the door anyway. With a shock, she saw his head was bandaged. "What happened?" she cried in alarm.

He said hello to Jace and Bo, then said to her, "Let's go for a walk."

She raised a brow. He did realize it was four in the morning, right? When he took her hand, she recalled that he hadn't been that surprised to see her at her sister's house.

The night was dark and cold, but with her hand in his, she felt warm and excited. Just being this close to him—

He pulled her into his arms and kissed her like he meant it.

"What was that about?" she asked breathlessly. Earlier at the bar, he'd said they couldn't be together ever.

"I'm just so glad to see you. The sheriff told me about what happened to you."

"The sheriff?" She listened as he filled her in on

what had transpired since she'd last seen him. "You could have been killed."

"I'm realizing that. But I think whoever killed Collin didn't want to add me their list."

Harper let out the breath she'd been holding. "So Collin is dead and whatever he was going to tell you…"

"Is gone with him. I'm just glad you're all right."

Overhead, the stars seemed brighter. She could hear the sound of the creek murmuring, the water silver in the moonlit night. A faint breeze whispered in the nearby pines. Harper wanted to stay right here in Brody's arms forever.

"The sheriff is right. We need to stay out of this. It has gotten even more dangerous than I ever imagined," Brody said.

"We must be close to finding out the truth or the events of tonight wouldn't have happened."

"I can't have you be in danger, Harper."

She looked into his handsome face. Her heart did its rendition of a jitterbug.

"We should get back in," he said, after another long moment.

She didn't want to leave his arms, but she was exhausted and she knew he must be, too. "I'm just glad *you're* all right."

He hugged her to him. Relishing in his warmth, she breathed in the male scent of him along with the spring night as if to remember it always.

Back at the house, Bo and Jace had conspicuously disappeared and the door to the guest room was invitingly open. Brody grinned and shook his head, his gaze locking with hers a few moments before he took her hand.

BRODY CLOSED THE bedroom door behind them and stood looking at Harper. "You're probably exhausted and need to get some sleep."

"Actually…" She gave him that crooked smile and all his resolve evaporated on a breath.

"You realize there is no going back once—"

Harper put a finger to his lips before she pressed her lips to his. She stepped away, the challenge in her gaze saying, "Well, Brody McTavish? You wanted to do the chasing."

He grabbed her, pressing her against the wall with his body before dropping his mouth to hers. She parted her lips, welcoming him as her arms looped around his neck.

He lost himself in the kiss, in the taste of her, the feel of her. Why had he fought this for so long? He wanted this woman. He had given up everything for her.

His hand worked its way under her shirt and bra to cup her warm breast. Her nipple responded, hardening to a peak under his palm.

He drew back from the kiss to look into her blue eyes. Desire burned there like a flame. "I don't want to be just another one of your suitors."

She shook her head. "It has always been you, Brody." She grabbed the front of his shirt. The snaps sang as she jerked it open and pressed her palms to his chest.

He kissed her again, deepening the kiss as his fingers worked at the buttons on her shirt. She slipped out of it, letting it drop to the floor an instant before her bra joined it. Breathing hard, he cupped her freed breasts in his hands, kissing each hard peak before taking it in his teeth. She moaned in response and fumbled at the buttons of his jeans.

HARPER HAD NEVER felt such urgency. She needed Brody's naked body against her own. She needed him to hold her, to caress her, to make love to her.

She couldn't take the chance that anything would interrupt them this time. She'd dreamed of this moment for years.

As he took her nipple in his mouth, she arched against him, the ache inside her growing with each second that passed. He trailed warm, sweet kisses up her throat. She shuddered with pleasure.

His mouth found hers again, teasing her with his tongue until she melted against him, her longing making her weak. "Brody," she pleaded.

He drew back to look at her and what she saw in his eyes made her heart beat even harder. Swinging her up into his arms, he carried her to the bed. She pulled him down with her, the two of them instantly getting tangled in the bed clothing.

"I don't want to rush this," he whispered against her temple.

"Brody," she pleaded again. "Don't rush it the second time."

He laughed, but she could hear the emotion in it. He wanted her as desperately as she wanted him right now.

Rolling her to her back, he leaned over her. She arched against him, her fingers digging into his back as he filled her. The waves of release came one after another, leaving her spent and feeling as if things were finally right in the world.

Later lying in his arms, the sunrise outside their window, she cuddled against Brody's bare chest and heard Bo and Jace in the kitchen making breakfast. "I suppose…"

"Yeah, I guess we better get up."

She could tell he didn't want to let go of her any more than she wanted him to. She had started to pull away when he caught her and drew her back.

"Harper, I still don't have anything."

"You have *me*," she said, and smiled.

He laughed. "Do I?"

"You know you do."

"Then we'll get through this together. Whatever I have to do."

She looked up into his handsome face and smiled. "My hero."

He laughed at that and gave her a gentle push away from him. "You keep looking at me like that and…"

CHAPTER TWENTY

MAGGIE CLOSED HER EYES and turned her face up to the hot summer sun. Next to her the clear cold water of the lake lapped gently at the shore as several ducks took flight.

"You're going to get more freckles."

She opened one eye, then closed it again with a groan. "What are you doing here?" She'd seen Sarah Hamilton around, but they'd never actually met. The fact that she was here didn't bode well. She thought of all the stories JD had told her about his wife's claims regarding the woman and sat up, opening her eyes.

"I could ask you the same thing," Sarah said as she stood next to the rock where Maggie sat. "He isn't coming today."

"I don't know what you're talking about." She pulled her knees up, aware that she was wearing only her undergarments and her pregnancy was starting to show. She pulled her shirt on. As she looked at the woman, she felt a shiver even though the sun was burning hot against her skin. Sarah glanced toward the lake, but Maggie knew her attention was on her. "For whatever reason you rode all the way up here, you wasted your time."

"You have to leave JD alone."

Maggie climbed off the large flat boulder and stepped into her jeans. "My life is none of your business."

"He's married," Sarah said, looking and sounding bored.

"So are you. So why worry so much about your father-in-law's future?"

"He's planning to run for president. You aren't in those plans."

Had JD really made the decision to run? Maggie knew that Sarah was behind the whole thing. She played up to him, telling him how much the country needed a man like him. Was Sarah really after JD, and her marriage to his son was just a ruse?

Sarah smiled, seeing her surprise. "I guess he didn't tell you he's decided to run," she said stepping to her. "It's over, Maggie. He sent me to tell you."

"You're the last person he would send," she said as she finished dressing. "He is starting to wonder if Grace just might be telling the truth about you. I wouldn't get too comfortable in that big house your husband is building for you."

Sarah looked down at the diamonds on her left-hand ring finger. "Buck is devoted to me. I'm not going anywhere. You, on the other hand, need to leave. Not just Hamilton Ranch property, but the state." She reached into the back pocket of her jeans and brought out a thick white envelope.

Maggie shook her head, telling herself this wasn't JD's doing.

"He wanted you to have this." She held out the envelope. "It's enough for you to start over somewhere far from Montana."

She didn't reach for the envelope. Instead, she took a step back, still shaking her head. She knew that JD *wasn't comfortable with the way things had been es-calating between them, but he wouldn't end it like this.*

"It's more money than you'll probably ever see," Sarah was saying. "JD wants to be president. He can't take you to the White House with him even if he wasn't married. This is your chance, Maggie. Be smart for once. Take the money and leave. If you don't..."

Maggie met the woman's blue gaze and felt another shiver move through her. Had this woman pushed Grace down the stairs just as she'd claimed? It was definitely a possibility given the look in Sarah's eyes. But if true, then this woman hadn't just fooled her husband but her father-in-law, as well.

"Why do you care so much about whether or not JD is elected president?" Maggie demanded.

Sarah merely smiled. "He's gone to Washington to make the announcement. He told me to tell you that he doesn't want you here when he comes back."

Maggie fought the tears that threatened. She would rather die than cry in front of this woman. "He's going to have to tell me that to my face."

Sarah put the envelope full of money on the rock next to her. "Do you really want it to come to that?" She shook her head. "If I were you, I wouldn't want to stick around and have everyone talking about what a fool I was. Don't make this any harder on yourself than it has to be."

"I love him." Her voice broke with emotion. "I don't want to live without him."

"He thought you might say that." Sarah reached behind her and pulled out a container of pills. She put them beside the money. "These don't make as much of a mess as a bullet. Your choice." With that, she turned and walked away.

WHILE BO AND Harper visited after breakfast, Brody went with Jace out to the barn to do chores. He filled his friend in on what had been going on.

"What am I going to do?" he asked when he finished telling Jace about his last encounter with his father and uncle.

"You're asking the wrong man. Look what I've been through with one of the Hamilton Girls."

"I'd say it turned out pretty good for you and Bo."

Jace smiled. "But our families weren't deathly opposed to us being together."

"So you're telling me—"

"Hell, Brody, you've been in love with that girl for as long as I can remember. If you truly love her, what choice do you have?"

Brody laughed. "No choice. I have to fight for her."

Jace nodded as he finished feeding the horses.

"I'm just worried. If it turns out that JD Hamilton and Maggie…"

"That was thirty-five years ago. So what if they fell in love? They wouldn't be the first man and woman involved in a forbidden relationship. We can't control who we fall in love with even though we wish we could sometimes. I did my best to get over Bo, but ultimately she was all I wanted. Up on that mountain…"

"You must have been terrified you would lose her."

"I was. But between the two of us, we survived the ordeal and look at us now." Jace smiled. "You might as well be the first to hear. Bo's pregnant. Twins."

Brody laughed and slapped his friend on the back. "Congratulations. I'm glad you got your happy ending, even if I'm not so sure it can happen for Harper and me. My family is one thing, but her father…"

"Buck isn't so bad. He's actually a nice guy, fair. I doubt any man would be good enough for his daughters."

Brody looked out toward the Crazies. "Let's just hope Harper's right and JD had nothing to do with Maggie's death."

AFTER ONLY A few hours' sleep, the sheriff arrived at his office to hear that the DNA results were in. None of them matched Maggie's fetus.

"I just saw the DNA results," Frank said when the coroner answered his phone.

"Not what you expected, huh."

"I'll be right over," Frank said, and hung up. All the way over to Charlie's office, the sheriff told himself that the person who impregnated Maggie wasn't necessarily her killer. Yet, if that person had been Senator JD Hamilton... But according to the tests, JD hadn't fathered the baby.

He'd been so sure that one of those DNA samples was going to supply them with the answer. Everyone already believed JD was guilty. Would they believe the results? Not likely. Frank hated to think what impact it might have on Buck and his bid for the Republican nomination in June.

After parking, he got out and entered the coroner's office to find Charlie sitting at his desk. "Help me understand this," Frank said.

"None of the samples you brought me were a match."

He let that sink in as he dropped into a chair across from Charlie. "But if I know anything about DNA, you wouldn't get an *exact* match from Buckmaster since he is JD's son, but some of the same markers should have been there, right?"

"Unless Buck isn't JD's son. Otherwise, JD was not the father of Maggie's baby."

Frank sat back with a curse. "I hadn't considered that Buck might not be JD's biological son." He swore again. "I'm going to have to get a judge to let me exhume JD's body." He pulled off his hat and raked his hand through his hair. "At least I am going to try."

"No other suspects?"

He let out a long breath. "One who refused to give me a DNA sample. I'll talk to the judge about him when I ask for the exhumations of JD Hamilton and Ty Jenkins. Ty killed himself not long after Maggie was raped."

Charlie jerked back in surprise at this news. "She was raped?"

Frank nodded. "Evidently, it was more than one offender involved, according to her doctor. There was bruising on her wrists and ankles where she'd been held down."

"So any one of them could have fathered the baby, including JD Hamilton—if he really was having an affair with her," Charlie said.

"Yep. Just as any one of them could have killed her. According to the doctor, the man who brought Maggie to her that night was none other than Senator JD Hamilton."

"How did that happen?"

"Your guess is as good as mine. But it makes sense that he wasn't involved in the rape."

"But it also makes it look as if he was involved with Maggie."

"Doesn't it." Frank put his hat back on. "I best get over and talk to the judge."

"You don't have much probable cause."

"No. I suspect I might get turned down flat and then I'll have to go to Buckmaster and try to sell him on the idea of the exhumation clearing his father."

"Good luck with that."

"THERE'S SOME THINGS I need to take care of," Brody said as they left Bo and Jace's house. "I can drop you off at your house first."

Harper wanted to ask him what things, but she figured it had something to do with his family and the ranch. Brody had always been told the ranch would one day be his. He'd spent years working it, believing that. Now he wasn't sure what his future held. She could tell he was worried and her assuring him that everything would be fine wasn't going to make him feel better.

At the house, she was relieved to see several of the staffs cars parked in front. Brody hadn't wanted to leave her until he searched the house, but she promised him she would be fine in broad daylight with staff around.

When she entered the house, the first thing she found was a note from her father.

Sorry to tell you this way, but your mother is going to be moving in. She didn't want to move in until she talked to you, though. I have to get back to DC for a few days, but will return as soon as possible. Please make her feel at home. Love, Dad

Harper read it twice. "Mother is moving in?" she said aloud to herself.

"She's down at the stables."

Looking up, she saw the housekeeper and felt a flush of embarrassment. She'd thought she was alone in the room.

"Oh, I'm sorry, you weren't talking to me?" the woman asked.

Harper laughed. "It's fine. That would have been my next question." She realized that one of the cars out front was her mother's. She hadn't recognized it because her mother was the last person she expected to see here.

What had changed that her mother was now moving in?

As she walked down to the stables, she admitted she was floored by this sudden turnaround. The last time she'd talked to her father, her mother wasn't moving in until after the primaries—at the earliest.

Also surprising was her mother being at the stables. Frowning, she looked up to see a rider headed toward the Crazies. *Her mother?* "Excuse me," she said to one of the wranglers by the barn. "Was that my mother who just left on a horse?"

"Sarah, right?"

"Right. Did she say where she was going?"

The wrangler shook his head. "Sorry."

Harper looked after her, more than a little confused. She'd heard her whole life that her mother was terrified of horses after being bucked off.

A cold dread settled in her stomach. Why would her mother lie about being afraid of horses? The woman riding the horse in the distance appeared to know perfectly well what she was doing—and where she was going.

"Sorry to bother you," she said to the wrangler. "You don't happen to know how to get to Mirror Lake, do you?"

He shook his head. "But I do have a map of the Crazy Mountains in my pickup. My brother camps up in the mountains all the time. He left it in my truck."

By the time the wrangler returned, Harper had her horse saddled and was ready to go. She knew a lot of the area from growing up here, but she had never been to Mirror Lake.

However, one glance at the map and she had a pretty good idea where her mother was headed—and how to beat her there.

FRANK HAD FEARED it would be an uphill battle to get the warrants he needed, and that's why he went to Judge Roy Nash.

"Sounds to me like you're using a shotgun approach when you need a rifle," the elderly judge said, eyeing him across the table.

Just because everyone in the county thought JD Hamilton was guilty, it didn't make it true. "I can't convict a man based on rumors," Frank said. "Also, I have reason to believe there is more to the story. Maggie was raped by two or more men five months before she was murdered."

"Five months," the judge repeated.

"It is possible one of these men was the father of her baby—and her killer."

Judge Nash nodded thoughtfully. "Sometimes it takes a shotgun when you're not sure what you're hunting for," he agreed. "I guess we see who puts up the biggest fight."

"There are too many variables not to go straight to the source."

"The source being the father of the next president of the United States."

"He still has to win," Frank said, and the judge laughed.

"Also, I want to exhume Ty Jenkins's body. He killed himself not long after the rape."

"Covering all your bets."

"Yes, I am, Judge. One of the suspects was murdered last night." He quickly filled him in. "I think the killer is still alive and might kill again unless I stop him. I need to know whose baby Maggie was carrying."

Leaving the office, he had his warrants and two graves to exhume. But his first stop was Kyle Parker's house. When Kyle saw him, he groaned, his expression bleak, but faced with going to jail, he had only one choice.

"What is it you're so afraid I'm going to find out?" Frank asked after Kyle reluctantly gave him his DNA sample.

Kyle shook his head and looked away.

"You know it could go easier on you if you told me. If you were one of the men who raped Maggie—"

"What?" Kyle cried. "That's ridiculous. And anyway, isn't there a statute of limitation on rape?"

"But not on murder."

"I'm not saying another word without my lawyer present."

HARPER REACHED THE lake to find her mother hadn't arrived yet. A part of her wanted to be wrong about Sarah

Johnson Hamilton. Even after everything Kat had told her, she wanted to give her mother the benefit of the doubt. No one wanted to believe that the woman who'd given them life possibly had a very, very dark side.

She left her horse in the trees away from the spot she recognized from Maggie's drawing of JD. Seeing the lake, the rocks, the scene, she realized probably the same thing her mother had.

Hurriedly she began to look in the rock crevices. She found what she was looking for only moments before she heard the sound of another horse making its way up the mountainside toward the lake, and she quickly hid.

From her hiding place, she watched her mother dismount and begin her search. Like her, she peered into the holes between the rocks. Her search looked as frantic as her own had been. But then again, her mother had more to lose if she didn't find it.

"Is this what you're looking for?" Harper held up the diary as she stepped out of her hiding place. Its cheap vinyl cover was soiled from having been hidden in the rocks. Fortunately water hadn't gotten to it over the years. Harper had been forced to break the lock since she hadn't thought to bring the key. But the lock was flimsy and popped open easily. The words inside were still plenty legible.

After a startled moment, her mother asked, "Where did you find it?"

Harper told her how she'd taken a shortcut to beat her to the spot and how the moment she'd seen the rock, she'd recognized it from the drawing Maggie had done of JD. It hadn't been that hard to find the diary once she realized this would be the logical place Maggie would hide it.

"When I saw you riding in this direction, I remembered what you said about them meeting up at Mirror Lake. I realized you were the one who'd been searching for the diary in the old Maynard House and in the Hamilton ranch house last night. It was your perfume I smelled right before you knocked me down."

Her mother looked away. "It was foolish of me. I'm sorry. I didn't see you in the dark last night."

She looked at the diary in her hands. "You've been busy looking for this, which means you knew about their affair." She met her mother's blue eyes, eyes so like her own. "You said you didn't know for sure. Why lie? Unless you have something to hide? What are you so afraid Maggie wrote in this diary about you?"

SARAH LOWERED HERSELF to a rock facing her daughter. Suddenly she felt exhausted. She breathed in the high mountain lake air and thought about the time she'd found Maggie up here waiting for JD. She looked out at the lake. Why was it that some of her memories were missing and others were crystal clear? This was one memory she wished she could forget.

"They were in love," she said, turning back to her daughter. "It would be hard for most people to accept, but they seemed...perfect for each other."

She could see that this wasn't what Harper had expected to hear. Sarah watched her daughter move to a rock closer to her. Her gaze went to the diary, clutched tightly in Harper's hands.

Her daughter followed her gaze and seemed to grip the diary even tighter. "Why would you think Maggie had written something in here about you?"

"Because we met up here once. I tried to buy her off."

Harper raised a brow.

"She refused the money. She refused to give up JD. She didn't care that she would destroy his marriage, his political career—"

"So you killed her."

Sarah flinched. "Is that what you think?" She shook her head, hurt that her daughter could think that of her. But under the circumstances, she shouldn't have been that surprised. "I didn't kill her."

"Then who did?"

She sighed and looked toward the lake again. Her gaze came back to Harper. "JD didn't do it. I knew the man. He could never have hurt her. He loved her."

"Grace?"

Sarah thought of the bitter woman. "Not alone."

Harper frowned. "JD wouldn't have helped her…" Her eyes widened. "Not Dad."

"I've always suspected Grace killed Maggie by accident and—"

Harper was on her feet. "No, Dad wouldn't do that."

"He loved his mother. I'm sure he felt he owed her after marrying me. He knew that he'd broken her heart."

"No, you're wrong."

"I pray I am," Sarah said. "But Grace had more of a hold on Buck than he ever wanted to admit. He was her baby boy and he knew that he'd broken her heart by marrying me."

Harper looked down at the diary in her hand. "You think there's something in here that—"

"You asked me if there was bad blood between the

families. There's something I didn't want to tell you. When Flannigan McTavish found out about his daughter and JD, he was livid. He came roaring up to the house looking for JD, saying he was going to kill him. JD had been down at the stables. Buck and I had taken the babies over… Buck tried to stop them, but the two men ended up in a fistfight. If Buck hadn't separated them…" Sighing, she continued, "Grace was watching from the window. I saw her standing up there. The look on her face… She was hoping Flannigan killed JD."

"That doesn't prove anything other than that she could stand and she was hateful. That doesn't mean she killed Maggie."

"Fortunately, none of the ranch hands saw the fight," Sarah continued. "Buck was beside himself, furious with his father and worried about his mother. JD was different after that. Maybe Maggie told him that I'd tried to buy her off." She shrugged. "I'm not proud of what I did, but she was destroying JD's marriage and any chance he had of being president if they were having an affair or, worse, if he left Grace for her."

"As it was, he pulled out of the race. Are you sure it mattered so much to him. Or was it only important to you?"

Sarah smiled. "You've been listening to your sister Kat. Yes, I wanted it for him. The man needed something and he couldn't have Maggie. He was a good man. He would have made a good president."

"Like Dad."

She shook her head, not surprised that Kat had poisoned Harper against her. "You think it is my obsession to see another Hamilton in the White House? I've never liked politics. I can't imagine living in DC. All that ambition to save the world? That's on the male side of the Hamilton family. Not mine."

Harper looked down at the diary in her hands. Sarah realized that her daughter hadn't had enough time to read much of the diary. "Is it possible Maggie knew about Grace's fall?" Harper asked.

Sarah saw what she was getting at. "You think I really did push your grandmother down the stairs?"

"I'm not sure what to think."

"Think about a woman who would do anything to keep her husband and son tied to her—even throw herself down a flight of stairs. Grace wanted to make JD quit the senate, to dote on her the rest of her life. She hated politics, hated me for encouraging him. She wanted his undivided attention and would do anything to get it."

"Even kill Maggie?"

"Yes. I suspect JD talked to Maggie about what was going on at home."

"And if Maggie wrote about it in this diary…"

"Then the murder trail will lead to Grace. If Maggie went over to the house to talk to her, to tell her about the baby she was carrying and there was a confrontation… Grace couldn't have managed disposing of the body alone, so the trail would eventually lead to your father," Sarah said. "Throw the diary in the lake. Destroy it before it destroys our family."

CHAPTER TWENTY-ONE

"I WASN'T SURE you would be here," Maggie said as she dismounted.

JD had been waiting for her after getting her message. He figured that she knew of the rumors running wild about them after her father had stormed over to the ranch, the confrontation ending in a fistfight that Buck had broken up.

Now he watched her, suddenly scared. "What's wrong? Is it the baby?"

She shook her head but didn't look at him.

"Sarah hasn't tried to buy you off again?"

Maggie turned to him. "Bobby Barnes has asked me to marry him."

"What?" The word came out on an expelled breath. He suddenly had to sit down. Stumbling to one of the rocks, he sat. "Bobby Barnes?" He looked up at her, squinting in the fall sun. Her back was to him. Just the sight of her... "Isn't he one of—" She'd never told him who the boys were who'd raped her.

"Bobby wasn't one of them."

JD wished he could believe that.

"He will give the baby a name."

"A name? You and your baby need more than a name."

She spun on him, green eyes blazing. "I don't have

a lot of options. I'm doing the best I can. My father..." Her voice broke.

"I know. Come here."

She stepped closer and he held out his hand. When she took it, he pulled her down on the rock beside him, still holding her hand tightly.

"I can help you."

Maggie shook her head and tried to pull free.

"You can't marry him."

She said nothing as she looked out at the lake.

"Maggie." It came out a plea. He couldn't bear the thought of her in a loveless marriage with Bobby Barnes.

She turned to him, her heart in her eyes. "Run away with me."

His own heart broke at her words. There was nothing he wanted more than to just take off with this woman. But even as he thought it, he knew how unfair that would be to her. Her life was just beginning. While only forty-two, his was probably more than half-over. Not to mention, he was married. He'd made promises to Grace and she needed him more now than she ever had.

"We could go to Hollywood. Every man there marries a younger woman," she said, but he could tell she was no longer serious. She knew that for them, there was no place to run. Since he'd tossed his hat into the ring for president, his face was everywhere.

He let go of her hand and she rose to her feet. "I want to run away with you. You can't know how desperately I want to."

She nodded, her back to him as she stood looking out at the lake. "But you can't. I know."

"Don't marry Bobby. I can give you money to help with the baby and—"

"No," she said, turning to face him. "I've made up my mind. I've put my father through enough as it is. He's old-school. It will be hard enough for him when everyone finds out that I was pregnant before the wedding."

JD tried to find something to say to change her mind, but there were no words and he knew it. "When?"

"Soon. I'm already showing."

"Are you sure you want to keep this baby?"

She placed a hand over her stomach. "She's mine."

"What if she's mine?"

"That's another reason I'm keeping her."

He tried to swallow the lump in his throat as he watched her swing back up into the saddle. He knew that she wouldn't be back to the lake. Neither would he. He couldn't bear it without her.

"I love you." He'd never said anything more true.

She smiled down at him. "I know. I love you, too." With that, she rode away.

THE SHERIFF HAD had a day of surprises. First Harper had shown up with Maggie's diary. He'd listened as she'd told him how she'd decided to check out the lake where she believed that JD and Maggie had spent time, telling him about a sketch she'd found that Maggie had done of JD at the very spot.

"And the diary was hidden in the rocks?" he'd asked, still finding it hard to believe. Also feeling there was something she *wasn't* telling him. "Remind me again how you knew she kept a diary?"

Harper had shrugged guiltily. "I found the key to it when Brody and I checked her room. We were just trying to help you."

"Uh-huh," he'd said. "And you probably read what was in the diary."

"I did read through it," she'd admitted. "She was in love with my grandfather. It was very sad because she knew they couldn't be together."

After she'd left his office, he'd spent the rest of the day reading the diary, until it was time to go home. It was clear to him, just as it had been to Harper, that Maggie had been in love with JD. Even though she didn't mention him by name, anyone reading this would have known she was talking about him.

He'd found the entry after she'd been raped. She hadn't mentioned who'd done it, just that the "He" in her life had found her and taken her to the doctor.

It was the last few entries in the diary that he was the most interested in. It seemed she'd been trying to decide what she should do, though she didn't mention the "problem." He assumed it was the pregnancy.

I asked him to run away with me but of course he can't. I told him what I was thinking about doing. He got really upset and begged me not to. I know I'm putting him in a terrible position. I hate seeing him like this. This is all my fault. But now I have to do what is best for him and my baby. Bobby loves me. He said he'll love the baby. My heart is breaking, but I'm strong. I can do this. I'll hide this diary where he can find it, and maybe someday he will. Then he'll know how much I loved him.

That was the last entry. Frank had hoped for more. What he read made it sound as if she'd put JD Hamilton in an untenable position. Days later, Maggie would be buried alive.

He'd thought about that all the way home. He couldn't get Maggie and JD out of his mind. It was probably because he understood that kind of longing for someone he had spent years yearning for only too well.

"I have a confession."

He'd been so lost in thought that Lynette startled him as she came into their living room. She handed him a cold beer, looking guilty.

As he twisted off the top of the bottle and took a sip of beer, he studied his wife. For weeks, he'd known she was hiding something from him. Lynette was great at ferreting out other people's secrets, but she wasn't good at keeping her own.

Frank had experienced different kinds of fear over the years as a lawman. A half dozen horrible thoughts raced through him. Was it possible Lynette wasn't happy? That there was another man? That she might be sick, might be dying? That she might have done something that he would have to arrest her for?

He clutched the cold, sweating bottle and said, "Yes?"

She reached into her pocket and produced a small white box.

Staring at it, he watched her open it, not sure what he expected might be inside. Certainly not what she pulled out. "A pendulum?"

She nodded, looking guilty. "I bought it when we

found out that Sarah had one branded on her behind and that it was a symbol of The Prophecy."

Of course Sarah had sworn she couldn't remember how the tattoo had gotten there or what it might mean, let alone why The Prophecy had targeted her. When one of the members had been caught, another killed and a third arrested, he'd asked that they be checked for the tattoo.

Sure enough, all of them had it—including Virginia Handley, the woman who confessed to being Red.

That had been enough evidence to convince Senator Buckmaster Hamilton that The Prophecy had "branded" Sarah in order to make it appear she was a member of the radical group, when she knew nothing about it.

Frank hadn't been so easily convinced. Because of it, his wife now had a pendulum? "This is your… secret? Your confession?"

She nodded.

"Why would you buy a pendulum?"

"To see if they work," she said, suddenly excited. She shoved him over on the couch to sit next to him. "It works. I'm telling you, I've tested it. You ask it a question and it tells you—"

"It talks?" He laughed, so relieved he wanted to take her in his arms and hug her.

"You ask it questions that can be answered by yes or no," she said. "I can tell that you're skeptical, but I swear to you, it's amazing. I ask it questions all the time. You've almost caught me a few times. I knew you'd make fun of me, so I quickly hid it."

That's why she'd been acting guilty the times he'd

caught her. "You can't really believe that piece of matter answers your questions."

"I can prove it. Ask it a question." She took the pendulum and held it at the end of the cord. The pointed end hovered over the top of the coffee table, moving slightly as she steadied her hand. "Remember, it has to be a question that can be answered with a yes or no."

He took a drink of his beer. He could see how determined she was. The last thing he wanted to do was make fun of her and yet she couldn't really believe in all this. Lynette was too smart to fall for such hocus-pocus.

She was looking at him, waiting. The pendulum hung from the line, the end of it barely moving with her breathing.

A question. "Does my wife love me?"

Lynette mugged a face at him and looked down at the pendulum. It didn't move for a few seconds. Then it slowly began to circle, the circle growing larger and larger before the pendulum settled down again.

"The answer is yes, as if you didn't know. That's the only question you had?" She sounded disappointed in him.

He looked at the pendulum as it stopped moving. He felt like a fool as he asked, "Did JD Hamilton kill Maggie McTavish?"

The pendulum began to move almost at once. It rocked back and forth, back and forth.

Lynette's eyes were large and shiny. "I told you." The pendulum stopped again. "Let's try this. Does Collin Wilson's death have anything to do with Maggie McTavish?"

The pendulum began to circle slowly, growing in speed and distance.

"All right, that's enough," Frank said, getting to his feet. "As long as I'm sheriff, I'm going to solve crimes the old-fashioned way."

"You just hate to admit that there might be more to all this," Lynette said as she gathered the pendulum and cord in her hand before dropping it back into the little white box.

"I'm just glad you still love me," he said, pulling her to him as she rose from the couch. "Now I'm going out to talk to my crows. They have their own theory on Maggie's death. Don't make that face at me. They're as reliable as your…pendulum." He smiled as he bent and kissed her. "I love you."

"I know. The pendulum told me." She laughed, making him feel a little better. She didn't entirely buy into all this, at least he hoped not.

But, like the pendulum, he also believed Collin's murder was tied somehow to Maggie. If only the pendulum could talk, he thought as he pushed open the door and, taking his beer, went out to visit with his crows perched on the phone line.

BRODY TOOK THE call when he saw it was Harper. "I can't talk long."

He was back at the ranch to get some things and he knew that at any minute his father and uncle could drive up. If they caught him talking to Harper it would only make this harder. He didn't want to put himself or them through that. "My father called. He wants to set up a time to meet here at my house. He wants to talk to me."

"You're getting your ranch back?"

"I don't know. Maybe." He felt as if he should be happier about that prospect, but the bond between him and his father and uncle felt irrevocably broken.

"I'm happy for you."

"I have to admit there have been moments when I just wanted to walk away. I'm angry with them and they're angry with me."

"I know what you mean." She told him about seeing her mother riding off on a horse after she'd heard her whole life that her mother was terrified of horses. "You found Maggie's diary," he interrupted when she got to that part. "Where is it?"

"I gave it to the sheriff. I tried to reach you first."

"I had my phone turned off. You looked at the diary before you gave it to him, right?"

"Maggie didn't name JD in it. Nor did she ever say who raped her. Her last entry was about letting go, giving up, doing what had be done. I wrote it down. Do you want to hear it?"

"Yes. If I hang up before you finish, you'll know my father dropped by."

Harper cleared her throat and began to read.

"So she was going to marry Bobby Barnes," he said. "I have to go. But I want to see you later. I miss you."

"Me, too. Call me."

"RUSSELL?" SARAH COULDN'T believe he'd called. All the messages she'd left him. All the times his phone had gone straight to voice mail. He hadn't answered any of her messages. Just the sound of his voice now made her want to cry. She'd missed him, missed the time they'd spent together as friends. "Are you still on the ship?"

"I haven't left yet."

She fell silent. Hadn't she suspected that he hadn't left? And yet, she'd hoped that he hadn't been able to return her calls because he hadn't been able to call from the ship.

"You haven't gone yet?" she repeated. Or he wasn't going at all. The rancher didn't seem like the kind to go on a cruise by himself. But she knew she'd hurt him badly and thought maybe he really did need a change of pace.

If he was still in Montana it more than likely had something to do with her. She'd broken their engagement, broken his heart, according to him. She hated herself for thinking that she could marry Russell when Buck had her heart and always would.

"Why not?" she asked.

"I couldn't leave, Sarah. Because you're going to need me."

She'd called to tell him that she was moving back in with Buck, that it would soon be all over the news. "Russell—"

"Dr. Venable is back in the States. He could even be back in Montana."

His words came as a shock. She wanted to argue that she didn't know any Dr. Venable, that he had nothing to do with her, but she saved her breath. Russell was convinced that Buck had worked with the doctor to steal her memories of the time before she'd tried to kill herself. Worse, according to what the sheriff had been able to learn about her, she'd spent the missing twenty-two years with a man named Dr. Venable in Brazil—apparently willingly, even though she swore she didn't know the man.

"How do you know that he's back?" she asked quietly.

"It doesn't matter. I know. I've given the information to the sheriff. He might be contacting you."

"What makes you think this doctor will come here?" she asked, praying he was wrong about everything, and yet she knew Russell was only doing all this because he cared.

"Sarah." She heard the frustration in his voice. "The sheriff told me that they now know where you were during those missing years. With Dr. Venable."

"He had no right to tell you that."

"I was the one who told him about my brain-wiping theory, Sarah. I'm the one who helped him track down this doctor. Anyway, there is no official investigation on the sheriff's part."

But that wasn't stopping the sheriff and everyone else from digging into her past. She resented the fact that other people knew more about her than she knew about herself. "He shouldn't have bothered you with any of this."

Russell let out a low chuckle. "He knows I love you."

She gripped the phone, pressing it against her cheek, and tried not to cry. Just hearing Russell's caring voice… "I love you, too." The admission was out before she could stop herself.

"I know, but you love Buckmaster Hamilton more."

A long silence followed since there was nothing she could say.

"I'm not leaving town, Sarah. I can't. You *are* going to need me."

"Russell, you can't—"

"That's just it. I can and I will wait. Who knows— you could be right, and you might never see Dr. Ven-

able again. If so, then you and your husband will soon
be living the dream in the White House." His tone said
he didn't believe that for a moment. "But if *I'm* right…
You have my number. When Dr. Venable shows up,
call me. You can't trust him. But you know you can
trust me, don't you."

"Yes."

CHAPTER TWENTY-TWO

GRACE SAW HER husband come home looking like a whipped dog. She watched him walk up from the barn after putting his horse and tack away. His footsteps were plodding, his head down and, for a moment, her heart went out to him.

He'd been ashamed of himself since that episode with Flannigan McTavish. She'd watched the two of them fighting in the dirt like fools. It had been bittersweet, since now her son knew while she'd known all along.

Maybe now her son would realize she'd been telling the truth about a lot of things. Not that she expected Buckmaster to come to his senses. What was it about men and the women they fell for?

"No fish today?" she said, unable to keep the sarcasm out of her voice as her husband walked in.

He didn't answer as he stuck his head into the refrigerator and dug around, coming out with a beer. He opened it and drained half of the bottle before he stepped into the living room, where she was waiting.

She wanted to demand to know what had happened. She could only guess. His cute little cowgirl had dumped him. Good. Grace wanted to clap and cheer and tell him what a fool he was. But even she couldn't beat a dead dog.

"Buckmaster dropped by earlier," she said. "The new house is coming along well. He's already adding on more rooms."

JD looked up.

"That's right. She's pregnant again. She's really rubbing it in, isn't she?"

Her husband groaned. "She isn't having children to spite you."

"Isn't she?" Grace smiled at that. Her husband wasn't just a fool. He was a blind fool. He'd fallen for Sarah's lies as easily as he must have fallen for that wild girl from next door.

The phone rang and he answered it. Another person wanting to give him money to run for president. She gritted her teeth as he thanked the caller and hung up. When he turned to her, she saw the future as if looking into a crystal ball. He'd lost that tramp from next door and now he was going to throw himself into the presidential race with Sarah and Buckmaster cheering him on.

The worst part was that he could win. People liked JD. Even if this scandal with the neighborhood tramp came out, JD would be able to convince the voting public that basically he was a good guy, because he was.

And she would lose him to politics again.

Over her dead body, she thought darkly.

BACK AT HIS office the next morning, Frank thumbed through the photographs from Claudia's high school years. She was a year younger than Maggie. Through the yearbook, he could track who was dating whom fairly easily. The school was small, the senior class even smaller.

His own class had had seven seniors so he knew everyone in the school.

He wasn't sure why he'd taken the albums. There were few photos of Maggie. Apparently she hadn't attended any of the school dances where Claudia had taken the most photos. But there were photos of boys Maggie had dated—and written in her diary about. Ty Jenkins, Kyle Parker, Bobby Barnes, Will Sanders, Collin Wilson.

All his instincts told him that these photo albums contained not just the key players in the two murders he had on his hands but, ultimately, the answers. Because it was such a small school, most of them had dated each other. Maggie had dated Ty, Bobby, Will, Collin and Kyle. When she'd broken up with them, they'd dated the other girls.

That was the problem with a small town. Not only did everyone know everyone else's business, but also there were a lot of tangled relationships because of the small pool to draw from. If only he could unravel the relationships to get to the truth. Wasn't that exactly what Harper and Brody had been trying to do with the yearbooks?

Somewhere in this mess was a killer. He just hoped he found the murderer before he killed again.

"I ran that DNA through the system like you asked," his undersheriff said from the doorway of his office. "We got a hit," Dillon said as he handed him the information.

Frank hadn't known what to expect when he'd asked to have Kyle Parker's DNA run. He suspected Kyle was one of the men who'd raped Maggie. Is that why Kyle hadn't wanted to give his DNA?

But he was surprised now to learn that it matched evidence taken at an old burglary case more than twenty years before. One of the burglars had cut himself getting out a window and left both blood and skin behind.

The statute of limitation had run out on that particular case. Wouldn't Kyle know that? Now Frank wondered if there was something else Kyle had to hide?

"Also, I talked to the coroner who handled both JD and Grace Hamilton's deaths," Dillon said. "He was suspicious that Grace had been on the second floor given that she'd been in a wheelchair for months. He said her daughter-in-law was the one who'd found her at the bottom of the stairs."

Frank looked up. "I thought JD found her."

"That's just it. I dug through notes taken after the accident. In the sheriff's report, JD said he found her. But he originally told the coroner that Sarah had gotten there just moments before him."

Frank rubbed the back of his neck. "Did either say why she was upstairs?"

Dillon shook his head. "Evidently no one asked them that."

"Well, we suspect she was able to walk. What about JD's accident?"

"It seems he lost control of the car and went into the river. It wasn't a suspected suicide, if that's what you're thinking, according to the coroner. There were brake marks in the gravel where he tried to get control. The coroner brought up the question of whether or not there might have been another car involved but was never able to prove it."

"Another car? Wife dies in a fall, husband dies shortly afterward in a car wreck."

"It happens when people are upset, not paying attention."

Dillon had turned his attention back to the DNA test results. "You think the old burglary is why Kyle didn't want to provide the DNA?"

"Maybe. I'm going to talk to his wife. Now that I have Maggie's diary, I know the night she was raped. I have a timeline that brings up some interesting… coincidences. There was a big dance that night at the school. According to the yearbook, Parker was dating his soon-to-be wife back then. She should remember if he was with her that night."

"All those years ago?" Dillon asked skeptically.

Frank laughed. "It was *high school.* Something about those years imprints itself on us more vividly than any other years in our lives. We were young, full of illusions, believed we were immortal and were so easily hurt. I suspect Maggie hurt someone and might not have realized just how badly until she found herself facing her killer."

After Dillon left, Frank went back to the photos. He was staring at photos of the senior dance, not realizing at first what he was seeing, when it finally registered.

He felt his heart do a little skip before he quickly pulled the photos from the album and headed for his patrol SUV.

HARPER PICKED UP the phone, hoping it was Brody. She hadn't heard from him and wondered if he'd met with his father about the ranch yet. She felt responsible first for bullying Brody into helping her look for Maggie's killer and, secondly, for putting him in an untenable situation with his family.

But the caller wasn't Brody. She didn't recognize the male voice.

"I have a delivery for Sarah Hamilton," the man said.

"Yes."

"I can't read the address. If I could speak with her."

"She doesn't live here. That is, not at the main ranch address, but you can deliver it here. I'll see that she gets it."

"I'm sorry but she needs to sign for it."

"Who is it was from?" Harper asked.

"Buckmaster Hamilton."

Her father had sent something to their mother that required a signature to deliver? Must be expensive, she thought as she told him the address of the house on the ranch where her mother was staying.

The driver asked for directions, which she gave him. "Thank you. The package needs to be delivered in the next twenty-four hours and it is already almost late."

Harper had reservations about giving out her mother's address after she hung up. What if it had been a reporter just wanting to find out where Sarah Hamilton was staying? Harper thought about calling her mother and warning her that a reporter might be showing up at her door. But Sarah had dealt with her share of reporters. She'd deal with this one. And maybe there really was a package and her father had just foolishly put down an address the carrier didn't recognize.

KAREN PARKER LOOKED up as Frank walked into the city library. It was early so the place was near empty. She'd been working diligently at her desk when he'd walked in, but when she saw him, she rose, pushing the papers aside. He reminded her of one of her strict teachers from high school—the scowl, the expectant look that said he knew she was about to break some rule.

"Good morning, Sheriff. Is there a book I can help you find?"

"Not this morning. I was hoping we could talk somewhere private."

She glanced toward the librarian's office, which was dark and empty. "I really shouldn't leave my desk."

"It won't take long and we'll be able to see if anyone needs your help."

With obvious reluctance she led him into the office. He closed the door and pulled out his notebook. She hovered behind the desk for a moment before sitting down. Her gaze kept going to her own desk as if willing someone to appear.

"I suppose you heard that Collin Wilson was killed."

She nodded, and for a moment he thought she might break down.

"I understand the two of you were good friends."

Karen quickly shook her head. "Not really. We just knew each other from high school."

"He was in your grade, right?"

"I guess so. What is this about?"

"Just trying to put some names together. Who were you dating your senior year?"

"My husband, Kyle. We got married shortly after graduation."

He nodded. "Wasn't there a graduation dance the first part of June that year?"

She frowned. "Yes."

"You went with Kyle."

"I suppose so."

"You don't remember?"

"I'm sure I did. Yes, I recall now."

"Who else was there?"

She fiddled with a pen on the desk for a moment. "The usual crowd."

"Bobby Barnes?" He ticked off his suspects and she nodded to each. "Some of them left early, right?"

Again she frowned. "I don't understand why you're asking me about this."

"I've spoken to several other people who recall a few of the boys leaving the dance early." It was a small white lie.

She settled back into the chair, now looking as if she felt trapped.

"This was the last dance of your high school year. I'm sure you remember whether or not it was just you girls standing around talking or if you danced the last dance with your soon-to-be husband."

When she shook her head, he pulled out the photos he'd taken from Claudia's album and spread them across the desk. "You can see that these taken from later in the night show you girls standing around, only a few people on the dance floor. Some of your dates were conspicuously missing."

Karen swallowed, appearing uncomfortable. She smelled a trap but she didn't seem to know why let alone how to get out of it. "I guess some of the boys did leave."

"Kyle?"

She nodded.

"Who went with him?" She started to shrug, but he

quickly said, "They would have left their dates. Small school, it would be hard not to know whether or not they were gone. Plus, I already have a pretty good idea who they were."

"Will Sanders and Ty Jenkins."

"Bobby Barnes wasn't with them?"

"No, he and Claudia got into a fight. He left alone as far as I know. Later, Claudia went after him and I didn't see either of them again."

"Why did your date leave?" he asked.

She hesitated. "They said they were going to get a friend of theirs to buy them some beer for later and they'd be back."

"Did they come back?"

Karen looked away. "No."

"You and Kyle argue about it?"

"Really, Sheriff, I can't see how this—"

"Did he know you were pregnant?"

That took her by surprise. "No, I told him later that night after I found him."

"Was he still with Ty and Will?"

"No, he was back at his place."

"Didn't you find that strange?"

"He'd had too much to drink and was sick, so no, I didn't."

Frank didn't take his gaze from her face. "Did he tell you what he'd been up to—besides drinking?"

"No and I didn't care. I had more important things on my mind."

Frank studied her. Did Kyle, drunk and sick, confess what he and the others had done? Or was she telling the truth and she really didn't know what her future husband and his friends had done that night?

CHAPTER TWENTY-THREE

JD THREW HIMSELF into trying to be the man that Grace had married. He got her a second, smaller wheelchair and started carrying her upstairs to their old bedroom where he would hold her and they could talk about the happy years.

She seemed better, although it was clear she didn't want him to get back into politics. He couldn't imagine his life on the ranch with only Grace now. Maggie had left a huge hole in his heart that ached constantly. There was definitely a part of him that needed politics. Otherwise, he wasn't sure he wanted to go on.

He thought about Maggie day and night and watched the local newspaper for the announcement of her upcoming marriage to Bobby Barnes. He still wasn't convinced that Bobby hadn't been one of the boys who'd raped her. How could she marry a man like that? But he knew the answer. She saw no other option and that alone caused his sleepless nights.

Grace seemed sweeter now that she had his undying attention. If she noticed that he no longer went up to the lake, she said nothing. Fall was now upon them, the nights growing colder, the days growing shorter. Soon it would be too cold to ride up into the mountains. Next summer, though, if he was still here on the ranch and not campaigning, she wouldn't be able to *help herself. She would ask why he no longer went up into the mountains fishing—even though he suspected she knew only too well. He knew he couldn't hide anything from her—especially his guilt.*

But he was glad about this change in her. She was nicer to Buck and Sarah and their grandchildren. He'd taken her over so she could tour their new house. "It's so...huge."

Sarah, whose latest pregnancy was showing, laughed. "I want to fill it with children. It's all I ever wanted." Then seeing Grace's expression, she'd moved quickly to her, crouching in front of the wheelchair. "I'm so sorry. I know how hard this must be for you. But God is giving you grandchildren. That has to help."

It didn't help, JD knew. "They all look too much like Sarah," Grace had said one day. "Children of the damned."

JD had ignored it and as he'd poured more love into the woman he'd married, he'd realized that Grace had become a bottomless vessel. There wasn't enough love in the world to fill her disappointment in the men in her life.

HARPER WAS ON her way out when her mother walked into the house. It seemed so strange to see her here. From the way she stopped just inside the door, it was even stranger for her.

"Did you get the package Dad sent?"

Her mother looked confused. "I don't know anything about a package. Look, Harper, I know you probably don't want to talk to me right now."

"If this is about the diary—"

"No, I'll tell your father everything when I see him. This is about Brody."

Harper sighed. "You might as well save your breath. Quite frankly, you're the last person I would take relationship advice from, no offense."

"None taken, but you're wrong. Could we sit down?"

"I thought you were moving in," Harper said, noticing that her mother hadn't brought anything with her.

"Not yet. Please." She motioned to a chair. Harper curled up in one of the large comfortable chairs. Her mother teetered on the edge of the couch across from her and seemed to be gathering her thoughts.

"The one thing I have a great deal of experience with is marrying into a family who didn't like me." Her words had hit their target. "It put so much pressure on our marriage. Buck loved his mother. It tore him apart the way she treated me. At some point, I think he started to question if there wasn't some truth in what Grace was saying about me. It was the most painful part of our marriage."

"You lived on the same ranch with them. Brody and I—"

"Will live *where*? On the ranch he inherits? You'll be in the same position I was. If Brody is as nice a man as you say, then imagine how hard it will be for him if his father and uncle never accept you."

Unfortunately, Harper could imagine it. She hadn't thought about where she and Brody would live. She hadn't gotten that far. All she knew was that she loved him and wanted to be with him always.

"Dad will give us some property." But the moment she said it, Harper knew that it wouldn't be what Brody wanted. He'd worked too hard on his family ranch. To lose it now… "Maybe his father and uncle will come around."

"Maybe in time. Maybe not. Grace never did. After she died…" Her mother looked away and Harper realized there were tears in her eyes. "JD was never the same. I think he never truly believed that I hadn't killed her."

"No, surely—"

"I was there the day she died. We were arguing. She headed for the stairs. I reached for her…."

"She was walking?" Harper asked, shocked by that news as well as the fact that her mother hadn't just been there. She'd been part of it.

"She wasn't that steady on her feet." Sarah shook her head. "Her hatred of me killed her. If I hadn't been there and tried to stop her…" She looked away for a moment. "I don't want that life for you. Or for Brody. You asked me once about bad blood between the families. Even if the sheriff proves that JD didn't kill Maggie, Flannigan will never forgive him."

"But in the diary, it is so clear that they loved each other," Harper protested.

"A forbidden love that ended badly."

Long after her mother left, Harper found herself thinking about what her mother had said. She didn't want Sarah to be right. And yet when she thought about Brody, she knew everything her mother had said was true. Brody loved his family. He'd chosen her over them and now he'd lost the ranch that he loved.

Even if they could find a way to make it work, if his family didn't come around… He was too proud to come to her with nothing. It would destroy their love. He had given up too much for her. She couldn't let him do that.

She picked up the phone and dialed his number. It went straight to voice mail. "I hadn't wanted to do this in a message, but maybe it is better this way. We can't see each other again. Our families will never get along. It's best if we part ways now. I'm sorry." She was choked up with tears by the time she disconnected. Burying her face in her hands, she headed upstairs wondering how she was going to live without him.

"YOUR STOMACH BOTHERING YOU?" Lynette asked him at lunch.

"Just not hungry." It wasn't like him and they both knew it. He loved to eat.

"It's those DNA results. You're going to get an ulcer. Everyone's talking about how you had JD Hamilton's body exhumed, and Ty Jenkins's, too. Amber was in the store saying she was going to sue. When are you supposed to hear?"

Frank had been waiting, growing more anxious by the hour. "I don't know."

Lynette let out a breath. "Well, when you do we'll finally know who fathered her baby."

He loved the way she said *we*. As if he could keep a lid on the results. The entire county was waiting.

"Did I hear that Buck has moved Sarah into the main house?" Lynette asked.

He looked at her in surprise. "He did?"

His wife smiled. She did love being ahead of him when it came to news. "That doesn't seem wise right before the primaries."

Lynette shrugged. "A few media sources mentioned that his second wife hasn't been in the ground long.

But mostly he is getting support for reuniting with his first wife. Everyone loves a love story."

"Apparently." He couldn't help being surprised by this news. "Buck is taking quite a chance." He wondered if it had been his idea or Sarah's. Was she pressuring him to get back together?

"Don't look so worried. He hasn't won the primaries yet."

"And I could be wrong about her," he said, even though they both knew better. Since Sarah's return to Montana, he'd suspected there was more to this than a love story. Unfortunately, he had no proof that Sarah's motives were anything other than wanting her family back.

"I need to get to the office," he said after finishing the can of orange soda she'd brought him and rising to his feet.

"You're going to be hungry in an hour."

"Probably. But I'll manage until dinner. You will be there, won't you?"

She laughed. "I wouldn't miss it for the world."

"Especially if I have news."

"Oh, I would imagine I'll know before you do."

He shook his head. He really needed to plug some leaks at his department and the coroner's.

On his way into town, Charlie called.

"Tell me," Frank said.

"I'd ask you if you were sitting down, but I know you are."

"Was JD the father?"

"It was Ty Jenkins."

Frank swore, and not because a part of him wasn't relieved that it wasn't JD Hamilton's baby. Hell, they couldn't even be sure that JD and Maggie had been lovers.

But he swore because now Ty Jenkins's suicide note made sense. He hadn't been able to live with what he'd done to Maggie. So if Ty was one of the rapists, then who else was involved?

He thought of Collin. Was that what he'd planned to tell Brody before he was killed?

"Opens a whole new can of worms, I take it?" Charlie said.

"My thoughts exactly. Thanks for the news." He started to say, *Let's try to keep this under wraps*, but didn't bother. Maybe it would scare the other rapists. He knew there was at least one more from what Dr. Franklin had told him. Given when the rape had occurred according to Maggie's diary, Ty had been one of the rapists.

So who else? And how did he find him? And the big question—was the rape the reason Maggie was killed?

BRODY LISTENED TO the message from Harper and swore. There was no way he was going to let her get away that easily. At the sound of a vehicle, he looked out, hoping it was her and that he could talk some sense into her. She was the one who'd said they should fight to be together. What had made her change her mind?

He recognized the pickup as he tried to call Harper back. It went straight to voice mail. He wasn't getting into this over the phone. As soon as his father left, he'd go find Harper.

Pocketing his phone, he opened the door to find his father standing on the porch. "Come to evict me?" He'd been packing up a few things, thinking it would be best if he moved out of his house until this was settled. He feared it was already settled. He had no right to the ranch or even the house he'd built. His only option was taking it to court and he wasn't apt to do that, not against family.

"Son, we need to talk."

"You were both pretty clear the last time we talked," he said, surprised to see his uncle Flannigan was with his father. His uncle slowly climbed out of the pickup but didn't approach the house. "Did you think you might need help throwing me off the ranch?"

"That isn't why we're here." His father pulled off his Stetson and turned the brim for a few moments in his fingers. "I'm sorry about everything that happened between us."

Brody looked toward his uncle, who was still standing by the truck. It was pretty clear he didn't feel the same way. "You always told me that this was my ranch. But the minute I didn't do something you wanted—"

"You turned against your own family," his uncle said.

Finn glanced back at his brother, sending him a look that made Flannigan turn away.

"The two of you disowned me and made it real clear I was no longer welcome on this ranch," Brody said. "I'm just here to get some of my things."

"That was wrong of us. Of both of us," his father said, glancing at Flan again, who said nothing. "I don't have to tell you how hard this has been on your uncle."

Brody could have argued it had been hard on them all, but in his heart, he knew none of them could feel the kind of loss Flannigan had, so he kept his mouth shut.

"We came by to tell you that the ranch is still yours," his father said.

"I'm going to have to get that in writing, since I can't trust that the next time I do something you don't approve of you'll kick me off again."

"That isn't going to happen," Finn assured him.

"Still. In writing."

His father looked back toward the pickup and his older brother. Flannigan didn't look happy but gave a slight nod and then got back in the truck.

"Also, I'm going to marry Harper," Brody said.

His father sighed. "Son—"

"It's nonnegotiable, so if that changes things, you let me know."

Finn nodded, but he didn't look happy.

"Uncle Flannigan is never going to accept it, is he?"

"Give it time. He loves you. He's still hurting." Finn put his hat back on and gave him a regretful smile. "I'll talk to him and get back to you. Again, I'm sorry."

Brody nodded and watched as his father and uncle left. He knew he should have been happier, but it was a bittersweet victory. He'd caused a schism in his family. He told himself it would take time to heal, but he wondered if that was even possible. Was there enough time left for his father and uncle before either older McTavish accepted Harper?

FRANK PULLED OUT the Ty Jenkins suicide file. The note Ty had written before hanging himself was on top. He picked it up, vaguely remembering the case from when he was a deputy.

Not much had been made of the note's bottom ragged edge. Looking at it, he wondered if the former sheriff had asked about the rest of the note. Clearly the bottom half had been torn off. Whoever had found Ty hadn't wanted whatever else the boy had written to be found by the sheriff.

In the file, he found what he was looking for. Ty's sister, Amber, had found him and cut down his body.

He made a call to the Dixie Cup Diner to find that Amber was home sick. Her house was by the river, a small out-of-the-way place, a car parked out front.

She answered on his third knock, wearing T-shirt and jeans. She didn't look sick, but she was the owner of the diner so she could call in sick whenever she wanted.

Opening the door only a few inches, she asked, "Yes?"

"I need to talk to you," Frank said, taking off his Stetson.

"I'm home sick and I—"

"This can't wait, I'm sorry."

He could see her debating letting him in for a few moments before she relented and opened the door.

The house smelled of freshly popped popcorn. The television was on to a soap opera that Lynette always watched and there was a large cola drink on the chair next to where Amber had been sitting.

She snapped off the television. "What is this about?"

Frank sat down in a chair near the one she'd been sitting in. He leaned forward to rest his elbows on his knees. "I need your help."

"I can't imagine how I could—"

"Maggie was raped five months before she was murdered."

Amber blinked as if surprised, but Frank saw that

she'd known. She seemed at a loss for words as she finally took her former seat. "What does that have—"

"I know your brother was one of the men."

She shook her head. "No, Ty—"

"Maggie was also five months pregnant when she was murdered. I have the DNA results from the baby. It was your brother's."

Tears welled in her eyes. Her lower lip began to tremble. "He didn't want to do it. They goaded him. He…" She looked away as she tried to pull herself together.

"It's why he killed himself. He couldn't live with what he'd done. What else did he write on his suicide note?"

She shook her head and said nothing.

"I know you ripped off the bottom of the note. Do you still have it?"

"I burned it."

"Who were the others? The ones who goaded him into it?"

Her face was hard as stone, her eyes glistening like flint, when she finally looked at him. "Kyle Parker and Will Sanders."

Not Bobby Barnes? "You're sure."

"I'm sure."

"Did he name them?"

"No, but I saw him with them the day before he killed himself. They were arguing. When they saw me they shut up, but they were bullying him. I heard them say they would kill him if he ever opened his mouth about it."

"You didn't know then what they were referring to?"

She shook her head. "Not until I read the suicide note. But it wasn't his fault. Maggie—"

"You aren't going to say she was asking for it, are you?"

Amber met his gaze. "If she hadn't been the way she was…"

Frank got to his feet. "She didn't ask to be raped by three men. Thank you for your help. I'll see myself out."

CHAPTER TWENTY-FOUR

GRACE KNEW SHE shouldn't have brought up Maggie and her upcoming marriage. Mabel Murphy had told her when she'd come to clean. Grace couldn't help rubbing it in her husband's face.

Now she grabbed JD's shirtsleeve as he tried to leave, pulling her to her feet. She took a few steps away from her wheelchair before he stopped and turned in surprise.

"You can walk." The shock on his face was quickly replaced with disgust as he freed his sleeve from her grip.

She stood there, her lie the elephant filling the room. "JD, you have to understand—"

"Oh, I understand, Grace. I finally understand. All of this, a ruse to what? Keep me tied to you?" He shook his head. "Why, Grace? I told you I would never leave you." He seemed to see the truth in her expression and let out a curse. "It was never about me. It was Buck. You did this to hang on to your son?"

She searched for the words to explain but knew he could never truly understand.

"You know what's heartbreaking, Grace? You still lost your son." He took a step back. "You pushed him away just as you have me."

She took a step toward him, reaching again for him.

He shook his head and retreated to the top of the stairs. "This whole charade..." He waved a hand through the air and she saw the future etched into his handsome face. "You're sick, Grace. I thought I could help you, but I was wrong. You don't give a damn about me."

"You can't leave me."

He laughed. "That's what I kept telling myself. But you know what? I can. I have a chance to be happy and damn if I'm not going to take it." JD turned then and started down the stairs.

"You're going to that redheaded harlot?" she cried.

"I am. I think I can make her happy. I'm damned sure going to try."

She rushed to the top of the stairs. "You can't leave me! If you do, Sarah will come back and kill me! JD! It's the truth."

He'd reached the bottom of the stairs, where he turned to look back up at her.

"You mean the truth like you can't walk, Grace?"

She met his gaze and knew she'd lost him. "You were just looking for an excuse to go to her. So go."

He hesitated, but only a moment, then he turned and stormed out.

Grace stumbled to the top of the stairs. She gripped the top railing, leaning over it and yelling down at him as the door banged closed.

Finally, she turned away, telling herself he would be back. He always came back. She'd only just reached the bedroom when she heard someone behind her and spun around.

"What are you doing here?" Grace demanded, star-

tled to see Sarah in the doorway. One look at her, and she knew that Sarah had heard the whole argument.

"I just saw JD leave. He asked me to check on you. He failed to mention that there'd been a miracle." She motioned toward the small, empty wheelchair JD had bought so they could be together on the second floor.

"You've always known I could walk." She narrowed her eyes at her daughter-in-law. "Why didn't you tell JD the first time you caught me standing?"

"I'm actually on your side."

Grace laughed. "The only side you're on is your own. You didn't tell because it must benefit you to have me married to him. Of course, the presidency. He has a much better chance with me by his side instead of that...redhead next door."

"I can see that you don't want company." Sarah turned and headed for the stairs. "So I can tell JD that you're fine."

Grace went after her. "I saw through you the first time I laid eyes on you. You didn't marry my son because you loved him. So why did you?"

Her daughter-in-law stopped at the top of the stairs. "Does it matter why I married him? Your son is happy. Isn't that enough for you?"

Incensed, she lunged for her daughter-in-law, wanting to shove her down the stairs and put an end to this.

But Sarah was younger, more agile. She dodged the attack, throwing Grace off balance. She teetered on the top step for a moment as she tried to regain her footing. When she realized she was going to fall, she reached for Sarah. Their fingers brushed. She looked up at Sarah that instant before she tumbled down the stairs. As she fell, Grace realized that Sarah's would be the last face she ever saw.

AFTER SHE'D LEFT Brody the message, Harper couldn't bear another minute in the house. She saddled up, just planning to go for a ride to clear her head. Her heart was breaking at the thought of never seeing Brody again. But in this case, she feared her mother was right.

He'd lost everything because of her. She was kidding herself thinking that the past and old secrets didn't matter. Maybe that's why she headed in the direction of the spot where she'd first seen him again. The day was warm, the sun high and bright in a robin-egg blue sky. Only a few clouds drifted on the breeze.

But over the Crazies, dark clouds were gathering, promising rain before the day was over.

As she rode, she thought about the last time she'd ridden this way. She'd been so happy that she'd been racing her horse across the pasture screaming her jubilation—and her life had collided with Brody's.

Maggie had brought them together only to tear them apart. She felt as if history kept repeating itself. Maggie and JD. Her and Brody. Neither got their happy ending.

She slowed her horse as she neared the hillside where they'd found Maggie's remains. Dismounting, she ground-tied her mare and walked the rest of the way. Maggie had been buried at the top of the hill. If it hadn't been for the rainstorm that washed her casket out...

The sheriff and coroner had taken away any sign of casket and remains, but there was a spot in the dried mud where she recalled the body had been lying that day.

She glanced up the hillside for a moment, thought

she saw movement. Was there someone up there? "Hello?" she called as she began to climb. It was steep as she wound her way through the dark pines. When she topped out on the barren hill, she stopped to catch her breath. Just as she suspected, there was a hole where Maggie had been buried. Soaked from the rain, the earth had sloughed off and slid down into the pines, taking the casket with it.

She looked around but saw no one. Had she only imagined movement? A flash of color? Apparently.

Standing up there, the wind buffeting her, she thought about Maggie. She felt as if she'd come to know her after reading her diary and sharing her despair. That filled her with a deep sadness, since in getting to know her she'd also gotten to know Brody better.

Harper brushed at her sudden tears and was about to start back down when she realized she wasn't alone. Turning, she blinked in surprise at the person holding a shovel handle in one dirty hand and a gun in the other. The gun was pointed at Harper's heart.

THE SHERIFF DROPPED by the lab to find the coroner finishing up. A tech was chipping away at the dried mud on the boards that had made up Maggie's casket.

Frank looked away. "I got another call from Flannigan McTavish," he told Charlie. "He wants to know when he can bury his daughter's remains."

"We have a few more things to do before they can be released. We're still sifting through the debris, but should be finished later today."

"I'll check back with you," Frank said.

"You all right?" Charlie asked.

"Just tired."

"This has been a rough one," the coroner agreed. "Makes me wonder why I keep doing this. But while horrifying, the case was also fascinating. That alone makes me think I should quit."

The sheriff nodded. "As awful as my job is sometimes, when we catch the bad guys, it makes it seem worth it."

Frank returned to his office, feeling old and tired and discouraged. Maggie had been able to tell them so much—and yet they still didn't know who'd killed her.

He was also no closer to finding out who had killed Collin Wilson. Dropping into his chair behind his desk, he noticed Collin Wilson's yearbook, which Harper had left with him.

Opening it, he thumbed through the senior section of it, stopping on a photo of Collin. Then studying Maggie's face. From her diary, he knew that she'd been through so much before her final hours.

His phone rang. He pushed the book aside, surprised to hear the coroner's voice on the other end of the line.

"I can't believe it, but we found something in the mud from when the casket broke open. It's a bracelet. But the name on it isn't Maggie. It's Karen."

Frank hung up and pulled the yearbook back over, found Karen's photo. Something gleamed on her right wrist. He took out his magnifying glass from inside the desk drawer.

The lettering was scrolled across the silver. *Karen.*

Karen. Harper was convinced Karen Parker had called Collin from the library the day she'd gotten the copies of the yearbook photos.

Karen. But she hadn't acted alone. Is that what Collin had wanted to confess?

BRODY SAW THAT Harper was calling and quickly picked up. "If you think for a minute that I am going to let you go—"

"I have Harper." Not her voice. Another female voice, but not one he recognized. "If you ever want to see her again, I suggest you listen carefully."

Brody listened, already heading for his pickup as he grasped the untenable situation. He tried not to drive too fast, afraid he would lose control on the gravel road. Karen had Harper and was threatening to kill her if he called the sheriff. He should come at once—and bring what he and Harper had taken from Maggie's grave the day they found it.

He hadn't known what she was talking about. They hadn't taken anything, but he wasn't going to argue that with her, not when Harper's life was at stake.

Brody took the back road, driving along the dirt track just as Maggie's killer had all those years ago. His mind raced as the pieces of the puzzle began to fall into place. The day Harper got copies of the yearbook photos, Karen had called Collin. Just as she must have called him the night she killed Maggie.

The wind howled on the hilltop as he crested the rise and saw the two figures silhouetted against the sky-line. Karen had the gun to Harper's head as he drove up, killed his engine and got out.

"You better have brought it," Karen said as he approached the pair.

Harper's eyes filled with tears at the sight of him. "I was afraid you wouldn't come after…after everything."

He shook his head. "Not rescue you? Not a chance."

"Enough. Where is it?" Karen demanded.

"She thinks we took her bracelet from Maggie's grave," Harper said.

"Why would you think that?" he asked Karen.

"Because Maggie grabbed it off my wrist that night. I didn't even realize it was missing until I got home and by then it was too late. She was dead and buried. I thought it would never turn up. Then the two of you found her body. I've looked everywhere, but it isn't here and since the sheriff hasn't found it, that means one of you took it."

"Sorry, but we don't have it," Brody said as he stepped closer. He knew he couldn't get hold of the gun, not with it pressed to Harper's temple, before Karen got off a shot.

"You're lying."

"Why would we lie?" Harper asked. "If we'd found anything we would have given it to the sheriff. We've been trying to find out what happened to Maggie. That's all we cared about."

"What *did* happen?" Brody asked.

Karen looked past him to the hole in the ground where Maggie had been buried. "I don't expect you to understand. She was going to ruin Kyle's life because of one stupid mistake."

"He and his friends raped her," Brody said, trying to keep the anger out of his voice.

"They'd been drinking. They were just fooling around when they grabbed her. They hadn't planned to do anything, but then she got mouthy with them."

"So they decided to rape her."

Karen had the good grace to avoid his gaze. "It was Will. He started it, demanding Kyle and Ty hold her down, then taunting them until they… Kyle was so sorry for what he'd done. He just wanted to forget it ever happened and then he found out that Maggie was pregnant and that it could be his baby." Her voice broke. "I told him the night it all happened that I was pregnant. I was afraid I was losing him. I loved him so much that I lied, knowing he would do the right thing and marry me."

"But five months later, Maggie would have been starting to show and you…" Harper stopped as Karen pressed the gun harder into her temple.

"A month after the wedding, I told him I miscarried," Karen said. "I had hoped to get pregnant so it wouldn't be a lie, but it didn't happen. Meanwhile, Maggie was maybe having Kyle's baby? He was convinced that was the case and was beside himself even before he heard that Bobby Barnes was going to marry her. He would have died before he let Bobby raise *his* child."

"So you decided to kill Maggie," Brody said.

"It wasn't like that. I just wanted to talk to her. I had saved some money. I asked her to meet me."

"Up here?" he asked.

She shook her head. "Outside of Big Timber. I didn't want Kyle to know. I offered her money to leave town and never come back. She laughed in my face." Karen's expression turned sour. "She threatened to go to the sheriff if Kyle or I ever bothered her again. As she started to walk away, I picked up a rock. I just wanted to stop her from ruining my life."

"What did you do after you killed her?" Brody asked.

"I couldn't believe what I'd done. I drove back to town. I knew I couldn't go to Kyle. He would never forgive me, believing I'd also killed his baby. I stopped by Bill's Auto. Collin was there working late. We were friends…"

"So he helped you," Brody said.

She nodded. "He found a box. We went back out there with his pickup. He said he knew the perfect place to bury her."

"On Hamilton Ranch so if she was ever found, it would look like my grandfather had killed her," Harper said.

Karen didn't seem to hear. She was lost in the past. "As Collin was starting to close the box, she grabbed my wrist. I screamed. I thought she was dead. We both did. I was trying to get free and screaming for Collin to help me. He grabbed the shovel…"

Brody closed his eyes. He'd heard the rumors that Maggie had been buried alive, but he'd thought that was all they were. Fury filled him, but when he opened his eyes and saw that Karen still had the gun to Harper's head, it instantly cooled.

"What did you do with Maggie's pickup?"

"Collin drove it into one of the reservoirs outside of town. I kept hoping it would be found and everyone would think she'd drowned," Karen said. "But as luck would have it, the two of you stumbled across her grave."

Maggie was dead. Karen and Collin had killed her. All Brody could think about was keeping Karen talking. He could see that she'd needed to tell someone in all these years. Tell her side of the story.

"Let me guess. Collin was going to tell me the truth," he said, knowing that Maggie's death wasn't the only one Karen had been responsible for.

"He had wanted to the night I thought I'd killed her. I couldn't. Collin was my friend, but once he realized that the truth was going to come out… I never thought it would come to this. The irony is that Kyle and I never had any children. I was infertile, but I couldn't admit that because of my lie about the pregnancy before we got married. So my husband spent the past thirty-five years fantasizing that Maggie was alive somewhere raising his child." Her laugh was bitter.

THE SHERIFF HAD been on his way to the library to pick up Karen when he'd gotten the call from Brody McTavish.

"Karen Parker has Harper out where Maggie was buried," he'd said, talking fast. Frank had heard the sound of a vehicle engine and the spray of gravel from the road. "I'm heading there now. I will leave my phone on. Hurry."

He'd quickly called on the patrol SUV radio for backup. "No sirens. We're going to have to take her on foot. I'm going to patch this call through so we can monitor what is happening as well as record it. I don't want anyone else getting killed."

Now as he and the others scrambled through the pines, the hilltop in sight, he prayed that Brody could keep Karen talking.

HARPER HAD BEEN listening quietly as the story unfolded. With the gun pressed to her temple, she could feel Karen's hand trembling. She met Brody's gaze. They had to do something and soon. Karen wasn't going to be able to hold it together much longer.

Looking down, Harper realized that she stood

within inches of the hole where Maggie had been buried. One wrong step and she would fall into it.

"So what is your plan? Killing us to cover up another murder makes no sense."

"I thought for sure I would hear from one of you after I heard about the body being found," Karen said. "When there was no mention of the bracelet by the sheriff, I figured you would try to blackmail me. Then Harper here shows up at the library wanting photos from the yearbook. I thought you were taunting me."

"So you called Collin. What was he supposed to do, scare her off?" Brody asked.

Harper edged a little closer to the hole. She knew this could be suicide, but if she threw herself into the empty grave and rolled, she could take the same path that the casket had down into the pines.

She doubted that Karen was much of a shot. Especially if taken by surprise. Brody was close enough that once Harper made her move he might be able to rush Karen. Harper met his gaze again and shifted her feet—a little closer to the hole, hoping he saw what she had planned.

"I told Collin to stay calm, but he got cold feet," Karen was saying. "I decided to take care of things myself. I borrowed his precious car, thinking I could put an end to your girlfriend. She's harder to get rid of than I thought. Then today she shows up here. Now you're telling me that neither of you have my bracelet."

"We don't," Brody said as he seemed to give Harper a slight nod. At least she hoped that was the case. "We had no idea you killed Maggie. I thought JD Hamilton had done it. That's what everyone thought. But if you kill us, the sheriff won't stop looking until he finds you. Killing the next president's daughter? A major mistake."

"Not if it looks like the two of you, star-crossed lovers, killed yourselves. Everyone knows how your families feel about each other. I heard that you've been kicked off your ranch," Karen said. "It makes sense that you would come here to do the deed. I almost feel sorry for you."

Harper knew she couldn't wait any longer. She had to do something. She could almost feel Karen's trigger finger itching to finish what she'd started thirty-five years ago.

She threw herself into the grave an instant before she heard the shot.

BRODY HAD SEEN what Harper planned to do. He knew it was risky, but he had no way of stopping her without giving her away. And he could tell that Karen wouldn't be distracted much longer even though she'd needed to get some of this off her chest. But with a thunderstorm moving in from the Crazies, time had run out. His only hope was reaching Karen before she could get off a shot.

As Harper dived into the grave, he rushed Karen. Both actions had taken her by surprise. He was on her in a heartbeat, but she'd already pulled the trigger before he reached her. The shot echoed along the ridgeline. He crashed into Karen, taking her down as he struggled to get the gun out of her hand.

"Are you all right?" he called. "Harper?" He couldn't see her and suddenly the hillside was alive with sheriff's deputies. One of them quickly moved him aside so he could cuff Karen. The deputy began to read Karen her rights as Brody got to his feet and looked over the side of the hill.

Harper had thrown herself into the grave, then rolled down the slope into the pines. Now she lay there unmoving. He scrambled down the hill, terrified that Karen's one shot had been fatal.

He reached her and rolled her over to find her eyes open. She was gasping for breath. "Are you hit?" he cried. "Harper, are you hit?" Behind him, the sheriff was asking the same question.

"No," she said. "The fall…it knocked…the wind… out of…me." He pulled her to him, holding her gently as she sucked in air. "Karen?"

"We have her," the sheriff said. "We also have her confession. Nice work," he said. "Now maybe the two of you can quit putting yourselves in danger. I'm going to need statements down at the office, if you're up to it."

Harper nodded as she caught her breath. "I just want this over with."

CHAPTER TWENTY-FIVE

JD LEFT THE HOUSE, *driving too fast. He had to get to Maggie. He had to stop her. The sun had set, leaving the Crazies black against the growing twilight. Long, eerie dark shadows from the stark, bare branches of the cottonwoods snaked across the narrow road.*

He knew going to the McTavish Ranch could get him shot, but he didn't care. He had to see her. He had to stop her from marrying Bobby. He'd been a fool not to realize that too much water had crossed under the bridge for him to make a life now with Grace. He'd broken his promise to her. He would have to live with that. Nor did he give a damn about being president if it meant not being with Maggie.

Stopping in a cloud of dust in front of Flannigan McTavish's house, he got out. "Maggie!" he called. "Maggie." He was running toward the porch when Flannigan stepped out holding a shotgun.

"She's not here."

"Where is she?"

"Like I'm going to tell you? What the hell do you want anyway?"

"I want your daughter. I want to make an honest woman out of her."

"It's too late for that."

"No," JD said, refusing to believe that. "I know I'm

*the last person you want to see your daughter with, but
I love her. She loves me and—"*

"She's just a child. She doesn't know who she loves."

*"She's eighteen, of legal age, and I can make her
happy."*

Flannigan raised the shotgun, pointing the serious
end of it in his direction. "Like I said, she's gone. She's
run off."

"Where?"

"If she wanted you to know she would have told
you."

"If you know—"

"I don't."

JD heard the pain in the man's voice. "I'm so sorry."

"Are you? You're why she's run off. Don't you think
I know what you did to her?"

"If you're talking about the rape—"

The shotgun went off, kicking up dirt in front of him
and pelting his jeans and boots with buckshot. "You ru-
ined her. Now get off my property before I shoot you."

JD left, but he didn't go home. He knew he would
have to eventually. He'd have to face Grace, face the
end of his marriage, face the end of his dreams. He was
forty-two and he felt as if his life was over.

He drove aimlessly for hours telling himself that if
he couldn't find Maggie, he had no reason to go on.
Then he drove home to find the sheriff waiting for him.

THE NEWS THAT Maggie's killer had been caught moved
through the county like a storm out of the Crazies.
It blew into the Beartooth General Store and spread
quickly through the valley. Nettie couldn't believe it.

She'd put her money on JD Hamilton. The phone at the store hadn't quit ringing off the hook.

"I just heard Kyle Parker was seen leaving his house with suitcases," one source told Nettie. "Packed up and moved out the moment he got the news. Apparently Karen is on her own now."

"I wonder if her public defender will ask for a change of venue," another woman said when she called the store to see what Nettie knew. "There is no way any juror in this county will want less than the death penalty for her. She was always so snooty at the library. She acted like we were going to steal the books. Once I had a late fee and you can't believe how she treated me. You'd think I'd killed someone."

Nettie tried to reach her husband to find out if it was true that he and several deputies had taken Karen into custody after she'd tried to kill Harper Hamilton and Brody McTavish. "Is it true Harper saved herself by diving into the grave?" she asked when Frank answered.

"Why don't you ask your pendulum," her husband said. "I'm kind of busy right now."

"I told you you'd catch Maggie's killer." She hung up an instant before Mabel Murphy came rushing in.

"Have you heard the news?" Mabel cried. "It's all over town!"

HARPER HEARD THE fear in her father's voice. "We're so glad you're all right," he said when he reached her by phone later at the house. His flight had just been called in DC. "What were you thinking? Frank said you went down to the grave site alone. Why would you do that?"

"It just felt…unfinished," she told him in her defense. "I'm not sure why I went there. I guess I had to see it again. I never expected to see Karen there."

"You watch enough movies, you should know the killer always returns to the scene of the crime," her father said.

"Well, it's over now," Harper said as she headed upstairs. All she wanted was a hot shower to get the dirt off of her. "Brody saved my life. If he hadn't called the sheriff and then tackled Karen before she could get off another shot..."

"You and Brody..."

"We won't be seeing each other again. Too much history that has nothing really to do with us."

"I see. Well, I'm just relieved that you're all right," her father said. "Has your mother moved in yet?"

"No. I talked to her earlier. She said she had to do a few things before she packed up. You're coming home later today?"

"I'm just about to get on my flight. The sheriff told me that Maggie was pregnant with Ty Jenkins's baby, not sure who that is," her father said.

Harper wasn't surprised. She'd been pretty sure Ty was one of the rapists. "Just a boy she knew from school who got in with the wrong crowd."

"The sheriff said he is going to try to press charges against Kyle Parker and Will Sanders for rape?"

"I'm not surprised," she said as she reached her bedroom.

"I would think the statute of limitation had run out, but he must think he has a case."

She thought of Karen. Her life had been destroyed by lies. First the lie about her pregnancy. Then encouraging Kyle not to come forward about his part in the rape—not to mention killing Maggie and dragging her best friend, Collin, into her lies and secrets.

"If Maggie hadn't been murdered, do you think JD would have run away with her?" she asked as she heard her father's flight loading.

"We'll never know."

"I guess not." Harper said goodbye, disconnected and turned on the shower.

She hadn't seen Brody except to thank him for saving her life before she'd been taken into the sheriff's office to make her statement. When she'd finished, she'd been told that his father had picked him up. Maybe their family could heal now that Maggie's killer was caught and the truth about her pregnancy was out.

Still, JD and Maggie had had a relationship. That would always be between the Hamiltons and the McTavishes. Flannigan would never forgive JD. And Harper would always just be a reminder.

Stripping off her soiled clothing, she stepped under the hot shower.

"WHERE'S HARPER?" BRODY demanded as he burst through the door of the Hamilton Ranch's main house.

"I've called security," the maid said, phone in hand. "You need to leave right now."

He looked toward the stairs. *"Harper?"* he called as he took the steps three at a time. *"Harper?"*

On the second floor, he heard running water and ran in that direction. Throwing open a door, he burst into a bedroom. The bathroom door stood open. He could hear the sound of a shower running.

"Harper?"

"Brody?" she said in a surprised voice over the sound of the shower. "What are you doing here?"

The water was running behind a glass-block wall. He saw a prism of flesh colors and asked himself what the hell he *was* doing? Any minute the security guards would be coming up here armed. He'd be lucky if he didn't get killed.

"You said I once advised you to go after what you wanted, come hell or high water," he said as he stepped into the bathroom. "Well, I'm taking my own advice. I want you!" he yelled over the running water just as she shut it off.

"Your family will never—"

"They will have to live with it and so will yours, because I'm going to marry you."

"Is that right?" she asked, peering around the glass-block wall between them.

He grabbed a big white fluffy towel from the rack and handed it to her. "Yeah, that's right. Our families are wrong. We belong together."

She stepped out, the towel wrapped around her. Her blond hair dripped in ringlets around her shoulders.

"Damn, you're beautiful."

Harper smiled and then two security guards burst into her bedroom. "It's all right," she told them before they could grab Brody.

"We have orders—"

"You have orders from me," Harper snapped. "I said it was fine."

"But your father—"

"Isn't here. And neither will either of you be tomorrow unless you leave right now," she said.

They both looked embarrassed as they holstered

their weapons, apologized and ducked back toward the door.

"Please close the door on your way out," Harper called. As they left, she turned to Brody. "Do I have to tell you all the reasons you and I can't—"

"We can make whatever kind of life we want. My father picked me up at the sheriff's department. I just sat down with him and my uncle at a lawyer's office to sign papers. The ranch is mine. No one can take it away from me ever again. I also made it clear that I'm going to marry you."

She sighed. "What if they never accept me?"

He shook his head. "Their loss. But I can tell you right now, they will fall in love with you, just as I have. Trust me. We now know that JD didn't kill her. Nor was she carrying his baby. Maggie can rest in peace. The past is buried for good. As for the future…the maid or those guards are going to call the senator."

Harper gave him that smile he'd fallen in love with so many years ago. "But it will be too late since he just got on a plane headed this way," she said as she locked the door.

"I love you, Harper Hamilton," Brody said, dropping to one knee. "Marry me." He held out a small jewelry box. "It's my mother's ring."

Tears welled in her eyes. "And I love you, Brody McTavish," she said, and dropped the towel.

"Is that a yes?" he asked with a laugh before he swung her up into his arms.

"I THOUGHT YOU were going to keep them apart?" Sarah said when Buck called to say he was at the main house with news about Brody and Harper.

He sighed. "Sarah, there is only so much I can do. Harper is a strong-willed woman. Hell, all our girls are."

"And you have no idea where she gets it from."

He chuckled at that. "She loves him and has for years. Anyway, would it be so terrible?"

"Brody's family will never accept it. I ran into Flannigan in town recently. Apparently his ill will toward your father goes back years. JD purchased some land that he wanted, then this thing with Maggie…"

Buck sighed again. "Given time…"

"Is that what Jerrod tells you? That any of this isn't going to hurt your campaign?"

"I'm more worried that my baby daughter is going to make a mistake she will regret the rest of her life."

"By marrying Brody McTavish? Or not marrying him?"

"Like I said, I'll talk to her, but from what I was told when I got the call from the house, it could be an uphill battle," Buck said. "Brody managed to get through security to see her. He's upstairs with her now."

"Remember when we were in love like that?" Sarah asked.

"I still feel that way." When she said nothing, he realized what she was waiting for. "You want me to do something daring and dangerous for you?"

"No, of course not." But he thought he heard regret in her voice.

"I defied my mother for you," he said. "That was pretty daring and dangerous." Sometimes, like lately, he regretted it. "Sarah, get packed and I'll come get you."

"No, I'll come over when I'm done."

He heard something in her voice and feared she might change her mind. He wanted her with him. "Well, don't take too long. There's a big storm coming. I know how you hate thunderstorms."

SARAH HAD HOPED that she could get the last of her things packed up before the thunderstorm hit. But she could hear the wind, feel the cold already creeping in through the cracks around the door. She moved away from the window, realizing she didn't have that much to pack.

She'd told Buck not to come over, that she'd be along when she was done packing. In truth, she'd wanted this time alone. She was finally going home. After all these years, she and Buck would be together in the house he'd built for them.

Even as she thought it, though, she knew it wouldn't ever be the same. Her daughters were grown and distant. Buck would win the primaries and want her on the campaign trail with him. And if he won the election...*when* he won the election...

The storm rattled the old glass in the front window as she came out of the bedroom with her suitcase. The wind bent the thick cottonwood limbs to almost breaking and sent twigs and leaves whirling through the air ahead of the rain. Pine boughs groaned and a shutter began to bang against the house.

Sarah hugged herself, feeling the electricity in the air long before she saw lightning flickering in the distance. She hated storms. They prickled at her nerves and made her jumpy and anxious.

She started to change her mind and call Buck to come get her. But before she could reach the phone, the first raindrops hit the glass like thrown pebbles startling her. The sky darkened, stealing the daylight. The thunderstorm roared, rain slashing down, the wind howling at the eaves.

A window not quite latched suddenly blew open, making her jump. The curtains billowed as she rushed to it, the rain cold and wet against her skin as she hurried to wrestle the window closed again.

As the cold droplets dimpled her skin with goose bumps, she thought of the last big rainstorm and what it had wrought.

With a wave of relief, she spotted the lights of a vehicle coming up the road. Buck hadn't listened to her. He'd decided to come get her anyway. She turned to pick up her suitcase and take one last look at the house where she'd been living.

Sarah started at the knock on her door. Buck wouldn't have knocked. Not unless she'd forgotten and locked the door. She rushed to it and threw it open only to rear back in shock.

The man standing in the doorway was elderly, his face weatherworn, his expression somber.

"Hello, Sarah."

She took a step back as she recognized him from the photograph she'd been shown of Dr. Ralph Venable, the man she'd allegedly spent her missing twenty-two years with.

A thought struck her. Harper had mentioned that someone was delivering a package from Buck. That she'd given the carrier Sarah's address. This package was not from Buck, she realized.

The man stepped into the house on a gust of wind,

closing the door behind him. "There is no reason to be afraid," he said quietly. "I'm here to help you."

She shook her head as she recalled what Russell had told her about Dr. Venable. He specialized in brain wiping. Was this the man who'd stolen her memories? Worse, planted new ones?

"You made me forget my life," she said, moving quickly to the kitchen, where she grabbed a carving knife and brandished it as he followed her. "You stole twenty-two years from me." Her voice broke with emotion. "I missed seeing my babies grow up. Tell me why I shouldn't kill you."

"Because you need me."

"Who hired you to do that to me?" she asked, terrified he would say it had been Buck—just as Russell had always said.

He shook his head almost sadly. "I saved your life, Sarah. That winter night you drove into the Yellowstone River, your car breaking through the ice, the water washing you downstream? I'm the person you called. You begged me to help you. I sent someone to pick you up and bring you to my clinic."

She had no memory of any of this, but all along, Russell had surmised this was exactly what had happened. Russell. If only he was here. She patted her pocket for her cell phone and realized she'd left it on top of her suitcase in the living room.

"You have no reason to fear me," the doctor said. "You and I are friends. You might not remember everything—"

"I don't remember any of it!" she cried. "You stole my memories."

"Only because you begged me to. You couldn't live with them. That's why you tried to kill yourself."

Sarah shook her head as she backed toward the living room, holding the knife out in front of her. He didn't seem afraid or even worried as she spotted her cell phone and snatched it up.

"Who are you going to call, Sarah? The sheriff? Your former husband? One of your daughters?"

She looked down at the cell screen, her fingers momentarily frozen over the keyboard. Russell. He'd said to call her. He'd known Dr. Venable would come for her again.

"They can't help you like I can. I can clear it all up for you. You want answers? I can provide them. I am the only one who can give them to you. Put down the phone, Sarah. I've come back to help you just as we planned."

She looked from the phone to his face. She knew this man. Even as she tried to deny what he was saying, she also knew it was true. She had called him that night. She had trusted him. Even if she didn't now, he had all the answers she desperately needed.

"You know why I tried to kill myself?" she asked, the knife wavering in her hand, the cell phone in the other forgotten for the moment.

He nodded. "I know everything from the first time you and I met all those years ago."

To her surprise, she began to cry. He stepped to her, taking the knife, then the cell phone, and putting them aside before he took her in his arms.

"It's all right, Sarah. You're going to be all right now. I'm here. I'm going to help you. It's time."

EPILOGUE

"MY DAUGHTER TELLS me she is in love with you," Buckmaster said to Brody as the family gathered in the living room.

Brody glanced past the man to where Harper was standing and felt his heart lift at the sight of her as it always did. "Is that right?"

"In fact, she tells me that the two of you are engaged. I'd like to know how you feel about my baby daughter?" the senator asked.

"I'm in love with her, as well."

"I see. And your family?"

"They'll come around in time once they see how happy I am with Harper," Brody said with more assurance than he felt.

"You know Sarah and I had a hard time because my mother never accepted her."

"And yet, here you are," Brody said. "You've been through a lot and yet you're together."

Buckmaster chuckled. "You have a point." He looked at Sarah and smiled, but Harper had told Brody that her mother had changed her mind about moving back in until they were married—after the primaries.

"Don't break my daughter's heart," Buckmaster said, and extended his hand. "You're always welcome here."

"Thank you, sir."

"And it's Buck."

"Soon to be Mr. President," Sarah said, taking Buck's arm.

"Let's not count our chickens just yet."

"Don't be so modest," she said. "The media recently printed—"

"Damn the media, no offense, Max."

"None taken, Senator."

Buckmaster raised his glass. "We're a family and by damned we're going to start living like one." His gaze lit on Sarah. "I will be marrying the love of my life as soon as the primaries are over. I expect you all to be there."

"Hear, hear!" everyone said.

Brody noticed that Sarah looked skeptical as Buckmaster pulled her to him for a hug. "We'll weather this, just as we have everything else that's been thrown at this family," the senator said.

His words met with approval from his daughters. All except Kat. She looked worried, but Max put an arm around her.

Brody saw Harper frown and step to her sister, taking her hand and looking at what was glittering on her ring finger. "Is that what I think it is?" she cried. "Kat?"

"We weren't going to announce our engagement until after the primaries, because we weren't sure this was the appropriate time," Max said.

Buckmaster laughed. "It's the perfect time."

Brody smiled as the other sisters huddled around Kat and Harper to look at their rings and talk weddings. He felt the warmth of this huge family and was relieved that he'd been welcomed into it. He thought of his father and uncle. Maybe someday they would come around. He hoped so, but he wasn't going to let them spoil what he and Harper had. They were going to make their own history.

He noticed that when no one was looking, Sarah looked worried. He saw her glancing out the window several times as if she was expecting someone.

The gathering had an air of excitement to it, and underlying tension. He hoped Harper didn't sense it. He wanted her to be happy today. As for the future, they would have to take it as it came.

"You can still change your mind," Brody whispered next to Harper as he cornered her later in the kitchen.

She turned to wrap her arms around his neck. "Not a chance, cowboy."

Outside thunder rumbled. A sudden streak of lightning lit the sky behind the windows. Brody pulled her close as they watched the storm come out of the Crazies, headed right for them.

* * * * *

Read on for a sneak peek at
INTO DUST,
the next installment in
THE MONTANA HAMILTONS
by New York Times *bestselling author*
B.J. Daniels

CHAPTER ONE

THE CEMETERY SEEMED unusually quiet. Jack Durand paused on the narrow walkway to glance toward the Houston skyline. He never came to Houston without stopping by his mother's grave. He liked to think of his mother here in this beautiful, peaceful place. And he always brought flowers. Today he'd brought her favorite, daisies.

While he hadn't planned on being in the city today, an unexpected errand had come up. Since he hadn't visited his mother's grave in several months, he was glad he'd decided to stop even though it meant being late getting back to the ranch.

He breathed in the sweet scent of freshly mown lawn as he moved again through shafts of sunlight fingering their way down through the branches of the huge oak trees. Long shadows fell across the path, offering a breath of cooler air. Fortunately, the summer day wasn't hot and the walk felt good after the long drive in from the ranch.

The silent gravestones and statues gleamed in the sun. His favorite were the angels. He liked the idea of all the angels here watching over his mother, he thought as he passed the small lake ringed with trees and followed the wide bend of Brays Bayou that wound along one side of property. A small flock of ducks took flight, flapping wildly and sending water droplets into the air.

He'd taken the long way because he needed to relax. He knew it was silly, but he didn't want his mother to see him upset. He'd promised her on her deathbed that he would try harder to get along with his father.

Ahead, he saw movement near his mother's grave and slowed. A man wearing a dark suit stood next to the angel statue that watched over her final resting place. The man wasn't looking at the grave or the angel. Instead, he appeared to simply be waiting impatiently. As he turned...

With a start, Jack recognized his father.

He thought he had to be mistaken at first. Tom Durand had made a point of telling him he would be in Los Angeles the next few days. Had his father's plans changed? Surely he would have no reason to lie about it.

Until recently, that his father might have lied would never have occurred to him. But things had been strained between them since he'd told him he wouldn't be taking over the family business.

It wasn't just seeing his father here when he should have been in Los Angeles. It was seeing him in this cemetery. He knew for a fact that his father hadn't been here since the funeral.

"I don't like cemeteries," he'd told his son when Jack had asked why he didn't visit his dead wife. "Anyway, what is the point? She's gone."

Jack felt close to his mother near her grave. "It's a sign of respect."

His father had shaken his head, clearly displeased with the conversation. "We all mourn in our own ways.

I like to remember your mother my own way, so lay off, okay?"

So why the change of heart? Not that Jack wasn't glad to see it. He knew that his parents had loved each other. Kate Durand had been sweet and loving, the perfect match for Tom, who was more distant and a workaholic.

Jack was debating joining him or leaving him to have this time alone with his wife, when he saw another man approaching his father. He quickly stepped behind a monument. Jack was far enough away that he didn't recognize the man right away. But while he couldn't see the man's face clearly from this distance, he recognized the man's limp.

Jack had seen him coming out of the family import-export business office one night after hours. He'd asked his father about him and been told Ed Urdahl worked on the docks.

Now he frowned as he considered why either of the men was here. His father hadn't looked at his wife's grave even once. Instead he seemed to be in the middle of an intense conversation with Ed. The conversation ended abruptly when his father reached into his jacket pocket and pulled out a thick envelope and handed it to the man.

He watched in astonishment as Ed pulled a wad of money from the envelope and proceeded to count it. Even from where he stood, Jack could tell that the gesture irritated his father. Tom Durand expected everyone to take what he said or did as gospel.

Ed finished counting the money, put it back in the envelope and stuffed it into his jacket pocket. His father seemed to be giving Ed orders. Then looking around as if worried they might have been seen, Tom Durand turned and walked away toward an exit on the other side of the cemetery—the one farthest from the main office. He didn't even give a backward glance to his wife's grave. Nor had he left any flowers for her. Clearly, his reason for being here had nothing to do with Kate Durand.

Jack was too stunned to move for a moment. What had that exchange been about? *Nothing legal*, he thought. A hard knot formed in his stomach. What was his father involved in?

He noticed that Ed was heading in an entirely different direction. Impulsively, he began to follow him, worrying as to what his father had paid the man to do.

Ed headed for a dark green car parked in the lot near where Jack himself had parked earlier. Jack exited the cemetery yards behind him and headed to his ranch pickup. Once behind the wheel, he followed as Ed left the cemetery.

Staying a few cars back, he tailed the man, all the time trying to convince himself that there was nothing strange about the meeting in the cemetery or about his father giving this man so much money. But it just didn't wash. His father hadn't been there to visit his dead wife. So what was Tom Durand up to?

Jack realized that Ed was headed for an older part of Houston that had been gentrified in recent years. A row of brownstones ran along a street shaded in trees. Small cafés and quaint shops were interspersed with the brownstones. Because it was late afternoon, the street wasn't busy.

Ed pulled over, parked and cut his engine. Jack turned into a space a few cars back, noticing that Ed still hadn't gotten out.

Had he spotted the tail? Jack waited, half expecting Ed to emerge and come stalking toward his truck. And what? Beat him up? Call his father?

So far all Ed had done from what Jack could tell was sit watching a brownstone across the street.

Jack continued to watch the green car, wondering how long he was going to sit here waiting for something to happen. This was crazy. He had no idea what had transpired at the cemetery. While the transaction had looked suspicious, maybe his father had really been visiting his mother's grave and told Ed to meet him there so he could pay him money he owed him. But for what that required such a large amount of cash?

Even as Jack thought it, he still didn't believe what he'd seen was innocent. He couldn't shake the feeling that his father had hired the man for some kind of job that involved whoever lived in that brownstone across the street.

He glanced at the time. Earlier when he'd decided to stop by the cemetery, he knew he'd be cutting it close to meet his appointment back at the ranch. He prided himself on his punctuality. But if he kept sitting here, he wouldn't make his appointment at all.

Jack reached for his cell phone. The least he could do was call and reschedule the appointment. But before he could key in the number, the door of the brownstone opened and a young woman with long blond hair came out.

As she started down the street in the opposite direction, Ed got out of his car. Jack watched him make a quick call on his cell phone as he began to follow the woman.

Read on for an excerpt from
THE MARSHAL'S JUSTICE
the next installment in the
APPALOOSA PASS RANCH *series*
by USA TODAY *bestselling author*
Delores Fossen

A shoot-out on the banks of Appaloosa Creek is the
last place Marshal Chase Crockett expects to find his
ex-lover, former criminal informant April Landis...

Chapter One

The shot cracked through the air. Mercy. That was definitely not what Marshal Chase Crockett wanted to hear.

Or see.

The bullet slammed into the woman he'd just spotted. Her gaze connected with Chase's a split second before she crumpled to the ground.

If she wasn't dead, she soon would be. Chase was sure of it.

He cursed when he couldn't go out into the clearing where she'd fallen and pull her out of the path of more gunfire. Cursed, too, that he hadn't been able to stop that bullet from hitting her in the first place.

How the devil had this happened?

He didn't have time to try to figure that out because the next bullet came right at him, and Chase had no choice but to dive behind a pile of rocks. Maybe he'd get a chance soon to return fire and make the shooter pay for what he had just done.

And what he'd done was shoot the criminal informant Deanne McKinley on the banks of Appaloosa Creek. A woman who had phoned Chase earlier and begged him to help her. If he'd just gotten her call a few minutes earlier, maybe he could have arrived in time to stop this.

Whatever *this* was.

Clearly someone wanted Deanne dead, and now whoever had attacked her was shooting at Chase, too.

"If you want to get out of this alive, you might as well give up now!" the gunman shouted.

Chase didn't recognize the voice, but he'd caught a glimpse of a guy wearing a ski mask before the man shot Deanne and then darted out of sight. He wasn't even sure if the idiot was yelling at him or Deanne. Chase didn't have nearly enough info, other than the call a half hour earlier from Deanne to tell him she was in trouble. She'd said someone was trying to kill her, that she needed his help.

Help was exactly what Chase had intended to give her when he'd arrived.

So far, all he'd managed to do was dodge bullets, but if he had anything to say about that, things were about to change.

Chase heard Deanne's hoarse moan, and she moved her hand to her chest. *Alive.* He had to do something now to keep it that way.

He didn't know the exact location of the shooter, but Chase fired two shots in the guy's general direction. In the same motion, he scrambled toward Deanne to try to pull her away.

Basically, it was a high-risk move with little chance of succeeding.

Or at least it should have been.

But another set of shots blasted through the air. Definitely not ones that Chase or the gunman had fired.

They'd come from a cluster of trees about thirty feet away, and the bullets had been aimed at the shooter.

Maybe backup had arrived a little sooner than Chase had thought it would. Or it could be a hunter or nearby rancher who'd heard sounds of the attack and had come to help. Either way, he'd take it.

Chase grabbed hold of Deanne's arm and pulled her behind a tree. It wasn't much cover, but it was better than her being out in the open.

He fired off another shot to keep the gunman at bay and sent a quick text requesting an ambulance along with the backup. It would no doubt be one of his brothers who responded to his request since all three of them were in local law enforcement. Chase only hoped the backup and the ambulance arrived in time.

It'd be close.

Deanne was bleeding out from the gunshot she'd taken to the chest. Chase did his best to add some pressure to the wound, but it was hard to do that without constricting her breathing. He didn't want her to suffocate.

More shots came from the gunman.

The idiot was moving closer to them, no doubt coming in for the kill.

Deanne mumbled something, something that Chase didn't catch, and without taking his attention off the area where the shooter was positioned, he leaned in closer, hoping to hear what Deanne was trying to say.

"Help," Deanne whispered.

"Help is on the way," he assured her. Chase wanted to say how sorry he was for what had happened to her. Deanne had a criminal past, but she didn't deserve this.

Deanne shook her head. "No, help *her*." Her gaze

drifted in the direction where those two other shots had been fired.

Each word she spoke was a struggle, and by the time she was done, Deanne was gasping for air. Still, she managed to say one last thing.

Something that twisted his stomach into a tight, hard knot.

No more breaths from Deanne. Her chest just stopped moving, and Chase could only watch the life drain from her eyes. Watch and mentally repeat what Deanne had said to him with her dying breath.

April's in trouble.

His gaze whipped in the direction of the second shooter. The person was still hidden behind a tree, but Chase had the sickening feeling that he knew who'd fired those two shots at the gunman.

Was April really out there?

Just the thought of it twisted and tightened that knot even more. There was plenty of bad blood between April and him. But a different kind of connection, too. One that would last a lifetime.

Because April was pregnant with Chase's baby.

However, April shouldn't be here. *Couldn't* be here. She was in WITSEC, tucked away somewhere safe with a new name and a location that even Chase didn't know. A necessary precaution so that no one could trace her by following him.

April was also nine months pregnant, ready to deliver any day now.

He waited until the original shooter fired another shot, and he used that to help him pinpoint the guy's position. Chase fired. He also got moving right away, heading toward those trees where the second shooter had been. Maybe, just maybe, he wouldn't find April there.

But if she was, then that meant something had gone wrong.

He tried to recall every word of the short phone conversation he'd had earlier with Deanne. She'd been frantic, said she was in her car, somewhere near the Appaloosa Creek Bridge, and that she was being tailed by a gunman wearing a ski mask.

Had Deanne said anything else?

No.

Definitely nothing about April being with her.

So, maybe he was wrong about April, and Deanne's words were merely the mumblings of a dying woman. And maybe that was one of his brothers out there helping him with the shots.

Chase scrambled his way through the trees and the underbrush, cursing the wet spring weather that'd clogged this part of the woods with mud and briars. It slowed him down.

He ducked behind a tree, fired off another shot and then had to reload. It was his last magazine so he'd have to be careful with the shots now and make every one count. Whoever was returning fire at Deanne's killer, however, didn't seem to have the problem of not enough ammunition. The person continued to shoot, spacing out the shots several seconds apart.

"Jericho?" Chase whispered, hoping his brother, the sheriff, was the one returning fire behind the sprawling oak that was now just a few yards away.

No answer.

And if it'd been Jericho, or his other brothers, Levi

or Jax, they would have responded somehow to let him know not to fire in their direction.

Chase kept moving, working his way through the muck, and he finally got in position to spot someone. It was late afternoon with still some sunlight, but the woods created some deep shadows. There was nowhere near enough light for him to see the person's face, but whoever it was wore all black.

He risked lifting his head just a little, to see how this shadowy figure would respond, but he or she didn't even seem to acknowledge Chase.

"I'm coming closer," Chase warned the person, hoping this didn't turn out to be a big mistake, and he scurried toward the tree.

Thank God the person didn't shoot him, but this definitely wasn't one of his brothers.

Not April, either.

Because while he still couldn't make out much of the person's face, he could see the silhouette of the body. Whoever this was darn sure wasn't nine months pregnant.

Chase scrambled the last few feet to the tree and landed on the ground right next to the person who was kneeling. However, his heart skipped a beat or two when he saw the ski mask. Identical to the one of the other shooter.

Hell.

He brought up his gun. Taking aim. Just as the person shoved up the ski mask to reveal her face.

April.

Yes, it was her all right. There was no mistaking her now. The black hair, the wide blue eyes. But she didn't have her attention fixed on him. It was on the other shooter.

"Is Deanne okay?" she asked on a rise of breath.

"No. She's dead."

April had no reaction to that. Well, none that he could pick out in the dusky light anyway. A surprise. Deanne and she weren't friends. Far from it after everything that'd happened, but still April had to be shocked by a woman's murder.

However, reactions and that ski mask weren't his only concern about this situation. Chase couldn't stop himself from looking in the direction of her stomach again. Definitely flat.

"The baby?" he managed to say.

His baby. The one that April should have been giving birth to any day now. But she certainly didn't have a newborn with her, and she didn't look as if she'd just delivered, either.

"Play along," she whispered, a split second before she hooked her left arm around his neck, dragged him in front of her and put her gun to his head.

"I have Marshal Crockett," April called out to someone.

"What the devil's going on here?" Chase snarled, and he shoved her away from him.

"You have to play along," April repeated. Definitely not the tone of a terrified woman on the run. Nor was that a weak grip she put on him when she yanked him back against her.

Damn. Was April up to her old tricks again?

"Put down your gun," she added in a whisper. "And whatever you do, don't shoot him."

Chase didn't get a chance to ask her anything else

because he heard the footsteps. Heavy, hurried ones. And he soon spotted the guy who'd been firing shots at him.

The very snake who'd killed Deanne.

Chase didn't put down his gun as April had demanded, but she shoved his hand by his side. Maybe so that his weapon would be out of sight. Or maybe because this was some kind of sick game she was playing.

The killer came right toward them, and the moment he spotted April—and the gun she had to Chase's head—he lifted his ski mask.

And he smiled.

Chase didn't recognize him. The guy was a stranger, but judging from his sheer size and the hardened look on his scarred face, this was a hired thug. He certainly didn't look like a man ready to negotiate surrender, not with that Kevlar vest and multiple guns holstered on his bulky body.

"Good job," the guy told April. "Well, sorta good. That wasn't you shooting at me, now was it?"

"I aimed over your head. I wanted Marshal Crockett to think I was trying to kill you so he'd come to me. It worked."

Oh, man. Was this really a trap? Possibly. But Chase kept going back to April's *play along* comment.

What kind of sick plan was this?

The man stared at her. A long time. As if he might challenge what she'd just told him. Then he shrugged. "Guess it did work. Now, take a hike so I can finish this. Unless you'd rather watch while I have a word with your ex-lover. It might involve a bullet or two."

Shaking her head, April stood. Slowly. "No, I'd

rather skip that part. Just give me what you promised, and I'll leave."

Chase stood, too, hoping it wasn't a mistake that he hadn't already put an end to this hulking clown. Or that he'd semitrusted April when she'd rattled off those whispered instructions about not shooting the guy.

"Give me what you promised," April demanded to the man.

Now Chase heard some emotion in her voice. Not in a good way, either. She was scared. Which meant whatever the heck was going on here was possibly about to take an even worse turn than it already had.

"You'll have to wait a little longer," the man said. He motioned for her to leave. "I'll meet you at your car, and you'll get it then."

Chase still didn't have a clue what this conversation was about, but he had no doubts that this bozo was about to try to kill him.

"You promised." April's voice was trembling now.

The man smiled again. There was no friendliness or humor in it. "And it's a promise I'll keep, okay? Just not right now at this second. I need to have that little chat with this cowboy cop first while you hurry along."

April stayed put, and even though Chase kept his attention on the man and couldn't see April, he thought she might be glaring at Deanne's killer. Chase was certainly doing his own share of glaring at both of them.

"I need you to find somebody in WITSEC," the killer told Chase. "April claimed she wasn't able to help, but since you're a marshal, I'm betting you got access to stuff that she doesn't. I need to find Quentin Landis."

Chase groaned. He shouldn't have been surprised

this was about Quentin. It usually was when April was involved.

Because Quentin was her brother.

Along with being a criminal. And the only reason Chase had met April to begin with was because he'd been investigating Quentin. However, at the time he had thought April was innocent and had no knowledge of her brother's criminal activity. He'd been dead wrong about that.

"You expect me just to tell you where he is?" Chase asked, making sure he let this jerk know that wasn't going to happen.

Quentin might be scum, but he was in WITSEC after turning state's evidence in an upcoming murder trial, and it was part of Chase's job to make sure that even scum stayed protected. Whether they deserved it or not.

The gunman stared at him. "Yeah. I didn't figure you'd cooperate, but we had to try, didn't we? Maybe if I put a few bullets in your kneecaps, you'll recall something."

"We?" Chase spared April a glance, but she only shook her head. He had no idea what that head shake meant.

Nor did he have time to figure it out.

"No!" April shouted. Not at Chase but at the gunman.

The gunman lifted his Glock and aimed it at Chase. Chase was doing the same to the killer with his own Smith & Wesson.

Chase beat him to it.

He didn't fire into the Kevlar vest, but instead he double tapped two shots to the gunman's head. And

Chase didn't miss. The man dropped like a sack of rocks just as Chase had intended.

With that taken care of, Chase turned to April. "Now, what the hell's going on?" he demanded.

But she didn't answer. Probably because of the hoarse sob that tore from her mouth. "Oh, God." And she kept repeating it.

She dropped to her knees, and she grabbed the dead man by the shoulders, lifting his torso off the ground. "Tell me where she is!" April yelled. "Tell me." The sobbing got worse when she put her fingers to his neck. "He's dead. He can't be dead."

It wasn't exactly the reaction Chase had expected since she knew this snake was a killer and had been prepared to kill again.

She looked up at him, tears shimmering in her eyes. "The baby."

All right. That got his attention. "*Our* baby?" Chase asked.

April nodded, and her breath shattered. "Someone took her. And that dead man was my best hope at finding our daughter."

Find out what happens next in
THE MARSHAL'S JUSTICE
by USA TODAY bestselling author
Delores Fossen
Available May 2016 wherever Harlequin Intrigue
books and ebooks are sold
www.Harlequin.com

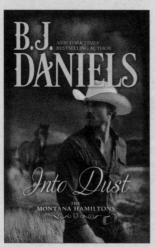

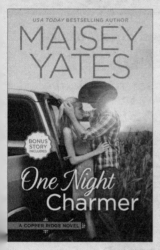

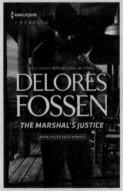

Meet the Carsons of Mustang Creek: three men who embody the West and define what it means to be a rancher, a cowboy and a hero in this brand-new series from *New York Times* bestselling author

LINDA LAEL MILLER

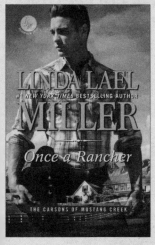

Slater Carson might be a filmmaker by trade, but he's still a cowboy at heart—and he knows the value of a hard day's work under the hot Wyoming sun. So when he sees troubled teen Ryder heading down a dangerous path, he offers the boy a job on the ranch he shares with his two younger brothers. And since Ryder's guardian is the gorgeous new Mustang Creek resort manager, Grace Emery, Slater figures it can't hurt to keep a closer eye on her, as well…

Grace Emery doesn't have time for romance. Between settling into her new job and caring for her ex-husband's rebellious son, her attraction to larger-than-life Slater is a distraction she can't afford. But when an unexpected threat emerges, she'll discover just how far Slater will go to protect what matters most—and that love is always worth fighting for.

Pick up your copy today!

Be sure to connect with us at:

Harlequin.com/Newsletters

Facebook.com/HarlequinBooks

Twitter.com/HQNBooks

HQN™

www.HQNBooks.com

PHLLM968

REQUEST YOUR
FREE BOOKS!

2 FREE NOVELS
FROM THE SUSPENSE COLLECTION
PLUS 2 FREE GIFTS!

YES! Please send me 2 FREE novels from the Suspense Collection and my 2 FREE gifts (gifts are worth about $10). After receiving them, if I don't wish to receive any more books, I can return the shipping statement marked "cancel." If I don't cancel, I will receive 4 brand-new novels every month and be billed just $6.49 per book in the U.S. or $6.99 per book in Canada. That's a savings of at least 19% off the cover price. It's quite a bargain! Shipping and handling is just 50¢ per book in the U.S. and 75¢ per book in Canada.* I understand that accepting the 2 free books and gifts places me under no obligation to buy anything. I can always return a shipment and cancel at any time. Even if I never buy another book, the two free books and gifts are mine to keep forever.

191/391 MDN GH4Z

Name _____ (PLEASE PRINT) _____

Address _____ Apt. # _____

City _____ State/Prov. _____ Zip/Postal Code _____

Signature (if under 18, a parent or guardian must sign)

Mail to the **Reader Service:**
IN U.S.A.: P.O. Box 1867, Buffalo, NY 14240-1867
IN CANADA: P.O. Box 609, Fort Erie, Ontario L2A 5X3

Want to try two free books from another line?
Call 1-800-873-8635 or visit www.ReaderService.com.

* Terms and prices subject to change without notice. Prices do not include applicable taxes. Sales tax applicable in N.Y. Canadian residents will be charged applicable taxes. Offer not valid in Quebec. This offer is limited to one order per household. Not valid for current subscribers to the Suspense Collection or the Romance/Suspense Collection. All orders subject to credit approval. Credit or debit balances in a customer's account(s) may be offset by any other outstanding balance owed by or to the customer. Please allow 4 to 6 weeks for delivery. Offer available while quantities last.

Your Privacy—The Reader Service is committed to protecting your privacy. Our Privacy Policy is available online at www.ReaderService.com or upon request from the Reader Service.

We make a portion of our mailing list available to reputable third parties that offer products we believe may interest you. If you prefer that we not exchange your name with third parties, or if you wish to clarify or modify your communication preferences, please visit us at www.ReaderService.com/consumerschoice or write to us at Reader Service Preference Service, P.O. Box 9062, Buffalo, NY 14240-9062. Include your complete name and address.

B.J. DANIELS

78855 LUCKY SHOT   ___ $7.99 U.S. ___ $9.99 CAN.

(limited quantities available)

TOTAL AMOUNT	$ _____
POSTAGE & HANDLING	$ _____
($1.00 FOR 1 BOOK, 50¢ for each additional)	
APPLICABLE TAXES*	$ _____
TOTAL PAYABLE	$ _____

(check or money order—please do not send cash)

To order, complete this form and send it, along with a check or money order for the total above, payable to HQN Books, to: **In the U.S.** 3010 Walden Avenue, P.O. Box 9077, Buffalo, NY 14269-9077 **In Canada:** P.O. Box 636, Fort Erie, Ontario, L2A 5X3.

Name: _____
Address: _____ City: _____
State/Prov.: _____ Zip/Postal Code: _____
Account Number (if applicable): _____

075 CSAS

       *New York residents remit applicable sales taxes.
     *Canadian residents remit applicable GST and provincial taxes.

HQN™

www.HQNBooks.com

PHBJD0416